# Claire Voyant

By Saralee Rosenberg

CLAIRE VOYANT
A LITTLE HELP FROM ABOVE

# Claire Voyant

**Saralee Rosenberg**

AVON
TRADE

*An Imprint of* HarperCollins*Publishers*

HarperCollins books may be purchased for education, business, or sales promotional use. For information please write: Special Markets Department, HarperCollins Publishers Inc., 10 East 53rd Street, New York, NY 10022.

FIRST EDITION

*Designed by Elizabeth M. Glover*

Library of Congress Cataloging-in-Publication Data

Rosenberg, Saralee H.
   Claire voyant / Saralee Rosenberg.—1st ed.
      p. cm.
   ISBN 0-06-058441-6 (pbk.)
   1. Grandfathers—Death—Fiction. 2. Plainview (N.Y.)—Fiction. 3. Young women—Fiction. 4. Air travel—Fiction. 5. Actresses—Fiction. I. Title.

PS3618.O833C55 2004
813'.6—dc22                                                              2004050231

04  05  06  07  08  WBC/RRD  10  9  8  7  6  5  4  3  2  1

*To Jenny and Harry Belinkoff*
*Your loving hearts live on*

*To James Owen O'Hagan*
*Your soulful voice is missed but not forgotten*

# *Acknowledgments*

I SALUTE THE INTERNET, MY TRUSTY PERSONAL ASSISTANT. FAST, smart, no attitude, works late, and never calls in sick. But when questions arise, there is nothing like talking to an expert. Thank you Dr. Jeff Zola, Dr. Brian Kaufman, Dr. Heidi Rosenberg, south Florida real estate maven Randy Levine, actress Jody Raymond, certified financial planner Lee Rosenberg, medium and clairvoyant Lori Belché, and the late Nancy Toomer, who taught me so much about the spirit world. May she rest in peace.

I love the WWF. No, not those guys. My Women Writer Friends. Especially the wit and wisdom of my mentor, Dr. Mickey Pearlman. Christine O'Hagan is a delight: Erma Bombeck funny, and a heart of gold. And to all my Power Punch gals, I am honored to be in your midst and your club.

The journey wouldn't be nearly as fun or rewarding without my dearest friends (in order of appearance): Judi Ratner, Deb Tomsky, Fern Drasin, Gloria Raskin, Patricia Hanley, Lenore French, Risa Sidrane, Ellen Gordon, Ellen Wolfson, Bonnie Hoffman, Sue Zola, Denise Morris, and Susan Kaufman. Thank you for the walking, talking, uplifting e-mails, and offers to buy chocolate.

I used to call my sister, Mira Temkin, the "forcer" because, as the older one, she thought rank had its privileges. But when she said I HAD to be a writer, I listened. She thinks even my grocery lists are funny (she hasn't seen my notes to school). Thanks for the endless love, honesty, and encouragement.

My parents, Harold and Doris Hymen, and my mother-in-law, Rita Rosenberg, say and do all the right things. Not too much, not too little. They love, they support, they brag. What more could a girl want?

With my wonderful, talented editor, Lyssa Keusch, I am never at a loss for words. She is part teacher, part friend, part boss, part cheerleader. I love her sharp instincts, and her great poise under pressure. I am privileged to be in her coveted stable of Avon authors. . . . Would still be VP, Carpools, without Deborah Schneider, my devoted agent and friend. She knows her business, she always takes my calls, and I've changed her middle name to Faith. Thank you God, and some nice folks from Highland Park, Illinois, for sending her my way. . . . Steve Fisher, at the Agency for the Performing Arts, is my valiant warrior in the quest to get Hollywood's attention. Couldn't ask for a smarter, more indomitable leader of the brigade. Go Steve!

My pride and joy, Zack, Alexandra, and Taryn, keep me young, alive, and humble. Very humble. After eating my cooking, they're just glad the doorbell works. With them I laugh, love, and endlessly enjoy. I am so blessed.

My husband, Lee, is a very accomplished businessman, but so supportive of my work, he'd do anything to help. Even the laundry ("Wait. Which one is the dryer?"). He's the best partner. Thoughtful, generous, dedicated, and he still makes me laugh. After twenty-seven years, that's saying a lot!

Finally, to all the wonderful readers who discovered *A Little Help from Above*, and loved it, you made my day by letting me know. Please continue to be my book angels, and spread the word that you found a new author you enjoy. And by all means, keep in touch via my website: *www.saraleerosenberg.com*.

Saralee Rosenberg
October 2004

P.S. Thank you, Jason Kaufman at Ta Da Designs (*Jason @ta-da.com*), for creating my fabulous site. You are so gifted. Just glad I didn't have to pay you by the compliment.

## Chapter 1

"WILL YOUR GRANDFATHER BE NEEDING ANY SPECIAL ASSISTANCE?"
The gate agent asked as she waited for my boarding pass to print out.

"My grandfather?" I said. Frankly, it was a little late for special assistance, as both of them were dead. I assumed she must be speaking
to the person behind me.

"Does he need a wheelchair? Extra time to board?" This time the
woman looked right at me, and without glancing at her airline ID, I
knew her name wasn't Patience.

Let me guess. She would walk off the job if she had to deal with one
more skinny blonde in Prada who couldn't grasp a simple concept.

Normally this sort of profiling offended me. It was bad enough
having just been felt up at the security check-in because my under-
wire bra set off the metal detector and I had to be ruled out as a ter-
rorist threat. But to be typecast as a bimbo by a woman who clearly
colored her own hair, that was just wrong. It reminded me of all the
times Hollywood producers wrote me off because I was more Darryl
Hannah than Julia Roberts, and they had like zero imagination.

"I'm sorry," I replied. "Are you talking to me?"

"Yes," she snapped. "That gentleman over there." She pointed to
an elderly man who was dozing in a corner chair. "Aren't you two
traveling together?"

"I don't know. Is he rich?"

"Ma'am, I have no idea. . . . Your seat assignment is next to his. I just assumed . . . I thought I noticed a resemblance."

I studied the silver-haired geezer whose pant waist was up to his *pupik*. "Yeah, I can see the confusion," I laughed. "We're practically twins."

"Sorry," she sighed. "It's been crazy today, with the rain and cancellations."

"Although I'll be honest"—I leaned in—"I did request to sit next to a hot single guy. I guess next time I should be more specific about the age."

"Believe me, you'll be happy." She handed me a boarding card. "I almost put you next to that lady with the screaming twins."

I spotted the young mother whose infants were wailing as if their bottles had been seized by security. So the agent was right. I loved babies, but if I had to listen to those shrill cries all the way from New York to Miami, I just might open the emergency exit door at thirty thousand feet. Better to take my chances with Gramps. Maybe he had a hot single grandson for me.

Unfortunately, I never got to ask. He seemed anxious to chat, but right after takeoff, instead of doing the cordial thing, I napped. Then, when the plane reached a comfortable cruising altitude, I leafed through *People* magazine and became fixated on this picture of Penny Nichol at her fiftieth birthday bash. I was wondering, was it just me, or had the legendary film actress gotten a little porky around the ass, when suddenly the elderly man seated next to me, the stranger mistaken for my grandfather, started waving, and collapsed on my tray table.

Damn! Too late for a do-over. There would be no reversing his heart attack, nor my abject indifference to him. And I felt terrible. For had I known that his last few hours on earth might be spent on American's Flight 1165, I would have been much friendlier. Offered him my bag of pretzels, or any section he wanted of my *New York Times*.

Trouble was, it never dawned on me that this could be his final boarding call. Yes, he looked to be in his mid-eighties. But there weren't any signs that his health was failing. No note pinned to his checkered blazer that read, CAUTION: THIS MAN IS A TICKING TIME BOMB.

My first and only indication of distress was when he gasped, clutched his shirt, and fell on top of my magazine. Shame on me. It was only after I realized that his bifocals had fallen in my coffee and his hand was resting in my crotch that I screamed for help.

Please don't think I'm a snob or insensitive to strangers. I'm always chatting with people with whom my only bond is that we're bracing for a bikini wax or sitting in a casting agent's office, hoping the audition won't be another waste of highlights and lip treatments.

Nor as a rule am I unkind to the elderly. I'm not the one groaning in line at the supermarket when the old ladies fumble for exact change. And never do I honk at senior motorists, even when the old farts need as much time to make a left turn as I need to brush my teeth.

But as I watched the lead flight attendant try to revive the dying man's heart using one of those new portable defibrillators, I asked myself a God-fearing question. How could I, Claire Greene, Very Nice Girl, have completely ignored a member of my species?

The truth? I thought no one would ever know. It's not like undercover flight attendants walk through the aisles with little notepads. *Unfriendly passenger in 8B. No interaction with seatmate, hogged the armrest, ripped several pages out of our magazines. . . .*

There's more. I had counted on being able to use my time on board to indulge in self-pity, not humor some old guy who was thrilled to have a captive audience for three hours. First he'd expect me to *kvell* at pictures of his brilliant and beautiful grandchildren, who in all likelihood only called around the annual Festival of Checkbook. Next would come the stories of his remarkable feats in the stock market. Finally, he'd drop the name of the world-renowned surgeon who was honored to perform his triple bypass for free (although if it was actually true that he got a freebie, it might explain why he was lying unconscious in the aisle of a 757).

Anyway, that was my state of mind. So when the man kept smiling at me, indicating his interest in starting a conversation, I'd said to myself, no thanks. What little solitude I got these days, I wasn't going to waste on some stranger I would never see again.

Funny thing is, I normally love to chitchat on planes. It's fun to network (maybe they'll be related to Spielberg) or to discover a mutual interest ("Oh, I know. Isn't Dr. Drasin's collagen lunch lift the best?"). And if there is no common ground, I'll play this game I made up called "Liar Liar," where I'll listen to the words, but check out the body language. If the two don't match, if the woman raving about her husband's successful import business is simultaneously twirling her hair and scratching her arm, I know that there is much more going on here than free trade with China.

But on this particular Monday in May, I was feeling tired, angry, bloated, anxious, depressed, unloved, a failure, sad, and did I mention bloated? Naturally the perfect antidote was devouring a bag of overpriced, high-calorie trail mix while flipping through the pages of *People*.

The new issue had darling Prince William on the cover, and I was fascinated to read that the royal grandson intended to find a real job after college, not squander his manhood by turning into another polo-playing, ribbon-cutting, fox-hunting philanderer like dear old dad.

So what if the story was a bloody lie? Focusing on hot Willie's future sure beat dwelling on mine. In no small part because my thirtieth birthday was in exactly six days, and not one lousy aspect of my life had gone according to plan.

My current occupation was out-of-work, straight-to-video actress, on leave from L.A. after years of trying to get noticed, and that was by my agent. My current address was my old bedroom in Plainview, Long Island, home to six CVS pharmacies and the high school football field where I lost my virginity (not exactly one of the "scheduled" homecoming festivities). And my current boyfriend? Definitely the strong, silent type, provided the batteries didn't die.

Not that I hadn't been lucky in love. Only a month before, I had a special sweetie. A sexy, successful movie producer named Aaron Darren (would I lie?), who indulged me with little goodies from

Gucci and Godiva, and who convinced me that our bond was eternal.

Not only had I blabbed to everyone that this was *the* guy, I hinted that he would soon be placing a ring on my finger. Maybe even at a theater near me. Only to leave the gym one morning and get this cryptic message on my cell phone. Something about my agent, Raquel, inviting him to check out a new ashram in Idaho with her. "I luv ya babe," Aaron said, "but this feels so right."

"Do you wish to erase this message?" the lady inside my phone asked sweetly. No, I wanted to keep it forever so I could play it any-time I needed to be reminded that love was a beautiful thing. And that any agent who stole my boyfriend was another name for maggot.

Maybe I would have reacted better to the bombing of my love life if my career hadn't been decimated the same week. Only six months earlier, after dozens of false starts, false hopes, and false breasts, my agent left me a voice mail: *I did it! I got you your breakout role.*

Naturally her assumption was that my talent and beauty were in-consequential to the deal, but who was I to argue? After two screen tests and a meeting with the director that, thankfully, did not involve a request for a blow job, I had landed a supporting role opposite Alan Handler. How perfect! A romantic comedy that would show-case my much-lauded comedic timing. "You're fucking Carol Bur-nett with tits!" Alan had swatted my ass.

Despite my maxed-out credit cards and a pile of nasty late notices (why do bills travel at twice the speed of checks?), I did a victory lap on Rodeo Drive, splurging on a new treatment to boost up my cheekbones, and a pair of Manolo Blahniks that cost more than my first semester at Indiana.

Sadly, my big debut was a wrap before principal shooting began, thanks to the studio's supposed script differences with the box-office bad boy. Except that I'd been around long enough to know the truth. The writers had so botched the latest draft, Alan didn't give a rat's ass if he was getting fifteen percent of the gross and all the Absolut he and his entourage could barf before dawn. His movie days would be numbered if he was the main engine of yet another infantile train wreck. Good-bye Alan.

In spite of studio assurances that a new star would be cast, a week later I read in *Variety* that the project was dead. My final dirty martini. I was broke and alone, and couldn't decide which was worse. Not having a boyfriend with a great car who always got an "A" table at Mr. Chows, or not having a way to support the high-maintenance rituals considered bare necessities for a Hollywood "B" list actress like myself.

I chose "B." If I couldn't afford basic upkeep to stave off all those nubile twenty-year-olds landing at LAX every day, the only parts, or guys, or parts of guys I would be able to score were the old, agentless actors with bad breath who did summer stock in the Berkshires.

*What's the use?* I e-mailed my father. *The last film I starred in was an X-ray. I'm thinking of moving home for a while.*

To my relief, my parents were fine with the decision, but only because they would rather talk to me than each other. You'd think that after more than three decades of marriage, they'd have run out of things to fight about. But it had been thirty-one long seasons of *The Lenny and Roberta Show*, and still no sign of reruns. He wanted to travel. She'd rather have a new kitchen. He hated her cooking. She hated his mother.

"Don't you ever get sick of listening to them?" I asked my brother, Adam, one night.

"Are you kidding?" He shrugged. "Last year they went for counseling and had to be nice to each other. It was the worst two weeks of my life. It was honey this, and sweetheart that. I wanted to gag."

And typical of my younger sister, Lindsey, who had always been a few sandwiches short of a picnic, she was clueless that anything was wrong outside her own universe. She was too busy carrying on that now that I was home, she had to vacate my closet and find another place to put the computer. "And I would appreciate it if you didn't hog the bathroom like you used to." She informed me on my first night back. "Some of us have to get to work in the morning."

*Work, my ass*, I thought. *You answer the phone at Daddy's office, and spend the rest of the day shopping online.*

"No way did I ever think Adam, Lindsey, and I would still be living at home in our twenties," I bitched to my childhood friend, Elyce Fo-gel at our old hangout, the Plainview Diner. "We're like the plates and silverware here. Relics from the eighties, but nowhere else to go."

"Could be worse." Elyce patted my hand. "At least none of you moved back, divorced with two kids, like at everyone else's house."

"No, I can't believe my parents aren't the ones who are divorced. All they do is fight."

"Oh, please. They've been like that since I met you. They're crazy about each other."

"You got the crazy part right. . . . I don't know. Maybe I should have toughed it out in L.A."

"Maybe you just need time to adjust. And look at the bright side. Now you can be in my bridal party."

"Oh, no, no, no. I mean, I'm honored, of course. I just wouldn't feel right taking someone else's place who, you know, is closer to you now."

"Are you kidding, Claire? Ask Ira. I was so excited to hear you were home. You're my oldest and dearest childhood friend."

"But I've never even met Ira. . . ."

"You're going to love him. He's so funny, and he's an accountant like your dad. Oh, and you should see his absolutely adorable cousin who is going to be our best man. . . . Could be a match made in heaven. You never know, right?"

*Oh, I know, all right.* "See, it's just that—"

"Look, if you're afraid this is going to turn into one of those huge, crazy affairs, I promise you, the Bergs are very classy. We've all agreed on small and tasteful."

"Terrific." I sipped my coffee. "How many on the guest list?"

"Three-twenty-five. Three-fifty tops."

"People?" I gulped.

"Yes, people!" Elyce laughed. "You are still such a rip."

"Gee. I always thought small and tasteful was forty of your near-est and dearest at a little seaside restaurant."

"Claire, oh my God. Are you insane? I've waited my whole life for this day!"

I had yet to break it to her that if Vera Wang personally designed my dress, I wouldn't subject myself to a torturous year of engagement parties, showers, and bridal registries. To say nothing of the urgent phone calls I'd have to take after the caterer shortened the cocktail hour and the videographer insisted on using floodlights, which didn't he know would melt the ice sculptures?

Not for me, thanks. I had done this tour of duty twice in my life, and in both cases the mission was a bust. The first friend accused me of trying to lure her fiancé away for a weekend of rough sex, and the other decided last minute that her mother was right, the guy was a nothing loser, and everyone would forgive and forget as long as she promptly returned all the gifts, except for that beautiful sterling gravy boat from Tiffany's, which if she was smart she would swear she never received.

I promised myself that as soon as I returned from Miami, I would explain to Elyce that although I was very happy for her and what's-his-name, I just wasn't in a bridal party frame of mind these days.

But what I was dying to say was, I couldn't believe people needed years to plan the affair. Jewish funerals were thrown together in less than forty-eight hours, and they had all the same things as a wedding. The rabbi, the chapel, flowers, speeches, limousines, guests. . . . And just like a funeral, once Elyce married this guy, her life was over.

Not that I would fret over her future. I had returned to New York on a "Me" mission. Goal #1: Fall in love. Goal #2: Pursue opportunities unique to the East: Broadway, commercials, and most definitely, a visit to *Law and Order*'s casting office in Chelsea Pier.

Unfortunately, after reading *BackStage* diligently, it appeared that the open-call season was over. The only promising tryout I could line up was located a little south of the city. Specifically, South Beach, Florida. And it wasn't exactly for a speaking part. More like a go-see at this hot modeling agency that specialized in booking asses for the studios.

You heard me. I was so desperate to break into movies, I was flying to Florida to drop my thong in front of the gay photographer who owned the agency. So that after a few test shots, he could give me his opinion if my aging but still pilates-tight *tuchas* was the perfect size, shape, and color producers would pay thousands for when their ass-ashamed stars needed an understudy, so to speak.

I had learned of this incredible "back door" opportunity when my former roommate in L.A., Sydney Sloan, instant-messaged me.

**SYDERELLA (11:56 PM):** u should go . . . butt doubles can make a quick 10gs

**CLAIREBEAR1(11:57 PM):** r u serious that's how much they'll pay u?

**SYDERELLA (11:57 PM):** i no this grl who made 20G to do a crappy little scene for Dana Donovan.

**CLAIREBEAR1 (11:57 PM):** a love scene?

**SYDERELLA (11:58 PM):** in the shower/// show her ass

**CLAIREBEAR1 (11:58 PM):** wow

**SYDERELLA (11:58 PM):** then Dana canned her . . . said her ass was 2 fat and pale . . . her fans would no its not hers . . . EGO bitch.

**CLAIREBEAR1(11:59 PM):** did she still get the $?

**SYDERELLA (11:59 PM):** hell yes.

Naturally, my parents thought the very idea of having my ass evaluated was ridiculous. Didn't I have any pride? (Not for twenty grand I didn't.) Didn't I care what the neighbors thought? (Translated: How could they brag I was in a movie if they had to ask everyone to close their eyes?) Didn't I want to help out Cousin Arnie who ran a drama school for kids? (Sorry, but my most valuable lesson was showing girls how to duct tape their breasts to give the appearance of being perkier.)

But after reminding my parents that I didn't need their approval, and that the connections the agency could make for me would be worth the humiliation, they backed down. Even agreed to pay for my airfare, provided I stayed with my grandmother (I call her Grams), and took her around to look at all the new assisted living centers going up in the area. It was a great plan.

Until I ended up seated next to a heart attack victim on a flight without a single medical professional on board. Only a group of anxious flight attendants who looked much happier passing out headsets than operating high-tech life-saving equipment.

Meanwhile, all I could think was, I sure hope God hadn't put me in 8B as punishment for my growing list of transgressions. Yes, I had run out on my creditors, abandoned my agent, been unsympathetic to my parents, and judgmental of Elyce. And yes, I had just ignored a perfectly nice person for no other reason than I was in a pissy mood.

So as I stood over the grayish-colored man whose name I never bothered to ask, I prayed for a miracle. *Please God. Revive this man's heart. Otherwise I'll never be able to live with the fact that his last few hours alive were spent with me, Claire Greene, Not Very Nice Girl.*

## Chapter 2

"HIS NAME IS ABRAHAM FABRIKANT," I BLURTED WHEN THE COPILOT emerged from the cockpit.

First Officer Freeman hadn't yet laid eyes on the old man lying face up in the aisle, but he looked sickly in anticipation of the moment. Then, mindful of his oath to stay cool so that passengers didn't panic, he crossed his arms, indicating his comfort level with the job his coworkers were performing in the forward galley. "I understand this is your grandfather?"

*Jeez. Not again.* "No sir. We just met." I sniffed into a cheap tissue from the lavatory. "She gave me his wallet and I found identification." I pointed to the perspiring flight attendant who was frantically alternating between administering CPR and shocking the man with the automated external defibrillator. "His driver's license is expired, but it says he lives in Miami."

First Officer Freeman didn't bother pretending that this little tidbit interested him. "The tower cleared us for an emergency landing in Jacksonville," he whispered to the crew. "Until then, do the best you can."

"It's too late." One of the flight attendants clutched the masks and gloves from the emergency Grab-n-Go kit. "There's no pulse or respiration. He's blue."

"Please don't give up on him," I cried. "I once was on *ER* and there was this scene where the third shock was the one that worked. . . . He told me his whole family is waiting for him. . . . It's . . . his birthday."

"Oh Christ. Second Code Red this month, too." The copilot looked away. "Well, it's best we're removing the body before the passengers get alarmed. Gayle, prepare the cabin for landing."

"No. Wait." I grabbed First Officer Freeman. "Look. I think his foot just moved."

"Maybe you should come sit over here." A flight attendant ushered me away. "Believe me, we're doing everything humanly possible."

"Then why isn't he responding?" I yelled so that other passengers heard. Maybe if they witnessed the airline's clear-cut negligence, they would demand an investigation. And the reinstatement of meals. And those really good macadamia nuts they used to pass out.

"Don't worry. We can't stop trying to revive a passenger until we land, even if we know he's gone," she sighed. "It's an FAA regulation."

"Oh." I buckled myself into a vacant seat. So if the old man died, I should presume it had nothing to do with the crew being heartless or incompetent. Simply, his time had come.

"I sure hope they know what they're doing," the man seated next to me said. "If it was a myocardial infarction and not ventricular fibrillation, that little machine can kill you."

"Are you a doctor?" I wondered how a knowledgeable medical person could just be sitting here, while a flight attendant more experienced in pouring coffee without spilling was trying to save a person's life.

"Nah. My brother sells defibs to casinos and airports. But it wouldn't matter if I was a doctor. The FAA won't let anyone other than the crew use them. Liability laws and all that crap."

"Makes sense," I said. "Why let a trained medical professional pitch in, when someone who's got to first read the manual can do the honors?"

A mother holding her infant son patted his back and leaned over to join the discussion. "I saw this thing on *20/20* or *Dateline,* or one of those, where you're supposed to get the victim to cough vigorously, and then take deep breaths so they get oxygen into their lungs."

*Good thinking! Let's wake him and ask him to cough!* I couldn't listen to these imbeciles gab, not while Mr. Fabric Softener, or whatever his name was, was teetering between here and the hereafter. I unfastened my seatbelt and returned to the scene.

When I'd first moved to L.A., I'd done a few walk-ons on *General Hospital*, and maybe that was about to serve some greater purpose. "Are those paddles in the right position?"

"Yes, of course," the exhausted flight attendant snapped.

"Because you didn't yell 'Clear' very loud. Maybe you're not doing it right."

"Somebody get this lady out of here!"

"No. Wait. See, I'm like that commercial. I'm not a doctor but I've played one on TV. And I remember they had me place one paddle on the right breast between the collarbone and the nipple—"

"Ma'am, please. You're interfering," First Officer Freeman scolded.

"I'm sorry." I started to sob. "He was such a nice man. A wonderful person."

"It's always the good ones who go first." He motioned the sign of the cross.

The first thing that struck me was that Mr. Fabrikant had been a living, breathing human being for over eighty years, but the instant that his heart stopped, he was just a body. "We'll have to remove the body through the center exit." "We'll have to ship the body back." So one minute you're a person, maybe the lone vote that changes the outcome of a Florida election, and the next minute you're a heavy object that needs to be bubble-wrapped and shipped Federal Express.

Maybe that's why I volunteered to get off in Jacksonville and remain with "the body" until family could collect their loved one. I hated thinking that we lost our humanity faster than one could say "will" and "testament." Besides, it would be nice to somehow sanctify this man's last day, although I had to admit that I had done nothing to sanctify it when he was still able to line up little pill bottles on his tray table.

First Officer Freeman thought better of my idea. No way did he want me having the chance to plant the idea in the family's head that something had gone terribly wrong on board. "Let me assure you that we have trained personnel to handle these matters." He patted my shoulder as if to demonstrate his airline's no-fail approach to consolation.

"I'm sorry," I said. "I feel I should be there for the family."

"Thinkin' maybe the old guy's kids will cut you in on the will, huh?"

*No, I'm thinkin' all men are idiots, and Mrs. Freeman married their king!* "No, of course not," I replied. "But if that man was my father, I'd want to hear exactly what happened."

Not that I knew myself. I hoped his loved ones would be too grief-stricken to press me for specifics, because I hated the idea of lying, on top of my original sin, ignoring. For sure I would make repentance my top priority so that I could face the family and still look in a mirror.

But no sooner did I exit the plane than I was paged to the Admirals Club to await the arrival of Mr. Fabrikant's next of kin. And, through no fault of my own, to receive the royal treatment. Apparently word was slow to get to God that His child Claire Greene was a selfish, pitiful member of the human race.

Once inside the lounge, an attendant brought me coffee and made sure that I felt comfortable seated near a TV. I was quite comfortable, thank you, but would I be violating any rules if I switched the channel from *CNN* to *The View*? No, I could do whatever helped me ease my grief. Did that include making out with Ben Affleck's brother, or whoever that stunning man was sitting alone over by the window?

How shallow could I get? It mattered not if the stranger with the red power tie was a good kisser. After being dumped by so many men, I didn't even know if I was a good kisser. I should be agonizing over my thoughtlessness and lack of decency, and what to say to Mr. Fabrikant's heartbroken family.

But tribulation would have to wait. For suddenly I was distracted by a young executive in head-to-toe black who was helping herself to bagels and muffins. I don't mean noshing. This girl was hoarding, dropping several napkin-wrapped items into her darling Dior bag. And, of course, I could relate, having done the very same thing on every movie set on which I'd ever worked.

Studios were notorious for hiring swank caterers to sate the appetites and whims of a hard-to-please cast and crew. Each day brought a new, delectable feast that was ours for the taking. So you bet that every other pauper and I making scale did our food shopping on those tables, bringing home a week's worth of dinner and snacks. How else to save up for eight-hundred-dollar pocketbooks that were all the rave until the next issue of *Vogue* hit the newsstands?

"Ms. Greene?" the receptionist called out. "You have a phone call."

It was an executive from American's headquarters in Dallas calling to say that she'd been able to reach Mr. Fabrikant's son, and that he would be en route to Jacksonville within the hour.

"Did you tell him the truth?" *Or did you say your father has taken a turn for the worse?* I knew about such calls. It's what the doctor told my mother the night that my Grandpa Harry died. Later we learned that he was already gone when the call was made, but hospital policy was to break the news in person.

"Naturally I told him the truth," the woman replied. "I informed him that his father suffered a heart attack while on board, and that we immediately requested to land."

"Yes, but does he know his father is dead?"

"The gentleman asked if his father survived, and I told him that he passed."

*That's what you said?* I thought. *He passed?* What a euphemism. It was one thing to pass gas, or pass a test, or pass the dry cleaner's on the way to the supermarket. But when a person we loved was taken from our midst, when the beating of his heart succumbed to a Godly force, that loved one had not passed. He had returned his soul to the loving house of our heavenly Creator. Where had I heard this before? Oh yes. My grandfather's funeral.

"How was he?" I asked. "After you told him."

The woman paused. "Between you and me? He cried like a baby. Then he told me it was very important that his father's body not be touched or examined until he arrived."

*Gee, he sounds sweet.* "Did you happen to mention that someone from the flight was waiting to meet him here?"

"Yes. And then he started crying again. He sounded so grateful."

*Run, Claire. Catch the next flight out before you have to pretend that you formed this incredible bond with Abe Fabrikant. If the son is even slightly intuitive, he'll know you're playing "Liar, Liar."*

"Well, what time *can* you be here?" My grandmother asked after I explained the little wrinkle in my travel plans. "I told Rose down the hall not to take me to the doctor because you would do it."

"I'm sorry, Grams. It's only eleven o'clock now. I'm sure I'll be in sometime this afternoon. Call the office and change the appointment for tomorrow."

"Ha! I'm never talking to his son-of-a-bitch office gal again. The other day she has the nerve to say to me, Mrs. Moss, your check came back. So I says, yeah, well, so did my arthritis."

"Oh no. Not more bounced checks. Mommy's going to kill you."

"What's the big hoo-ha? One to the doctor, the other to the drugstore. Serves those sons-of-bitches right. They make all us sick customers walk way the hell to the back for medicine, but the idiots who come in to buy cigarettes? They get to pay up front!"

Hmm. I'd have to give her that one.

"And those sons-of-bitches at the bank? All a bunch of no-good idiots. They leave the doors wide open so anyone can rob the joint. But the pens? Them they chain to the counter. . . . So this fella on the plane. The one who died. You knew him?"

"No, of course not. He just happened to be in the seat next to mine."

"But me you know your whole life, right?"

"Uh-huh." *Twenty dollars says I know where you're going with this.*

"Now a total stranger is more important than your own grandmother?"

Vintage Gertie, the country's top travel agent for guilt trips. "No, Grams. I didn't say he was more important. I just didn't think it was right to leave him here all alone."

"Like he'd know the difference? Where did you say he was from?"

"Miami."

"Oh. Miami? Uh-huh. Did he happen to mention his name?"

"We talked about a lot of things." I coughed. "The weather. His hobbies. His old neighborhood in Brooklyn."

"Where in Brooklyn? Flatbush? Coney Island?"

"Yeah, Grams. Coney Island."

"I wonder if he knew my cousin Estelle. Did you ask him?"

*Absolutely. I said to him, maybe you know my grandmother's cousin Estelle, a woman she hasn't seen in twenty years.* "No, I didn't get a chance. I'll explain everything when I get in."

"Well, don't spend the whole day there. I made your favorite meatloaf."

"Oh good." *I'm sure the sugar-free, low-sodium, low-fat, no-cholesterol version is even better than the original recipe, which used to make me puke.*

After an Advil chaser, I started making calls. First one was to Raphael de Miro, the owner of the modeling agency, to inform him of my unexpected delay. I couldn't tell if he believed my crazy story. But then he told me that something similar had actually happened to a friend of his. And to be careful, because the family of that deceased person accused his friend of poisoning their mother's wine when she went to the lavatory.

"Oh my God. That's terrible," I said. "What happened?"

"I really don't know, darling. It was probably true."

Next I called my father's office, never expecting it would be harder to get through to him than the in-demand Mr. de Miro.

"Who may I say is calling?"

"Linds, it's me. Don't you know my voice?"

"I'm sorry. Who is this?"

"Your sister? I live down the hall from you? I have to talk to Daddy."

"He's in a meeting right now. Can I take a message?"

"Yes. Tell him that his younger daughter reminds me of Claudia Schiffer."

"Really?"

"Absolutely."

"Because of my highlights, or because I've been bleaching my teeth?"

"Because you have Schiffer brains. What are you doing?"

"I don't know. Daddy yelled at me before because I don't sound professional enough."

"Oh. Well, I'm sure he didn't mean with family. Just please put him on. It's important."

"I don't think he wants to talk to you right now. He's sort of pissed."

"Why? What did I do?"

"It's a long story . . . Oh wait. He's coming out of his office." Lindsey cleared her throat. "I'll see if he can take your call now. And thank you for calling Greene and Levinson."

I had no idea what Lindsey was getting at. My father rarely got angry with me anymore. Unless by some odd coincidence he found out my nude scene with George Clooney was in his apartment, not a film like I'd suggested. But that little lie notwithstanding, I knew he'd be pleased by my Good Samaritan deed, as it would give him bragging rights on his next golf outing.

Except that I never got the chance to tell him why I was sitting around an airport lounge in Jacksonville, because he was too busy yelling at me. So Lindsey was right. He was mad at me. And what a coincidence. It was all thanks to her.

It seemed that after I left home this morning, my darling little sister couldn't wait to tell them that I had refused my oldest childhood friend's invitation to stand up at her wedding.

Of course! I'd forgotten that she and Elyce's younger sister, Monica, still hung out together, and that word of my insolence would make front-page news in the *Plainview Gazette*: CLAIRE GREENE TURNS BACK ON BEST FRIEND. WEDDING PLANS RUINED.

"How could you say no?" my father asked. "It's not like you to hurt someone's feelings."

"I didn't say no, exactly. I just didn't say yes. You know how much I hate big weddings. The music is awful, and you have to smile every time the happy couple walks by, and tell them how much you love the food and the flowers, and everything is so beautiful. . . ."

"When did you become so cynical and angry?"

"After the Supreme Court gave us a cheerleader for President who bombed his SATs."

"I'm serious, honey. Your mother seems to think you're depressed."

"You'd be depressed, too, if you had to show up in public wearing lime-green chiffon."

"Look. If it's the money you're worried about, we'll pay for everything."

"I appreciate that. But why do you care if I do this or not?"

"Because we're loyal people, Claire . . . and Ira's father sends me a lot of business."

"So fine. We'll all go to the wedding, act happy, and you'll give them a very generous gift."

"I don't understand how you could deny Elyce this happiness. Adam and Lindsey would never do such a thing to a good friend."

"Oh my God. Why do you always compare me to them? Trust me, Dad. They're hardly poster children for model behavior, yet I'm the one you pick on."

"I don't pick on you. It's just, with you, I always have to point out the painfully obvious. But tell you what. If you say yes, next month I'll set you up in an apartment in the city."

"Tell Elyce I'm a size six."

Oh God. Had I really just agreed to be a bridesmaid, and run for fittings, and give my opinion on floral arrangements, and be available for frantic late-night calls whenever Ira went out of town and Elyce couldn't find him ("He promised he'd be back at his hotel by eleven")?

But here is what bothered me more. The fact that my parents thought of me as angry and cynical. I was sarcastic, definitely. But never bitter. In fact, I subscribed to the Single Girl's Credo. Better to laugh at desperate moments than to cry and ruin a perfectly good Botox treatment.

Like after the time I found out a studio lawyer I'd been dating had a serious drug dependency. I just thought his mood swings and teeth grinding were a result of his high-stress legal life. But when I found him snorting coke at seven o'clock on a Sunday morning, the bell went off.

Did I bawl my eyes out? No. Did I play the role of rock-star wife and plead with him to go into treatment? Certainly not. I grabbed my clothes and said, "Steven, if I wanted to date a cold man with slush for brains, I would have moved back to New York and slept with a snowman."

And that time I got a job working in the men's department at Saks? I dreaded going in because my boss was this two-faced psycho-bitch who had no idea what shirt looked good with what tie, but who never failed to remind my customers that I was still in the training program.

Still, I maintained a positive outlook, as the commissions were high, and I'd already gotten a chance to do close-up work with James Brolin and Sean Connery. In fact, after outfitting each of them, I stuck my glossy and résumé in their bags. The unadvertised free gift with purchase.

Which explains why I got fired. But did I have a temper tantrum or cry for mercy? No. I ran after said boss and yelled, "Wait! Can I trade this job for what's behind door number two?"

So you see? I wasn't really the angry type. More like tired. Tired of people who always assumed their needs were more important than mine. Tired of hearing thoughtless words from insensitive people. Tired of dealing with those who never extended themselves, but who felt entitled to receive the royal treatment.

Oh God. What if Mr. Fabrikant had decided that after eighty years, he was tired of the same things? What if he looked at me, so self-absorbed and aloof, and said enough was enough? If one person couldn't even be bothered to say hello to another person anymore, what was the point of living?

On the other hand, my father would probably tell me to stop dwelling on my mistakes and simply chalk this day up to being a good learning experience. He was a big believer in those life-altering, fall-on-your-sword events that if they didn't kill you, made you stronger.

But here was my own personal experience with experience. All it did was help me recognize the same dumb-ass mistakes when I made them again. Which inevitably I always did.

# Chapter 3

I'LL ADMIT TO HAVING WOUND UP IN A LOT OF STRANGE PLACES UNDER strange circumstances in my time. The as-yet-unexplained morning I woke up in the back of Brad Pitt's truck wearing only a bedsheet and a Burger King crown. Or the time I went hiking with friends in Jackson Hole, got lost looking for a place to pee, and walked onto some recluse's property who had a rifle and no interest in hearing how much I liked his flak jacket with the NIXON FOR PRESIDENT buttons.

Not exactly the sort of skirmish a civilian girl from Long Island had been trained to handle. Frankly, the only battle for which I'd been prepared was fighting over a parking spot at the Roosevelt Field Mall the week before Christmas.

So I suppose as unexpected excursions went, spending the morning in Jacksonville, Florida, wasn't the worst detour. In fact, I was sort of getting off on hanging out in a comfortable airport lounge frequented by bonus-happy executots. It was just unfortunate that I hadn't dressed better for the occasion, as I was the only one in the room wearing flip-flops and shorts.

Nor had I walked in holding the requisite bag of electronic toys, or tried to close a million-dollar deal on my cell phone. Although if I'd wanted, surely I could have pretended to be in a scene, and acted the role of a corporate ass-kicker taking a much-needed vacation day. *"I swear, they had to literally push me out of the office."*

But who was I kidding? No Palm Pilot or cell phone could mask my unaccomplished past. Compared to all these magazine covers in the flesh, I looked old and obsolete. Dowdy Miss Claire, director of the Sharper Image Nursery School.

Then, in the middle of my self-pity party, I got this strange vision of two tall men walking in a dark hallway, and they were headed in my direction.

"Ms. Greene?"

"Yes?" I walked over to the reception desk.

"The family has left the morgue. They're on their way up to meet you."

The woman made it sound so official, I felt bad for not preparing any welcoming remarks, as if dignitaries were visiting my country. I also wished she'd given me more than thirty seconds' notice so that I could have put myself together. For just as I reached for my pocketbook, two stunning men entered, and I had to force myself to place my tongue back in my mouth.

Not even their sullen expressions and hushed tones could detract from their sexual lure. Abe Fabrikant's next of kin were hot! How did I know that they were related to the deceased? The older of the two men carried the same canvas bag that Mr. Fabrikant had tucked under his seat.

I guessed the son to be in his late fifties, although his taut abs and snow-cone biceps spoke volumes about the benefits of sticking with a gym. The younger man—a grandson, I presumed—was a head taller, and closer to my age. And although leaner and lankier than his father, he, too, had six-pack abs, shoe-polish-black hair, and a George Hamilton tan. (Hey. Didn't I wish for a grandson?)

Put either of them in Italian suits, and they would pass for morning talk show hunks. The kind you just knew smelled good and said the right things before sex. I could tell because of the flowers that Junior Stud was clenching.

Amazing how fast word spread in the Jewish community. Loved ones had already started calling the caterers, liquor stores, and florists, who heard the word *shiva* and jumped into their *We're sorry* *for your loss, that'll be $260* mode. Unless . . . Oh no. Was that bouquet for me?

After the receptionist pointed in my direction, I tucked my hair behind my ear and smoothed my shirt. Didn't matter. I still looked like a *shlump* who'd rolled out of bed and caught the first flight out to Miami, never once stopping to think that this might be the day I met the crown princes of Dade County.

As they walked toward me, I felt a chill. There was a certain familiarity to these strangers, impossible as that was. For if I'd known men this attractive, wouldn't I have remembered? Then it hit me. A minute ago I'd had this strange vision of two tall men approaching, and here they were.

I guess you could call it a premonition, not that I had much experience with this sort of phenomenon. To the contrary, I had zero psychic abilities, as was evidenced by the fact that I had both bought a Kia and voted for Bush.

"Claire Greene?" The older man removed his shades, revealing red, swollen eyes.

I nodded yes, and he hugged me so tight I could hardly breathe. "Thank you so much for everything you've done."

"It was really nothing." So far I wasn't lying.

"No. No," he insisted. "You are a wonderful person. Please." He took the bouquet. "We'd like you to have this small token of our appreciation."

"Thank you." *You don't know how small a token I deserve.*

"I'm Ben Fabrikant, and this is my son, Dr. Drew Fabrikant."

"Hi, Dr. Fabrikant. I'm Claire, and I'm very sorry for your family's loss." I extended my hand and didn't want to let go. He had a warm jock grasp and a dazzling, dentist-chair smile.

"Please. Call me Drew. . . . We were so relieved when we heard a stranger tried to come to my Pops' aid. He was such a great man. . . ."

Ben couldn't contain himself at the reference to his father in past tense, and began sobbing on Drew's shoulder. So I reached into my pocketbook for tissues, but pulled out Mr. Fabrikant's wallet instead. Right! The flight attendant had asked me to search it for identification.

"I'm sorry." Ben took a deep breath. "We are in such shock. I mean, he wasn't well, but we just spoke to him this morning. He sounded fine."

"You're never prepared for the call." Drew sniffed.

"Of course not," I said. *Hey. You think you were surprised?*

"Is that my Pops' wallet?" Drew eyed the worn leather billfold.

"Yes. The flight attendant asked me to hold on to it."

"I told you no one stole it." He punched his father's arm. "Didn't I say it would turn up?"

"Yes, you did." Ben turned to me. "When we didn't find it on him, naturally we thought someone stole it. Not that he carried much money around. A few credit cards. . . ."

"And 'My Sky,'" Drew added. "This poem he liked. It's like his American Express card. He never left home without it."

*Oh my God. The man walked around with poetry in his pocket? I hate myself!*

"I still can't believe Aunt Charlotte invited him to the party." Drew looked upward, as if he might catch a glimpse of the gate for departing souls.

"She's unbelievable." Ben shook his head. "We begged her not to, didn't we? We said please don't send Pops the invitation because you know him. He'll come."

"He never missed an occasion," Drew sniffed. "Did he tell you why he was in New York?"

Shouldn't that be something I knew? If only I'd asked, "So what brings you to New York?"

"His great-granddaughter's first birthday," Drew continued. "We said, Pops, it's not necessary. It's just a little party in Aunt Charlotte's backyard. If only it had been any other weekend, I could have gone with him."

"Drew's fiancée had her bridal shower yesterday," Ben explained.

Damn! He was engaged. Was my timing in life always going to be this bad?

"Did he . . . happen to say anything about our family?" Drew hesitated.

"Yes. He seemed so proud of all of you." What was a little white lie if it eased their pain?

Ben closed his eyes. "He did love all of us, especially this guy." He punched Drew's arm. "Mr. Lacrosse Star. Mr. First in His Class at Podiatry School."

Bummer. Not a *real* doctor. But who was I to be a snob? I didn't even have a job, let alone one that people viewed as second-rate. Even my brother, Adam, was more gainfully employed than me. Then, as if on cue, my cell phone rang, and it was the prodigal brother himself.

"Thanks for blocking me in with your car, moron. Where the hell are your keys?"

"Excuse me." I signaled to Ben and Drew that it was an important call. Ha! "Check the rack by the TV in the kitchen," I whispered. "That's where I always hang them."

"Well, guess again, genius! They're not there, and I gotta be at work in twenty minutes. Where else should I look?"

"I have no idea. Maybe Lindsey or Mommy took them, but they're not on me." *I hope.* Oh no. What if they were still in my pocketbook? I'd been so busy running around packing last night, and the cab came so early this morning, maybe I'd had a brain freeze and forgotten to leave them.

"I already asked, and they haven't seen them. Just tell me where the spare is."

"The spare?" I gulped. *You mean the key I lost ages ago, and never got around to copying?*

"You freakin' idiot. You don't have another key?"

"It was on my to-do list."

"Yeah, well, add hiring a bodyguard to that list. How the hell am I supposed to get around?"

"I don't know. Call AAA. Don't they open cars all the time?"

"Gee. Why didn't I think of that? I'll get in your car and be able to drive NOWHERE!"

"I'm really sorry, Adam. Maybe call Honda. . . ."

Then it was like, boom, another vision. I was picturing the windbreaker I'd worn yesterday, and if there was a God, maybe I'd left the keys in a pocket. I wasn't sure what made me think of it, but Adam checked, and amazingly, there they were.

"Thanks for the heart attack," he grumbled.

"Funny you should mention that," I sighed. "Believe it or not, the man next to me on my flight just dropped dead from one, and I got off in Jacksonville to be with the family."

"Gross! You had to sit next to a dead guy? I woulda made them stick him in an overhead bin or something."

"Which is why it's looking doubtful kids will ever get a day off of school in your honor. Anyway, sorry about the scare."

"Whatever."

"My kid brother." I pointed to the phone when I returned. "He called to express his condolences."

"We've been rude, Claire," Ben sighed. "We haven't even asked about your family."

"There's nothing much to tell, really. We're from Plainview, Long Island. It's my parents, my brother, sister, and me. My dad is an accountant, and my mom . . . is not."

"If they raised a daughter like you, I'm sure they're nice. Come. We'll grab a bite and talk."

"Oh no. I couldn't eat. I'm still a little queasy." *From pigging out on bagels in the lounge.*

"Of course you're still upset. One of the flight attendants told us that you went nuts on them. Like you were trying to will my dad to live." Ben shook his head in admiration.

*Guilt will do that to you.* "It's just that he seemed so concerned about all of you."

"He loved family," Drew sobbed. "He couldn't do enough for us. Whatever we needed. . . ."

"We were everything to him." Ben hugged his son to his breast.

My God. I hadn't been around this much father/son love since . . . ever. My father and brother had mostly snarled at one another when they weren't taking swings at each other's heads. In fact, I could swear the last peck on the cheek my father gave Adam was at his bar mitzvah during the candle-lighting ceremony . . . after the photographer suggested that it would make a nice pose.

Can you imagine? It didn't dawn on a proud father to kiss his only son on such an important day, until he was reminded that the picture would look good in the photo album?

How could our two families be so different? The Fabrikants' hearts were humming like finely tuned engines, while my family was hopelessly disengaged. That's when I realized I had to do whatever I could to comfort them. This kind of profound love and devotion should be celebrated, and I, Claire, was going to help, even if I had to lie about what really happened on their patriarch's final journey.

Unfortunately, each time I deceived Ben and Drew, I realized that the key to being a better-than-average liar was having a great memory. But I have Nouns Disease. Difficulty remembering persons, places, or things.

So although we were sipping iced lattes at Starbucks, I was in a sweat. They wanted details. Had Abe said anything about not feeling well? Did he eat his snack? What was he reading? Did he happen to mention if he was happy in his new assisted living center? He wasn't one to complain. Did he show her pictures of his five grandchildren and two great-grandchildren?

Big problem. How would I remember everything that I was making up on the spot? It was hard enough remembering things that actually happened to me. On the other hand, thanks to my acting talent, I was a better liar than I thought. I not only answered their questions with a straight face, I concocted cute little stories, making it sound as though Abe and I had connected like dots.

In fact, Ben and Drew were ecstatic when I told them how he had helped me finish the *Times'* crossword puzzle in under an hour. They had no idea that he'd even liked crossword puzzles, but I said he'd mentioned that it was his favorite thing to do because it kept his mind sharp.

Mind you, I hadn't worked on a crossword puzzle since I was

eight. So who knew if taking an hour to complete one meant we were qualified to join Mensa, or were borderline retarded? All I knew was that Ben was deeply moved. "My old man never ceased to amaze me," he cried.

Understand that this was difficult work, lying. At any moment I could mention something that would blow my cover. Reveal myself for the fraud that I was. My only hope was that in their fragile state of mind, anything suspect I said would bypass their antennas.

Turns out I liked Ben and Drew. They were sweet and funny, and it would be the easiest thing to fall in love with either one. As I listened to their wonderful stories about Abe, and watched their eyes well up each time they realized that he was gone, I fantasized about which one would I prefer to date. The suave, handsome older man who appreciated the seductive qualities of moonlight and love songs? Or the young devil with bedroom hands who could get creative with whipped cream?

I know. I have a really sick mind. These poor men were in mourning, and all I could think about was indulging my fantasies. But what stopped the ride on the love train were the constant interruptions.

First an airline representative informed us that we'd been booked on the next flight to Miami, with Mr. Fabrikant's white cardboard casket to be placed in cargo. It was a somber moment, but one we had anticipated. Then there was a barrage of calls.

I heard from my mother, who had just heard from her mother, and was it true that an old man on the flight died on my lap, and did American plan to refund my airfare because I'd been so inconvenienced? "My friend Paula got two free tickets after their dog died on a United flight."

My father called to urge me to be careful about what I told the family, because if they sued the airline for negligence, they'd call me as a material witness, and I'd have to fly back and forth to Florida to testify. "I'm telling you right now, Claire. Once they subpoena you, you'll be tied up in litigation for years."

My friend and former roommate, Sydney, called to see how my ass audition went, only to hear my strange tale and offer me advice. "Engaged means shit. If you like this Dr. Drew character, slip him your number. Maybe it's an on-again-off-again-type thing."

But from what I could tell, the fiancée seemed to have a pretty good grip. She must have called six times in a half hour, and each time he ended the conversation with an "I love you." Although by that last good-bye, he reminded me of a smitten Mr. Movie Fone. Robotic devotion.

The best call, however, came from Ben's sister in California, who had just heard the devastating news and was preparing to fly home. I could only hear his side of the conversation, naturally, but when I heard the words *postproduction* and *director*, my curiosity was piqued. Was his sister in the business?

"This must be so hard for you," I sighed. "But at least you have family to help you through. Is your mother alive?"

"No," Ben sighed. "I guess you could say we're orphans now."

"So it's you, Charlotte in New York, and the sister who just called from California?"

"Impressive." Drew smiled. "It took me much longer to get the family straight."

"His mother was a young widow when we got married. . . . But he's been my son from the day I held him . . . and my father was crazy about you. Right, Drew?"

"That was my Pops." His eyes glazed.

I nodded sympathetically, too, but my mind was racing. "So, Ben. Your sister in California? Where does she live? It's funny, because I just moved back from there."

Ben looked at Drew.

"Uh, she's in Southern California." He cleared his throat. "But she also has a home here."

Bingo. Anyone who could afford two houses located in the priciest parts of the country had to be in the business.

"That's so funny," I said. "I lived in Southern California. Just outside of Santa Monica, actually. I'm an actress. Well, I was. I'm sort of in between gigs right now. That's why I moved home. But no kidding. One call from the coast, and I'd never look back."

"I thought you looked familiar," Drew said.

"Really? Because I felt the same about you. As soon as I saw the two of you it was like, whoa, where do I know them from?"

"I know what it is." Drew snapped his fingers. "You remind me a little of my Aunt Penny. Don't you think, Dad?"

Ben studied my face. "Maybe a little. It's hard to say."

"Is she the aunt from California?"

"Yeah. Although she's a lot older than you, of course," he replied. "I don't know. It's just something about your eyes. . . ."

Suddenly Ben stood and looked at his watch. "We should go check on our flight. Drew, you check to see if our tickets are ready. I'll go back downstairs and make sure everything is set with . . . Dad. Claire, why don't we meet up with you in a half hour by the gate?"

"Fine. It'll give me time to make some calls. . . . I was supposed to have this go-see at a modeling agency in South Beach."

"They'd be crazy not to hire you." Drew winked.

"Let's go." Ben hustled his demonstrative son out. "See you in a few, okay?"

"You bet." I waved.

What just happened? All I did was ask a simple question about Aunt Penny, and off they went. Think. Who could it be? Penny Marshall? Puh-leese. I'd be really upset if Dr. Drew thought I looked like her. Penny Danziger, the president of Red Lion Pictures? No way. She was a beautiful girl, but from the Philippines. Penny Nichol? Now, that would be incredible. And come to think of it, until she had that last face-lift and came out looking like Alien Joan Rivers, people told me how much I resembled her. But how could she be related to the Fabrikants? By their name I knew they were Jewish. But Ms. Nichol? Definitely not a member of the tribe.

My thoughts were interrupted by yet another call, and to my surprise, it was Grams. Until now she'd refused to dial my cell. Once Dan Rather reported cell phones were the leading cause of brain cancer, that was it.

"There's zero risk if you're the one on the regular phone," I would remind her.

"So what's with the dead guy?" she asked.

"He's still dead," I laughed. *And thanks for your deep expression of sympathy.* "But I'm on a one-fifty flight, so figure by the time I get my bags, a cab, and stop at the modeling agency, I should be to you around seven-thirty, eight."

"*Oy.* So late? What should I do with the meatloaf?"

*Do you really want me to answer that?* "Freeze it, maybe? I'm not very hungry."

"Anyway, Rose down the hall asked me to ask the man's name who died. She wants to make sure it's not her cousin Sol, 'cause he was fly-ing back from New York today, too."

"Nope. This man's name was Fabrikant. Abe Fabrikant."

"Wadjasay?"

*Turn up your hearing aid.* "Abraham Fabrikant." I spoke louder. "From Miami."

Silence was followed by three *oy vey is mer*'s.

"What's the matter, Grams?"

"*Oy yoy yoy yoy yoy.* . . . *Gutenu* . . . *vey is mer* . . ."

"Enough with the oying already. Did you know him?"

"That stupid son-of-a-bitch. . . . I can't believe what I'm hearing."

"Who is he . . . was he?"

"I can't say another word. *Oy, oy, oy!* I think I'm going to *plotz!* Of all people to die on you. . . . Claire, don't say nothin' to your parents about this, hear me?"

"Okay, you're starting to freak me out a little here. Are you saying we knew this man?"

"And don't talk to the family again. Zip your lip. You don't know nothin' about nothin'. . . . And let's hope it stays that way."

# Chapter 4

I SWEAR TO GOD, MY GRANDMOTHER COULD BE A CHARACTER IN A BOOK. According to my mother, Roberta—her eldest, and consequently the one who has had to live with her the longest—every day brought new battles with the butcher, the baker, and the candlestick maker. This one was a lousy son-of-a-bitch, and that one a *narishkeit* (yiddish for "asshole"). And somebody was always trying to make a fool out of her, to which my Grandpa Harry would yell, "Believe me, Gert. You do that all on your own!"

I had seen enough evidence growing up to suspect that between her long bouts of depression and her paranoid view of the world, Prozac would have been a helpful staple in her medicine cabinet. But in her day, who ever heard of being diagnosed with mental illness? People were written off as *meshuginas*. Oddballs you ignored when they started acting a little crazy.

And, understandably, after the tragic death of her twenty-four-year old son Gary, she was even more difficult to deal with. She'd run to the cemetery every morning and curse God for sparing him from Vietnam but not keeping him out of harm's way on the Long Island Expressway. Then she'd go to work and yell at the kids who came into their Valley Stream shoe store with no intention of buying.

"Leave them!" Grandpa Harry would say. "Later they'll come back with their parents."

My Aunt Iris and my mom pleaded with her to get help, but she'd go berserk at the mention of seeing a psychiatrist. "What's to discuss? My only son is gone. Is he going to bring him back? No. So that son-of-a-bitch can rot in hell if he thinks he can sit on his fat *heiny* and judge me."

And so it went, until Gertie finally reached the age where craziness was standard fare, along with gout, arthritis, and high blood pressure. Particularly in Florida, where the state bird is a cuckoo.

And even though her ranting and raving were annoying, and we dreaded taking her out in public (apologies to that nice waiter at the Cheesecake Factory who may never recover from being called a lazy *fageleh* whose brains fell out after poking all those holes in his head), it seemed like everyone else's grandparents were just as crazy.

That's why the more I thought about her reaction to hearing the name Abe Fabrikant, the easier it was for me to blow it off. She was probably confusing the man with the son-of-a-bitch butcher in Canarsie from forty years ago who used to cheat by weighing the meat with the bones.

Meanwhile, it was time to catch up with Ben and Drew, and although I felt out of sorts from all the stress and commotion, I hadn't expected to start hallucinating. But as I got closer to the gate and saw Drew, arms around his sobbing father, I could have sworn I also saw the deceased hovering.

I blinked a few times, but honest to God, I was looking right at Mr. Fabrikant. Surely his son and grandson were aware of his presence, as they were directly in his shadow. But something told me that this was my own personal aberration. My own exclusive sighting. Served me right for watching *The Sixth Sense* all those times. Now I was seeing dead people.

"Boo!" I felt a tap on my shoulder.

"Oh jeez!" I jumped. So this is what heart failure felt like.

"Oh my God. It is you, right? Claire Greene?"

"Julia?"

"I can't believe it." She nodded like a bobble-head doll.

"How are you?" I hugged her.

"I'm sorry. Did I scare you? It's just that I thought I recognized you over at Starbucks, but I wasn't sure because it's been like, what? Ten years? Anyway, I said to my mother, I think that's my old friend Claire, from I.U. Mommy. Come over here. It *was* her. . . . What are you doing here?"

"You wouldn't believe me if I told you. You?"

"Well, my whole family was supposed to be getting together, then my dad got sick, and my sister couldn't find anyone to watch her kids. . . . Wait. Are you on the flight to Kennedy?"

"No. Miami. To visit my grandmother. I'm going to help her—"

"Hello, darling." Kiss kiss. "Look at you. Still looking like a sorority girl. Thin and gorgeous as ever. One day you have to tell me your secret."

"Hi, Mrs. Farber. You look great, too."

"So tell me, dear. How is your family? Are you married?" Detective Farber surveyed my ringless fingers.

"Family is good, thanks, and almost." I giggled like a schoolgirl. "I'm here with my fiancé and his father. They came to speak at this big medical convention."

"Oh my God. He's a doctor?" Julia squealed. "That is so amazing. So is my fiancé, Joel Goldstone. He's specializing in male infertility. He's in this big practice in the city."

"Really? That's unbelievable. Mine is a . . . brain surgeon." *You didn't just say that.* "So wait. Tell me again. Why are you here?"

"Remember my little brother Jonathan?"

"Sure." *The brat who stuffed the toilets with Play-Doh during parents weekend.*

"Well, he's not little anymore. He's six-three, and he graduated law school yesterday, and next month he's moving back to New York to work down on Wall Street. Can you believe it?"

"Yeah. It's a shame you're involved," Mrs. Farber pouted. "He'd go wild for you."

*Yup. The day just keeps getting better and better.*

"Claire? Come on." I turned around and Drew was signaling me. "We really have to go."

"Drew, honey. Come over here. I have friends I want you to meet." I prayed he couldn't hear me.

"Oh my God. That's him?" Julia squealed. "He's adorable. You must be so happy."

I looked over my shoulder, and miraculously he signaled that they were getting on the plane.

"Damn! I guess he wants to get his father seated. We think he picked up a bug at the hotel or something. He wasn't feeling well this morning. . . . Anyway, it was great seeing you."

"Well, hold on," Julia said. "Let's exchange e-mails. Or write down your phone number."

"Actually, I'm back home right now . . . until, you know, Drew and I finalize our plans."

"So wait. Do you still live in Plainview? Because do you remember my cousin, Elyce Fogel? She's from there, too. In fact, weren't you two really good friends at one time?"

"Uh-huh."

"I don't know if you heard, but she just got engaged."

"I did hear that, actually. I think to an Ira somebody."

"Right. Ira Berg. And it's the most amazing thing, because he was one of Joel's best friends at Cornell, and they just asked him to stand up at the wedding. So maybe when we get back, I'll call you, and all of us can go out. Wouldn't that be so much fun?"

"Absolutely!" *If I haven't followed Virginia Woolf into the River Ouse with rocks in my pockets.*

Just call me Pinocchio. I had lied more in this one morning than in an entire lifetime. And these weren't just ordinary, everyday fibs like the kind that kept you out of trouble with your boss or your best friend. This was outright deception of mythical proportions.

Not only had I befriended an elderly gentleman and convinced his family that he adored me, I was also engaged to a man I met an hour ago, who unbeknownst to him, had earned a medical degree, and was so respected in his field, he was speaking to colleagues at a convention.

It made me wonder if I'd missed my true calling. Maybe I should have tried my hand at screenwriting instead of acting, as I certainly didn't seem to be at a loss for material. But who was I kidding? I had gotten in way over my head with my Good Samaritan charade, and now it was spiraling out of control.

It's no wonder that by the second leg of my journey, I was feeling completely unhinged. My saving grace was that as a courtesy, American had bumped us up to first class, the free drink capital of the world. Ben and Drew downed vodka and tonics like they were pouring out of Buckingham Fountain. And on the other side of the aisle, I had requested three white wine spritzers and a straw.

So you can imagine that when Ben dozed off and Drew leaned over to whisper something, I wasn't my exactly on high alert. I was actually trying to nap myself, while trying not to drool with my mouth open. But when I heard him say the words "Aunt Penny" and "you'll never guess," I sat up.

"Remember before when you asked about her, and my dad just got up and left?"

I nodded.

"It's because he didn't want to tell you who she is."

*Well, thank you, Captain Obvious.* "Are we talking America's Ten Most Wanted list?"

"No. Nothing like that." Drew chuckled. "The thing is, she's sort of a famous celebrity."

"Sort of? You mean it's like a part-time thing?"

"No, it's definitely an all-the-time thing."

"So should we play charades, or can I start taking wild-ass guesses?"

"Not necessary." He smiled. "I'll tell you. Just promise not to freak out on me."

"I'm cool. In my line of work I meet tons of celebrities. They're just like you and me."

He leaned in and whispered a name in my ear. "Except for her," I gulped. "Oh my God."

Drew tried to shush me, but at that point I couldn't stop the Ohmygodathon. Could you blame me? I had just learned that the man who had died on my lap was the father of the legendary Golden Globe–winning actress Penny Nichol.

"I expected you to be excited, but . . ."

"It's not what you think. I mean, don't get me wrong. I love her. She's my idol. But there's something I have to tell you, and now *you* have to promise not to freak out."

"Okay. . . ."

"This is so bizarre, I'm shaking." I placed my hand over my heart. "Okay. . . . When we were on the plane, it so happened that I was reading *People* magazine, and I was looking at this picture of your Aunt Penny at her birthday party, and thinking, wow doesn't she look amazing at fifty!" *You are such a liar.* "Then all of a sudden, your grandfather collapses, and lands right smack on her picture."

"You're fucking kidding me!"

Drew's loudness stirred Ben. "What's going on?"

"I told Claire about Aunt Penny."

Ben raised an eyebrow.

"What the hell is the difference? She's in the business."

"Exactly." Ben whispered. "Isn't that why we agreed not to say anything?"

"Hey, look. She just tried to save Pops' life, okay? Be nice. And listen to what she told me."

Ben looked at me to make sure there were no hard feelings for withholding his sister's identity, and I smiled. As if I'd ever try to take advantage of the personal connection.

"I'm paraphrasing," Drew continued. "But basically Claire just told me that when they were on the plane, she was looking at Aunt Penny in *People*, and that's when Pops *plotzed* on the page."

Ben laughed. "Claire, do you swear you're not making that up?"

"Why would I lie?" *I've already reached my quota for the day.*

"Was he looking at the picture with you?" Drew asked.

"I don't think so. He'd been nodding on and off for a few minutes."

"Even if he did see it, he wouldn't have recognized her anyway." Ben sneered.

"She's had some work done." Drew lowered his voice.

*No, my car has had some work done. Penny had a major overhaul, according to my sources who frequent the same Beverly Hills plastic surgeons.*

"Do you mind if I ask you something?" Ben said.

"Not at all."

"When my dad talked about the family, did he happen to mention anything . . . about Penny?"

Even in my inebriated state, I knew a loaded question when it was pointed at my head. "No. Not a single word." *At last. The truth.*

Ben looked relieved, and I could tell that I'd just saved him thousands in therapy.

"He did talk a lot about you though." I smiled. "In fact, I remember thinking, wow, he seems so proud of his son's accomplishments." *Please don't be a convicted felon out on parole.*

Now Ben beamed, and I thought, *Hey, maybe I could become a professional liar.* I was obviously quite good at it, and look how helpful I was being.

"See? I told you he wasn't mad anymore." Drew smacked his father's arm. "He was worried that Pops died angry at him because we'd moved him into an assisted living center."

"It was nothing like a nursing home," Ben blurted.

"Actually he told me how much he loved it there," I said. "He had started to make friends and—"

"Really?" Ben said. "That's strange. Because the last time I spoke to the administrators, they said that he almost never came out of his apartment, he didn't want to go on any outings—"

*Ooops. Delete, delete, delete.* "You know? He did say that. But then he met a nice man down the hall, they started playing cards, and next thing he knew, he had all these new friends."

"Isn't that great, Dad? See? You were worried for nothing."

"I can't tell you how much this means to me." Ben took my hand.

"Hey, you know what?" Drew leaned in. "I was just thinking. Maybe we should have Claire speak at the funeral."

*Oh fuck!* "Oh no, no, no. I couldn't possibly do that. I mean, he was such a nice man, and we had a wonderful few hours together, but—"

"That's what I mean." Drew stopped me. "My Pops' last few hours on earth were incredible, all because of you. Dad, don't you think everyone would want to hear Claire tell the story?"

"I don't know. It might be a nice touch."

"No, wait." I had to stop this runaway train. "I mean I'm honored, of course. I just wouldn't feel right taking someone else's place who, you know, was closer to him."

Great. Now my sentences were repeating on me like pepperoni. That's exactly what I'd said to Elyce when I tried to get out of being her bridesmaid. Little did I know that I'd suddenly be in such demand to appear in weddings and funerals. Whatever happened to the old-fashioned rule of asking people you actually knew?

"But you're the only one who shared his final moments." Drew gave me puppy dog eyes. "I know it would mean a lot to our family."

"Well, look," Ben offered. "We obviously haven't had time to finalize the arrangements, but we did book the funeral chapel for Wednesday morning. Why don't you think about it?"

*Ha! What did I tell you? A perfectly nice funeral is being put together in less than two days. Why not a wedding? Wait until I tell Elyce.*

Meanwhile, I told Ben and Drew that I was deeply touched by their wanting to include me in the service, but that I'd only planned to be in Florida for a few days to help my grandmother and might have a possible modeling assignment. Not to mention I hadn't brought a single thing to wear that would be suitable for a funeral. Three damn good reasons, but not why I was hedging.

The bottom line was that I may have been able to snow these guys because they were in mourning and vulnerable. But no matter how good an actress I was, I just couldn't see myself getting up to make a speech filled with bald-faced lies to perpetuate the notion that Abe Fabrikant and I were buddies. I was a fraud, not a fool.

And yet in spite of all that, I heard myself say yes. Not because of Ben's generous offer to pay for a shopping spree and a trip to his wife's hairstylist. Not because of Drew's tight hug, although his woodsy aftershave made me weak. Not even because this would be a once-in-a-lifetime opportunity to ingratiate myself with Penny the Great, tempting as that was.

It was something more mysterious and unexplainable. A voice in my head that nearly cast me off my seat. The voice of a man saying *please* over and over again like a mantra.

Was my Grandpa Harry trying to reach me from the other side? Doubtful, as he hadn't seemed all that interested in me when he was on this side. Besides, the voice I was hearing was gentle and soothing, not shrill like I remembered hearing as a kid. The word *please* more like a message of peace than a stern lecture from the late Harry Moss. And then it hit me. If I wasn't hearing from my grandfather, maybe I was hearing from Drew's.

Why this was happening to me, I had no idea. I wasn't one of those spiritual can't-think-without-my-green-tea kind of people who ran to psychic fairs on weekends or who consulted Sir Singh, the Tarot card reader, before making a major purchase. I never had premonitions or saw auras. Hell, I never even opened fortune cookies.

And if Abe Fabrikant was going to make the effort to contact someone on earth, first appearing to me in human form, then whispering messages, why would he choose me, Claire-Awful-Person-Greene? I was his last impression of the human race, and hardly the way I'd think he'd want to remember us.

Then again, who was I to question the will of a spirit? If he was trying to communicate with me for whatever reason, I had better pay attention. Maybe he had an important message for me. Although with my luck, the message would sound like a threat from the Wicked Witch of Miami. "Speak at my funeral, and I'll get you, my pretty."

*Good job, Abe. The dead guy one. Claire nothing.*

# Chapter 5

"If treffic stays good, we be et South Beach in blink of yur eye," my chauffeur said. "Do you like more air?"

"No, thanks, Viktor." I leaned back and closed my eyes. "Everything is perfect."

And I wasn't saying that just to be polite, like the time my deli-owner boyfriend Max surprised me with one of those hideous Coach pocketbooks with the million *C*'s, and I had to jump up and down like an excited schoolgirl (he actually told me to say the *C* stood for Claire, as if anyone over the age of eleven wasn't familiar with the designer signature).

Seriously, the death of Abe Fabrikant notwithstanding, this day was starting to feel like the grand prize from one of those stupid reality shows. How else to explain that I was heading down 95 South to Raphael de Miro's studio in a white stretch limousine, sipping chilled champagne and with feet on the seat, watching my friend Renee get slapped on *One Life to Live*?

Or that when I called the temperamental Mr. de Miro to plead my case to let me do the test shoot later in the day, he couldn't have been lovelier? "Whenever you get here, dear," he said.

What was wrong with this picture? For starters, I wasn't used to riding in the back of a limo alone. Usually I was some rich guy's eye candy for the night, too busy fending off the customary predate groping and grinding to enjoy the trip.

As for the nice treatment from Raphael? A real mystery. My friend Sydney had warned that the prickly photographer had once left Heidi Klum in a fetal position because he didn't care for her work. "They don't call him Saddam Scavullo for nothing."

Meanwhile, I was trying to make sense of my quandary. It seemed the more I lied, the better the treatment. The Fabrikants thought I was Claire, Queen of Kindness. I thought I was a royal ass.

Extreme guilt forced me to mull over the possible repercussions if I should suddenly confess the truth to Ben and Drew. But what would I say? *Did I happen to mention I have a multiple personality disorder, and now that I'm somebody else, I just remembered I didn't get friendly with Mr. Fabrikant? In fact, it turns out, I never said a fucking word to him?*

Couldn't do it. For as soon as I agreed to speak at the funeral, they were so in love with me, so intent on repaying my good deeds, I blew the chance to rescind my story. And just as well. For when Drew heard I was cabbing it down to South Beach, then heading to my grandmother's place in North Miami, he said, "Nothing doing. The least we can do is get you a limo."

Frankly, I didn't put up a fuss for two reasons. I was happy to save the minimum eighty dollars it would have cost me to schlep all over town. And second, when Drew told me not to worry because the family owned a fleet of cars, it dawned on me that luxury transportation might be a mere segment of their holdings. Could you blame me for being curious about what else was under their conglomerate hood?

Until that moment, I swear I had no idea that the Fabrikants were loaded. Yes, Ben and Drew were smartly dressed, but they were wearing Florida casual. And with the way that Ralph Lauren discounted these days, for all I knew, they shopped at Marshall's like everyone else.

So when I asked my driver to tell me about this nice family he worked for, I wasn't expecting to hear that the Fabrikants were south Florida's answer to the Gatsbys. That their name was synonymous with opulent wealth because Ben managed to use his entrepreneurial instincts to parlay the profits from his father's furniture business into a chain of exclusive clubs all over town where celebrities and the paparazzi gathered nightly.

In fact, his newest club, By the C (*C* for Cuba; now, that was adorable), had just been named by *Florida* magazine as Miami Beach's number one go-to place for the toweled-off crowd and was so coveted by club-hoppers that when it was closed temporarily due to a kitchen fire, the other Ocean Drive nightspots were thankful for even the short reprieve.

"I wotch and I learn. In thees country, a kesh business is the way to go." Viktor talked to me through the rearview mirror. "What ken the government do? Collect money they don't know ehbout? No. Em I right?"

*Okay, Viktor. Here's a little English test. Spell* IRS, tax evasion *and* jail. "Well, I'm sure the Fabrikants are very honest businesspeople."

"Who ken afford to be honest? You get keeled in texes. I say, give us more tex credits. Give us more deductions. Em I right?"

"Amen to that." *Why was it that the only people who knew how to run the country either cut hair or drove limos?* "So you were saying before, Ben practically owns the Miami night scene?"

"He hez so much businesses, he ken't keep them all straight. But to tell the truth, Abe was my real Ameriken hero," Viktor sniffed. "He give my father job, he help bring my femily here. He bought us house. . . . A better men there never was. Em I right?"

"A saint." I gulped. *Shit, Claire! Next big lightning storm, and guess who's gonna be toast?*

"I'm so sed he's gone." Viktor bowed his head. Not a good thing for a driver who is cruising at seventy miles per hour. "But the rest of thi bunch?" He suddenly came to. "Crazy, crazy, crazy."

"Really? They seem pretty normal to me."

Not so, according to the well-informed Viktor, who was clearly unfamiliar with confidentiality agreements, as there didn't seem to be much he was afraid to say. Particularly on the subject of Ben's marital history.

Seems Ben's first wife, Doreen, the doctor's daughter, divorced him after catching him, drawers down, in a little bedroom duet with Desiree, the Dominican dancer.

A year later, against his family's wishes, Ben married this Desiree lady. Only to have the union last about as long as a Beatles album, thanks to a freak boating accident on the Intercoastal. Sadly, the poor girl had a few too many, and did a "Natalie Wood" over the side of Ben's yacht. The police reports said it was accidental, but job-secure Viktor had no problem speculating that the tragedy could have been avoided if Mr. Ben hadn't pushed her. "Strong winds, my ess."

Not a big believer in long mourning periods, Ben started dating even before his black funeral suit came back from the cleaners. This time, a swimsuit model and spokesperson for a chain of tanning salons caught his eye. "He called her fifties wrepped in hundreds." Viktor sighed.

Little did Ben know that the former Shari Deveraux was not only a single parent, but a grieving widow like himself. And with such a common bond, they clung to one another as if they were the last lovers for miles. Even after Shari's young son Andrew was brought into the picture, Ben insisted that he had never been more in love, and proposed yet again.

"My father say to heem. Mr. Ben, if you get the meelk for free, why buy the cow?"

But in spite of that expert marital advice, Ben, Shari, and Drew walked down the rose-strewn aisle together and were the toast of the town. Nothing was more coveted than an invitation to party at their lavish waterfront home in Gables Estates, or to travel the seas in their ninety-foot Cheoy Lee yacht.

But even the good life, like cow's milk, can have a limited shelf life. And if you believed Viktor and the local gossip columns, the marriage was curdling, thanks to their twelve-year age difference and Shari's difficulty sticking to those little vows recited before God at the wedding.

"Some days I ken't keep treck who iz in beck." Viktor snapped his gum. "Who iz the decorator, the lover, the lawyer, the trainer. . . . End now their little girl, Delia, is like her mother with the parties and the drinking. . . . It's crazy, em I right?"

As if this weren't enough of a guide to the "Lifestyles of the Rich and *Ferklempt*," here is what Viktor had to say about the dashing Dr. Drew:

He and his fiancée, Marly Becker, met on blind date, arranged by their fathers, no less. Apparently, Ben had been doing business for years with Milt Becker, the owner of the largest linen supply company in south Florida, when they discovered they both had single kids on the prowl.

Although neither father expected the couple to click, a year later Drew proposed on bended knee. Unfortunately, the romantic act must have cut off his circulation, for a few months later he got cold feet and started calling old girlfriends, one of whom used the same manicurist as Marly.

And as any girl knows, news in the nail business travels faster than a fill-in. Once the two customers discovered their mutual love interest, Marly drove over to By the C, chucked her perfect four-karat solitaire engagement ring into the five-hundred-gallon aquarium, and waved her ringless finger in Drew's direction. He would never look at fishing the same way again.

Eventually he came to his senses and begged forgiveness from her and her mother, Sharon. Soon the Becker girls were working on take two of the November nuptials, and one thing was certain. Marly's mother was her best friend, and therefore her matron of honor. Not that Drew saw anything wrong with that.

At this point, I was glad to be nearing Casa de Miro, because my head was spinning from having listened to thirty minutes of rapid-fire details about these mega-rich, out-of-their-minds Floridians who only a few hours earlier I never even knew existed.

Whenever Grandma Gertie did this to me, chewed my ear off with stories about the people in her building and their *meshugina* spouses and former spouses and siblings and children and cleaning ladies and cleaning ladies' children, I'd yell, "TMI, Grams. Too much information."

"I gotta hand it you, Viktor," I said when he pulled up in front of the pink stucco building in the middle of bustling Collins Avenue. "You're a fountain of information."

"It's my business to know what goes on. People like to esk me, 'How do they live?'"

"I'm sorry?"

"Thi *Sun,* thi *Enquirer,* thi *Globe* . . ."

"So, wait. You're saying you're on more than one payroll?"

Viktor shrugged. "I have femily to help take care of. My muther, my father, my brother, hees wife, their one son . . ."

"But what about your loyalty to Abe? You just told me he did everything for your family."

Viktor touched his heart. "And I never say bed word about heem . . . may God rest his soul."

"I see. And Ben has no idea you leak like a faucet?"

"He trusts me like hees son. You don't say nothin', em I right?"

"Who, me? Of course not. I don't even know these people."

"Okay, good. Here's my card. If you ever need to know something, Viktor find out for you."

"For a slight fee."

"It's the Ameriken way. No? I have a family to take care of. My muther, my father, my brother, hees wife, their one son . . ."

"Yeah, yeah." I grabbed his card. "I get the picture."

As I waited for Viktor to open my door, the meter was still running on the Fabrikants' dime, so I went for a freebie. "What are the odds on Drew and Marly?" I asked casually. "You think they'll get married this time?"

"Ah!" Viktor eyed me. "So you like heem?"

"No. Of course not. I'm just curious. Because the family is so nuts."

He turned to make sure our conversation was private, as the number one rule of dishing dirt was having an exclusive. "I hear heem say he no like the sex. . . . She no like to go down there." He pointed to his crotch.

"Gee. Maybe if it was fifties wrapped in hundreds, she'd dive right in." *Em I right?*

Viktor needed a second to get my humor. "Good one. I like thet. Maybe I tell heem to try."

"You do that," I said, suddenly staring up at my boy/man driver, wondering how I could have missed the fact that he was easily six-three, fair-haired, with ocean-blue eyes, and bulging pecs beneath his perfectly pressed shirt.

Having served time in L.A.'s menial job land, it shouldn't have surprised me that I hadn't noticed him at first. The eternal lament of hired help was that we were practically invisible. Except to horny guests who thought that touching breasts or patting asses were harmless gestures we secretly enjoyed.

"Maybe one day Viktor take you to dinner." He pumped his biceps. "Big strong man. Gentle heart. You like thet?"

"I'm sorry? Oh no. I mean, you're adorable, of course. But I'm getting engaged soon." *Once again the phantom fiancé strikes. And please, Viktor. Don't escort me into the building. My luck, they'll take one look at you and discover the ass they were looking for all along.*

My friend Sydney tells everyone that I'm practically computer-generated in perfection. Five-nine, 110 pounds. Curves in places men love. Natural blonde. Two breasts, both still in their natural habitats. Looked like this since ninth grade. So no one ever believes me when I say that I'm insecure about my looks.

Not that I didn't think I turned heads. Why else would Dolce & Gabbana have given me preferential treatment (free clothes) for agreeing to be Exhibit A on the Hollywood party circuit? It was just that after having lived in L.A, I discovered that beauty was a cheap commodity. Absolutely everyone and their colorist were stunning. So no matter how great your body, face, or hair, you were only one chair away from someone making you feel like Sandra Bernhard without makeup.

It's why I obsessed on my flaws. The narrowly spaced eyes, the wide-body forehead, and feet the size of a tribal conga leader's. My biggest fear was that I'd wake up one day, and those would be the only things people noticed about me.

But the one body part I considered my winning hand was my butt, which was small, tight, and thankfully cellulite-free. Mind you, I worked very hard to keep it looking like a baby's bottom. I jogged, did Pilates, drank a gallon of water a day, and fried foods never passed my lips.

So when I walked into Casa de Miro, I wasn't expecting to feel intimidated. After all, my bottom was top shelf. But after gaping at the lineup of framed glossies on the wall, I had to admit that my puny ass wasn't in the same league. Whatever made me think I could succeed in this bodacious booty boutique?

"Claire?" A dark-haired, pretty-in-pink stud greeted me, his just-facialed skin not even scraping my face with the obligatory air kiss. "Hmm. You smell yummy . . . Dante & Vita?"

"No. Ben & Jerry's."

"What?" He feigned shock. "A model who eats?"

"Every Tuesday." I smacked my lips. "Is it almost time?"

Pretty boy clapped. "I do love a beautiful girl with a sense of humor. . . . Pablo Casale, Mr. de Miro's personal assistant." He kissed my hand.

"Yes. Hi. We spoke on the phone. I apologize for being so late. Is he pissed at me? You wouldn't believe the day I've had—"

"Calm down, darling. Pablo just moved a few things around on the schedule, and voilà, time for Claire. . . . And may I say, he is so looking forward to meeting you."

"He is?" I looked around to see if anyone was eavesdropping. "Do you mind if I ask why?"

"Are you serious? You only tried to save the life of one of his favorite people."

"I'm sorry? He knows—knew—Mr. Fabrikant?"

"Knew him?" Pablo gasped. "He's been sitting in his office bawling like a baby since we heard the story on the news this morning."

"What story?"

"About you and the plane ride, and how you tried to revive him with your bare hands."

"Are you kidding me? They said that on the news? Why?"

"Oh right. You're not from here. . . . Well, because everyone adored Abe. And now, my darling *bubeleh*, it looks like you're going to be a little local celeb."

"Oh no no no no. I swear. I'm just your basic Good Samaritan. . . . Why is everyone making such a huge fucking deal over this, pardon my French? I mean, he was a nice guy and all, but it's not like he tried to save the world."

"Actually, he was a hero to Jews everywhere."

"Why?" I started to sweat. "Did he invent the cure for indigestion?"

"No, silly. He gave away his millions to save the lives of Jewish activists in Russia, Germany, Spain, Portugal, Argentina . . ."

"Really? He never said a word about that." *Or anything else, for that matter.*

"Then he'd bring the families to Florida, help them settle in, start their lives over. . . . So down here he's like the Messiah."

"He certainly was an amazing man." *Dear God, Yom Kippur is four months from now. Got any other days of atonement that start a little sooner? Love, Claire.*

"Let Raphael tell you the story of how Abe managed to smuggle the entire de Miro clan out of Buenos Aires right before they were taken away in the middle of the night by—"

"Wait, wait, wait. Raphael is Jewish?"

"Of course, darling."

"But his name sounds Hispanic or Cuban, or, I don't know . . . something Latin."

"Didn't Mommy and Daddy ever send you to Sunday school?" Pablo sighed. "Jews descended from everywhere. Not just Brooklyn. Raphael comes from a long line of those Marranos. The secret Jews who pretended to be Christian so they didn't get their heads chopped off . . . the artist Miro, even Rita Moreno. Oh, and Fidel Castro."

"No way. Castro is a Jew, too?"

"They think on his mother's side. . . . Anyway, back in the late forties, the de Miros left Lisbon for Buenos Aires, then Raphael's father and uncles got into deep shit with Eva Peron—"

"Oooh. I remember her. The one with the shoe fetish."

"Sorry. Incorrecto." Pablo made an annoying buzzer sound. "That was Imelda Marcos."

"Right. Of course. The heiress to Neiman Marcos."

He blinked. "You are joking, right?"

"Absolutely." *Not.* "Just having a little fun . . . trying to collect myself. I'm actually not feeling that great. I think I'm going to puke."

"Oh no. No puking. No, no, no. We have a strict policy now. No more two-finger girls—"

"Would you stop? I'm not bulimic. I'm in shock. I'm sad." *I feel like flypaper for freaks.*

"Well, of course you are." He hugged me. "What was Pablo thinking? Let me make you a Bloody Mary. Or how about—"

"Telling me the truth. Will Raphael love my ass?"

"Oh dear." He took a deep breath. "Well, it's just my opinion. I mean, don't get me wrong. You're a knockout. Good posture. Excellent skin tone. But, like, where were you ten years ago?"

"So basically you're telling me this is going to be a waste of time?"

"Well, no. We do occasionally get requests for older—"

"Pablo!" a man's voice bellowed from beyond.

"Coming, Raphael," Pablo singsonged. "You know what? Let's just go in there and do it."

"How do I look?" I chewed at my pinky nail. "Got any last-minute advice?"

"You're to die for." He fluffed my hair. "But I do have an eensy-weensie suggestion."

"Really?"

"Yes. Our last office manager ran out of here Friday threatening to kill herself. Third girl in six months. Now, in case he offers you the job, don't take a dime less than thirty."

"Oh, don't worry. I'm not a nine-to-fiver. In fact, lately I've been very busy with my film work."

"So the reason you flew all the way down here was because . . ."

"My whole life I've dreamed of showing off my ass to millions of moviegoers?"

"Oh, pish tish, Claire. Your last screen credit was two years ago, it was that awful remake of *Deliverance*, and you didn't even get an upgrade from a U5."

"Fine. So I had under five lines. But the director said I was damn convincing as a townie. . . . Jeez! I can't believe you checked me out."

"God bless Google." He winked. "The better to see you with, my dear."

I looked away. How embarrassing to be caught in a lie, although compared to the doozies I'd already told today, this was nothing. Still, I didn't appreciate my in-the-Dumpster career being scrutinized by Pink Pablo over here. How qualified did I have to be to pull down my thong?

"Never scrunch the forehead, darling. It invites Mr. Wrinkle. . . . Anyway, I knew Sharon Stone and Sandra Bullock back in their B-movie-queen years. They spent all day on their feet waiting tables, and Lord knows what they had to do on their backs . . . so it's not like I don't get the whole struggling-actress thing."

"You know what, Pablo? I appreciate the pep talk. I do. But frankly, you know shit."

"I was merely trying to point out—"

"That what? That it's okay to judge me because I've had a run of bad luck? Because I refuse to do porn, or cable films where the director yells, 'Open wide,' and he's not talking about my mouth? Believe me, you wouldn't be so quick to condemn if you knew what it was like to be almost thirty and not remember the last time someone gave you a goddamn break!

"You have no idea what it's like to put yourself out there year after year, literally hang your heart and soul out to dry, only to be overlooked, underpaid, stood up, felt up, compromised, criticized, lied to, shit on, laughed at, disregarded, denigrated, shunned, stunned, fondled, fooled . . . and believe it or not, I'm one of the smart ones.

"In high school I was in National Honors Society. Did you find that out on the Internet? I have a degree in theater, I've tested amazing for three sitcom pilots, I've done a dozen commercials, modeled since I'm fourteen. I'm funny, I'm beautiful. So I don't need to stand here and listen to some flaming fag who is never going to be anything more than a lover's gofer tell me that my time is up and I should go home until it's time to be wheeled out for the Old-Timers' Game."

Pablo bowed his head. His lower lip trembled.

"Oh my God." I burst into tears. "I am so sorry, Pablo. I swear I didn't mean to say that. I was having a hormonal meltdown. . . . My meds wore off. . . ."

Pablo wouldn't even look at me. Apparently I wasn't finished groveling.

"It's been the most awful day. . . . I'm still so crazed from what happened to me on the plane. . . . Such a dear, sweet man, and then boom, there's a dead guy on my lap. . . . And you have no idea how nervous I was to coriosity Raphael. And did I mention how depressed I've been since moving back home? Every morning I wake up in my old room and think, this has to be a nightmare 'cause they never even bothered to buy a new mattress, so every night I'm sleeping in a ditch. And the bedspread is still the same crappy one my mother bought at Alexander's, which I knew, even as a kid, came from the clearance bin. . . . And I think, how did this happen to me, Claire Greene . . . most likely to be a huge star? Washed up at twenty-nine."

Pablo dabbed his brow with his pinky, miraculously regaining his composure. "What can I tell you, hon? Some days are real mood-crappers."

"More like some years are real mood-crappers. But that is no reason to pick on a nice person like yourself. . . . Please forgive me, okay? Otherwise, I swear, I'll march right over to the nearest Baskin-Robbins and buy the biggy size banana split with the hot fudge."

"Let's just drop it, okay?" He faked a smile. "I get where you're coming from. I was merely trying to give you a heads-up. Raphael is a very sensitive man who doesn't take well to people going batshit on him."

"Me go batshit?" I laughed. "Never! But tell me this. And I'm asking only out of curiosity. Why can't he keep the help?"

"Are you loco? The man's a whack job. Brilliant, but completely *ferkahct.* All day long he screams, he carries on, he can't ever find what he's looking for, and it's always your fault—"

"Pablo!" The booming voice practically made the windows rattle. "These aren't the comp cards I wanted. And where the hell are yesterday's call sheets?"

"Coming, Raphael."

*Who would be crazy enough to work for this maniac?* I thought. But to be nice, I said, "Wow. He speaks perfect English."

"Let me guess." Pablo rolled his eyes. "You were expecting Ricky Ricardo. . . . I said his parents were immigrants. But he was born here. Just like you and me."

"Pablo! Goddamn it! Get Scorsese on the phone before his masseuse shows up."

I grabbed his arm. "Did he just say Scorsese?"

"Yeah. Marty is a good client of the firm's. So is Oliver Stone, Ron Howard, Spielberg . . ."

"Really?" I swallowed. "How are the benefits?"

# Chapter 6

I WAS CERTAINLY LEARNING A VALUABLE LESSON. NEVER TRUST A DAY that started out like any other, 'cause faster than you could say "I'm screwed," your plane of existence could be thrust into a graveyard spiral that left you disoriented and desperate for a view of the horizon line.

This little epiphany occurred, not on my doomed flight, but while sipping lemonade on a sun-drenched deck overlooking the majestic Biscayne Bay. For given the inane discussion I was having with the great Raphael de Miro, who to my amazement was only slightly older than me, I felt like I was flying through a dark haze without an instrument panel to save me from the crash and burn.

After he thanked me for being so good to his family's beloved champion, Abe, and made polite chitchat about my work experiences in L.A., our conversation began to tailspin, and nothing I said could make it fly right.

Boy Wonder knew I had come all this way to land a body double job, yet he was pressing me on my culinary skills. Was I familiar with Thai cooking? Could I tell the difference between cumin and cilantro? Did I prefer hand chopping to food processors?

"To be perfectly honest, Mr. De Niro, recipes are like science fiction to me. I get to the end and think, well now that's never going to happen."

"de Miro."

"Excuse me?"

"You called me Mr. De Niro. Like Bobby. It's de Miro."

"Oops. Sorry. Typical me. One-track mind. Always thinking about the business."

"So you're saying you don't enjoy cooking." His wiry fingers tap-danced on the table.

"I'm saying my idea of the perfect house is six bathrooms, no kitchen."

"Can you at least operate a microwave?" he sniffed.

"Of course. But my real strength is vending machines."

Jeez. Not even a smile. What made him Lord of the Lens? I was expecting a guy ready to be brought to pasture, not someone in his early thirties. A man who towered over his subjects, not came up to their waists. No wonder he was hiding in Miami.

"Do you know anything about photography?" He spooned out a lemon pit from his glass.

"I know that I miss Fotomat. Oh, and the disposables just came out in digital."

Raphael's left eye twitched. "Are you familiar with various procedures such as—"

"All of them . . . liposuction, chemical peels, quadruple thigh passes . . ."

Now he stared at me as if I'd just arrived from planet Zoloft. "I meant are you familiar with basic accounting procedures, word processing programs—"

"No. But I can IM six people at one time without screwing up a single conversation."

"You're not even remotely qualified for an office management position?"

"That's what I'm saying."

"I'll offer you twenty-five thousand to start."

"No way. I could spend more than that on shoes."

"May I remind you that you have no qualifications?"

"May I remind you that I came here to do some test shots . . . and to get rid of this wedgie?"

Finally a smile. "I admire your *chutzpah*, Claire. And you obviously know the business. I'm thinking Pablo could teach you the rest."

"And I'm thinking, when did I lose control of this go-see? All I wanted to do was make a few bucks modeling, and instead I'm sitting here defending myself because I didn't train with Emeril."

"I won't lie. You're a beautiful girl. Stunning, actually. Just not body double material."

"Let me guess. I'm too old."

"No. Too thin."

"Well, now, there's something you don't hear at a modeling agency every day. Too thin?"

"Your arms have no definition, you have this little nothing *tuchas*, I can't tell about your thighs yet, but your shoulders are bony—"

"That's my crime? Bony shoulders?"

"This is one business where you're not the sum of your parts, love. Look at J. Lo. Nice face, but she's got an ass like a three-car caboose. Jamie Lee Curtis has more rolls than a bakery. Brooke Shields, Elizabeth Hurley, Cindy Crawford, even Pamela Anderson . . . they all wanted Anita Hart as their butt double. Believe me, after fifteen years, I know what works on the big screen. . . . Maybe you should consider catalog work."

"You're killing me, Mr. de Miro. I'm a respected actress, not a lingerie model for Sears."

"According to Pablo, right now you're neither. That's why I thought you'd be interested—"

"In what? Finding out that after running rings around most other actresses, the only thing I'm qualified to do is answer phones and fetch Starbucks at some loony bin agency that pays shitty?"

"I assure you our salaries are commensurate with living costs down here."

"Not my living costs. Do you have any idea what Botox injections go for these days?"

"I see that you're not afraid to speak candidly. . . . Most people are afraid of me, you know."

"Because they had no idea you just started shaving. And besides, now that I know you can't help me—"

"I can help you. Thirty thousand. Final offer."

"Why do you want me to work for you at all? You said yourself I'm totally unqualified."

"Because at the moment I am positively desperate for someone with brains who can run the day-to-day. Pablo is a pushover, and the last three girls . . . one stupider than the next."

"Is it all grunt work, or would I get to interact with Mr. Scorcese?"

Raphael laughed. "My dear, who do you think its job will be to tell him to fuck off?"

"Are you serious? I would get to tell Marty Scorcese to fuck off?"

"Nicely, of course. Along with all the other pains in the asses you'll have to deal with. Models, booking agents, casting directors, producers, directors. . . . We're now one of the largest agencies in the country for body doubles."

"That's great. . . . Why did you ask if I could cook?"

"I like lunch served fresh."

"Me, too. God bless takeout."

"It gets very expensive."

"So does paying me forty grand a year, then sticking me in the kitchen to whip up paella?"

"Thirty-five, and I adore paella."

"Me, too! But here's the thing. I don't cook. I don't even defrost. Once I burned a salad. . . . The other problem is I'd need a place to live."

"Where are you staying now?"

"With my grandmother."

"Move in with her."

"I like it. I do. Rooming with an eighty-four-year-old woman who spends half her day pissing in her pants, and the other half looking for her teeth."

"You'll be very happy here." Raphael kissed my hand. "I give you my word."

"Is that what you told the last three girls?"

"Of course."

"And where are they today?"

"I had them all killed."

I was relieved that Viktor did not take offense when I got back into the limousine, closed my eyes, and begged for privacy. Thank God, because I was thinking that if I got dragged into even one more surreal conversation today, I would start looking for my biggest artery and a razor blade.

First there were all those wackos on my flight down. Then the phone call with my father about Elyce's wedding . . . Adam with the whole missing-car-key business . . . Grams with the meatloaf, and freaking out about Abe Fabrikant . . . meeting Ben and Drew and setting a hundred lies in motion . . . bumping into Julia Farber (wonder if Dr. Fiancé knows she once majored in ménage à trois). Then came Drew's request for me to speak at the funeral (Who asks a complete stranger to do a eulogy?). And finally, the war of words with Viktor the Mouth, Pink Panther Pablo, and Raphael de Lunatic . . . oh my God . . . had I actually agreed to consider working for him?

And yet, what did it all matter? The one conversation that should have happened, the only one-on-one that would have enriched my life and restored my faith in mankind, never took place. And it certainly wasn't because I'd had my fill of great humanitarians. In L.A., you qualified as a hero if you got a friend Marc Jacobs at wholesale.

Sadly, all I had to show for my lone encounter with the great Abe Fabrikant were the *if only*'s. If only I'd been a decent human being instead of a self-absorbed little putz. If only I'd stayed on the plane and not lied to his grieving family. If only I'd redeemed myself by confessing the truth to Ben and Drew, maybe I wouldn't be feeling the unexplainable nearness of something practically on top of me.

I opened my eyes, startled by the fact that everything was as it should be. Viktor was behind the wheel heading north on 95, yakking on his cell. I was alone in the back seat. Yet as sure as the sun was shining, I somehow knew I had company.

I don't know what made me poke around. There was nothing to see or touch. And how stupid I must have looked, waving my hand in the air, a maestro without music. Still, I just couldn't shake the feeling that there was an enormous energy force beside me that wanted to make its presence known. A cold, improbable heaviness invading my space, mimicking my uneven breaths.

My instinct was to cry out, but my voice was still. My heart pounded, yet I did not know what I feared. The chilled cabin air was tempered by an aura that warmed my skin.

"Mr. Fabrikant?" I whispered, actually expecting a reply.

"You okay beck there?" Viktor lowered the privacy window.

"Fine. I think. . . . I don't know. . . . Do you believe in ghosts?"

"Of course. In Russia, we have our *barabashkas*, our little house ghosts. You leave, they don't. Then there's all thi stories about the ghost of Rasputin. You remember heem? The poet and the devil. Oh. And maybe you like to read excellent Russian literature like Gogol's *The Dead Souls*. . . ."

*Absolutely! Let's stop at the library.* "What about ghosts of people who die on your lap?" I took a deep breath. "What do they call that in Russia?"

"In Russia?" Viktor chuckled. "They call thet beeg trouble."

"Uh-huh."

"Maybe yur just heving bed dream."

"I guess so. . . . Are we almost there?"

"If treffic stays good, we be et your grendmotherz—"

"Yeah, yeah. In blink of yur eye."

I reached for my cell phone. Maybe a familiar activity would shoo away the hair-raising thought that to grandmother's house I was going, only not alone. But with seven missed messages, three of which were from Elyce, I wasn't sure which scared me more, the bride or the boogeyman.

Turns out hearing Elyce's orgasmic voice was bone-chilling. "Oh my God, I'm so excited you're going to be in the wedding." Beep. "Call me right away so I know when to set up your first fitting at Kleinfeld's." Beep. "Wait until you see the bridesmaids' dresses. They're to die for." (If ever there was an expression I didn't want to hear . . . )

On the good-news front, it occurred to me that if I accepted the job offer from Mr. de Miro, I'd have a great reason not to be part of the Fogel/Berg nuptials. How could Elyce expect me to be a dutiful bridesmaid from fourteen hundred miles away? It would be difficult for me to help plan her shower. And what about all those pesky fittings?

But did I really want to commit to living in Florida, working in slave mode for a bunch of hotheaded homosexuals, just to avoid a wedding party? What about my shot at the Big Apple? It was too soon to cave. Not too soon, however, to reach Gram's high-rise apartment building, and to have the fun begin.

"I ken't bee-leeve it." Viktor laughed. "There's an old lady stending outside in thi hot sun with a plate of food. . . . What is she doing? Looking for her next husband?"

I glanced out my window and groaned. "No, unfortunately. She's looking for me.

"Grams, you didn't have to bring the meatloaf down," I scolded her in the elevator. "Unless you were planning to mail it to the starving children in Europe."

"Excuse me, Miss Skinny Minny. I thought you'd be hungry." Her once-steady hands shook as she clutched the plate of home cooking.

"Yeah, but I'm not four anymore. I can wait until I get to a table."

She mumbled something about her table, and I noticed she seemed agitated, but I was more focused on taking a nap and a bath and then phoning Sydney back in L.A. to tell her about my bewildering day. Maybe she'd consult with her astrology guru and ask if there was some weird planetary thing going on in my birth sign that was creating havoc in my personal cosmos.

"You girls are so thin nowadays." Grams looked me over as if I were a paltry chicken at Publix. "I tell everyone. Try my granddaughter's diet. You eat nothing. Soon you disappear."

"Would you stop? I'm in great shape. I eat healthy. I'm fine."

Jeez. My family's obsession with food was scary, especially after I moved back to New York and saw that they'd all been supersized.

And no wonder. Every night was either eat out or take in. *Feel like pizza? No. We had that last night.*

"I thought you went for a modeling job." Grams interrupted my thoughts.

"I did. Well, not a job, exactly. More like a test. An interview."

"And that's how you dressed? Like you came from one of those acrobatic classes?"

"You mean aerobics?" I chuckled as Grams fumbled for her keys. But when I looked at my ratty gym shorts I knew she was right. I'd had every intention of changing into this pink fishnet and fringe mini, the very dress Adam Sandler said was so hot it would set off the sprinkler system.

Damn! I'd been in the business long enough to know that fashion statements were paramount to success. Not even a temporary lapse of designer judgment could escape ridicule, unless you traveled in Gywneth Paltro's celebrity circle. Then you could be the laughing-stock at the Oscars, and it wouldn't downgrade your stock one bit.

But up-and-comers like myself were always subject to scrutiny, so I could only imagine what Raphael, Pablo, and even Viktor were say-ing with regard to my cheap ensemble. Pablo probably did an imita-tion red-carpet twirl. "Who needs Valentino? I'm wearing Target."

"Now, don't get all *ferklempt*. It's no big hoo-ha." Grams inter-rupted my thoughts.

"What?" I said.

Apparently, having tuned out her incessant chatter, I'd missed the part where she mentioned something about her furniture. So the last thing I expected when she opened her door was to see nothing but packing boxes, two lawn chairs, and the TV with a *yahrzeit* candle burning on top.

"Grams! What the hell happened?" I threw my bags down. "Were you robbed?"

"I just told you. I decided to get rid of a few things."

"A few things? There's nothing left. Where's your dining room set? And the living room furniture?" So much for hoping she'd taken a sudden interest in computers and had created a nice little setup in the guest room. "Oh God. Please tell me you still have beds." I raced inside her room.

"You'd be surprised how comfortable the floor is." She followed me in. "And let me tell you. It's a pleasure not to have to bend over to make a goddamn bed every morning. Eighty years of tucking this and pulling that . . . terrible for the stenosis on my left side . . . no, thank you."

"This is insane!" I opened her closet door to find empty hangers. "Where are your clothes?"

"How much does one person need? A few things, really. . . ."

"Have you totally lost your mind? You can't just decide to get rid of all your possessions."

"Ridiculous the crap I saved for all these years. Who needs it?"

"I can't believe you did this and didn't tell anyone."

"Who listens to me? Nobody! I keep saying I don't like it here anymore. I want to get the hell out of this joint. Seventeen years. It's enough already."

I quickly surveyed the barren room and clung to the closet doorknob to steady myself. Gone was the imposing cherry maple bedroom set and her tiny silver dressing table with the dainty perfume bottles. Gone was her cherished rocker, the chair where she lovingly nursed her three children, and for years mourned the loss of her only son.

"I don't understand why you did this," I mumbled. "You have so many friends here."

"Shows you what you know," she snorted.

"Mrs. Greenbaum would miss you."

"Not so much. She died a year and a half ago. Colon cancer."

"Oh. Well, what about that nice man from Chicago with the two shih tzus?"

"Marvin Plotzer. Dead. A stroke in the bathtub. Oy. Such a *shanda* he had with his rotten children. They never came. Never called."

"Okay. What about what's-her-name? The lady whose son is the big dentist in Boynton?"

"Edith. She moved."

"Oh."

"Then she died . . . a massive coronary right in the middle of her mah-Jongg game."

"So there's no one left."

"Dead, dead, dead. They're all dead."

"No, wait. No, they're not. What about Rose down the hall? This morning you said yourself she was driving you to the doctor. She still has to be alive."

"Ha! Her arms are so weak she can't hold a cup of coffee. Her arthritis is so bad she can't turn her neck. Her blood pressure medication makes her dizzy, she's got cataracts in both eyes—"

"And that's who drives you everywhere? How can she still have a license?"

"Who said anything about a license? And listen to this. Yesterday she comes over and I say to her, Rose, you're not wearing any pants, and she looks at me like I grew two heads, but I know what I'm talking about 'cause her heiny's showing, and she's talking about going to the market. And believe you me, she's not the only one who's lost her mind down here. They're all batty."

*Except you, of course. You're still perfectly sane.* Naturally, I felt for her. It must be awful to lose all your friends. To know that the next *shiva* might be your own. Meanwhile, what a travesty to reach the stage of life where your presence in the universe meant so little to so few. Where the bustling, ever-changing world not only left you sidelined but rendered completely irrelevant. Functionally obsolescent. Of no use to anyone besides the doctors who profit from your misery.

I studied my grandmother's face. Really took a good look at her tired eyes and sagging cheeks, the once-silvery hair that had lost its tarnish. For as long as I could remember, she had stood so tall and proud, a bean pole among her fleshy contemporaries. Whereas they had wingspans for arms, Grams's remained pencil-thin. Whereas she had always seemed dignified in posture and poise, now she appeared almost minute, her narrow frame hunched, her regal fingers short and swollen.

And here I was, depressed about turning thirty and competing for film work with a bunch of latent teenagers who didn't know directors' chairs from musical chairs, while my grandmother struggled every day to hold on to the remains of her dignity, or at least her memory.

"All right. I get the point." I looked around the room. "You want to move. But you gotta be realistic. You can't just sell your stuff and walk away. You have no place else to go."

"Don't worry, darling. We'll find something. Tomorrow we'll borrow Rose's car."

"Fine, but this isn't like shopping for a dress. You can't just walk in and buy something off the rack. You have to look around, compare prices. . . . I gotta call Mommy. She is going to freak—"

"No," Grams yelled so loud I jumped.

"Yes." I started to fumble in my purse for my cell. I didn't mean to speak to her like she was a child, but one of us had to play the part of the grown-up.

"She doesn't listen. She doesn't care if I live or die. This is none of her goddamn business."

"It is her goddamn business, and I'll make her understand. I promise. . . . Where are you going?" I followed her into the kitchen and watched as she rifled through a drawer.

Meanwhile, I dialed my mother's cell.

"Put that thing down," Grams yelled, pointing something small and silver at my head.

"Oh my God!" I shrieked. "What the hell are you doing? That's a gun."

"You don't think I know that?"

"Is it loaded?"

"I don't know that."

"OH MY GOD. Give it to me, damn it. You could kill me." I moved closer.

"Drop it!" She waved the gun in my face. "You can't call home, you hear me?"

"Loud and clear." I tossed the phone on to the countertop. *This isn't happening. I'm looking at the barrel of a revolver because my eighty-four-year-old grandmother thinks we're Bonnie and Claire.* "Just give me the gun, Grams. Oh my God . . . where the hell did you get that thing?"

"From Mr. Morales's son."

"Who?"

"The super. His son just got married. He needed furniture, so I says to him take mine. I'm moving anyway. Then he tells me he don't have any money, but he's got a gun he can give me."

"That's absolutely nuts. There's probably an all-points bulletin out for that thing. What do you bet he killed someone with it and had to get rid of the evidence? . . . I can't believe you."

"So let the son-of-a-bitch cops arrest me and throw away the key," she cried. "Then nobody has to bother with me anymore. I'll have a nice place to live . . . and I won't need no furniture!"

"Grams, give me the gun right this minute," I said softly. "I won't call Mommy. I promise."

Just as she was about to hand it over, my cell rang.

"Can I at least see who it is?"

"No. First I gotta tell you a story."

"Great! I'm being held hostage so my grandmother can read me *Cinderella*."

"No, ma'am. Not a fairy tale. A true story . . . about that Mr. Fabrikant. The stupid son-of-a-bitch who died on the plane."

"I still can't believe you knew him too. Were you close?"

"Never met the man."

"Yet you have a story to tell me about him."

"It'll make your hair curl. Ya better sit down."

"Where?" I looked around the empty kitchen. "Where would you like me to sit?"

"Don't matter. You're gonna fall on the floor no matter what."

## Chapter 7

I'VE ALWAYS SAID, DON'T ARGUE WITH AN ELDERLY RELATIVE WHO HAS just pointed a gun at your head. If she pulls the trigger, both you and the point you wanted to make will be moot. So when Grandma Gertie ordered me into the living room to sit on her scratchy blue plaid lawn chairs, I sat.

The good news was that I could stop fearing for my life, as we had called a truce, agreeing to leave our weapons on the kitchen counter. Then I served us cups of hot tea and laced hers with a sleeping pill.

Do you honestly think that after the day I'd just had, I would let her yak my ear off with some crazy story about a man she never met but still despised? Then try to fall asleep while a loaded Saturday Night Special was as close as the toaster? I was spent, not stupid. Besides, how could Abe Fabrikant possibly be a bad guy, when according to the rest of the world, he was a saint?

As we sipped tea, the darkened stillness of the room lulled our frayed nerves. The flickering glow of the *yahrtzeit* candle illuminated our shadows. It was then that I realized that although Grams had sold off her couches and coffee tables, she hadn't entirely erased her past. Her treasured family photos remained on the walls, proof that she hadn't always lived among the ruins of old age.

One of my favorites was taken on Labor Day when I was maybe seven or eight. It was a great shot of me, Adam, and Lindsey with her and Papa Harry at Coney Island, on a hot but happy evening. We were ushering out the summer with double-scooped ice-cream cones when a bearded stranger witnessed our rollicking and offered to snap a picture.

We never actually expected the man with the huge camera to make good on his promise to develop the film and mail us a copy. But a week later, a brown envelope arrived, postmarked Carmel, California. And inside was a luxuriously big eight-by-ten in rich sepia (maybe the greatest glossy of my life) with a note that read, "*Summer Smiles*" *by Ansel Adams*. I swear to God.

So it was no wonder that whenever I visited Grams and studied the now-infamous photo, I tended not to pay much attention to the other, less extraordinary ones. The usual fare of wedding pictures from the 1920s, where the bride and groom were posed and serious, as if they were preparing to take an oath of office, not profess true love. Where at nineteen, they had already experienced such a lifetime of struggles, they looked old and worn beyond their years.

And of course there were the modern-day shots. The bar and bat mitzvahs of me, Adam, and Lindsey, and our first cousins Alison and Hilary. With each successive affair, the girls' dresses got fancier, the hair bigger. Compared to our ancestors, who looked practically patriarchal in grade school, our faces looked young and exuberant. Our minds focused on our five-hour parties, and the Viennese dessert tables that cost more than our grandparents' first house.

But tonight, a picture I'd seen a million times and ignored suddenly piqued my curiosity. It was a studio portrait of my mother with her younger sister, Iris, and their baby brother, Gary. Three tiny cherubs jammed tightly together for a pose. And in the shadows, I'm sure, Grams praying to God that he spare these beautiful children any harm or misfortune. But it was not to be.

It dawned on me that I knew very little about my late Uncle Gary, as his name was rarely mentioned, unlike other dead relatives whose memories were invoked at family gatherings. The only fact I knew for sure was that he survived Vietnam, but not a car crash a few months later.

But now as I studied the picture of Gertie and Harry Moss's three small children, and the memorial candle burning beneath it, I knew, of course, that it had to be Uncle Gary's *yahrtzeit*. The annual remembrance on the anniversary of his death. For I distinctly remember my Papa Harry's pine casket being lowered into the hard, cold December ground.

I leaned over to ask Grams about her beloved boy, but her short, noisy snorts told me she was lights out. Perfect! The sleeping pill had worked. Now I could make her a soft bed of pillows and blankets on the floor, then call my mother.

I had every right to ream her out for being so neglectful and self-absorbed that she was oblivious to the fact that Grams was slowly losing both her mind and her will to live.

Then it hit me that this might be a wee bit hypocritical. In spite of what I'd led the Fabrikants to believe, I was hardly a good example of the caring, compassionate caregiver. And, too, I supposed Grams shouldn't be my mother's sole responsibility. She and Aunt Iris should be equal partners.

I shuddered just thinking about the scene twenty years from now when it was my, Adam, and Lindsey's turn to look after never-happy Roberta and know-it-all Lenny. Our luck, they'd be divorced and living in separate nursing homes, competing for the title of biggest pain in the ass.

And if I had to take bets, Adam would wipe his hands of the whole mess, citing it as the daughters' job, while Lindsey would probably space out and forget that she had parents altogether. Until the call came from the attorney that it was time for the reading of the will.

*Some bright future I've got*, I thought as I tiptoed into the kitchen to get my phone. I was about to dial home when I noticed the voice-mail icon and discovered the call I'd missed while at gunpoint was from Drew Fabrikant. We had exchanged cell numbers before saying our good-byes at the airport, but I didn't expect to hear from him so soon. If there was a God, he had called to tell me the family had second thoughts about my speaking at the funeral.

\* \* \*

"Are you okay?" Drew asked when I reached him in his car. "You sound upset."

*No. Indecisive. Should I kill myself or order in? Suicide or sushi?* "It's been a long day."

"Can I do anything for you? Get anything for you?"

*Yeah. See if within the next twenty-four hours you can drum up a furnished apartment with padded walls.* "I'm sure I'll feel better tomorrow. How are you doing? How is your dad?"

"He's a mess. My mom's a mess. My sister, Delia, is in a fetal position. We're all in shock. But that's not why I called. . . . We just found something out that kind of surprised us. I think we should talk."

"Talk?" Oh good. Here came the end to the perfect day. They'd found out I was a big liar, and as punishment I would have to wear a scarlet letter and reimburse them for Viktor and the limo.

"Actually, I was sort of hoping I could see you," he continued. "There's something I'd like to show you."

*It better not be your penis, 'cause I'm in no mood for those games!* "Right now?" I gulped.

"Are you busy?"

*Yeah. I'm babysitting a crazed killer. Don't let the Depends fool you.* "I guess not. I mean, I'm really tired, and my grandmother is sleeping now. She might get upset if she woke up and I wasn't here."

"Could you leave her a note?"

"It's that important?"

"Yes."

"Then can you lay it on the line with me? 'Cause I am so on overload. Am I in trouble?"

"In trouble?" he said. "Why would you think that?"

"No reason. It's just . . . to be perfectly honest? I'm sort of a mess myself."

"I understand. It was a difficult day."

"Drew, you don't even know the half of it."

Just releasing those words, and realizing there was a sympathetic person at the other end of the line, was all it took. The emotional dam broke, and it was a gusher. I just couldn't bear one more minute of this insane, out-of-control day.

I started babbling about ghosts, guns, and grandmothers. About a job I didn't want but was afraid to turn down. About a bridal party I should have turned down but didn't. About turning thirty while getting a sneak preview of eighty. And that was after having this nice man die on my lap.

"I'm not far from your building," Drew said. "I can be there in ten minutes."

"I'm sorry." I wiped my wet hand on my shirt. "How do you know where I'm staying?"

"Viktor told me where he dropped you off."

"Right. Good old Viktor. Okay, look. You've been very sweet to me. I guess I could go with you for a little while. I just need to call home, get dressed . . . I'll leave a note for Grams. Is Marly with you?"

"No."

"No?"

"She had some gifts to return with her mom. From the engagement party."

"Uh-huh." *Great. He's going to make his move now. Maybe I'll bring the family gun.*

One reasonably expects that a young stud with mega-rich parents will pull up in a Mercedes or a Porsche. Not a Cadillac. Not even a late-model Cadillac. But there was Drew, behind the wheel of a gleaming Eldorado. And before I could utter an insult about him being too young for a Jew Canoe, he told me that this was like traffic court. He was guilty with an explanation.

It so happened that, just as I predicted, he did drive a Mercedes convertible. And a vintage red Porsche on weekends. But his fondest memories were of riding around town with his Pops in his latest Cadillac, windows down, radio up, searching for hot bagels and hotter babes. He was only thirteen at the time, but he never forgot how great it was to come home with a dozen assorted and, on a good day, a pretty girl's phone number.

Drew's mother, however, was less than amused with her father-in-law's juvenile antics when two of those girls' names were included, undetected, on the guest list of friends for Drew's bar mitzvah. Especially after they showed up at the kids' table wearing halter dresses and stilettos.

"Are you serious?" I squealed. "You invited hookers to your bar mitzvah?"

"Miami's finest."

"Oh my God. Do you mind if I ask what they gave you as gifts?"

Drew's laugh was so spontaneous and hearty, I momentarily forgot what ailed me.

As did he, apparently. But then it was time to return to his original story. About following the casket from the airport to the funeral home, then running over to his grandfather's apartment to pick up a few possessions. "When I found the car keys by his bed, I said to myself, what the hell? Why shouldn't I drive the Caddy? It's still my favorite set of wheels."

"I can see why." I rubbed the buttery leather interior. "Thirty-two-valve Northstar V-8 engine, three hundred horsepower, three hundred pounds of torque. . . ."

"Wait a minute. Were you that girl in *My Cousin Vinny*?"

"No. My grandfather on my father's side never drove anything but a Caddy. Sevilles, De Ville's. So is this what you wanted to show me?"

"No, something even better. Something I think will make you very happy."

"Veal parmigiana with angel hair and a side of garlic knots?"

"No way. Models don't eat like that."

"This one does. In fact, just today a famous fashion photographer told me I was too thin."

"That's crazy. You're perfect."

"Thanks, but I guess plus-size modeling is out of the question. And that's where all the 'big' money is."

"Big money." Drew laughed. "Good one."

But my sense of humor wasn't the only thing that surprised him. Over dinner at a quaint bistro he swore he had never met a girl who could, or would, out-eat him. Salad fanatics, all of them. Yet it wasn't the food that made the meal. It was the conversation. The ease with which we talked and laughed, and with apologies to Martha Stewart, the way we chowed down as if our forks were shovels.

As he talked, I realized how very different he was than the men I had known. He hadn't salivated on me like a lion eyeing raw meat, or compared my breast size to the last three girls he dated. He was kind without being solicitous. Intelligent but not condescending. Stunning but unassuming (unlike the vain men of L.A. who wore furs, pampered their skin, and swore on their Speedos that they didn't believe in cosmetic surgery).

Oddly, the only time Drew grew tense was when I mentioned his fiancée.

"Marly? Yeah, she's great." Drew chugged his beer, then pulled out a picture from his wallet. "This was taken last year on a cruise to Mexico."

"She's beautiful," I said. She reminded me a little of Courtney Cox. Petite. A hundred and five pounds. Dark brown hair, great green eyes. Their kids would be stunning.

"Yeah, she is." He nodded. "You'll love her. Everyone loves her. She does this amazing needlework with her mom. They've got pillows and wall hangings in every room of the house."

"Oh. Do they own a shop or anything?"

"No . . . it's more a hobby, I guess."

"So what does Marly do?"

"Do? You mean for a job?"

*This oughta be good.* I nodded yes.

"She sometimes works for her dad. He runs a commercial linen business."

Jeez. Another Lindsey. *I think I'll come in on Tuesday for a few hours after my manicure. . . .*

"That's nice," I said. "My sister works for my dad, too. Of course, I'm sure Marly's father gives her real responsibilities."

"Absolutely. She's vice president of buying."

"Oh. That is a big job."

"Yeah. She buys coffee, lunch, office supplies . . ."

"Be nice," I laughed. "I'm sure she's very bright and talented."

"Every day she proves she's a helluva lot smarter than me."

He just didn't say how.

"So let me see your family," Drew said.

"Mine? Oh. I'm not the picture-carrying type. I change pocket-books a lot." *And believe me, they're nothing to look at.*

"Really? You don't carry a single picture?"

"Well, maybe one." I rummaged through my wallet, and lo and behold found an old photo.

"This one's from a few years ago." I wiped off the smudges. "It was taken at my sister's graduation from Towson University in Maryland. Those're my parents. That's Adam and Lindsey."

It's funny what happens when you show someone a picture of an unattractive subject. They want to be polite, but honestly, what can you say about an ugly baby, for instance, or in the case of my family, a short, dumpy, curly-headed quartet?

"I'm sure they're very nice people," he offered. "But it's funny. You look nothing like them."

"Ya think? Actually, the big joke in my family is that I was born to aliens from the planet Spend-on-Me."

"Hey, that's where Marly's from . . . just kidding. But no, really. There's no family resemblance here at all."

"Yeah, but I inherited other things. Like my dad's ability to make a bad situation worse."

"No way. That runs in my family, too. If you say one wrong thing to my mother, she never lets you hear the end of it. Then three days later she's still on your case, and you can't even remember what the hell you said in the first place. Drives me nuts."

"Oh, I know. If, God forbid, you tell my mother the steak was tough, she'll make you eat it every night for the next week until you swear up and down that A-1 should name a sauce after her."

Drew laughed. "My dad thinks the reason I studied genetics in college was to figure out how I could possibly be related to her."

"Lot more to it than forty-six chromosomes." I stirred my straw.

"You got that right. . . . Actually, it's not that unusual for offspring to more closely resemble grandparents, aunts, uncles. I bet you look like one of them."

"Oh God. I hope not my Aunt Marilyn, my father's sister. She's got less hair on her head than on her face."

I really didn't mean to say anything that mean, let alone at the exact moment Drew downed a glass of water, for he laughed so hard, it sprayed through his nose and mouth.

"So then after podiatry school you went to charm school?" I teased.

Now I was laughing so hard, my sides ached. I couldn't remember the last time I'd had this much fun. And it was just a guess, but he looked like neither could he.

# Chapter 8

IN A MILLION YEARS I NEVER WOULD HAVE GUESSED THAT DREW'S BIG secret, the thing he had to show and tell me, was his grandfather's apartment in this brand-new assisted living center in Coral Gables. In fact, he was practically giddy when we pulled up. Maybe he thought that since Abe and I had become fast friends, I'd want to learn more about him. But that did not explain why, when we checked in with the security guard, he introduced me as his cousin from New York.

"Your cousin?" I said as we walked through the marble-tiled atrium lobby.

"Trust me, it's easier this way. Everyone here knows Marly. . . ."

"Am I a younger cousin or an older cousin?"

"Why, Claire—you're the baby in the family. The late-in-life accident."

"Gee. I really am starting to feel like a member of the family. When I checked in at La Guardia this morning, the gate agent thought Abe was my grandfather."

"How come?"

"I guess because our seats were next to each other. Oh, and she even said we looked alike."

"Could be worse," Drew said. "At least she didn't think you were his wife."

\*   \*   \*

Drew was right. Abe's apartment was worth seeing. The rooms were bright and spacious, the living room overlooked a large lagoon, and the kitchen appliances were so new, the manufacturers' labels had yet to be removed.

What I loved best, though, was the absence of old-people smell. That mysterious sour odor that smacked you in the face when you walked into a room with heavy, decrepit postwar furniture. Everything here was magically clean and stinky-free.

"I'll take it," I mumbled under my breath.

"Good," he replied.

"What?"

"That's what I needed to tell you. The thing I found out when I came over here before."

"I'm sorry?"

"Your grandmother. You said she was looking for an assisted living center. She could move into this one."

"What? Oh no. No, no, no, no. I mean, the place is beautiful, don't get me wrong. It's perfect, in fact. But she's on a fixed income. I'm sure the rent would be—"

"Taken care of," Drew said. "She wouldn't have to pay a dime."

"I don't understand. Was she the hundredth caller?"

"No. See, when I went down to the office before, they pulled up Pops' records, and it showed he was only here about six weeks, but apparently paid for a whole year up front, which surprised the hell out of us because we weren't sure he was going to stay. Anyway, I got to thinking. Why let the place sit empty? Claire's trying to help her grandmother find an apartment just like this."

"You mean they won't give you your money back?"

"No refunds after thirty days."

"Are you serious? You should sue."

"I'm joking." Drew cupped my chin. "Of course we could break the lease."

"But you don't want to?"

"To be honest, it's not like my family needs the money. Anyway, I mentioned the idea to my dad, and he said it's exactly the kind of thing Pops would have done, and if she's happy here, we'll just set it up so his estate pays her expenses as long as she stays."

"Oh my God," I cried. "Oh my God." I was literally shaking. *Didn't I wish for this kind of miracle only an hour ago?*

"Those are the good kind of tears, right? Sometimes with Marly I get them mixed up."

I nodded yes. "This is unbelievable. Absolutely unbelievable."

"Do you think she'd like it here? They do an awful lot for the residents. They take them to the movies, to the doctor . . ."

"Are you kidding?" I started to walk around, surveying the apartment from the perspective of a *kvetchy* tenant. It was huge compared to where Grams lived now. Plenty of closets, a large bathroom—no, wait, two bathrooms, one adjoining the bedroom and another down the hall. And what was this? A second room? It was smaller, but Abe had set it up as a den with a pull-out couch. Perfectly suitable for a guest.

"This place is amazing," I sniffed. "What about all the furniture?"

"It'll stay. What would we do with it? . . . Why? You don't think she'll like it?"

"Oh no. She'll love it. It's so much nicer than what she has now." *If you only knew.* "By any chance, do you happen to know if there is an age restriction here?"

"Probably. We just assumed she was elderly."

"She's eighty-four."

"That oughta do it."

"What about thirty?"

"Who's thirty?"

"Me. Next week."

"And you feel you're in need of assisted living?"

"Drew, right now I need all the help I can get."

Nothing is more frustrating than going out of your way to do right by people, then having your good intentions bite you in the ass anyway. No matter that it had been the longest day of my life, I'd still made it my business to keep my family informed.

Three times I left detailed messages on my mother's cell. Twice I left a message on the home answering machine. Once I paged my dad. And I tried Adam's and Lindsey's cells, too, but no one bothered calling me back.

So when early the next morning my cell phone rang and I heard my mother screaming in my ear, my first question was, what was she yelling at me for? My second question was, where the hell was I? Oh yes. Grams' apartment. Sleeping on the floor of her bedroom, door locked, with a high-powered revolver under my pillow.

"What do you mean, you gave her a sleeping pill?" My mother cried. "What were you trying to do? Kill her?"

"She started it," I whined.

"Have you lost your mind? You can't mix sleeping pills with all her medications. It could send her into cardiac arrest."

"I'm sorry. I didn't think it was a big deal, okay? I'm sure she's fine."

"You mean you don't know if she's fine?"

"She's still asleep on the living room floor."

"The living room floor? What did she do? Fall again?"

"What the hell is going on down there?" My father picked up the extension in the bedroom. "I knew we shouldn't have trusted you to handle this."

Welcome to *The Lenny and Roberta Show*, starring two crazy people who criticize me, then turn on each other.

"If you'll stop yelling at me, I'll be happy to tell you everything," I said.

"Yeah, Lenny. Enough with the *shrying*. I want to hear what Claire has to say."

"Who's yelling? You're the one who's yelling. Claire, tell us what happened already. You're making me late for the office."

I sat up on my blanket. "Okay. Well, I'll spare you all the gory details about the day I had because you wouldn't believe me if I told you. I'll just start with the little surprise I found after I got dropped off here last night."

"Last night?" My mother interrupted. "What did you do all day?"

"I had the go-see with the photographer, remember? Anyway,

when Grams opened her door, all I saw were boxes, her TV, and those god-awful lawn chairs from the house in Valley Stream. Why? Because she sold every stitch of furniture, and most of her clothes. No, I stand corrected. She gave them to the super's son as a wedding present in exchange for his gun."

"Wha'd she say?" My mother asked my father.

"A gun!" My father yelled. "She has a gun. . . . Claire, what kind is it?"

"Daddy, c'mon. I wouldn't know a Saturday Night Special from a Sunday brunch."

"Wh-what does she need a gun for?" my mother stammered. "The neighborhood got so bad?"

"The neighborhood is fine. I don't know why she wanted it, but she pulled it on me."

"What's she saying, Lenny? You know I can't hear a damn thing when you pick up in the bedroom. But why should you care? As long as you can hear."

"I think she just said Gert pulled a gun on her."

"*Oy*, Claire! You know how easy she gets herself all riled up. What did you say to her?"

"Oh my God. I didn't say or do anything, okay? All I did was walk in the door and ask if she'd been robbed. And then she went on and on about how all of her friends are dead, and how you never listen to her anymore, and you don't care whether she lives or dies, so I go to call you, right, and she runs into the kitchen and pulls out this handgun."

"She said I don't care whether she lives or dies?" my mother seethed. "The nerve of her. All I do is call her, call her doctors, call her home health aides. . . . I'm worried sick about her day and night."

"Mommy, could we please not make this about you?"

"Exactly," my father chimed in. "Every time, you have to turn things into how it affects you."

"Lenny, did I ask for your opinion?"

"Fine," he yelled back. "You handle this. But I told you not to send Claire down there alone. Didn't I say to you, go with her just in case? . . . Claire, listen to me. We're not blaming you, honey. Thank God you're there. Are you okay?"

"Couldn't be better. Thanks for asking . . . but Daddy, wait. Don't go. I have something amazing to tell you, and I want you both to hear. I found a great place for her to move."

"What move?" My mother didn't let me finish. "She can't move. She's got a lease."

"Mom, you're not listening. She can't be alone anymore. We don't give a shit about a lease."

"That's easy for you to say," my father grumbled. "I'm the one who gets stuck with all the bills. Paying off sky-high credit cards with twenty-one percent interest, and leases on cars we only got to use for three months because someone forgot to take the keys out of the ignition so it got stolen, but all right, we're all entitled to make a little mistake now and then—"

"I told you a hundred times I did not forget to take the keys out," my mother yelled. "They got stuck in there or something. I don't know. It was a very hot day. . . ."

"I'm warning both of you," I said, "if you don't shut up and let me finish, I'm hanging up and I swear, you'll never hear from either me or Grams again."

Bingo. Twice in one phone call I got their undivided attention.

"Okay, so as I was saying, last night the grandson of the man who died on me offered to let Grams move into his grandfather's assisted living apartment, and you have to see this place. In fact, it's so big and nice, I was thinking, and I know this is going to sound crazy, but unless they find out it's against the rules, maybe I'll move in with her for a little while because I was sort of offered a job down here at that modeling agency, and I haven't decided what to do yet, but it's a possibility—"

"Where is this place?" my mother asked. "In a decent neighborhood?"

*Excuse me. Did you hear a word I said? I just told you I'm considering moving to Florida and living with your mother, and your first question is about the location?* "It's down in Coral Gables."

"*Oy*. It's all Spanish down there now. And so far," she complained.

"So far?" I replied. "Oh my God. What are you worried about? That her commute will be too long? What do you care where it's located? The place is brand-new, they offer a million services, and you should see how huge the apartment is. Plus, it's fully furnished, which, may I remind you, is a beautiful thing, because let's review, class: YOUR MOTHER IS SLEEPING ON THE FLOOR."

"How much?" my father, the accountant, asked, already calculating twelve months' rent.

"Okay, see? That's the best part. It'll be free."

"There's no such thing as free."

"Yes, there is, Daddy. The Fabrikants love me so much for trying to help Abe, they'll do anything for me. So when they found out that my grandmother needed a place to live . . ."

Silence. "Hello?" I said. "Hello?"

Oh God. Of all times to lose the signal.

I decided to see if *The Lenny and Roberta Show* would call me back first so we didn't have to go around and around with the busy signals and the voice mails. Meanwhile, I'd go check on Grams and hope to God that I hadn't accidentally killed her.

Admittedly it took me longer to arouse her than I expected, which made me work up a bit of a sweat because could you just imagine *that* phone call home: *Mommy, you were right. Never mix sleeping pills with Cumadin.* But at least when she awoke, she was not only alert, but in decent spirits and hungry for breakfast.

Turns out she loved the nice cup of tea I made her last night. In fact, she hadn't slept that good in years, and wanted to know what brand it was so she could try it again.

It was only after a few minutes of getting her up and moving that I realized I hadn't heard back from my parents. Strange. I would have thought that after hearing the words *free rent*, my father would have returned the call immediately. On the other hand, given my parents' history of petty bickering, they were probably fighting about something ridiculous, and it was Grams who?

Why should they care where the beloved matriarch of the family lived? Why should they care what a struggle it was for her to function? Let someone else worry whether she remembered to take her medicine or see the doctor. Didn't they realize what a lousy example they were setting for their children?

Meanwhile, I was about to tell Grams to put on her last remaining outfit so I could take her to breakfast and surprise her with some great news when my cell rang.

"Claire. It's Dad. I'm going to ask you a very important question, and I need you to speak slowly and clearly when you answer."

"Hey, Dad. Nice of you to remember I was in the middle of telling you some really big news."

"Drop the smart-ass crap, would ya? You may have opened up a can of worms here, and it could mean serious trouble. . . . Please repeat the name of the man who died."

"Sure. No problem. His name was Abraham Fabrikant. From Miami. A very wealthy humanitarian who helped save the lives of all these—"

"Oh my God. *Oy, oy, oy.* I can't believe what I'm hearing. This isn't happening."

"Actually, that's what Grams said when I told her his name . . . but I don't get it. Did we know him? Because if we did, I swear I don't ever remember hearing you mention him."

"Claire, listen to me, and listen good. For your own sake, I do not want you to have any more contact with this family. Do you understand? These are not good people."

"I don't know what you're talking about. So far they've been wonderful to me. Yesterday they gave me a limo and a driver for the whole day, they offered to let Grams move into Mr. Fabrikant's apartment for free no matter how long she lives there, they invited me to speak at the funeral—"

"Speak at the funeral? Are you out of your mind?"

I had to hold the phone from my ear or risk permanent hearing loss.

"Please. I'm begging you," he said. "No more contact. Your mother and I will be on the next flight down. We'll take care of everything. And don't mention any of this funeral business to your grandmother, because I'm telling you right now, this will be the death of her, too. No wonder she threatened to kill herself—"

"Hey, wait. She pointed the gun at my head, not hers."

"Exactly. Because you brought this mess into the house, like we needed to deal with even more craziness right now."

"Would you stop blaming this on me? It's not my fault a man died, it's not my fault that Grams has been neglected, it's not my fault that—"

"Whatever. Just tell me if the gun is loaded."

"How the hell should I know?"

"Don't be fresh. Just find a good hiding place so she can't get a hold of it again. *Oy givalt.* I needed this today like I needed a hole in the head. I got clients coming in from New Jersey . . . I'm still way behind after tax season . . . Roberta! We're going to Florida. Pack the bags. I'll call JetBlue. . . . No, not Adam and Lindsey, too. Did you hear me say anything about this being a vacation to Disney?"

Okay, you think this was sounding bad? Not two minutes later, Drew called. Did I happen to remember the name of the nice man down the hall who played cards with his Pops, because Channel 6 was planning to do a story for the evening news, and they wanted to interview the two of us together.

Believe me, I seriously considered finding out if that damn gun was loaded.

# Chapter 9

SURE AS I PREDICTED, GRAMS HAD NO INTEREST IN PAYING GOOD money to eat at some restaurant where the son-of-a-bitch waiters never got the order right and the bagels were stale. But if I couldn't talk my grandmother into going out for a nice breakfast, what hope did I have of getting her to take a walk with me to look for a Starbucks? Trouble was, I was starting to feel a little shaky without my triple grande cinnamon nonfat latte and dreaded the headbanger I'd surely get if I had to survive on her brand X decaf and lactose-free milk substitute crap.

I would just tell her I was going out for my daily jog and hopefully find that my favorite caffeine oasis had opened nearby. Although what were the chances that a place that charged a minimum three dollars for a cup of coffee would survive in a neighborhood with elderly patrons who wouldn't pay that much if Juan Valdez personally ground the beans?

Unfortunately, now that she was feeling so refreshed after her good night's sleep, she decided to whip us up a batch of her famous buckwheat pancakes. I didn't have the heart to tell her the only thing they were famous for was weighing you down for two days. But to be polite, and because I wanted her to be in good spirits when I told her that my parents were en route to Florida, I said I would be glad to eat pancakes after my run.

But what to do with the gun? Pack the pistol in my bra? Leave it with the doorman? ("Excuse me, would you mind holding this?") Couldn't hide it under a couch. There was no couch. Or any furniture. Speaking of which, where did she plan to serve breakfast? Would we be eating every meal standing up? Of course not, she said. There was a bridge table and chairs in the front closet. Did I think she was crazy? Matter of fact yes!

I suddenly thought of the laundry hamper. That was my mother's favorite hiding spot when she was on Weight Watchers and needed a safe haven for her contraband Snickers bars. I just had to hope Grams had no plans to do laundry.

I'll admit that my jogging attire attracts attention. It's skimpy. It's tight. And the Lycra content is so high, I have to stay away from lit cigarettes for fear I'll blow like a Firestone tire. But in my defense, the shorts and jog bra are comfortable and they inspire me to run for miles.

But when I got outside and looked at my watch, I realized I was kidding myself if I thought I could get a run in. Grams was probably pouring batter on the griddle right now and had no idea a five-mile jog took more than five minutes. I should probably just go find a place for coffee before she came down looking for me, holding a plate of pancakes.

Too bad Viktor would miss that little reprise. Or maybe he wouldn't.

After squinting, I thought I recognized a familiar white stretch parked in the circular driveway. Sure enough, there was Viktor, newspaper in hand. I tapped on the window.

"Good morning, Miss Claire. Yur feeling better today, em I right?"

"Much better, thanks. What are you doing here?"

"Mr. Ben seys to wait here for when yur ready. Yur to go shopping . . . get your hair blown up."

My hair blown up? Oh, right. Ben had told me to buy something to wear to the funeral, and then to have my hair done. But no way could I pull that off now. Not with the Fabrikant name causing such a furor, not with my parents arriving in a few hours, not with me being so worried that Grams would find the gun.

"Oh, end Drew sez to get eh second outfit for the television news tonight."

"No, no, no, no. There is no television news tonight." What a disaster, I thought. It was bad enough I was going to be lying to Abe's family and friends at the funeral. The least I could do was draw the line at defrauding the viewing public.

"Viktor, I gotta be honest. I'm in little bit of a bind here. My grandmother isn't feeling well. In fact, I'm on my way to the drugstore to pick up some medicine for her. And my parents are flying in this afternoon because they're very concerned. So I can't leave. But maybe you can do me a favor."

"Viktor ken do enything."

*I have no doubt.* "Please tell Drew I'm very sorry, but Abe never mentioned the name of the man who he played cards with, and I'm too overwhelmed with grief to speak to the media right now."

"You don't look, how you say, overwhelmed." He took in an eyeful of my breasts.

"Yeah, well, I am, okay? And tell Ben I appreciate his generous offer to let me spend the day shopping, but I don't have time. I was thinking maybe you could pick out something."

"Me go to thi store? I don't know enything about yur clothes."

"It's easy. All I need is basic black. Here. Give me a piece of paper and a pen. I'll write down what I need: black skirt, size six; black T-shirt in small, V-neck preferable over round neck; black mules, size ten—"

"Mules?" He wrinkled his nose. "Where do I find thet? The Miami Zoo?"

"Sorry," I laughed. "Mules are ladies' shoes. Open-backed. Try Neiman Marcus, Saks, I don't really care. Then be a doll and leave everything with the doorman, okay?"

"End what about yur hair?"

"Don't worry. I'll blow it up myself."

"Okay, but I'm not the best et this. . . . Maybe I take yur measurements."

*Yeah, that's going to happen.* "You'll be fine. Just ask the sales ladies for help. Meanwhile, do you think you could take me to the nearest Starbucks?"

"In this neighborhood, are you joking? End what about yur grendmotherz medicine?"

"Oh yeah. The medicine."

"And you hev no purse. No money."

"Oh my God. You're right. I can't believe where my head is. I forgot my pocketbook."

In spite of the fact that the sun was burning my back, the look in Viktor's questioning eyes gave me a chill. I may have liked playing "Liar Liar," but that didn't mean I couldn't be a contestant myself. I just hoped that he wouldn't share any suspicions about me to the Fabrikants. Then again, Mr. Let-Me-Spill-It-to-the-*Enquirer* should be more concerned about what I had on him, rather than the other way around.

"Not to worry." Viktor opened the car door for me. "I ken take care of yur every need."

"Really? Can you divert a JetBlue flight that's en route from New York?"

Amazing what the mind can handle when the body gets its caffeine fix. Viktor knew of a little Italian coffeehouse down Biscayne Boulevard that served an eye-popping brew. Now I would be able to handle eating Grams' huge, dry pancakes and listening to her crazy story about Abe. Or so I thought. When I returned, I found her fast asleep at the bridge table, a stack of pancakes on my plate.

Naturally, given what I'd been through, and my mother's warning about mixing prescription meds with sleeping pills, I went into panic mode. Thank God that after a little nudging I was able to rouse her. But this time, instead of being chipper, she was on a warpath. What did I think? She would wait around all day for me to show up to eat? (It was eight-fifteen in the morning.) And how dare I call my parents after she forbade me? (Apparently they called and admitted to being on the way to the airport.) And why did I steal her gun? Didn't I know I could accidentally kill someone (unlike her, who pointed the thing at my head)?

"Grams, get a grip, okay? I have something really important to talk to you about."

"Eat your pancakes before they get ice cold."

"Fine." I cut the stack into tiny pieces. "It's great news, actually. Solves all your problems."

"What problems? So my arthritis acts up every once in a while. Not so terrible."

"I'm talking about your apartment problems. The fact that you want to move, but it has to be a place with special services."

She shot up so fast, the flimsy card table shook. "Where's the gun?" she huffed. " 'Cause I'm gonna kill myself right now! You're not putting me in one of those goddamn nursing homes where the son-of-a-bitch orderlies steal your things and the big black Haitian ladies touch your private parts when they give you a bath. That's the thanks I get for keeping this family together—"

"Grams, sit down. I'm not talking about putting you in a nursing home. After you fell asleep last night, I went out and found a beautiful assisted living center for you. The apartment is big and brand-new, there's a nice pool, they take you to the doctor . . . it's even furnished. You'll love it there."

"How much? 'Cause I'm not made of money, you know."

"That's the best part. It's actually less than you pay now."

"Is that right?"

I nodded. "Would you like to go over and see it later?"

She ran over to hug me. "You were always my favorite. My little *shayna punim*. I would say to Harry, you'll see. Claire will be the one who looks after me in my old age, not our *fershtunkeneh* daughters, what do they care?"

"I'm so glad you're excited, because when I saw this place, I couldn't believe how perfect it was for you." *And maybe me.*

"Where is it? Close by? Because you know me. I'll want to come back to visit my friends."

*What friends? Yesterday you told me they were all dead.* "I'm sure that won't be a problem."

"How did you find an apartment so fast? Was there an advertisement in the paper?"

"No . . . it wasn't in the paper. The friend that I made yesterday. He told me about it."

"That's what I always say." She clapped. "It's not what you know, it's who you know. So who's the friend? A young man, maybe? You know, a girl your age should be settled down already. Not running around like a teenager."

"Would you stop? I've got another few years before Social Security kicks in. Anyway, this guy is already engaged."

"Too bad. Who's the fella?"

"Funny you should ask." I cleared my throat. "It's Abe Fabrikant's grandson, Drew. He offered you Abe's apartment as a way thanking me for trying to help on the plane."

"What? *Oy, oy, oy.* Didn't I tell you never to mention that son-of-a-bitch's name again?" She pointed her arthritic finger in my face. "And who said you could stick your nose in my business? I'll find my own place to live, thank you very much."

"Grams, calm down. What are you getting so crazy for? I'm just trying to help you."

"Ha! You want to help me? Then stay away from those lousy, good-for-nothing—"

"I don't understand. You keep telling me you never met Mr. Fabrikant, so how would you even know what he or his family are like? You're probably confusing him with someone else."

"Oh, it's him, all right," Grams sniffed. "Believe you me, missy. I am not confused!"

# Chapter 10

WHY IS IT THAT WHEN AN OLD PERSON TELLS A STORY, THERE IS NO such thing as cutting to the chase? They much prefer the big buildup, like the endless previews shown before the feature film. Ten minutes can go by, and still no movie. But if I had known then what I know now, if I had any inkling what my grandmother was about to tell me, I would have told her to take all the time in the world. For the instant the words were spoken, my world would never be the same.

"If it was up to me, you would have heard this a long time ago. When you were a little girl. But who listens to me? What does the grandma know?"

"Fine, fine, fine. I get the point. We should always listen to you."

A dry, chalky piece of pancake got caught in my throat. Oh, for the days when she remembered step two: mix ingredients.

"You never knew my Gary. A beautiful boy. Smart. Good heart. Such a *mensch*."

"I don't mean to be rude, Grams, but I know this part, and I really want to jump in the shower."

"When he came home from the army, such a lost soul. Didn't know whether to finish college, get a job, work with Grandpa Harry at the shoe store. . . . We told him, go to school. You're whole life is ahead of you. You could be a teacher, an accountant, maybe even a lawyer."

"You know the Jewish position on fetuses. They're not considered viable until law school."

I presumed Grams couldn't hear my little sidebars because she hadn't cranked up her hearing aid yet. No doubt the expression "give a shout out" started with some little kid trying to talk to his hearing-impaired grandma.

"So anyway," Grams continued, "he finally decides he'll go to school in the city. Why he had to *schlep* all the way to Manhattan, I don't know. Long Island had plenty of nice colleges. Your cousin Mark. You know, Sydelle and Marvin's son . . . he got a fine education there. Became a dentist. But Gary, he had his own way of doing things, a stubborn mule like his father."

"Grams, you're killing me. Get to the part where the story starts."

"Believe me, this *is* where the story starts. . . . So Gary's going back and forth to the city, he's making friends, some I didn't care for, I can tell you that. With their loud music, and boys wanting to look like girls with those long ponytails. . . . But Gary, he looked real nice. Clean-cut like a young man should. I guess the army taught him good."

I was trying to be patient, but I was starting to feel like I was driving behind an old guy in a Caddy. Didn't look good for making the light. No wonder I preferred phone calls over visits. At least I could pluck my eyebrows or read *Vogue* while she went on and on.

"Anyway, one day he comes home and says he met a girl. Very smart and pretty. So naturally I say, bring her for dinner. But he says no 'cause she's a picky eater, and he thinks maybe I'm going to try to stuff her, which broke my heart, because *that* I would never do. Have you ever seen me push food?"

*My whole life.* "Never."

"Then one day he shows up with her, like it would have been too much trouble to call first? No. He's gotta walk through the front door, and say, 'Ma, I'm home.' And I run out from the kitchen 'cause I don't know why he's announcing himself, and there she is. The most beautiful girl I ever saw. Tall. Big bosoms. Looked like a movie star."

I snuck a peek at my watch. I really hoped this was going somewhere.

"So they stay for dinner, and I'm running around trying to put together something nice, maybe a brisket, a chicken with roasted potatoes, I don't remember, and she sits down at the kitchen table and says to me how much she likes Gary, how he's been real sweet to her, and then I look up, and I see she's crying. Who the hell knew why?"

"She was pregnant?" I yawned.

"Who told you?" Her eyes could not veil fear. "Iris the big-mouth?"

"No, Grams. C'mon. This is a dime-a-dozen story. The girl gets knocked up, and can't tell her parents, so she goes to the boy's parents and says she needs money for an abortion."

"Exactly!"

"What was she? Eighteen?"

"Nearly twenty. And old enough to know better."

"Oh, stop. She was a baby herself. Probably scared out of her mind. She had to be thinking, do I really want to screw up my whole life because of a little, careless mistake I made?"

"Is that so, Miss Big Shot with all the answers? You think that's how the world works? You make a little mistake? A butcher takes a knife to you. One, two, three. No more mistake?"

"I'm not saying that's what I'd do. I'm saying if I was nineteen, I would have been just as freaked out. But I bet I can tell you what you said to her. 'Look here, Missy,'" I mimicked her raspy, tarred voice. "'Life is precious, so don't think you can just walk in here, ask us for money, then run off to some back room down on the Bowery.'"

Grams pouted.

"Okay. Sorry. I'm stealing your thunder. I'll let you tell the rest." But from the way her nostrils flared, I knew I'd pushed too far.

"You think you know everything?" She waved her fist. "Well, I'll let you in on a little secret, Missy. You don't know nothin'! 'Cause this is not what you call one of them dime-a-dozen stories. This is my story." She began to cry. "Do you hear me? MY story!"

"Sorry, Grams." I followed her into the bathroom. "C'mon. Don't cry. Now I feel awful."

"Good! 'Cause this is very hard for me." She blew her nose. "And believe me. I warned your mother and Aunt Iris. I said, I am not going to my grave with this, you understand?"

"Yes, yes. They understand. Now let's go sit down in your nice lawn chairs. You can tell me everything, and I promise not to interrupt." *God help me.*

I sat her in the chair, no longer in shock that two pieces of outdoor furniture constituted her entire living room set. That and the big RCA TV, with the *yahrtzeit* candle that had flickered through the night. Soon the tiny wick would curl, and a puff of black smoke would billow from the thick glass. A flame snuffed out swiftly and without warning, like the child whose memory it honored.

Oh God. What was wrong with me that I had just sat there and made light of her heartbreaking past? I guess I assumed that after all these years, the pain had subsided. But from the sorrow in Grams' eyes, the way she slumped in the flimsy metal chair, clearly I was wrong.

I thought it might rejuvenate her to let some light into the room, so I tugged at the chain and drew open the stiff plastic blinds. Sun poured in, yet an ominous darkness enveloped the room, as if the brightness could not keep doom from descending upon us. Frankly, it scared the crap out of me.

As did the realization that Grams had just yelled at me the way I went nuts on Pablo when I thought he was judging me. Hadn't I accused him of being clueless and arrogant for presuming to know what my life had been like? Except that I was no better. I had just made my grandmother feel as though the details of her story were mundane and predictable.

How odd that in spite of our fifty-year age gap, our lives were starting to parallel one another's. We both felt past our prime, misunderstood, and resentful of having painful experiences dismissed by people who thought that the statute of limitations on feeling bad had run out.

"Okay." I clapped. "After these words from our sponsor, we now continue with our story."

"Uch, forget about it. Why open a can of worms? It's too late. What's done is done."

"No, please. I really want to hear this. I used to ask my mom about Uncle Gary all the time, but she refused to tell me anything. You're my only hope."

It took some coaxing, but after reminding her she just said she didn't want to go to her grave with this story, she agreed to keep talking.

"So anyway," she sighed, "we spent the whole night trying to tell the girl to talk to her folks. But no, she says she can't do that because they're different than Harry and me. They save people. They don't believe in . . . what did she call it? . . . early termination. Like we're talking about a savings bond. Anyway, she says they won't under-stand. But I say, a parent is a parent. No matter what, they love you. They'll forgive you. But she insists no they won't . . . and that was that."

"So, wait. She had the abortion?"

"Well, she went to the place . . . it was the Sunday right after Thanksgiving. I remember 'cause it was pouring, and Gary called me from a pay phone. He was standing there, shivering, and he said, 'Ma, we're coming home.' She couldn't go through with it . . . make us a nice Sunday dinner, but no more turkey. We're sick of it."

"Oh wow. So she did have the baby. That was good. Right?"

"To be honest, it wasn't good at first. She moved into Gary's bed-room, and all they did was fight. I tell you, every night we'd hear them. She's crying, he's throwing things . . . and I was afraid, you see, because I loved my son, but he could blow up like a firecracker . . . a terrible temper. Not that she didn't deserve a good *zetz* across the face with that big mouth of hers. But I'd say to Grandpa, *oy*, I pray to God one day he doesn't kill her."

Okay, now I understood where this was going. Grams' only son had killed his pregnant girlfriend. Then, to retaliate, her family took a contract out on his life. Which would certainly explain why nobody ever wanted to talk about Gary. His story was scandalous, shameful, bad for the Jews.

How clever of me to figure everything out. But it was only because

I'd read so many scripts, and knew there were maybe a dozen original plots. Everything else was just a variation on the same theme. Boy meets girl. Boy screws girl. Girl's parents seek revenge. Boy is sorry he ever met girl.

"Finally they settled down and got used to the idea they're having a baby," Grams went on. "So we said, what about getting married, but that they don't want to hear because they're hippy-dippys, and what's marriage got to do with babies? And besides, she's gotta open her big trap and tell us she's not planning on keeping it because she wants to finish school. Like the world would end if she didn't study the theater? You like acting? I said. Go see a show."

"Gee, thanks, Grams," I laughed. "Good to know you support the arts."

"Arts, schmarts. I was trying to tell her she shouldn't be wasting her time sitting around some hole-in-the-wall theater down on Fourteenth Street. But you know me. I don't like to push."

*Oh, I know.*

"Meanwhile, the girl won't tell us nothin' about her family. Where they live. What they do, 'cause she's afraid we'll call 'em. But at least, thank God, we found out she was a Jewish girl."

"I can see where that would make everything better."

"What?"

"Nothing. Go on."

"So anyway, a few months go by, and now she's big as a two-story house."

"How come you keep saying *she*, Grams? You used to yell at me all the time for doing that. '*She* has a name, Claire . . . where are your manners, missy?'"

"Sure, she had a name," Grams sighed. "Used to like that name, too. Penelope."

"Oh, yuck. Are you serious? Penelope? That's an awful name."

"Maybe to match the awful person she was."

"You didn't like her?"

"What was to like? Such a cold fish. . . . She did something so terrible you can't even imagine."

"Oh God. Please don't tell me she hurt the baby."

"Worse than that."

"She killed the baby?" I reached for Grams' hand. This was the last thing I expected to hear.

"No, no. Nothing like that. Bite your tongue."

"So what did she do?"

"Well, after the baby was born—"

"Boy or girl?"

"A sweet little girl. An angel. Not fussy. Except Penelope wanted nothing to do with her."

"Probably because she knew she was going to give her up for adoption."

"Turns out she couldn't go through with that, either. On account of Gary. Once he held his daughter, he went crazy for her. All of a sudden he wants to get married. Be a family man. . . . But Miss Stinker says to us, he can keep her for a while and see how it goes. Like the baby's a new Buick you take for a test drive."

"What a bitch. . . . But whatever. What did they name the baby?"

"Well, that's a whole 'nother story . . . *oy* . . . until they could finally agree. . . . But thank God they stopped fighting and picked one . . . Hannah."

"Oooh, now, that's pretty. Biblical yet modern. Classy but warm . . . Hannah Moss. I like it."

"No."

"No?"

"All of a sudden Penelope decides she wants Hannah to have *her* last name."

"Why?"

"Who the hell knows? She always had a bug up her ass about this, that, or the other thing."

"Well, it was the seventies. Women's lib and all. . . . So what was Penelope's last name?"

Grams stood. "You'll never in a million years believe."

It startled me how small and demure she looked compared to the imposing figure she'd cut in her younger days. Eventually I met her eye to eye, then passed her completely, but when I was younger and would look up, she always seemed soldier tall, though never at ease.

"Fabrikant," she whispered.

"I'm sorry?" Maybe I was the one who needed a hearing aid.

"Penelope Fabrikant . . . that was her name."

"Are you kidding me?" I gasped. "That's . . . I don't know . . . really bizarre."

"Why God is still punishing us, I have no idea. He doesn't think we suffered enough?"

"Wait, wait, wait. That's why you're all so freaked out? Because you think she might have been related to Abe Fabrikant?"

"There's nothin' to think about."

"Oh, please. That's nuts. I mean, granted, it isn't a common name. But honestly, what are the odds there's a connection here?"

"I'll tell you the odds." Grams collapsed in the chair and knotted the tissue around her thumb. "Sit down."

"I am sitting," I said. "See? I'm right here next to you." *Yup. We're getting you into this assisted living facility in the nick of time.*

"No, I mean sit on the floor."

"Why?"

" 'Cause you're too big for me now . . . for when you fall."

"I'm going to fall?"

"I know how you don't like nothin' with a scary ending."

"Okay, you do realize I'm not a kid anymore, right? It's not like that night we watched *Psycho* and I screamed so loud your crazy neighbor started banging on the door. What was her name? The one with that big birthmark in the middle of her cheek?"

"Mrs. Alberti."

"Yeah. Good old Mrs. Alberti. Remember she said she thought there was a murder going on?"

"That was fun-nee." Grams slapped her knee. "Barges in with that head full of curlers, and the furry slippers with those dogs on her toes. . . . Like that would scare off a killer."

"I still can't believe you let me stay up so late to watch *Psycho*. Of all movies, Grams. My God, how old was I? Eight? Nine?"

"Six and a half."

"No way."

"Sure. I remember 'cause it was right after your mother had that bad accident in Waldbaum's parking lot. Nobody told me at first. They knew what it would do to me. Brought back all the terrible memories of Gary's crash. . . . Anyway, I was staying with you kids, but every night, I'd watch a little television. Sometimes a good picture would come on. Half the time I'd find you curled up next to me on the couch . . . you and me . . . we always got along good 'cause we knew the rest of the family was nuts."

"Just keep going with the story." I squeezed her hand. "I promise I won't scream."

"That's what you always said," she sighed. "So where was I?"

My speciality. When someone yelled "Line," I always knew where we were. "You're at the part where Penelope just had the baby."

"Yeah. Yeah . . . so now we're home with Hannah, and everybody is crazy about her. She started out this little nothing *pishelach*, but in a few weeks she's got nice color, she's eating . . . she didn't like to sleep so much, but Gary, he was good. He could hold you in a certain way, like a football, and like magic, no more crying."

"Wait, Grams. You mean Hannah. He could hold Hannah."

"What?"

"Just now . . . when you were telling the story. You were talking about Uncle Gary. How he could make the baby stop crying, and you said 'you.' But his daughter was Hannah."

"I did?"

"Yeah."

"*Oy, oy, oy.*" She tapped the side of her head. "My mind. Sometimes it goes a little haywire. Grandpa Harry, he always used to say, 'Gert, you don't know how to tell a story.'"

"You're doing fine. Just keep going." But for the first time that I could recall, Grams was at a loss for words. "Yoo-hoo? Anyone home? You were just getting to the good part. Don't zone out on me now."

"Sorry. I can't seem to remember the rest. I'm old, you know . . . memory loss . . ."

"Oh, give me a break. You're sharp as a tack when you want to be. What happened next?"

"Finish your pancakes."

"If you finish the story."

"Maybe another time. I gotta take my pills now, otherwise I'm no good for the day."

"But you can't just leave me hanging. It's like when I read a new script. I can't stand the suspense, so I go right to the end. Just tell me what happened to Penelope and Hannah. When's the last time you saw them? How come nobody ever talks about them? God, it must be terrible for you to have this other granddaughter you never get to see."

"I see her," she blurted.

"Are you serious? You know where Hannah is?"

She nodded.

"I don't believe it. You're telling me I have a first cousin who would be about my age, but nobody ever said, hey, you know what? Maybe she and Claire should meet?"

Grams' eyes welled up. "When she was little, she was with me every day."

"You mean in your heart."

"I mean I'd drive over to her house, or she'd get dropped off by me."

"Wait, wait, wait. That's not even possible. I was at your house every day, and I never saw another little girl. Don't you think I would have noticed? Said, hey, Grams. Who's the spare kid?"

". . . I took her to the park, to ballet classes. I taught her to read, took her to our house in the mountains every summer. . . ."

"Okay, now you're really starting to freak me out. It was me, Adam, and Lindsey up in the Catskills. And then Aunt Iris and Uncle Herbie would bring Alison and Hilary after camp. Trust me. There was no little girl named Hannah."

"Yes, there was." Grams' lips quivered. "We called her by a different name."

"Well, that makes absolutely no sense."

"We had a big problem after she was born, see," she sobbed. "A mess like you wouldn't believe. First we bury our son. Then we sit *shiva*. Then, next thing we know, Penelope runs away in the middle of the night."

"Are you serious? She ran away with the baby?"

"WITHOUT the baby!"

"Oh my God. That's awful."

"We found this cockamamie note in the stroller saying Hannah was better off without her. And that was that . . . a seven-week-old baby's got no father, no mother. . . ."

"What did you do? Did Penelope come back? What happened to Hannah?"

Grams took a deep breath. "What happened to her is . . . now she's this beautiful young lady."

"Well, wait. How do you know that?"

"I know because I see her from time to time."

"This is nuts. If the two of you have a relationship, how come you never mentioned her before? Where does she live? What does she look like?"

"What does she look like? Actually"—she blinked—"she looks like . . . you."

"Me? Really?"

"I bet I couldn't tell you apart."

"They say everyone has a twin." I shrugged. "I just wish you'd let me meet her."

"Fine. You want to meet her?" Grams led me by the hand into the bathroom. "Let's go."

"What are you doing? Where are we going?"

"I'm introducing you to Hannah." She cupped my chin. "Take a good look in the mirror."

" 'Take a good look in the mirror,' " I mimicked her. "Don't take this wrong, Grams. But you've completely gone off the deep end."

"I know, my *shayna madel*. But listen to me. You wanted to meet Hannah, and here she is."

It took me a moment to follow her twisted trail. Then a ripple of nausea roared through my innards like a monstrous wave crashing into shore. "OH MY GOD!" I grabbed hold of the sink to catch my fall. "OH MY GOD!" My heart nearly pounded out of my chest. "Me?" I shrieked. "Me?"

Grams looked away, too frightened to examine the crime scene.

"NO!" I screamed. "No, no, no, no. . . . How can I be Hannah? I'm Claire. Claire Greene."

"No, darling. You're both."

"I'm both?" I repeated before slumping onto the toilet seat and crying into a towel. How could I be both? My parents were Lenny and Roberta. My brother was Adam, my sister was Lindsey . . . Grams was out of her mind. She was doing this to get attention. Or maybe she was overdosing on all those drugs she took. Soon she would be one of those unforgettable *20/20* stories: "Florida's delusional, granny-tripping psychopaths."

"A million times I said to your mother, tell her already," Grams rambled. "And she'd say, what good's it gonna do her? And I'd say, if it was you, wouldn't you want to know the truth? And she'd say no. And then I'd say, fine. If you're not gonna tell her, I'll tell her. . . ."

I stopped listening. All I could think was if I wasn't me, if I was really someone else, then it was time to find out if the gun in the hamper was loaded, for surely I would never recover from the shock that my whole life had been one huge lie. Or that I had been so deaf, dumb, and blind I needed an eighty-four-year-old woman to point out what should have been obvious.

Suddenly images clicked in my head like a roll of film being developed. One at a time a vivid picture slid down the shoot: my mother's refusal to talk about her kid brother . . . Grams' slip of the tongue about Uncle Gary holding me . . . the young, unwed mother who ran away without her baby . . . the way I stuck out in family photos like a green bean among fat tomatoes . . . Grams' relationship with Hannah that was identical to her relationship with me . . . my family's spooked reaction to hearing the name Fabrikant. . . .

I flipped up the toilet seat lid and upchucked fear and phlegm.

"*Oy.* Look what you're doing," Grams scolded. "I just washed the floor, and the girl don't come till Friday."

"Hey! Fuck the floor, okay?" I yelled into the cavernous blue bowl.

"This is what I was afraid of . . . you getting sick over this."

"What the hell did you expect?" I gagged. "You've had thirty years to get used to the idea . . . I've had, what? Thirty seconds. I can't fucking believe this. . . . I'm adopted . . . adopted. . . ."

"Better than being thrown out with the garbage."

"Oh my God, that's right . . . I was almost an abortion."

"I prayed every night she'd change her mind."

"Do you swear you're telling me the truth?" I shouted, my hair sticky with retch. "This isn't your way of getting back at us because you think no one cares about you?"

"It's the God's honest truth, honey." She grabbed more tissues. "It's a shock. I know."

"A shock?" I choked. "No. Uh-uh. Sorry. A shock is when you win a contest or . . . or you flunk your road test! This is a fucking nightmare. How could I be someone else? I'm Claire Greene!"

I flushed the toilet, then balanced on my knees, the cool tiles digging into my skin. "This is insane. I don't know who I am! What my real name is. . . . Wait. What *is* my real name?"

"*Oy.* You're not gonna like this."

"Oh. Like it's any better to find out you've been deceived your whole life?"

"So fine. You wanna hear your name? I'll tell you your name. You were born Hannah Claire."

"Hannah Claire what?" I pounded my fist on the wall.

"Hannah Claire . . . Fabrikant."

I let out a wail so shrill and piercing, the sound reverberated through the near-vacant apartment. And though my raw throat burned with dread, there was something else I had to know. "And who was Abe?"

Grams steadied herself by clinging to the bathroom door. "You'll never believe."

"Who was he, goddamn it?" I yelled. "Tell me right now!"

"I'm trying, believe me." She hollered back. "*Oy.* Of all the people to drop dead on your lap, God had to make him Penelope's idiot father!"

"OH MY GOD!"

"How's that for a fine how do you do? You finally meet your grandfather, then ker-plop, he's gone. Well, at least thank God you got to talk to him for a while."

"Nooooooo." I vomited again, then collapsed on the foul-smelling floor. Suddenly I recalled yesterday's conversation at La Guardia.

*"Will your grandfather be needing any special assistance?" the gate agent had asked as she waited for my boarding pass to print out. "My grandfather?" I said. Frankly, it was a little late for special assistance, as both of them were dead. "Aren't you two traveling together? . . . Your seat assignment is next to his . . . I thought I noticed a resemblance."*

What a nightmare. My life had just become a Stephen King novel. The wicked gate agent seats an unsuspecting girl next to a stranger, who is really her grandfather. Then he dies on her lap, and comes back to haunt her. Damn! The only thing I hated more than Stephen King was irony!

# Chapter 11

IMMEDIATELY FOLLOWING AN ACCIDENT, SURVIVORS SAY THAT THEY experience a series of involuntary responses. The body's way of coping with the sudden impact of catastrophic injuries. So when I was clobbered by the emotional equivalent of a six-car pileup, instinctively I wanted to downshift into a fight-or-flight mode. But my grandmother said, "No ma'am. Nothin' doing." I could not go to the aftershock party like everyone else. Better I should wash my face, sit down at the table, and finish my pancakes.

"Eat pancakes?" I just looked at her. "Are you freakin' kidding me?"

"Trust me. You'll feel better."

"Why? Are they made with Paxil?" I knew my grandmother had a few short circuits, but even she should be able to appreciate that it would take me years, not minutes, to recover from this horrifying discovery. And enough money to keep one lucky therapist busy till the day he or she died.

"What good's it gonna do you to sit and sulk?" Grams tried to woo me from my fetal position in the corner of her bedroom.

"Gee, I don't know," I cried. "I haven't had a chance to try."

"Maybe you'll feel better if you hear the whole story."

"Oooh. That's what I was thinking. Let's talk over cyanide cocktails."

But before I could sidle up to the bar there was a knock at the door. My grandmother's next-door neighbor, Lillian, had heard screams and wanted us to know we had nothing to worry about. She had just called the police.

Talk about irony. Grams had once told me she was going to call the cops on Lillian. To report her suspicions of a busy brothel. How else to explain the comings and goings of so many men, and the sounds of Sinatra blaring at eight o'clock in the morning?

From my floor-level view in the bedroom, I could tell that Lillian had rushed right over, as she was still in uniform. There she stood in a black see-through nightie, which, trust me, you didn't want to see through. And wasn't one leg of hers shorter than the other? Only in Miami could an aging gimp prostitute with penciled-on eyebrows have a steady following.

Then I felt shame and confusion. I was in the middle of a life-altering crisis. I should be smashing the last of Grams' lamps. Threatening to use the gun in the hamper. Not concerning myself with an old lady who had found a clever way to supplement her Social Security income.

"What do you mean, Claire knows everything now?" Lillian's bellow got my attention. "*Oy vey*, Gert! Roberta's gonna wring your little neck."

"He dropped dead on her lap, for Christ's sake. I should just say nothing?"

"Well, if you ask me, she got this far without knowing the truth— why rock the boat?"

"You don't know Claire. She's my tough one. She'll be fine."

"I hope you're right. 'Cause all you hear on the news today are stories about adopted kids going crazy looking for their real families. They go searching on that damn Intercom. . . . Turns everyone's life upside down. Who needs it?"

"It's not the Intercom, you old fool. It's the Interstate. . . . And Claire won't be out there looking for no one! She's got all the family she needs!"

Now I trembled in the corner, while gagging into a washcloth. Grams was wrong. I would be exactly like those kids who scoured the

country in search of their true identity. It reminded me of that
adorable book I made her read me every night. The one about the
little baby duck who fell from the tree and didn't know who his
mother was. What was the name of it? Duh, Claire! *Are You My
Mother?* How freaky that a story I loved so much as a child would
turn out to be MY story, too.

> *He could not fly, but he could walk. "Now I will go and find my
> mother," he said.*
> *He did not know what his mother looked like. He went right by
> her. He did not see her.*
> *He came to a kitten. "Are you my mother?" he said to the kitten.*

I had visions of tapping women on the shoulder at nail salons.
"Excuse me. By any chance are you my mother?" Or at the gym. "Hi.
You wouldn't happen to be my mother?" It made me feel so lost and
alone.

Furthermore, if a virtual stranger, Lillian the Lover, could be
privy to my *E! True Hollywood Story*, who else knew the truth? Adam
and Lindsey? All my aunts, uncles, and cousins (were they still even
related to me)? Family friends? My orthodontist? Everyone but me?

"Well, thanks for your two cents, Lil," Grams spit. "Is that how
much you get to kiss mens' pee-pees?"

"Why, I never!" Lillian gasped.

"That's not what I hear!"

"This is the thanks I get for trying to be a good neighbor!" The
lady in black stormed out.

"You wanna be a good neighbor?" Grams yelled. "Open your
door and close your legs!"

"Who the hell needs that *meshugina* tellin' me what's good for
you?" Grams walked into the bedroom and stood over me, hands
over hips, just like when I was four and banished to the corner for
drawing on her living room walls. "Damn right we're your family.
Nothing changes that."

"I can't believe the happy hooker knew before I did." I gagged on my tears. "That's what you do all day? Talk about your pitiful grand-daughter with the deep, dark secret?"

"This is Florida." Grams shrugged. "It's a right-to-talk state."

"You don't know how stupid I feel." Tears were free-falling on my lap. "How did I not figure this out myself? I never looked like them . . . never related to them. . . . I can't believe they kept this from me all these years."

"Ach! What do they ever agree on? Nothing! Was it a good time? A bad time? Were you too young? Too old? Too tall, too short? Too this, too that?"

"But if they'd just told me when I was little, I'd be over it by now!"

"That's what *I* said." She threw up her arms.

"Wait, wait, wait." I took a deep breath. "Are Adam and Lindsey adopted, too?"

She shook her head.

"Oh my God," I screamed. "You know what this means, Grams? It means my entire life has been one huge, fucking lie. Nothing that happened, happened to me. Do you understand? The whole time I was someone else. This person who was being betrayed."

"Baloney! You don't know nothin'!" She rammed her hands in her apron pockets and walked out. "Nothin' at all!"

"Oh, believe me, I know all I need to know!" I cried.

I might have sat sobbing in the corner for days if not for four pre-cipitously timed calls. It made me wonder if their synchronization had somehow been orchestrated by a higher power.

At first it took me a moment to realize my cell was even ringing. Then I was in too much of a fog to remember to look at the caller ID. Pity, I could have avoided another isn't-this-so-exciting call from Elyce, the 24/7 fiancée.

Thank God she was finally able to reach me, she said. And did I get her other messages? She wasn't sure because sometimes when you're out of town, the voice mails don't go through, and there was so much she had to tell me, and she hoped that I absolutely loved the dress she'd chosen for me, and not to worry, she wasn't going to make us all look like cookie-cutter bridesmaids.

"Elyce. Wait. Hold on," I butted in. "I'm sorry to have to tell you this." (I was still crying, so the tears weren't fake.) There's been a terrible tragedy. A death in the family. *My real family.* So this isn't a good time. In fact, now I'm not even sure if I'm coming back to New York. *Ever.* I'm really sorry. I don't want to ruin your big day, but I think you should probably ask someone else."

But no, of course she wouldn't dream of asking anyone else. She was sorry for my loss, but certainly by a year from November I'd be fine, and not to worry, she'd have Kleinfeld's put a hold on the dress until I got back, and please, if there was anything she could do to help, I should let her know, because as her oldest and dearest friend, she wanted me to know that I was like family to her.

Great. Now I was like family to everyone.

Just as I wondered how to beg off, the doorbell saved the day. "Elyce, I really have to go, hon. The police are arresting my grandmother for illegal possession of a firearm."

A normal person would concede that this was an emergency situation, but not the ever-helpful Elyce. She wouldn't hang up until informing me that Ira's uncle was a big trial lawyer in Boca, and to let her know if we needed representation.

"We're fine," Grams said to the cops when I walked in. "But if you want to crack a really big case"—she loved her Ed Sullivan voice—"check out next door. Action like you wouldn't believe."

"Sorry for the false alarm, Officers," I sniffed. "I'm the one who screamed before. We just received word about a death in the family . . . my grandfather."

Naturally they were trained to be respectful of my loss, but from the way the two high-testosterone cops ogled me in my running gear, the only thing they looked sorry about was not being able to cuff me and turn me into a squeeze toy in the back of the squad car.

It took several minutes to satisfy their curiosity about the furnitureless apartment and to snoop around under the guise of doing a thorough investigation. Thankfully they weren't all that thorough, as they didn't think to check a laundry hamper for an unlicensed weapon.

I had never been so grateful to see two people leave. Finally I could jump in the shower and have my much-deserved meltdown. And not a moment too soon, as I so reeked of puke; my body odor offended even me. But then there were further delays, like on a smog alert day at LAX.

God help me, but of all times for Pablo to call and ask if I'd made a decision about coming to work for them . . . Given my mental state, frankly I'd forgotten we'd even met, let alone discussed employment opportunities. But before I could answer, he wanted to remind me of a few things.

One, he had seniority over me; two, he got first crack at the comp tickets to any premieres; and three, if I hadn't guessed, he was in a loving, committed relationship with Raphael that he did not want to have fucked up by some petty coworker who had jealous fits over the preferential treatment.

"I'll be honest, Pablo." I blew into a tissue. "I've just received some very shocking news about my family, and I haven't had time to think about this."

"Well, what's to think about, sweet stuff? It's a great job, great pay, great people . . ."

"It's none of those things, and you know it."

"True. But we were hoping you'd look past that."

"To be honest, I don't think I'd like working down here."

"Oh pish-tish. Who doesn't want to work in the Sunshine State? We've got the greatest beaches, the hottest clubs, no snow. And here's a real attention-getter. No state income tax."

*Oooh. Big plus. I worry constantly about my tax bracket.* "That's all great, but I'm freaked out at the moment . . . not a good time to be working for Photographer Barbie."

"He's really a wonderful person, Claire. And think of the possibilities. Sometimes we're the first to know which producers are casting for what roles. It could give you a real leg up."

"Is that true?"

"Of course it's true. Pablo doesn't lie. Well, maybe a little fib now and then, but I swear on my cutie petutie, you could be in the heart of the action working here. *Variety* has nothin' on us!"

"Okay," I sighed.

"Okay as in, yes, I'll do it, or okay as in, I'll think about it some more?"

"Okay as in, I'm about to have a meltdown. Why not get paid while I'm losing my mind?"

"Oh, that's marvy! Raphael will be just tickled when I tell him. Be here at ten tomorrow."

"No. Sorry. I need the day off. For Abe Fabrikant's funeral." *My grandfather's funeral.*

"No, no, no. Uh-uh, darling. No vacation days for the first two months."

"Bullshit. You can't count it as a vacation day if I didn't even start yet. I'll come in for a few days next week, see if I like the job, then decide if it's worth it to go get my stuff in New York."

"Oh, fine. But I may have to note this little postponement in your permanent record."

"You do that, Pablo. Then take your little pen and shove it up your cutie petutie."

I was two steps from the bathroom when my cell rang again. Of all people, it was Marly Becker. Seems Viktor was needed at the airport, so she had volunteered to shop for me. The dear girl knew every inch of designer selling space in Miami, and was actually calling from the Versace boutique to ask my style preferences. And was I sure I wore a size six, because Drew had happened to mention that I was a rather large girl.

*My ass he said that,* I thought. But, of course, it would be impolite to kick a gift card in the mouth. (Versace? Oh my God, I adored Versace). And why be petty and tell her that Drew alluded to the fact that she was lazy, manipulative, and felt entitled to everything served on a Tiffany platter?

I frankly don't know how I had the wherewithal to hold a girl-type conversation, but somehow I managed to sound not only polite, but coherent. Then I actually heard myself say how much I appreciated her help, and I was sure whatever she picked out would be perfect, and to please have Viktor leave any packages with the doorman because I was taking my grandmother to the doctor.

Finally I could get into the shower. Then I heard my cell ring yet again. Was I stupid enough to run back out in a small bath towel? No, that's why God invented voice mail.

On the other hand, what if it was someone I wanted to talk to? Someone to whom I could unburden myself, confide my devastating secret? It would certainly calm my nerves to hear a compassionate, sensitive voice on the other end. Someone who could reassure me that the rest of my life was not doomed. Someone like Sydney. Or Drew.

*Oops. Don't get ahead of yourself there,* I thought. *He'll probably turn out to be like the rest of his species. Amazing at first impressions, lousy at sustaining the charm. A great listener at the beginning, altogether deaf by the end.* Then there was that little matter of his being engaged. And yet I ran for that phone like it was my last free minutes forever.

"Hi," Drew said. "Did I get you at a bad time?"

*Yes! I was hoping it was you.* "Well, I'm kind of standing here in a towel. I was just about to jump in the shower." *Oooh. Bad move. Poor guy will get blue balls from the mental image. Go on. Tell him how bad you smell.*

But being the gentleman Drew was, he let it go. "Should I call you back?"

"No, I'm fine." *I was just thinking of creative ways to end my life.* "How are you doing?"

"We've been really busy with all the arrangements. Not much time to think, which I guess is good. . . . Look, I only have a minute, but I wanted to find out if maybe you and your grandmother could come to my dad's for dinner tonight. Everyone wants to meet you."

"Dinner?" *Excellent. Another occasion for which I have absolutely nothing to wear.*

"Nothing fancy. The owner of the Rascal House is sending over some platters."

"Thanks for thinking of us, but I'm afraid we can't. My grandmother's not feeling well. In fact, my parents . . ." I hesitated. I'd said the *p* word a million times, but now it sounded vulgar and inappropriate. "They're flying down as we speak."

"Oh. Well, what if they watch her and you come by yourself? Viktor could pick you up."

"Drew, it's just not a good time right now . . . weird stuff going on with my family." *And yours!*

"Okay. Well, look, I wasn't supposed to say anything. . . . You have to promise not to repeat this . . . but I told my Aunt Penny the whole story about you, how you tried to save Pops' life, and that you're a struggling actress, and, well . . . she wants to do something to repay your kindness."

"She does?" *Are we talking cash reward, or valuable introductions?*

"Yeah. But she really wants to tell you herself."

"Okay."

"Oh, screw it. What's the difference who tells you?"

"Uh-huh . . ."

"See, she might be producing her first feature film next year. Part of a two-picture deal with Universal starring her, Meryl Streep, and I think Nick Nolte. No, wait. Maybe it was Nick Cage. Whatever. She'll tell you."

"UH-HUH . . ."

"Anyway, she's going to be casting for the part of her daughter, and I happened to mention that I thought you'd be perfect for the role because you two even look alike. So she said she would talk to you, maybe have you do a cold reading if you were interested."

"Interested? Oh my God. Of course I'm interested. I don't know what to say."

"That's why I wanted you to come for dinner. It'll be totally nuts after the funeral. And you know how crazy *shiva* calls get. At least tonight you'd get a chance—"

"What time?" I cut him off.

"Six? Six-thirty?" Drew laughed. "Now do you think you can make it?"

"Yes."

"But pretend you had no idea, okay? Be cool. Aunt Penny is very big on dramatic gestures."

"What?"

"Don't let on that you know. She likes to ride in on her white horse. . . . Are you even listening to me? Claire . . . I seem to be losing you."

"Huh? Oh. Sorry . . . I . . . um . . . dropped my towel."

"No, I'm sorry," he said. Though he didn't say why. "See you tonight."

Be careful what you wish for. Isn't that what they say?

You know how desperately I wanted to get a film offer. And now, equally important, a shower. Just five minutes of solitude with steamy water rushing down my back so that I could collect myself. Prepare for the most important meeting of my life. Decide what to say to my so-called parents before telling them I doubted I would ever forgive them for deceiving me.

That was the plan. Cleanse. Rejuvenate. Prepare for battle. Passing out in the shower was not on the agenda. But as the tension began to dissipate under the hot spray and I could fantasize about the stimulating chat I would have with Penny Nichol, a bone-chilling thought occurred to me. One that would turn an already eerie series of events into a grim, terrifying reality.

It began as a random stream of consciousness about the strange circumstances surrounding Abe Fabrikant's final moments. If it had been a Hollywood script whipped up by the wacky Coen brothers, the reviews would have said, "Clever, but unrealistic. This could never happen."

But it had happened, and I couldn't stop focusing on the absurdity of it. There I was on a plane, reading some stupid article about Penny Nichol's fiftieth birthday celebration, while unbeknownst to me her father was seated to my left and in the middle of having a fatal heart attack. But wait, wait, wait . . . how could he be HER father, and MY grandfather . . . unless . . . I was HER daughter? Impossible! Grams told me the name of the girl was Penelope. Yes, that's right. She said Abe's daughter was Penelope Fabrikant. Penelope refused to talk to her parents about having an abortion because their whole thing was saving people, not killing them. . . . But wait. Wasn't Abe supposedly this great humanitarian? . . . And hadn't Grams said the reason Penelope didn't want to keep the baby was because she was more interested in becoming an actress?

*Do the math*, I thought. *You've got a fifty-year-old star, minus something that happened thirty years ago. That equals twenty. The age Penelope was when she had her baby.* People were always saying how much I looked like Penny. It's just something about your eyes . . ."

Penny . . . Penelope . . . such similar names. How could they both be Abe's daughters? Unless . . . OH MY GOD . . .

*Then the little duck came to a beautiful actress who pulled in $23 million for her last two pictures, and just got a producing deal with a major studio.*

*"ARE YOU MY MOTHER?" the little duck said to the actress.*

*"You know who I am?" she said to her baby.*

*"You are a Hollywood star who is adored by late-night talk show hosts. You are my mother. . . . And now you want to check me out to see if I could play your daughter in a film."*

*"Yes, I suppose so."*

*"How funny is that? If you had been a decent human being, and not a goddamn Long Island duck, I could have played your daughter for the past thirty years."*

After that little imaginary scene, I screamed to the high heavens, then grabbed hold of the faded blue plastic shower curtain. So Grams was right. She said I would faint when I heard the miserable truth about my past, and I did. But let's see how long it would take her to go down for the count after I told her I thought I knew what happened to that awful Penelope Fabrikant.

# Chapter 12

HAD THIS PARTICULAR PREDICAMENT NOT HAPPENED TO ME, I WOULD have found it hilarious. Right out of sitcom land. A pretty girl faints in a running shower and gets dragged to safety by two EMS guys who thought they won the lottery. According to the dispatcher, a call had come in about resuscitating an old woman who fell in the tub. Instead they found a naked model. Ka-ching!

Even more humiliating, when they asked Grams to find clothes for me, she ran for one of her cotton housedresses. The kind that had sucking candies in the pocket and carried the scent of eau de old lady. But the best part was finding myself in a pair of underpants so huge, two of my legs could have fit through one hole.

I felt like Dorothy, fresh from Oz. Between my lovely octogenarian ensemble and the realization that a crowd had assembled around me, it was a wonder I didn't pass out again.

There stood Grams, Lillian (now in civilian attire), the EMS guys, a few assorted neighbors who wanted to know where all the furniture went, and those same annoying cops, who, upon learning of more trouble in 6F, returned to investigate.

In my first seconds of consciousness, they all appeared filtered and blurry, as if the wrong lens had been popped on a camera body. I heard voices, but the sounds were muffled and unfamiliar. Slowly, the veil of ignorance was lifted, and tiny puzzle pieces snapped into place. It was morning in Florida. I knew that because my nose was stuffed and my eyes itched. I also had a serious migraine. But why was I lying on the floor? Oh yeah. Grams wasn't into furniture anymore. And now I remembered that wasn't the only kind of lying. My parents weren't really my parents . . . I wasn't really Claire Greene. I was an old woman with zero taste in clothes.

"What the hell am I wearing?" My hoarse voice croaked.

"She's up!" Grams clapped. "She woke up."

"Get this thing off of me." I tugged at the snaps.

"What! It's my best housedress . . . butterscotch candies in the pocket . . . your favorite."

"Maybe later." I tried stretching the stiff cotton shift past my knees. "What happened?"

"*Oy, oy, oy*, Claire." Grams' pale skin telegraphed her fright. "You fainted in the shower. Thank God you didn't lock the door like when you were little. . . . You scared me half to death."

"Wait, wait, wait. Wasn't it the other way around? You scared me after telling me—"

"*Oy*. These crazy kids today." She cut me off. "Running in the hot sun, starving themselves . . ."

"I'm Enrique." A paramedic placed a blood pressure cuff on my arm. "How are you feeling?"

"A little dizzy. I have a headache. My throat is killing me."

"That's all to be expected. You vomited when you fell . . . aspirated down the lungs. . . ."

I shivered. "Could I please have some juice, Grams?"

"What kind? I got orange, tomato, prune—no, wait, the orange wasn't on special last week—"

"Anything but prune." I studied Enrique's eyes to see how concerned he looked.

"Don't worry, Claire. I got plenty of orange juice," Lillian piped in. "And I'm right next door. Who doesn't have orange juice? We're in Florida, for God's sake."

"We got a little apple juice left." A small bald man raised his hand.

"That's not good for fainting, Herb," his wife argued. "She needs something nice and strong to get her energy back."

"Like a martini," I mumbled. "Make mine a double."

"Don't worry, sweetheart." She patted my hand. "I'll get you a V-8. You'll be up in no time."

*Yeah. To shit my brains out.*

"Can you tell us what happened?" The paramedic asked. "Do you know what brought this on?"

"I'll tell you exactly," Grams said. "She eats like a bird. Goes a whole day with nothing."

"Would you stop? I have a very good appetite." I turned to him. "It's just that I hadn't gotten a chance to eat yet this morning, and then I learned some very shocking news—"

"But she's going to be okay, right, Doc?" Grams butted in.

"I'm sure she'll be fine, ma'am." He chuckled at the reference to his presumed medical degree. "Claire, are you taking any medications, any anxiety pills, antidepressants—"

"No, but soon I'll be taking all of them."

"Are you experiencing any other symptoms? Nausea, blurred vision, extreme fatigue—"

"All of the above, but so would you if you found out—"

"She suffered severe emotional trauma this morning," Lillian stated for the court.

"Lillian, go get the juice," Grams bellowed. "And mind your own goddamn business."

The paramedic rolled his eyes. "Is there any possibility you're pregnant?"

"No, a course not," Grams answered. "What kind a question is that to ask a young girl? Do you see a wedding ring?"

I had to snicker. Did she really think I was still a virgin? Good God. If anyone should know you didn't need a marriage license to have a baby, it was her. I was living proof!

"No, I'm not pregnant," I said.

"Well, that's good, because you took quite a spill there. . . . We'd like to run you over to Aventura Hospital now. Have them examine you for any possible internal injuries, run some tests."

"No, that's okay. Really. I'm fine. I just need to eat something.

Have some juice . . . find my real clothes before someone thinks I'm well preserved for eighty. . . ."

"I don't know, miss. You've got a pretty decent-sized contusion on the back of your head. And a fall like yours can lead to all kinds of problems. Spinal, neck, and back pain, blood clots, you name it. If I was you, I'd be seen, just as a precaution."

"Okay, but I'm not letting them admit me."

"That's up to the neurology consult—"

"Because I have a very important meeting this evening, and I can't—"

"What kinda meeting?" Grams asked. "Your parents are coming in."

*Some parents!* "I don't care. I was invited to the Fabrikants' for dinner, and I'm going."

"See! What did I tell you, Gert?" Lillian poked her shoulder. "Didn't I say this would be nothing but trouble?"

"It's nothing but trouble every time you open your big trap. Claire, why *schlep* there for supper? I made that nice meatloaf you like."

*Perfect! Serve it to my wonderful parents.* "I'm not going over to eat, Grams. I'm going to . . ."

She looked so panicky and bewildered, I didn't have the heart to finish my sentence.

"If we're taking you over to Aventura, we really should be going." Enrique packed his bag.

"Give me a minute to find my clothes. I am not going out in public like this."

"What! It's my best housedress!"

"You want us to drive you, Gert?" Herb, the good neighbor, asked.

"What for? I'll ride with Claire in the ambulance. I don't take up much space."

"But how will you and Claire get home, dear?" Mrs. Herb asked. "You don't have a car."

"Go with them, Grams," I said. "It's a good idea."

"I don't know. Now I'm thinkin' maybe it's better if I wait here for Leonard and Roberta. They might worry if we're not home."

"So? Who gives a shit what they think?"

"See?" Lillian shook her finger in Grams' face. "What did I tell you? She's starting with the attitude. From now on it's gonna be nothin' but aggravation."

I was not a frequent fainter. In fact, up until this day, the only other time I could recall blacking out was when I was twenty-three and about to marry Marc Melman, a stunning and brilliant law student at GW I'd met at a bar in D.C. one weekend while I was visiting a sorority sister.

Still, I never expected that within months I would be wearing a three-carat rock that made my friends' engagement rings look like those little starter stones from the mall. I was a lucky girl, all right. Everyone loved Marc. Envisioned our amazing life together. The beautiful family, the fancy sports cars, the amazing house in suburban Virginia once he made partner.

In fact, everything was going swell until Marc convinced me that he and I weren't really the "big wedding" types. I frankly hadn't known that about myself. But I was young then. And so intent on being the dutiful fiancée. Suddenly I didn't care about the Carolina Herrera silk gown that according to *Brides* magazine would cost more than my first semester at Indiana. Our love transcended overpriced apparel.

Only trouble then was I had this ever-so-slight question about my intended's sexual preference. Especially one night when I realized Marc was having a far better time with the bartender than with me. That's when the bells went off. And they weren't wedding bells.

I tossed my too-die-for diamond in his beer and joined the legion of "almost brides." The wedding dropouts who never looked back and, in my case, who never dreamed of a big wedding again. Especially after finding out from the "almost best man" that my instincts were right on.

So no, I wasn't in the habit of fainting, I told Enrique in the ambulance. "Twice every thirty years is hardly a trend."

"Calm down." He checked my pulse. "You took a big spill, but you're gonna be fine."

"Then why is my neck in a collar?"

"Because with head traumas, there is always the possibility of spinal cord injuries."

"But look." I sat up. "See? I'm fine."

"Lie still, okay? After the fall you took, you're lucky to be in one piece."

"Oh, I know. I'm feeling very lucky."

So lucky that I started praying to the Angel of Death. If he was in the neighborhood, and it wasn't too much trouble, maybe he could stop by, as I had decided I was ready to return to the other side. No need for any theatrics. Didn't have to see the white lights, or feel my body and soul separate. I would just check out quietly rather than have to suffer the rest of my days in pain.

This sounds melodramatic, I know. And where was the gratitude that I didn't have a truly life-threatening disease or injury? Trouble was, I couldn't help myself. Once again I felt like Dorothy, after finding out how much Oz sucked.

The Wicked Witch of the West was presumably my birth mother, now operating under an altered name and face. Lenny and Roberta were the cowardly lions for deceiving me. And the nice wizard, Abe Fabrikant, was about to be buried six feet under. So if I couldn't be back in Kansas with Toto, couldn't I just click my ruby slippers and be DOA at Aventura Hospital?

"Feeling sorry for yourself?" An old man examined my skin condition and respiration.

"Maybe," I said, trying to place his soft, translucent face.

"Sounds to me like self-pity."

"Really? And what makes you the expert?"

"I'm quite familiar with the expressions people make when they're feeling troubled."

"You're confusing it with pain. I have a major headache. What happened to Enrique?"

"I'm helping him out for a little while," he answered in a deep, radio-announcer voice.

"Who are you? Do I know you?" Where had I seen those broad jowls and twinkly blue eyes?

"We met briefly," he sighed. "I see that you're wondering what you did to deserve all this."

"That's right. I'm feeling a little sorry for myself. But how great would you feel after finding out that everything you thought was true and good in your life was just one huge cover-up? A lie."

"Even the truth is never what it seems. And you were not lied to."

"How do you know?" I blinked really hard, unsure of to whom or to what I was talking.

"I know this: It's too soon to be the judge and the jury. Take your time before rendering a verdict."

I shivered as I reached over to touch the man's white, silky hair. "Mr. Fabrikant?"

"No, it's Enrique." He gently placed my arm by my side. "Do you know where you are?"

"I think so. Yes . . . no. Not sure. . . ."

I suddenly felt my eyes roll behind my head and my skin turn clammy.

"Aw, crap." Enrique yelled up to the driver, "She's going into shock." He grabbed the oxygen mask from the wall panel and placed the cup over my nose and mouth. "What the hell just happened to her? It's like she was fine, and then she got spooked by something."

If ever there was an understatement!

## Chapter 13

"Wait, wait, wait." I sat up in bed to argue at eye level with the ER nurse. "You just told me my vital signs are back to normal. Blood pressure is good. Nothing fishy in my urine . . . *no more hallucinations* . . . why can't I leave?"

"Because I'm recommending that you be seen by Dr. Hanley. She's an excellent neurologist on staff. She'll probably order a head CT scan."

"Sounds fun . . . but it will have to wait until tomorrow. No, wait. I have a funeral. How's Thursday? Is she here on Thursdays?"

"Miss Greene, please. I understand that you want to go home, believe me. No one wants to spend the day in an emergency room. But now that you're here, you really should be throughly examined. We're very concerned about—"

"Yes, yes, yes. I know. Internal injuries. But I'm fine. I'm not even dizzy anymore."

"You can't wait another ten minutes to see Dr. Hanley? She's on her way down from surgery."

"I have no insurance." *That will scare her!*

"Don't worry. Your parents are in the waiting room. They said they'd take care of everything."

"My parents are here? Damn!"

"They seem very concerned."

"Of course. That's their specialty! Acting concerned. . . . Look, I know you're just doing your job, and I respect that. But there is someplace I really, really have to be in a little while."

"What time?" The nurse checked her watch.

Lovely! This was going to be like bear-wrestling, minus the beer. "I'm getting picked up around five-thirty. But you know the drill. First I have to shower, get dressed, do my makeup, my hair . . ."

"And this date is more important than your safety and well-being?"

*Now I get it. You used to teach sixth-grade health.* "It's not a date. It's a meeting. And yes, as a matter of fact, it's very important to me on both a personal and a professional level. See how smart I sound? How brain-impaired could I be?"

"Okay," she sighed. "You win. I'll sign your discharge papers, but you have to promise to call Dr. Hanley's office first thing tomorrow to set up an appointment." She scribbled a number on a pad. "And have these two prescriptions filled right away." She tore two more sheets off the pad. "And call us immediately if you experience any symptoms. Fever, nausea, vomiting, dizziness, dry mouth, fatigue, blurred vision . . . I'm giving you my private number here." She wrote it down on the same paper. "So don't give me any BS about not being able to get through the switchboard."

"Yes, ma'am!" I saluted. "Thank you so much, Nurse. I really appreciate your support."

"And go easy on your parents." She patted my arm. "They seem genuinely concerned."

"Absolutely. . . . Is there like a back-door exit, or some other way out of here?"

"Not unless you're being rolled out on a gurney with a tag around your toe."

Yes, I'm an actress. And a damn good one. I'm versatile, quick on my feet, and if I do say so, very intuitive. I "get" the subtle nuances the writer intended. But no matter how many times I'd read Uta Hagen's *A Challenge for the Actor,* no matter how many actors' studios I'd attended, I didn't think I could walk out there and maintain the kind of subversive cool needed to greet my parents and not unleash a torrent of angry words.

For at that moment I felt so numb and disconnected, I was sure this unscripted, unrehearsed scene could easily turn into a final curtain. And if I deserved anything, it was a chance to have more than twenty coherent seconds to absorb all that had happened to me.

One day I was humming along as Claire Greene, actress/failure, and next thing I knew, this macabre chain of events completely knocked me off my not-shapely-enough-to-be-in-a-movie ass, and I was suddenly Alice in Disasterland. Somehow I had slid down the wrong hole, because I recognized nothing and no one. This was NOT MY LIFE.

My life was in L.A., and I wanted to be back there. Speed dating in Westwood. Shopping for booby dresses on Melrose with Sydney. Having a romantic dinner in one of those huge hideaway booths at the Bungalow Club. Or, the best indulgence, splurging on a $350 haircut at José Eber, just 'cause.

That's where I belonged. Not in some emergency room in Miami. And yet, that's where I was. Praying that I survived the ordeals to come after walking out of the ER. Almost immediately I heard the sound of my mother's voice. That whiny, high-pitched tone that always signaled some level of disapproval.

I took a deep breath. *Claire,* I told myself, *it's too soon to fold. You are great Kate Hepburn in* The Philadelphia Story. *Ingrid Bergman in* Casablanca. *Penny Nichol in* Don't Do as I Do. *On second thought, scratch that.*

"Claire. We're over here." My mother waved as if I were a sailor coming ashore after years at sea. "Don't move. We'll come to you."

"Hi." I stiffened as the Greene/Moss family trio hugged me.

"Oh my God, Claire. You look terrible," she gasped. "Pale as a ghost."

"Thanks."

"What did they tell you?" my father, Mr. Cut-to-the-Chase, asked. "Are you going to be okay? Do you need any surgery? Physical therapy?"

"I'm fine."

"Well, thank God for that."

"I just have to call this neurologist in a few days."

"*Oy*, here we go with the specialists," my mother groaned. "First they make you crazy with getting the referrals, then they tell you there's no co-pay, but a month later they send a bill for five dollars. . . . Let's just make sure this doctor is on our plan."

"Yeah," my father said. "And what about the billing department? Do we need to stop in before you leave?"

"No, Dad. That's why they call it billing. Because they bill you."

"Okay, good, then." My mother clapped. "How about we all go out for a nice dinner?"

"What time is it?" I asked.

"Almost three," my father said. "Too early for dinner."

"Fine." My mother agreed. "Then we'll drive down to South Beach and have a nice lunch."

"What's the matter?" My father sneered. "Afraid of missing a meal?"

"No. Afraid of thinking of someone other than yourself? Claire hasn't eaten all day."

"Oh. Right. Sure. Yeah. Fine. Let's go for lunch. But I'm not *schlepping* all the way down to the beach to pay twelve dollars for a lousy chicken Caesar salad that's got three little pieces of chicken."

"Ha! Since when do you order a salad? You'll get a cheeseburger deluxe platter like always."

*Just keep breathing, Claire. In. Out. In. Out.* "Can we please go back to Grams' now?"

"Don't you want to stop for a bite?" My mother pleaded. "You really have to start taking better care of yourself."

"This had nothing to do with how I take care of myself, Mommy." I choked on the *M* word.

"Yeah," Grams said. "It's because the son-of-bitch cleaning girl made the tub so slippery. Every week I tell her, rinse it good. You want me to fall and break my neck? And see what happened?"

"So you'll find a new girl." My father shrugged, as if the answer to all his mother-in-law's problems were a better class of household help.

"Can we please leave now?" I said. "I have something to do later, and I need to get ready."

"Where are you rushing?" my mother whined. "You just got out of the hospital."

"No, I just got out of the ER. It's not the same thing . . . and I have a business meeting."

"What kind of business meeting?" My father looked at his watch again. "You don't even have a job. Which reminds me. I do have a job . . . and Marvin is probably tearing his hair out trying to juggle my appointments and his. I'd better call the office. . . . Okay. Let's get the hell out of here. . . . I can't even make a lousy cell phone call in this place."

"Nobody can," I sniffed. "It's a hospital . . . hello?"

"Well, whatever. . . . Hey. This will cheer you up, Claire. I picked up a convertible at the airport. I had to pay through the nose, but I figured, what the hell? How often do you get to ride with the top down?"

"Yeah, because nobody drives a convertible in California."

"Well, you don't live there anymore. . . . I just thought—"

"Cut the crapola, missy." Grams gave me the eye.

"That was very sweet of you," I sighed. "Nothing better than a convertible ride."

"Please tell me you didn't tell them you told me," I whispered to Grams as we walked through the parking lot. " 'Cause I am not ready to deal with any of this shit right now. You got it?"

"What do you mean, me tell 'em? You should be the one to tell 'em."

"Me? Why should I do it? You're the one who opened this whole can of worms."

"What are you girls whispering about?" My mother caught up to us. "Everything okay?"

"Fine," I replied. "Never been better. You?"

But before I could say another word, my father was demanding details on this so-called business meeting I was attending. What was so important that I had to drop everything and run? If he had to cancel all his appointments, the least I could do was stick around to explain what the hell was going on with Grams' apartment and the gun.

*And what about my plane ride?* I thought. *Don't you want to hear all about my Close Encounter of the Third Grandfather? After all, he was the real reason you two rushed down here.*

"I'll explain everything in the car." I resisted the urge to get nasty. "But I'm leaving at five."

"Well, if you ask me, I think you should cancel," Grams said when we reached the car. "Whadaya gotta go and start trouble for?"

"I'm not starting trouble, and nobody asked you."

"*Oy.* You call this an automobile?" Grams suddenly focused on the silver convertible. "How we all gonna fit in there? It looks like one of them little cars at the circus. The ones the midgets go in."

"There's plenty of room, Gert," my father snapped. "It's a five-passenger vehicle."

"Yeah, but have you looked in the mirror lately? You and Roberta got so fat, you're like two people each."

"WE'LL ALL FIT, GERT!" He enunciated each word. "Get in!"

"Ma. Enough already. You sit in front. I'll go in the back with Claire."

*Just keep breathing, Claire. In. Out. In. Out.*

Grams belted herself in, then gave me her famous look. The one that meant, *Don't say nothin' about nothin', you hear?* Then she barked an order at my father. "Watch your speed, sonny boy. My luck, you'll hit a tree and I'll fly out."

"Oh," I said. "Then maybe we should switch."

Wow, wow, wow. Say what you would about Marly having been born Couture, Princess of Entitlement. The girl could shop! I gasped when the doorman handed me three large shopping bags and a note that said, *Hope you love everything. See you tonight.* She signed her name starting with a big, loopy *M*, and ended with a chain of *X*'s and *O*'s.

When I peeked inside, there was an assortment of T-shirts, skirts, slacks, a jacket, and the most amazing black patent mules I'd ever seen. Good Lord. How much had she spent? Easily a few thousand dollars. And was she suggesting it was all mine to keep? I swear, if I didn't know all too well the repercussions of fainting, I would have passed out again.

"What is all that *chazeray*?" My father saw the Versace logo on one of the bags and immediately assumed that the contents had somehow cost him.

"A friend did me a favor," I said matter-of-factly.

"What friend? You've been here less than two days. And besides, you don't know anyone down here."

"Lenny, stop badgering her," my mother yelled. "If she says she has friends, she has friends. Why do you always have to question her? Not everything is your business."

"Yeah!" he snorted. "Until she needs money. Then it's suddenly my business!"

I frankly thought I'd done a decent job preparing them for seeing Grams' empty apartment. In fact, I know I had specifically said that all the furniture was gone, and that there were packed boxes everywhere. And yet, from the way they reacted when they walked through the door, you would have thought it was coming as a complete surprise.

My mother shrieked, my father cursed, and Grams started yelling at both of them to keep their goddamn voices down before nosy-neighbor Lillian called the cops again.

"You've done it, Gert. You've completely lost your mind!" My father's temples pulsed.

"Mother, this is so insulting. How could you get rid of all your good pieces and not even ask me if I wanted any of them? You know how much Iris loved your dressing table, and I would have gladly taken the dining room set."

"Mommy, stop it," I said. "This is not about you." *This is a recording*.

"Exactly," my father agreed. "It's not about you, Roberta. . . . But no matter what, Gert, you have to get it all back. Call José, or Jesús, or whoever the hell you gave it to, and tell him you made a big mistake, and you need everything back right away."

"No!" Grams cried. "I can't do that. He don't live around here."

"Well, how far away could he live? He didn't ship the stuff to Cuba! He probably strapped it to the back of a pickup and drove it somewhere. So call him up and tell him to get the hell back here."

"Lives near Stewart someplace. . . ."

"Perfect." He clapped. "It's straight up 95. He could make it back in two hours without traffic."

"I don't ever want it back, see, 'cause I don't want to live here no more. I don't care for the building."

"What the hell is wrong with the building?" he argued. "I noticed some nice new plantings out front. And the carpeting in the hallway looked very clean this time."

"Everyone is dead, Dad," I said. "She's trying to tell you it's depressing here. She has no friends left. She has to depend on strange people to take her everywhere, and I do mean strange. The only neighbor who still drives is Rose down the hall, and she forgets to put on her pants."

"Oh. So, fine. We'll help her find another place. But she's still going to need her furniture."

"No, I won't," Grams said. "Claire found me a place that's already got furniture."

"What are you talking about?" My father looked bewildered. "How could Claire find you a place, Gert? She's only been here two days, and one of those days was spent in an emergency room."

"A friend of Claire's knew about it."

"Again with the friends!" My father threw up his hands. "Claire, is this by chance the same friend who did your shopping, or a different friend? 'Cause I'm wondering where all these people are coming from. Roberta, were you aware that your daughter was so popular in Miami?"

"How should I know? She tells me *bupkas*!"

"It's because of what happened on the plane," Gert said quietly. "It's . . . the dead man's place."

*Oh God. The San Andreas fault has just ruptured. No way to stop the tremors now.*

"The dead man's place?" My father's face reddened.

"Claire, let me make you a bite to eat." My mother headed to the kitchen. "Maybe a nice tuna fish sandwich. Ma, you got fresh bread for a change?"

" 'Course I got fresh bread. It's in the freezer. You just gotta let it sit on the counter awhile."

"Wait. Hold on there, Gert." His pitch registered an octave higher. "This man who died . . . didn't we agree we were going to have nothing to do with the family? I mean, he was a complete stranger, of course," he said for my benefit.

"You can stop your tap-dancing, Lenny," Grams yelled. "I told Claire everything this morning. The whole stinkin' story about her and Gary and Penelope—"

"Oh my God." My mother grabbed hold of my father's arm. "You did what?"

"For Christ's sake, Gert!" he screamed. "How could you be so ir-responsible? Claire, honey. You know your grandmother. Does she ever get a story straight? Never!"

But like voyeurs surveying a wreck, they glanced at me out of the corners of their terrified eyes.

"If you hadn't noticed, she's a grown-up now," Grams practically spit. "Old enough to know the truth. Claire, tell 'em what I told you."

Tell them what? Every regrettable word of a story I should have heard twenty years ago? They already knew the facts inside out. Why should I repeat them? So that they could be let off the hook from hav-ing to explain their god-awful decisions in their own pitiful words?

As the seconds ticked away, the tension mounted, and I knew they were expecting me to say or do something. But what? Go on a deadly rampage with the gun? Fall into a pitiful, crying heap like Little Sally Saucer? Scream and kick like that time at Toys "R" Us when they wouldn't buy me a bike?

If a tantrum didn't require so much work, I might have gone that route. But I was feeling so incapacitated, the only thing I could muster the strength to do was bend over, pick up my pocketbook and my shopping bags, and head toward the door.

"Wait. Claire. Where are you going?" My father followed me.

"I can't do this." I choked back tears. "I can't talk to you right now. I can't even look at you. . . . I don't understand anything, other than I am exhausted and heartbroken. I just know I don't want to be in the same room as you."

"I hear ya, but you have to believe us. We thought—"

"Spare me, Dad! I'm not interested in your side of the story right now. In fact, I wouldn't give a shit if I ever heard what you had to say. The only thing I know for sure is that there is someplace else I'd rather be."

"Well, fine. Where do you have to go?" He tried to stop me. "I'll take you there."

"No."

"Then how will you get there? You don't have a car."

"I've got a ride." I opened the door.

"What time will you be back?" My mother ran over. "We can go out for a nice dinner. Anywhere you like. We'll talk. We'll tell you everything. Anything you want to know." She grabbed hold of me. "We're sorry. Very, very sorry, Claire." She began to cry. "I wanted to tell you, believe me. For years I pleaded with your father. But you know him, Mr. Know-it-all, always thinks he's the smart one. . . . Please. Don't walk out the door angry. . . . Lenny, stop her."

"No," he said in his indignant, how-dare-you-question-me tone he always used when he was losing an argument. "Let her go, Roberta. Obviously she needs to go sulk in a corner somewhere."

"Excuse me." I glared. "But I'm not going anywhere to sulk. I'm going over to my friend's house . . . to meet my *real* family."

# Chapter 14

AH, GENETICS! DREW HAD BASICALLY JUST TOLD ME THAT "AUNT Penny" was very big on dramatic gestures and didn't like having her thunder stolen. So maybe there really was something to that whole like-mother-like-daughter thing. It seemed I'd inherited her ability to make sweeping statements and grand exits. For after dropping that little bombshell on my parents and grandmother about going to meet my new family, never had I seen three mouths opened wider.

But then, typical of me, once the big climactic scene was over, I didn't know what to do with myself. Grab a cab and head to the airport? I swear I could hear L.A. calling my name. And what I wouldn't give to be back with my friends.

Oh, and this time I would be sure to find work. Pablo had gotten me thinking that I could get an office job, maybe even for one of the film studios. At least until I was back on my acting feet.

Meanwhile, I would crash at Sydney's. Or, wait, wait, wait—I could ask my newly discovered mother if I could move in with her. What do you bet she lived in a fabulous McMansion in Malibu or Benedict Canyon? Surely she had an extra guest house she could spare. And how cool would this be? We'd hang out together. Make up for all the lost years. Really bond. . . .

On the other hand, maybe the fall in the shower had done some serious brain damage, for clearly I'd lost touch with reality. Why would Ms. Nichol ever jeopardize her stellar reputation by admitting to having abandoned her tiny infant? She didn't need Peggy Siegal, the PR maven, to tell her to deny any connection between us. In fact, I could just see the interview with Diane Sawyer now.

Penny would tell all of America that I was your typical low-rent extortionist. A money-grubbing loser who thought that this little scheme was my only shot at cashing in on hush money, or getting my fifteen minutes of fame. "Ms. Greene is Tanya Harding without the hammer," she'd sniff.

Oh God. What if that was true? Not the part about me looking for fame and fortune. What if there wasn't actually a biological link between us? At the moment I had no tangible proof. No smoking-gun birth certificate that said, *This woman is definitely your mother*. Just a string of assumptions based on all these odd coincidences, and a smattering of circumstantial evidence.

So I had better be open to the idea of mistaken identity, that there might be another Penelope Fabrikant running around with nary a thought of her out-of-wedlock baby. My luck, she would probably be this strung-out alcoholic who lived in a trailer park with her boyfriend and a dog.

I was so sad and confused, I didn't realize I'd taken the elevator down, walked out the front door, and was now standing in front of a Greek coffee shop that was easily a half mile from Grams' building. Ah, but the smell of food was so tantalizing. And come to think of it, I was famished. Maybe I would feel better after some nourishment. A home-cooked meal served without a helping of guilt or a side of aggravation.

Unfortunately, the dark-haired man behind the cash register seemed more interested in reading the sports page than in feeding a hungry patron. Talk about southern hospitality! When I cleared my throat to announce my presence, he shoved a menu in my direction. "We're outa lamb," he grunted.

*But not flies.* I swatted two off my arm. And was it warm in here, or was I just flushed from all the craziness? Whatever. My coffee was fresh, and the Greek salad delicious, just the way my father liked it. Huge and cheap. But oops. Scratch that. Who cared what he liked anymore?

Point being, it was the first time in two days that I remembered what normal and calm felt like. Although that little bubble burst the instant my cell rang.

Funny thing about being an actress. We hear a ringing phone, and our hearts jump. Could this be the big break we've been waiting for? So there's almost never a time when we don't answer, unfortunately.

"What is it, Mother?" I didn't have to act annoyed. I *was* annoyed.

"Where are you?"

"I'm not telling."

"I don't know what you're getting so crazy about. Didn't we give you a good home, a fine education, nice vacations, a nose job for your sixteenth birthday, which may I remind you came out much better than Jennifer Zucker's because at least your father knew how to pick a decent surgeon?"

"Oh, I agree. It was a wonderful life. . . . You gave me everything but the truth."

"Grams had no right to say anything to you."

"That's right. You should have."

"Fine. But that other family? Awful people, Claire. Trust me. Don't get involved."

"Nope. Can't trust you. I may never trust you. And please don't call me again. I won't pick up."

"You're being foolish."

"Foolish?" I yelled, glad that at this in-between hour in the afternoon, I was the only customer. For now my raised voice was only disturbing a disinterested owner and a bunch of flies. "What you and Daddy did was disgraceful."

I heard a muffled sound. "Claire, this is your father." His tone was gruff, as if I were still ten and easily intimidated. "You have no right to speak to us this way. We didn't raise you to be rude. . . . And you have no idea what we've been through all these years. How difficult it's been for us."

"Oh, I'm sorry. How much do I owe you? I'll send you a check for your time and trouble."

"That's a bunch of crap, and you—"

Nope. Sorry. Didn't want to hear the end of his stupid sentence. That's what the "end" button on the cell was for. And what bullshit to suggest that they were the innocent victims here, while the Fabrikants were monsters.

On the other hand, their level of concern convinced me that this was no case of mistaken identity. The Miami Fabrikants had to be the same people my parents feared they were, otherwise they wouldn't be this freaked out.

"More coffee, miss?" The owner stood at the table with a hot pot.

"Definitely." I pushed my cup closer.

"A bad day for the pretty lady?" He filled it without spilling a drop. "Uh-huh."

"Every family fights. It's normal. We love them, we hate them. Believe me, I could tell you stories." He laughed. "It could always be worse."

"Well, thanks for the Greek philosophy, but not in this case."

He smiled. "Things will work out okay."

"Really? How do you know?"

"Because you give good aura."

*Is that like giving good head?* "Thanks for noticing. I sure hope you're right."

"Can I ask you question?"

*Only if you don't sit down.* "Okay."

"Do you believe in love at first sight?"

*Oh God. Of all days to be hit on. Check, please.* "No. No, I don't."

"Because I think the problem is you fell in love, but you don't want to admit it."

"And you know this because . . . how?"

"Let's just say I have a good sense about these things. Customers come from miles. They say to me, 'Costa, the food is so-so, but the predictions? The best!'"

"Is that right? Well, then, here's a question, since you're so psychic. If you were on a plane, and the old man next to you suddenly dropped dead on your lap, and afterwards you found out from your grandmother that, surprise, surprise, this man was actually your grandfather, and that your parents weren't really your parents, they sort of inherited you, and that your real father was dead, and your real mother was now this big, famous Hollywood star who abandoned you because you were too much trouble to raise, and that after figuring this all out, you fell in the shower and almost cracked your head open, and had to be rushed to the emergency room . . . would you be thinking about love?"

"Can I get you anything else, miss?" The man blinked. "Or just the check?"

I dug for Viktor's card in my pocketbook and dialed his cell. Never was I so glad to hear a crazy man's voice. And bless his little soul, he had been waiting to hear from me. Was I feeling better? Was my grandmother feeling better? Did I get the packages he left?

Yes, yes, yes, I told him. But was it possible for him to pick me up at the House of Athens Coffee Shop on Northeast 188th, and then take me someplace where I could shower and change before going over to the Fabrikants' for dinner?

"Miss Claire," Viktor said, "wat is going wrong with you today? Why ken't you shower at your grendmotherz place?"

"Viktor, there are so many problems over there, you wouldn't believe."

"Uch. Thet's the bed thing about rentals . . . thi landlords. They fix nothin' until the lawyer calls. Em I right?"

"As always."

"So I hev idea. How ebout I take you to Drew's place? He's not using thi shower now."

"Oh no, no, no. I couldn't do that. It would be such an imposition. I was thinking . . . Oh, jeez. I don't know what I was thinking. I guess you can't very well rent a hotel room for half an hour."

"Oh, believe me. In Miami you ken."

"Yes, but I don't have the money. What about a JCC or . . . I know—a country club with lax security?"

"I could take you to my house, but we only hev tub. Believe me, you'll be very heppy at Drew's."

"But I don't want to bother him. He's got enough on his head without worrying that he left the place a mess, or that Marly will get mad."

"He won't be beck until tonight. He iz busy with heez father all day. I hev keys to all their places. It's no beeg deal. I've done it."

"Are you serious? You've stopped there to shower? He doesn't mind?"

"He doesn't know. He hez a maid. If something iz dirty, she cleans."

"But don't you think he'll be mad if he finds out we snuck in?"

"Em I crazy? He only wants to make you heppy, Miss Claire."

*Well, I only want to make me heppy, too.* "If you say so . . . and I won't be long. In and out."

"I like eh woman who thinks like eh man." Viktor laughed. "I'm on my way."

I have seen some fairly amazing bachelor pads in my day, and regardless of whether the place was a hotel room, a condo, or a sixteen-room estate, I could count on the same basic three things: great views, a huge bed, and enough high-tech toys to rival the local Best Buy (because size does matter, especially when it comes to plasma TVs).

And yet, when Viktor took me south of Fifth, then led me from the underground garage in Drew's condominium complex to the private elevator which shot us up to the penthouse floor, I was blown away. His apartment, if you could even call it that, was a spectacularly designed, three-thousand-square-foot mecca of delight.

Between the ocean views, which the floor-to-ceiling windows made hard to miss, the rich, tasteful furnishings, the vast, open rooms, the assortment of Brookstone gadgets, and the ultimate indulgence, a wall of vending machines in his playroom, he would be crazy to share it with anyone.

"Oh my God," I must have repeated a dozen times. "This is all for one person?"

"Not bed for a kid who was born to a dencer and a plumber, em I right?"

A dancer and a plumber? Oh right. Drew wasn't born into money.

His widowed mother had played Chutes and Ladders for Husbands, and with one roll of the dice, shot all the way to the top.

"This kitchen is absolutely amazing." I rubbed the Italian marble countertops. "So Drew likes to cook?"

"He no hev time. But Marly, she ken *potchke* in here all day—an excellent cook."

"Oh," I blurted. "She lives here, too?"

"Not officially, no. Of course, efter they get married . . ."

"Lucky girl," I sighed. "So where should I shower, and how much time do I have?"

Viktor looked at his watch. "How about I ken pick you up in forty-five minutes?"

"Perfect." I nodded.

"End take my advice, Mr. Drew's bathroom has excellent shower. Thi water, it spleshes from all around. Top, bottom, everywhere. Thi other showers . . . not so special."

"Ah-hah. And what about towels? Maybe I'll take them with me so they're not lying around."

"Believe me, Drew iz too busy to notice who used this towel, who used thet towel."

"Okay. Anything else I should know? Alarm codes, light switches . . . how should I lock up?"

"I'll do it when I come beck up. And don't forget. He hez peppermint soap . . . try it. You'll smell like kendy store."

*Oooh. Good thinking. Then he'll never suspect I was here.*

Of course, I snooped around. Oh, come on. You would have done the exact same thing, and you know it. What girl wouldn't want the unofficial tour? Besides, I might never get another chance to open Drew's closets, medicine chests, and the all-important refrigerator. The true indication of whether he was still allowed to think for himself.

And the verdict? According to the contents of his mammoth Sub Zero, his life was over. The shelves were lined with fruit, yogurt, and salad makings, and one entire door panel stocked Diet Coke and bottled Evian. Yes, there was beer, but it all screamed *light*. And the freezer test didn't bode well, either. Unless his midnight cravings included lemon sorbet and Healthy Choice chicken enchiladas.

There were other signs that Marly was calling the shots. Exquisitely framed photos of the happy couple were perched on every available surface. And here was a big surprise: Those famous needlework pillows of hers were casually adorned on all the couches and chairs.

My favorites designs were stitched in splashes of peach, turquoise, and yellow. Miami-flavored ice cream on cozy little canvases. It was the inscriptions that made me want to puke.

*Duty makes you do things well, but loves makes you do them beautifully* (translated: Why screw your secretary when you can have me?). *Thy friendship be forever true* (translated: You cheat on me again, you're dead meat). Which was lovingly situated next to *Marly and Drew together forever* (translated: Or this time my lawyer will eat your prenup for breakfast).

But the most revealing of all was the heart-shaped pillow on the couch by Drew's computer. It read, *And they lived happily ever after*. And in a tiny heart, their little initials were stitched. *MF. DF.*

Wait, wait, wait. She wasn't an *F* yet. She was still a *B* for Becker. How presumptuous of Marly to be advertising her new last initial before the wedding. Still, I had to hand it to her. They'd hit a big bump in the relationship road, and somehow she'd managed to get Drew to drive back to her. (Maybe that's why he said she was so much smarter than him.)

I could only hope that one day I would be this sure of a relationship. Or at least confident enough to go through every room of my boyfriend's bachelor pad, girl it all up, and not panic that maybe I'd jeopardized his testosterone level.

Viktor was right. Drew's bathroom was so heavenly and unique, I felt like an awestruck tourist. Too bad I couldn't buy postcards at the gift shop, or at least have snapped a few souvenir shots of my own. Sydney would have gotten such a kick out of seeing the gold-leaf basins, the domed skylights, and the private bidet for the ladies.

And that was before discovering the doors leading to the sauna, the his-and-her toilets, the dressing areas, and my favorite find, a special room for spa treatments and massages.

But what we both would have drooled over was the cylindrical shower stall situated right in the center of the bathroom. I swear it looked like it could sleep six, and fly to the moon.

I had never been this excited to bathe. I just hoped that (1) I could manage to take an entire shower without fainting, and (2) I could figure out how to turn the damn faucets on without the powerful showerheads blowing me right out the door.

To my surprise, it was child's play. And I couldn't help but giggle like a child. This was heaven. A vichy shower, hot steam, and three choices of body washes, including the peppermint scent that Viktor liked so much. I never wanted to come out. In fact, the only thing that was missing was an attendant to hand me a warm, plush towel. . . .

. . . Or maybe not. The glass doors were now so moist with vapor, funny shadows appeared, and I swear to God I saw an attendant waiting for me . . . a male attendant.

A MALE ATTENDANT? Please God. Let it be another hallucination, like in the ambulance. But from what I could make out through the billowing steam, I was not imagining this. And then it hit me. Viktor! Who else knew I would be here alone . . . and naked? The psycho driver had set me up: Kept the keys. Told me not to bother with a hotel. It was fine to shower at Drew's. And told me to be sure to use this bathroom, *the others weren't as special*. Oh God . . . and to try the peppermint soap, so I smelled nice when the kinky bastard raped me . . . or worse.

As the figure move closer, I started to scream. I couldn't believe it. My young life was going to end bloody, just like the shower scene in *Psycho*. The very movie that had tormented me since childhood. Yet Janet Leigh's cries sounded like a whimper compared to mine.

Then the shower door opened, and even in my unclad and vulnerable state, my instinct was to try to strangle the man with my bare hands. But he was too strong to overtake. In a second, my left arm was behind my back and I felt the man's hot breath on me. I was just about to aim for his groin when I heard my name . . . with no trace of a Russian accent.

"Drew?" I pushed the steam away. "Oh my God. You scared the crap out of me!"

"I scared you?" He laughed, obviously relieved.

"What are you doing here?" I was practically panting.

"Shouldn't I be asking you that?" He let go. "I live here. Remember?"

He tried to be a gentleman, but a wet, naked blonde is pretty much at the top of the male fantasy chain, and the guy was only human. "What are *you* doing here?" His voice was softer now.

"I'm sorry. I am so sorry. You have to let me explain. I'm in the middle of a huge mess with my family, and I needed a place to shower. Viktor didn't think you'd mind—"

"It's okay. It's fine." He reached for a towel. "Here. Put this on. You're shivering. I'm just glad you weren't . . . I thought it was somebody else."

*An old girlfriend, perhaps?* "Thank you." I wrapped myself in the soft bath sheet. "We thought you weren't coming back until later."

"I wasn't supposed to. But Marly and her mom thought I should put on something nicer for tonight."

Poor guy was screwed! For the rest of his married life, he would be double-teamed. But why rub it in?

"It's so funny." I switched gears. "I was just thinking, the only possible thing this bathroom was missing was an attendant."

"Anytime." He blushed. "You have an amazing—"

"Ah, ah, ah." I shook my finger. "That's no way to talk to your first cousin."

"My first cousin?" He laughed. "Oh, right. Last night at Pops' place. . . . But that was just a story I made up."

"So we thought," I sighed. "But what would you say if I told you it might be true?"

# Chapter 15

TALK ABOUT *COMPROMISING POSITIONS*. GREAT BOOK, BUT I DON'T remember Susan Isaacs putting her main character in the humiliating situation in which I found myself.

While standing in nothing but a towel in Drew's bathroom, and just after dropping that little announcement to him about the possibility that we were related, guess who walked in? Marly and her mother, Sharon the Shadow. "Oh shit," was right.

Oddly, instead of my focusing on the fact that this was a very embarrassing, hard-to-explain situation, all I did was stare. The two looked so much alike, with their tiny birdlike frames and features. Small hands, small feet (how I envied anyone who didn't walk around with short skis at the ends of their ankles), great green eyes the color of dill, and silky auburn hair that had that did-they-or-didn't-they-just-spend-sixty-bucks-on-a-blowout-look. Even their little Louie pocketbooks matched.

It's not that I didn't know girls who were knockoffs of their mothers. It's that I was suddenly blue. I had never experienced that sort of connectedness, the biological billboard that flashed: *We belong to each other*. I would have loved for my mother and I to look like we played on the same team.

Meanwhile, this mother-daughter team had locked arms and was demanding an explanation. I did my best to keep my story simple, that Viktor made the suggestion I shower here, but a nervous Drew was more anxious to get his point across, which was that he had no idea I would be here. In fact, he thought I was an intruder.

A hysterical Marly didn't buy it. She'd been here before and automatically assumed the worst. Sharon, too, was beside herself: How many second chances did Drew think he was going to get, and didn't he realize the wedding invitations were going to be mailed in six weeks, and why the hell did he have to be what her late mother called "such a hard dog to keep on the porch"?

As I looked on, I was so overcome with anguish, so fatigued, I just wanted to curl up in a big fluffy spa robe and time-travel back to L.A.

Back to the days when I'd complain to Sydney that nothing exciting ever happened to me.

Back to when I'd watch Dr. Phil and throw Nerf balls at the TV every time he reduced a New Jersey housewife to tears.

Back to driving on the 405 in my trusty Honda Accord, coffee-stained carpets and all, but with my cherished CD collection, and the box of Coffee Nips hidden in the storage bin.

Back to Santa Monica, eating at a hot new restaurant with friends, while secretly sending daggers to the girls who were lucky enough to have even ugly dates paying those eye-popping checks.

Back to those fancy red-carpet movie premieres that took all day to get ready for, and that offered the hope of being spotted by a producer who happened to be on the lookout for an actress for her next film who looked just like me.

I did not want to be in deep distress thinking that my real mother had abandoned me, or that my new home address would be an assisted living center, where I'd be required to play bingo and never eat dinner after six again.

I wanted to pretend that these past few days in hell were an aberration. A little blip on life's radar that would one day be fodder for a short story I'd call, "If Only I'd Sat in 9B."

If only, indeed.

\* \* \*

"I can explain everything," I finally cried over the din in the bathroom. "Please. Just let me tell you what happened. But first, is there a bathrobe I can put on?"

Marly sniffed and ran to Drew's dressing room. "Here." She handed me a white terry robe. "Take Drew's. Mine wouldn't fit you."

"Thank you." I smiled graciously, though I felt like bitch-slapping her for that unkind cut. Instead, I did something out of Sydney's uninhibited playbook. I casually dropped my towel. Treated them all to an R-rated full-frontal nudity scene before putting on the robe.

"Oh my God," Sharon cried.

"I can't believe this is happening." Marly gawked longer than anyone, then ran out.

"Marly, wait." Drew followed. "She thinks we're cousins."

"You are one piece of work," Sharon, the mother bear, growled before joining her at-risk cub.

"First, let me apologize for all the chaos." I had somehow managed to get everyone to assemble around the kitchen table. "Believe me. The last thing I wanted was to create more stress for you at this very difficult time."

"Are you still going to speak at the funeral?" Marly sniffed. "Because I don't think you should."

"I don't even see why she should *be* at the funeral." Sharon bore her voo-doo eyes into Drew's forehead. "It's really for family, and friends of the family."

"Will you two just calm down and let Claire talk?" Drew said. "She was about to say something very interesting to me when you walked in, and I want to hear it."

"It was probably a proposition," Sharon mumbled.

"Okay, knock it off, Mrs. Becker," I said. "I've been through absolute hell these past few days, and I know the situation here doesn't look great, but believe me, I am not trying to steal your daughter's fiancé, because it so happens that I am very much in love with a man back in L.A., a very rich and handsome talent agent who proposed to me a few months ago, but I wasn't ready to commit, and now that I've had time to think about it, I realize that I do love him very much and I want to be his wife. So I would appreciate the benefit of the doubt here."

"Oh." A relieved-looking mother patted my hand. "Then I apologize."

"Thank you." I took a deep breath. "Okay, I'll skip the whole episode with my grandmother and the gun, because I know you are all expected for dinner in an hour, and I don't want to keep you."

"Well, wait. You're invited, too," Drew said. "Remember? Aunt Penny wants to meet you?"

"If she doesn't want to go, why are you pushing her?" Marly folded her arms in such a way that I couldn't miss her blinding engagement ring. *Is that to wear or skate on?*

"Hold on," I said. "Please stop assuming the worst. I promise things will look a lot different after you hear my predicament. And frankly, I could use some advice."

Silence. Who among them didn't think that they were experts on a host of delicate issues?

"Okay. The first thing you need to understand is that I never heard the name Abe Fabrikant in my life. Then, after he died, and I called my grandmother to tell her why I would be late, she asked me his name. So I told her, and she could hardly talk. And the same with my parents.

"I kept saying, I'm sorry, did we know this man? But they wouldn't answer me. They just kept insisting that I have nothing to do with the family, which I thought was strange, since all of you had been so wonderful to me.

"Finally, this morning, my grandmother sat me down, and out of the blue she tells me something about my past that at first I didn't believe. I was sure she'd lost her mind. But then I started to put the pieces of the puzzle together and realized she *was* telling me the truth. And that's when I passed out in the shower and had to be rushed to the hospital."

"Today?" Marly raised a freshly waxed eyebrow. "You were rushed to a hospital today?"

"Yes. That's right. I spent about three hours in the ER at Aventura Hospital, right by my grandmother's apartment. They wanted to admit me for observation, but I felt fine, so I put up a fight, and they let me go. If you don't believe me, I can show you my discharge papers."

Marly and her mother exchanged glances. Should they call my bluff?

"Oh, come on, you two," Drew shouted. "Give her a break. She's got nothing up her sleeve."

"I'd just like to see proof," Marly whined. "She says she has it, so let's see it."

"Fine." I got up to find my pocketbook. "I have all the paperwork. My prescriptions, the name of the specialist I have to call on Thursday . . ."

"Sit down, Claire." Drew reached for my hand. "It's okay. We believe you."

Sharon and Marly exchanged glances.

I felt like crying. Not because they were acting like judge and jury, trying to convict me of having an agenda. What saddened me was that they were so obviously attached at the hip, unlike my mother and myself. Whereas Sharon viewed the intimate details of her daughter's life as under her jurisdiction, my mother had never concerned herself with my love life, and now I finally knew why.

My gloomy expression caught Sharon's attention.

"Are you feeling okay, dear?" Sharon tried to take the high road with her conciliatory tone.

"Not really. No." I sighed. "I fell back on my head, and I've got this huge bump that's really sore. My throat is killing me, I've got a headache that won't go away, my butt is bruised, I'm really tired . . . but it doesn't matter. I just need for all of you to believe me. I swear I'm telling the truth."

"Nobody is saying you're a liar," Drew tried.

*Fool!*

"So what exactly did your grandmother tell you?" he asked. "I mean, why did you faint?"

Crap! Why had I opened my big mouth? It was nuts to expose this open wound to strangers, especially before I'd had time to let the facts sink in. For I knew that the instant the words were dumped like a bag of tarnished silver, they could never be thrown back in to the drawer.

In fact, the very idea that in the span of a few seconds I could utter some choice words and instantly turn lives upside down, but mostly my own, was more than I could handle.

"I can't say it." I cried into my hands as my body shook. "It's so awful."

"Claire, dear. Calm down." Sharon ran to get tissues. "It can't be that bad. Just get it out. It'll make you feel better."

I shook my head no.

"Is somebody sick? Is it cancer? Did your father lose his job?"

"Nothing like that." I blew my nose. "It's . . . much worse."

"Claire, we can't help you if we don't know what the problem is," Drew offered.

"You can't help me even if you do," I sobbed. "It's so awful. . . . See, I just found out . . . I'm . . . my parents . . . I still can't believe this is happening. I thought I was normal like everyone else, but I'm not. . . . I was adopted."

"Are you serious?" Marly looked at her watch. "And you never knew that?"

*No, dumb-ass. Would I be this upset if I found out when I was five?* "I had no idea." I wiped my eyes. "I mean, I always knew I didn't look like my parents, but a lot of kids don't."

"That's right." Drew nodded. "Claire showed me a family picture. She looks nothing like them."

"Truthfully, it's not the worst thing that could happen," Marly the psychiatrist said. "Look at Drew. He's adopted, and he turned out fine."

"Yes, because he knew all along!" I so wanted to bitch-slap her. "But I'm going to be thirty years old in a few days, and I had no idea, okay? It's different when it comes from out of left field."

"You poor thing." Sharon shook her head. "Does your grandmother know who your real parents are? I mean, not that your parents aren't your real parents, of course. Obviously they raised you."

"This is the part that is so crazy." I took a deep breath. "The reason my family is so flipped out is because . . . see, my grandmother had a son, Gary. My mother's younger brother. And after he got back from Vietnam, he started dating this college girl, she got pregnant with me, he talked her out of having an abortion, but then he died in this awful car crash on the Long Island Expressway when I was only a few weeks old."

"Are you serious?" Drew whistled. "That's horrible."

"I know, but you haven't heard the rest of it," I said. "The girl that Uncle Gary, or actually my biological father, was involved with was a girl from Florida who was going to school in New York. She was studying to be an actress."

"Oh, that's so funny," Marly the brain surgeon said. "Drew mentioned that you're an actress."

*Is that all he mentioned?* "The girl was from a very wealthy family. She was afraid to tell her parents that she was pregnant. She said they'd never understand."

"Did your grandmother happen to mention her name?" Drew leaned in. "If she was from Florida . . . I don't know, maybe we could go on the Internet and try and help you find her."

"Oh, believe me. You won't have to look far."

"You mean you know who she is?" Sharon placed her hand on her chest.

I nodded. "And so do you."

"Well, then tell us already." Marly the lawyer threw up her hands. "We're late."

"Oh God. You're never going to believe this, but her name was Penelope . . . Fabrikant."

"What?" Drew shot up. "That's impossible. That's my Aunt Penny's real name."

"Oh my God," Marly the genetics expert said. "Oh my God."

"I can't believe what I'm hearing," Sharon said. "Are you saying they're the same person?"

I nodded. "And when I realized it myself . . . put two and two together, I fainted in the shower."

"So wait." Marly the reporter was suddenly, miraculously interested in my story. "If it's true what you're saying, that means that the two of you would be related?" She pointed to Drew and me.

"Exactly." I patted her arm. "If the story is true, my real father is dead, and my real mother is—I still can't believe it—his Aunt Penny."

"Isn't that something?" Sharon clapped. "Not just related, but first cousins."

*Oh, stop gloating. I know what you're thinking.*

"You poor, sweet thing." Marly my new best friend came over to hug me. "I feel so sorry for you. You must be in complete shock."

"Well wait. Hold on." Drew said. "Don't you think if Aunt Penny had a baby thirty years ago, that by now she would have at least talked about her?"

I almost laughed. After the sneak preview in the bathroom, Drew was apparently still holding on to the hope that I was wrong about our being related. And Sharon the Mama Bear knew it, too.

"Not necessarily, dear," she said firmly. "A lot of women Penny's age had children out of wedlock and simply closed the door on that chapter in their life. It's the children who go crazy looking for their birth parents. Not the other way around."

"So as far as you know, she has no idea who or where you are," Drew said.

"Exactly. See, when this whole thing happened, she was living with my grandparents. And I guess a few days after the funeral, she left a note in my stroller and took off in the middle of the night."

"And that was it?" Sharon asked. "She never came back? Never contacted your family?"

"Yeah, then after it was obvious that she'd left for good, my Aunt Roberta and her new husband, Lenny, adopted me and changed my name."

"Changed it from what?" Drew asked. "Did she tell you?"

"Yes . . . it's just so hard for me to say."

"Of course it is, dear," Sharon practically purred. "The whole thing is such a terrible shock."

"Are you a Fabrikant?" Drew pressed on.

Whoa. Had I misread him? Did his interest in this story have anything to do with the sudden possibility that he would have to split his rightful inheritance? "Yes, I'm a Fabrikant," I answered. "She named me Hannah . . . Hannah Claire Fabrikant."

"She named you Hannah? That's bizarre."

"Why?" I bit my lip. "Is there another one?"

"No. I mean yes. Well, there was. She's been dead for many years. My dad and my Aunt Penny's grandmother was Hannah. I grew up hearing the stories. It was Bubba Hannah this and Bubba Hannah that. . . ."

"Isn't that something?" Sharon smiled. "This story gets more interesting by the minute."

*Oh, stop. We all know where you're coming from.* Still, I gasped, too. The facts were unraveling at a rapid pace, fitting together like a giant jigsaw.

"Wait until my dad hears this." Drew whistled. "I wonder if he even knew about you."

"Oh, wait. This is so cute, Claire." Marly the college professor clapped. "That would make Drew's dad your Uncle Ben. Like the rice."

Sharon delighted in her daughter's witty repartee, and an obliged Drew chuckled.

"So what are you going to do now?" he probed. "Do your parents know you know?"

"That's what started this whole commotion. When I called them this morning to tell them about Abe's apartment, they realized that I'd connected with Penelope's family and decided to grab the first flight out of New York. I guess they were afraid that someone from your side might tell me the truth, and if that happened, they wanted to be here to tell me their version of the story. They just never expected my grandmother would be the one to spill the beans, or that I'd end up in some emergency room. It was really awful when I got discharged.

"I couldn't look them in the eye, couldn't talk to them. I tried, but after a while I knew I had to get the hell away, so I called Viktor and asked if there was any place he could bring me to shower and change. Collect myself."

"Oh." Marly sighed.

"So you see? Nothing was going on here. I was just so desperate for someplace to hide. You can understand that, right?"

"Of course we can." Sharon came over to hug me. "What a terrible ordeal for any child to have to go through, especially after the experience you already had on the flight. Who would ever believe such a thing? Your own grandfather, a stranger, seated next to you on a plane. I tell you, the older I get, the more I wonder about the world . . . what God has in store for us. . . . Oooh, darling. You feel warm to me." She felt my forehead. "Claire, you're burning up. Don't you feel it?"

"I guess I felt a little hot before." I shrugged. "But it always takes me time to adjust to the humidity down here."

"No, dear. You're definitely feverish. Let's call the doctor. You could have an infection brewing."

"I'll be fine. Two Tylenol, and I'll be good as new. . . . I am very tired, though. Do you think it would be okay if I laid down for a little while?"

Sharon and Drew looked at Marly. How would the judge rule?

"I guess it's fine," she sighed. But, of course, she knew if she dared object, she'd be overruled.

"The only thing that bothers me," Drew said, "is I think Sharon is right, Claire. Maybe you should call the hospital first. Find out what they want you to do. . . . We really have to get over to my parents now. The Rabbi is waiting for us. But Viktor could run you over there."

"You can't be too careful, dear." Sharon seconded her own motion. "Just go back over there, get checked out, and then have him bring you back here."

"Or back to our house," Marly offered. "Wherever you think you'd be more comfortable."

"Would you stop already?" Drew finally lost his cool. "You heard her. We're COUSINS, okay? Nothing is going to happen, and I don't appreciate being second-guessed all the time. This is bullshit, Marly, and it's really starting to grow old."

"Drew, calm down, dear," Sharon said. "You can understand her position. That was quite a scene we walked in on before—"

"Butt out, Sharon," he said. "I know exactly how it looked, but it's all been explained. . . . Shit. I can't take this anymore. The two of you are driving me out of my mind."

*You go, girlfriend*, I almost said. But I was too caught up in the mother/daughter huddle in the corner. Without so much as uttering a word, they had taken a page from a relationship playbook, circa 1955. Retreat. Back off. Too much was at stake to have it all blow up again.

"I really appreciate everyone's concern," I finally said. "I do. It means a lot to me. But if I could just rest for a little while, I really think I'll be okay. And if I'm still not feeling right, you have my word I'll call the doctor. Just point me in the direction of a couch."

"No. That's ridiculous," Drew said. "Use my bed. You're not feeling well. Why should you be uncomfortable? When I get back, if you're out cold, I'll sleep on the couch."

We all expected Marly to object. But one look from Drew kept her mute. Good to see his balls weren't totally in the vise yet.

"You girls go on," he instructed. "I'll change and meet you over there. And don't say a word to anyone, do you hear me? This is Claire's decision how she wants to handle it."

"Of course it is, dear. We understand," the newly obedient Sharon said.

"We'll wait for you downstairs," Marly said. "You know I don't like walking into your parents' house alone."

"You're not alone," he grumbled. "Your mother is with you."

Funny how the pendulum can suddenly swing. One minute Drew was this gracious, I-aim-to-please kind of guy, and the next minute he was the drill Sergeant telling the Marly twins how high to jump. Kind of like pornography. Eventually everyone got their chance to be on top.

\* \* \*

"So before when you were talking," Drew said after I crawled into his bed, "about the man you're in love with back in L.A. The very rich and handsome talent agent. Was that true? Are you going to marry him?"

"Nope." I fluffed the down comforter. "There is no guy. I made the whole thing up. I hated to lie, but it seemed like the only way to get them off my back."

"I thought so." He chuckled. "Not that you weren't totally convincing."

"Really? You didn't buy it?"

"Not one word."

"And I call myself an actress. . . . How come?"

"Because when we had dinner last night, you never mentioned anything about being involved. And if I've learned anything, it's when a woman is in love, she just goes on and on about the guy. You can't shut her up."

"Good point."

"And your body language. Not exactly the look of love."

"Why? What did I do?"

"It's what you didn't do after you brought him up. You didn't smile, your eyes didn't get all sparkly. You didn't even look happy."

"Do you think Marly and her mom caught on?"

"Doesn't matter. It won't change anything for them."

"Does it change anything for you?"

"Not sure."

"What about the fact that we're kissing cousins?"

He hesitated. "I like the kissing part."

"You do?"

"Yes." He bent down and placed his soft lips on mine for a lot longer than a first cousin should. And being the slut that I was, I kissed him back. Hungrily, in fact. It was so nice to feel passion and heat, even if my skin was already burning with fever.

"Get some rest." He stroked my cheek, and looked at me with equal parts exhilaration and fear. "I'll be back as soon as I can to check on you."

I couldn't move. His tender touch had left me breathless and con-fused. Good God. What had I just done? My life was about to get very complicated without any sort of sexual entanglements, espe-cially with an engaged man to whom I was technically related.

But who was I kidding? Drew Fabrikant rocked my soul and had from the minute I saw him at the Jacksonville airport. Still, there was something I needed to know. "Why did you just do that?" I touched my lips. "Why did you kiss me?"

"I don't know." He stopped. "I guess in case I never got another chance." ·

# Chapter 16

I UNDERSTAND THAT MY GRANDFATHER, ABE'S, FUNERAL WAS LOVELY. A testimony to the indomitable spirit of a boy who escaped Nazi Germany. A boy who chose to embrace life, rather than spend it mourning his unthinkable losses. A boy who devoted his entire life to helping others escape the life-threatening conditions brought on by demon dictators.

Unfortunately, I didn't get to hear any of this firsthand, as I was not among the mourners. Seems I was lying unconscious in a hospital bed. Not at Aventura Hospital, where I'd first been taken. Rather, I'd been upgraded to the more prestigious Mt. Sinai, where I could be cared for by the Fabrikants' private physicians.

The fact that I was unaware of any of this was a little confusing. Last I knew, I was safely tucked in Drew's bed, confident that after the Tylenol kicked in, I would just get up and try to deal with my very real nightmare.

Instead, I awoke to the sight of my father hunched in a big leather chair, staring out the window. "I am such an ass," I thought I heard him mumble. But surely I was mistaken. Admission of guilt was rare. Still, it was worth pursuing, even in my groggy stupor.

"Why? What did you do this time?"

"I can't believe it. I hit a lady smack in the jaw. I've never hit a lady in my life. . . . Oh my God!" He jumped out of his chair, kissed my forehead, and ran to the door. "Nurse!" he yelled. "Nurse! She's up.

My daughter is up. She's talking. Get the doctor. Get my wife." He rushed back to my bedside. "You have no idea how worried we were about you . . . we thought we were going to lose you."

"Where am I?" I sounded like I had a mouth full of novocaine.

"You're in a hospital. A really good hospital in Florida. You wouldn't believe what they charge a night here. Like it's the goddamn Ritz-Carlton. But who cares about that? Thank God you woke up."

"Everything hurts," I grumbled. "My head, my throat, my chest . . ."

"No kidding it hurts." He ran back to the door. "Nurse! Somebody medical. My daughter woke up. . . . Jesus Christ." He banged the wall. "Five hundred big ones a night, and you still can't get any goddamn help when you need it."

"What are all these tubes?"

"Don't touch those!" He ran to my side. "Claire, listen. You're a mess, honey. You've been unconscious for two days, you got pneumonia after you swallowed your own vomit, and the bacteria got stuck in your lungs, or something like that, and then they had to drill a hole in the back of your head to drain out the fluid from the blood clot, which could have killed you if they didn't get to it in time . . . a subdermal hematoma they called it—"

"Huh?"

"But don't worry. You're going to be fine. The doctors said if you didn't go into a deep coma, your chances for a normal recovery were excellent."

"Where's Mommy?"

"She's coming. They're getting her. She's probably down in the cafeteria stuffing her face—"

"I heard that." My mother rushed in. "*Oy*, Claire . . . thank God you're up. And for your information, mister, I was down the hall speaking to one of the nurses about my migraines, which I wouldn't have if you weren't always carrying on like such a lunatic."

"Oh, good. We solved the case of the missing nurses. They're off gabbing instead of working."

"Don't be ridiculous. The care here is excellent. And stop blaming me for everything. You're the one who always gets Claire so crazy."

"Me get her crazy? All I try to do is reason with her."

"I think I'm going to throw up." I leaned over the bed.

"DOES ANYBODY WORK HERE?" My father's voice bellowed.

"Stop shouting, Lenny," my mother shouted back. "You're in a hospital, for Christ's sake. Here. Press this buzzer, and they come right away."

It only took a minute before not one, but two doctors and a nurse came to check on me. But according to my father, we'd been trying to get someone's goddamn attention for nearly a half an hour. Fortunately, they knew enough to let the big-mouth New Yorker vent, as their greater concern was the status of the beautiful model who was somehow related to the very philanthropic Fabrikants.

The reason I had no recollection of what happened next is apparently that I blacked out again. My brain's way of shielding me from having to listen to my idiot parents. All I know is that when I awoke for the second time, I was much happier to see a different man sitting in the chair.

"Hey." I waved.

"How are you?" He looked as frightened as the flight attendants who were hoping not to pronounce a man dead at thirty thousand feet. "Don't move. Let me get the nurse."

"What are you doing here?" my voice croaked.

"You know who I am?"

"Drew."

"Oh wow. You remember me. Because they weren't sure . . ."

"Drew Fabrikant," I said. "Abe's grandson."

"Right." He hesitated. "This is great. You keep going in and out of consciousness . . . the doctors are really baffled . . . we've been keeping a vigil . . . we were all pretty scared."

"Like who?"

"All of us. Me, my parents, Marly and Sharon, your parents, of course . . . they just left to go pick up your brother and sister at the airport."

"Why?"

"Because they wouldn't let Viktor go. They insisted—"

"No, why are they coming?"

"Because . . . see, what happened . . . your condition . . . the doctors said . . ."

"You thought I was going to die."

"I gotta be honest. It's been touch and go . . . you weren't responding . . . Let me go get the nurse."

"No wait." I tugged at his arm. "I feel so much better. My chest was killing me before . . . it hurt to breathe . . . but now . . . not so bad."

"That's great, Claire. I'm very relieved. But I really should get someone—"

"Hold on. I want to ask you something."

"About . . . Aunt Penny?"

"No . . . about us."

"Us? Oh. I was kind of hoping you wouldn't remember any of that. Look, I'm really sorry. I never should have . . . I wasn't thinking . . . it was pretty stupid, actually."

"Are we married?"

"No." He laughed. "Call me old-fashioned, but I'm one of those guys who thinks it's better if the brides are conscious. . . . Why would you think that?"

"Because I saw that we were."

"Claire, c'mon. You've been in a coma. It was just a dream. I'm engaged to Marly, remember?"

"But I'm telling you, I saw us together. We were married."

"Look . . . I know we could have feelings for each other, but things are already so crazy. Your father . . . it was pretty unbelievable . . . he caused some scene here the other night . . ."

"What did he do?" I tried to sit up.

"Lie still. You're all attached to tubes and everything. I'm getting someone right now."

"But wait. I'm not kidding. I saw us. We were married."

"Don't you have to be Mormon to have two wives?" Drew chuckled as he headed out. "Especially if one of them is your first cousin?"

\* \* \*

"Claire, come on. You need to drink this." My mother was pushing a straw in my face. "The doctors don't want you to get dehydrated again."

"Uch." I tried to sip, but my throat burned, and cold orange juice was hardly the perfect antidote.

"What if I go get her Starbucks?" My sister Lindsey yawned. "She loves lattes."

"Oh, I wouldn't advise that," Sharon said. "The caffeine might not mix with all her medications."

"We could ask," Marly offered. "I'll check with the nurses' station."

"What time is it?" I asked, not really knowing why it mattered.

"Nine-thirty in the morning," Lindsey grumbled.

"And it's Sunday." Sharon smiled. "It's your birthday, Claire. Happy birthday."

"Yes, happy birthday," my mother said.

"Yeah. Happy birthday." Lindsey chucked my shoulder. "You wanna go hit the bars? Free drinks today."

"Love to." I smiled. "Where's Daddy and Adam?"

"With Grams." My mother coughed. "Seeing about a new place for her to live."

*A new place for her to live?* My grandmother had lived in the same apartment on Country Club Drive for seventeen years. Why would she move now? I waited for my mother to explain, but she was examining the contents of her pocketbook. And Lindsey, who never had anything substantive to add to a conversation, but talked anyway, was unusually quiet.

Then it was if a power surge tripped a switch, and the memory chip in my head turned on. The details were still fuzzy, but I was starting to remember. My grandmother hated where she lived . . . she'd gotten rid of all her things . . . she needed a place to go . . . an assisted living center was available . . . it belonged to Abe Fabrikant . . . the man who died on me . . . my grandfather . . . that's why I was in the hospital . . . I'd fainted from the shock of figuring out the truth . . . my mother and father were not my authentic parents . . . they were understudies for my real parents, one of whom was unable, the other, unwilling, to fulfill their duties. *At this performance, the role of Claire's mother will be played by Roberta Greene.*

As for the Marly twins? Think . . . why were they here? Of course! Keep your friends close, and your enemies closer. The only way to stop me from becoming the majority stockholder in the Drew Corporation was to keep tabs on my recovery.

In fact, I'd bet the Fabrikant family farm that they were up to no good. There was just too much at stake here. The chance for Marly to marry into money, to live among the other wealthy scions of Florida, to complain about the high cost of maintaining a yacht and the difficulty in finding good help.

No way could they take the chance that I fully recuperated and competed for Drew's affections. I wouldn't put it past them that they had come in hopes of finding me alone so that they could pull the plug, then watch me die a slow, painful death.

Oh God! The idea that today was my birthday, that I was spending it in a hospital after coming out of a coma, and that I had no one in my corner who really cared about me, made me think I should let the Marly twins do the dirty work and just get rid of me.

"Get out!" I cried. "All of you, just get the hell out of here!"

"What did we do?" my mother asked. "We're just sitting here talking."

"I don't want to see any of you," I cried. "Please leave!"

"That's the thanks we get for *schlepping* here day after day." My mother stood, hands on hips. "You wouldn't believe what it costs to park the car, or get a lousy cup of coffee."

"Roberta, calm down," Sharon said. "Remember what the doctors said. She could be easily agitated."

"I am not agitated. I just don't see why you have to be here. I was doing fine without you."

"Hello? No, you weren't." Lindsey shuffled. "You were in a coma. They told us you might . . . you know. Check out."

"Yeah. And you were probably all thinking, good, who needs her? She's nothing but a burden and a nuisance."

"You're talking nonsense!" my mother barked. "We've been praying to God that you got better. Your father even went down to the chapel to talk to the rabbi."

"Sure!" I sniffed. "He's a big fan of religion, as long as he doesn't have to pay dues and contribute to a building fund."

"Enough with the insults!" she ordered. "We all have feelings, you know."

"Me, too!" I flung the TV controller at her.

"But I don't have to go, right?" Lindsey played with a hangnail. "You want me to stay?"

"No!"

"Why? What did I do?"

"Did you get me a birthday gift?"

"No. 'Cause . . . you know . . . I waited to see if you were going to croak first."

"GET OUT! ALL OF YOU JUST GET OUT!"

You can't blame a girl for losing track of time. Especially when she's lying in a hospital bed, struggling to recover from a near-fatal fall. And I didn't know if it was because I was a Very Important Patient or the staff was this attentive to everyone, but I had no idea how an ill person was supposed to regain her strength if she couldn't be left to rest for even five minutes.

The nurses were the worst, insisting that they needed my temperature, blood pressure, and how was I doing with that stool sample? Then the interns would come charging in to poke and prod, like I was a med-school cadaver. "Excuse me," I'd scream. "Is there a sign outside my door that says OPEN HOUSE?" And let's not forget the doctors who would casually stroll in, pull up a chair, and ask a lot of irrelevant questions, as if I were a defendant in a murder trial.

Frankly, I was so emotionally and physically drained, I didn't care if I lived or died. Until I saw Drew standing at the door with flowers and a box of candy.

"Hey." He knocked. "Coast clear?"

I smiled yes.

"I wasn't sure," he teased. "I heard this was a combat zone."

"A what? Oh, that. I'm better now."

"Glad to hear it." He walked over and kissed my cheek.

"Everyone's probably pissed at me, right?"

"Nah. Don't worry. We all know you've been to hell and back."

"It's so weird. Sometimes I feel fine. Like myself. Other times I feel completely out of it. Paranoid and delusional. . . . Like the other day when Marly and her mom were here? I actually thought that they'd come to kill me."

"Believe it or not, that was this morning. But don't worry about them. They're very concerned about you. You're family now." He laughed. "Otherwise they would have come to kill you."

It felt so good to laugh. And for that one brief moment of lightness, I was grateful.

"Anyway, happy birthday." He tossed what looked like a perfectly fresh bouquet into the trash, replacing it with the most magnificent arrangement of roses.

"Thank you. Wow. Those are beautiful. And so huge. How many are there?"

"Eighteen." Drew saved me the trouble of counting. "Marly thinks twelve is too ordinary."

*Yeah, and ordinary is a terrible sin.* "Well, it's a beautiful bouquet, and I'm very touched. Thank you again."

"My pleasure."

"So is it still my birthday?"

He looked at his watch. "For a whole 'nother five hours."

"Oh God. Hands down, it's been the absolute worst birthday of my life."

"Hey, we were just glad it wasn't the last birthday of your life." He slumped in the guest chair. "Believe me, one funeral a week is enough."

"I see that," I said. "You look like hell."

"Well, then we're twins, 'cause you look like crap yourself."

"Yeah, but I have a good excuse."

"So do I." He sighed. "So do I."

"I'm sorry. Forgive me. I remember. Your grandfather just died."

"Funny thing about that." Drew sighed again. "Turns out you were right . . . so did yours."

We let the enormity of that statement linger, as the implications were so devastating, neither of us could fathom where to start. Until I realized there was something I absolutely had to know.

"Does she . . . does Penny know about me?"

He nodded.

"What happened?" I hoisted myself up. "How did she find out?"

"It's a long story, Claire . . . probably not a good idea right now . . . you've been through so much."

"No, please. Tell me what's going on."

"It's not my place. You really should wait and discuss all of this with your parents."

"Uch, don't even use that word. They don't deserve it."

"Claire, c'mon. However weird your life started out, they raised you. They love you. You're their daughter. Nothing has changed."

"Maybe for them nothing has changed."

"Look, I'm not telling you that this whole thing isn't crazy. But maybe you just need to give it some time before you write off your family. They're all you know, and—"

I cut him off. "Has she come to see me?"

He didn't answer.

"Well, has she asked about me? Does she want to see me?"

"She had to fly back to L.A." Drew looked down. "Something sort of came up . . . she had to deal with it right away."

"Are you serious? She left without seeing me? Oh my God. . . ."

"It's not that she didn't want to see you," he said. "It's just that it . . . well, it was sort of a medical emergency."

"A medical emergency? You mean she finally realized she had no heart?"

"She has a heart, Claire . . . it was actually a problem with her face."

"Oh. She found out she had two of them?"

"Trust me. It's not what you think."

"The hell it isn't. Is she even human? I'm her daughter, okay?

Doesn't that mean anything to her? Why does she keep running away from me?"

"She's not running away, I swear. It's just that . . . Oh God . . . I really didn't want to be the one to have to tell you this. But you know the night you were supposed to come over for dinner? Right before Pops' funeral? Then you ended up falling asleep in my bed. Remember? You were so tired, and you had a high fever, and you just wanted to sleep. . . . Turns out this blood clot had formed on the back of your head, and if I hadn't gotten home when I did, it could have burst, and you would have died in my bed.

"I called for an ambulance, they rushed you to the hospital, then Viktor went to find your parents. Then, when everyone got to the hospital, your father walks in, took one look at Aunt Penny, and—"

"Smacks her right in the jaw?"

"Yeah. That's right. He told you?"

"Not exactly. He told me he hit a woman. He didn't say who. . . . I just figured it out now."

"He didn't just hit her, Claire. He threw a left hook that broke her jaw in two places."

"Oh my God."

"But thank God she was in a hospital so they could treat her. She actually had to have her jaw wired, and that's how she ended up going to the funeral—with a mouth full of metal."

*Serves her right!* "Oh my God!"

"That's why she flew right home. So she could see her plastic surgeon . . . because . . . well, her face-lift got pretty messed up. She's got some serious complications." Drew sighed. "And now so does your dad, because she's threatening to press charges. Maybe even sue him for damages."

"Are you serious? She wants to take legal action against the one guy who was willing to raise me after she took off and never came back? That's . . . I don't know . . . really sick!"

"I agree."

"You do? But she's your aunt."

"It still doesn't mean she's right. Look . . . I know our situations are totally different, but they sort of started out the same. I mean, my real father died when I was a baby, too. But then my mom married Ben, and after a while, it didn't matter how our family came together. He treated me like his son, I loved him back . . . it wasn't complicated. He was my dad."

"Yes, but you knew the truth the whole time. You weren't lied to, you weren't—"

"Oh, believe me, I get why you're angry. And when you leave here, you'll take however much time you need in therapy to deal with all this shit. I'm just saying, try to remember that he's not the one who gave you away. He's the one who raised you, who loved you—"

"Yes, but—"

"Nothing. I mean, I know he's loud and crazy and you can't tell him anything. But I saw the look on his face when he threw that punch, and there's no doubt in my mind, the man has never thought of you as anything other than his daughter. He would do anything to protect you."

"I know," I cried. "What I don't know is how I'll ever forgive either of them for betraying me."

"I'm not saying they were right. I'm saying you're still you. What you look like, how you think, what's important to you. It doesn't matter what your name was."

"It's not that simple. Don't you see? It's like when I was a baby, I got handed the script that was supposed to be my story. So I learned all my lines, and understood my role, and figured out how to deal with all the other characters, but then after thirty years of being in the same goddamn show, one day I turn the page and find out that I'd gotten it all wrong. My real story was nothing like the script."

"I don't think that's true. It's the same story, just the unabridged version, maybe. But whatever. It doesn't mean you can't have a happy ending."

"It doesn't?" I stared at him.

"Absolutely not. In fact, you of all people deserve a happy ending." Drew handed me tissues, and after a loud nose blow, which I'm sure was very sexy, I couldn't stop staring at this wonderfully sensitive man I barely knew but already adored. A man who could see me at my absolute worst and not seem to notice or care. How awesome it would be to have someone in my life this intelligent and understanding . . . after I got out of jail for strangling my parents.

# Chapter 17

It took thirty years, but I was finally thrown a surprise party. Not the kind where twenty people jumped out from behind the couch and scared me to death. Not even the kind where I suspected something fishy was going on but couldn't fathom the incompetent people I knew pulling off anything requiring that much attention to detail.

No. My surprise party was different in that it began quietly, in a private hospital room, without food, music, decorations, and with only a single guest. Someone who was hardly in a festive mood himself.

After listening patiently to my sad tale, Drew told me that he, too, was exhausted from the events of the past week. And also a little down. Over the past year, he'd been having second thoughts about working with his father, and even contemplated going back into podiatry. "But how could I leave him now? His father just died, and if his only son doesn't want to be business partners anymore, he's going to feel so abandoned."

I was about to go into my famous sometimes-you-have-to-follow-your-heart speech when my family arrived, carrying balloons and a cake. Not that it helped liven the party. If they'd walked in with Chippendale dancers it wouldn't have mattered. Sulking was a plane you wanted to fly solo.

I made a few snippy comments, but not even my normally combative father picked up his verbal sword to joust. Drew squirmed, while my mother busied herself straightening up the clutter in the room. What was wrong with this picture? Shouldn't Adam and Lindsey be fighting, or at least calling one another by their rightful names, Fatmoronloser and Dumbass? And where was Grams' big mouth when I needed it most?

Was I actually wishing for my family to behave as badly as they normally did? Anything to distract me from letting my emotional dam burst. For there was so much I needed to say to them. But not from a hospital bed. And not on my birthday.

To break the ice, I was about to ask Grams what I'd missed on *Days of our Lives* when I realized that she was the quietest of them all. In fact, she looked downright glum. No doubt my parents were making her pay dearly for having pried open the big family secret. In fact, they had probably moved her into an assisted living doghouse by now.

But there was no time for small talk, as more guests had arrived. The way they streamed in, it looked like an opening of another Ben Fabrikant club. So much for the hospital's strict rules limiting the number of visitors at one time. Everyone on the rope line had made it past the nurse/bouncers.

Viktor was the first to hand me a gift. "Heppy birthday to thi girl who hez everything." He pecked my cheek and handed me a pile of the latest tabloids to hit the newsstands.

"Thanks, Viktor. With any luck, there's a shot of Antonio Banderas in a Speedo."

"No, but there is excellent story about yur mother, Penny. Maybe you like to read about her."

Oh my God. Tell me he didn't just say that. But from the way Drew turned ashen and my father looked as if he were going to throw another punch, I hadn't heard wrong.

Fortunately, that's when Marly walked in, bookended by her parents, Sharon and Milt, and her younger sister, Marissa. They were followed by Ben, his wife, Shari (aka Drew's mom), and their daughter Delia aka Miss Why-Did-I-Have-to-Come-Here.

Whereas I should have acted appreciative that all of these

strangers had given up their Sunday night for me, instead I became fixated on the ladies' jewelry. It just amazed me how different their opinions were on what constituted good taste.

Then, as I was about to check out how badly the men had accessorized, it occurred to me that one more party guest had just arrived. Only this one was presumed dead and buried.

To his credit and my relief, Abe didn't go the Hitchcock route. He neither rattled the blinds nor made the lights flicker. He simply nuzzled up next to me and surrounded my space with a warm, powerful energy. And by virtue of the fact that no one screamed, I knew that I was the only one who sensed his presence.

The fact that I didn't startle everyone by jumping out of bed or shrieking at the top of my lungs was amazing, given my history of hysteria over things considerably less frightening.

Understand that I slept with the lights on until I was eighteen, and the only reason I stopped was because my bitchy, boyfriendless roommate at IU threatened to throw my study lamp out the third floor of McNutt Hall unless I turned it off so she could get some sleep.

So you'd think that having a dead man hanging around my personal energy field would set me over the edge. Yet I remained calm. Not because I was getting used to Abe showing up. It was because there was something about his aura that made me feel safe, as if I were in his protective custody.

"Hi, Grandpa Abe," I whispered.

"What did you say, Claire?" My father signaled that he couldn't hear above the crowd noise.

"Nothing." I shivered. What was I supposed to do? Confess that I thought my deceased grandfather was here and in some sort of unexplainable way was trying to comfort me?

"Claire?" My mother bent over me. "You're shaking like a leaf. What's wrong? Should I go get a nurse?"

"No."

"But you looked like you were about to go into convulsions or something."

"You stay, Roberta," Sharon said. "I'll go get someone."

"Don't. I'm fine."

"Yur not looking ez good ez before," Viktor said. "Maybe something is happening to you."

"I'm just tired."

"From what, for God's sake?" My father came over. "All you've done is sleep and eat—"

"Lenny, sha!" My mothered eyed him. "Don't start."

"C'mon, Claire. Let's sit up now." He fluffed my pillows and hoisted me so I was in an upright position. "All these nice people came to see you. Hey, why don't we all sing?" He turned to the guests. "Let's hear a good, rousing rendition of happy birthday. That'll cheer you up, right, honey?"

"No."

"We'll deal with this crap later, okay?" he whispered through clenched teeth. "But don't be rude. You're embarrassing the hell out of me."

*Oh no. We can't have that, now, can we?*

I felt like I was fifteen all over again. The only thing that had ever mattered to my father was that Adam, Lindsey, and I "be good" for company. Even if he hated who my mother invited—and he hated most everyone—we still had to clean our rooms, set the table with the "good" dishes, and put on decent clothes. ("Get back in your room young lady, and find an article of clothing that covers your *pupik!*")

But obviously this hadn't worked in reverse. He didn't seem to care one bit that I was humiliated for not having figured that I was born to other parents. In fact, I could just hear my father's snippy retort. "What the hell difference does it make how you got here? Take out the garbage."

The very thought of that upcoming conversation made me want to stuff my face.

"Can I please have some of that candy?" I pointed to the wrapped box that Drew had brought.

"After we cut the cake," my father said.

"Lenny, she's not a child. If she wants some candy, she should have some candy."

"I didn't say she couldn't have it. I'm saying, these people don't want to spend all night here. Let's get on with the show. Anyone got a match?"

"That's sure a shitload of candles." Adam pointed to the cake. "There go the smoke detectors."

"Adam. The mouth. Watch the mouth. . . . Whose got a light?"

Viktor and Milt drew lighters from their pockets as if they were in a showdown at high noon.

"No, wait." I tugged at my father's hand. "I'm so in the mood for caramel, you have no idea."

"I'm sorry to disappoint you, Claire." Drew coughed. "But it's not candy."

"It's not?" I grabbed the narrow box off the night table and shook it. "What is it, then?"

"Oh jeez," my father said. "It's a gift of some sort. What difference does it make what it is? You can open it after we do the cake. We got you one of those chocolate banana concoctions."

"What are you talking about?" my mother said. "You weren't even at the bakery. Don't listen to him, Claire. *I* picked it out. It's pralines and cream. Your favorite."

"You're sure this isn't candy?" I shook the box again.

"We could go see if the gift shop is still open." Marly reached for Drew's hand. "I mean, they probably don't sell Godiva or anything . . ."

"Hold on, Marly." Ben pointed to the box. "Drew? That's not what I think it is, is it?"

Drew looked away.

"Damn it, son! Didn't we discuss this? And didn't we agree this is not the time—"

"I heard what you had to say, but I think you're wrong," Drew replied.

"Oh, please? Tell me what it is," I said. "I hate surprises."

"You do?" Drew took back the box. "Then you know what? Your dad's right. Let's all sing happy birthday and cut the cake."

"No." I grabbed it back. "We want what's in the box. We don't care about the cake."

"Oh my God." My father started to perspire. "Who the hell is *we*, Claire?"

"Mr. Fabrikant. Grandpa Abe. Whatever. He says we want what's in the box."

"Well, isn't this just great? Now she's hearing voices. Should we call a doctor or an exorcist?"

"Can you tell us what's happening, Claire?" Ben's voice cracked.

"Yeah." Drew jumped on the bed like a little kid. "What's going on?"

"I'll tell you what's going on," my father said. "She's lost her mind . . . 'We want what's in the box,'" he mimicked me. "Hey, here's an idea. Since Abe wants to play *Let's Make a Deal*, ask him if he'd rather have what's behind door number three."

"Stop it, Lenny! She's just having a little hallucination."

"A little hallucination? I'm sorry. Is it just me, or does anyone else think that's a problem?"

"What are you getting so worked up about? You heard what the doctors said. Patients with head traumas are a little *ferkakt* for a while . . . until the swelling around the brain goes down."

"I'm not *ferkakt*, Mother. Trust me. I'm a lot saner than either of you."

"Oh shit," Adam whispered to Lindsey. "This is gonna get ugly."

"Oh, I see," my father said. "We're nuts, but meanwhile, you're the one who thinks there's a ghost in the room. . . . Not that anyone here is going to buy into that crap. Except for your mother, of course," he sneered. "We all know how she feels about that wacko John Edward . . . and thank God for TiVo so we don't ever have to miss even a single episode for the next ten years."

"You like John Edward?" I asked my mother.

"I think he's wonderful . . . how he helps so many people."

"Oh, me, too." Sharon nodded. "At first I wasn't sure if he was for real, but then a friend of mine who lost her husband flew to New York and ended up being one of the ones he picked on the show. She said he was amazing."

"Yeah, he's great," I said. "So, wait." I looked at my mother. "You've got 'em all on TiVo?"

She hesitated before nodding yes.

"Good to know!"

"Oh my God. Am I the only normal, rational person left in my family?" my father asked.

"That's a laugh," Grams snorted. "You're crazier than all of 'em."

"Is that so, Gert? So you think that, what? I should just go along with the crowd? Sorry. I don't buy it that a man who was just buried six feet under isn't really dead."

"It's 'cause you have like zero spirituality, Daddy," Lindsey whined. "You don't believe in anything."

"For your information, young lady, I happen to be a very spiritual person."

"Yeah, right." Adam slapped his back. "The only spirits you like are eighty-proof."

Everyone laughed, but you'd have to be dead not to feel the tension mounting. This was not exactly the frolicking, good-deed-charity-event-for-the-sick-girl that Ben and Drew had planned. I was afraid not to say something.

"Believe whatever you want, Daddy. But Abe has been with me since he died on my lap."

*Except that.*

"He has?" Ben and Drew asked.

"Yes." I blushed. *Nice ice-breaker, Claire. Keep talking. Because it's not like these people weren't already thinking you're a California airhead.*

But what I really felt bad about was that I hadn't intended to "out" poor Abe. What if he'd wanted to keep our out-of-body relationship confidential, and I'd just violated some sacred trust? This was all my dad's fault. If he hadn't pushed me to a breaking point like he always did, I wouldn't have felt compelled to say something to annoy him.

Now I understood how my mother must have felt all these years being on the receiving end of his scoffing tirades. Nothing she ever said or did was right. How had she slept next to him for thirty years and not suffocated him with a pillow yet?

I took a deep breath and explained that I didn't care who believed me. As unfathomable as it was, what had been happening to me was very real. I had seen the ghost of Abe at the airport. I'd felt his presence when Drew asked me to speak at the funeral, and then again in the limo when Viktor was driving me to South Beach. In fact, I was fairly certain that he was with me right now.

No one said a word. It was a game of chicken. Whoever spoke up first in support of me would be the next one to be scorned.

"So like what's he doing right now?" Drew whispered. "Do you think he can hear us?"

"I don't know. Do you want to try to say something to him?"

"Oh, for Christ's sake." My father threw up his hands. "This is such bullshit! Look, everyone. I apologize. I know Claire has been through a lot, but you don't need to indulge her like this. We'll get her whatever medications she needs to—"

"Excuse me," Ben said, "but if you don't mind, I'd like to hear what she has to say."

"Me, too," Drew said. "Hey, Pops." He looked around, not sure where to direct his eyes. "What's it like up there? Have you seen Mama yet? How are the babes? Hot as hell, probably. Right?"

Even my father chuckled. But what caused his head to spin was the sound of my laugh. It was more a loud belly roll than my normal, low-pitched cackle.

"That was weird." He eyed me.

"What?"

"The way you just laughed. It didn't even sound like you. It sounded more like a man."

"Really?"

"You didn't notice?" He looked spooked. "Did anyone else notice?"

Viktor raised his hand. "My head. It did a double-take. She leffed like Abe, em I right?"

"Do it again, Claire," Drew said. "I missed it."

"I don't know if I can."

"Can you ask . . . is there a way . . . how do we know if he's really here?" Ben treaded cautiously.

"It's hard to explain," I sighed. "I just feel this energy. And I hear his voice. . . ."

"Don't forget she spent six years out in California." My father made the sign of the cuckoo.

"So wait," Ben said. "You're saying you're having a conversation with him right now?"

"It's weird, but I think I am."

"Amazing." His eyes welled. "We love you, Dad. We miss you so much."

"I'm curious. Does he sound like he did on the plane?" Drew asked.

"On the plane?" I gulped.

"Yeah. You spent all that time talking to him. Does he sound the same as he did . . . before?"

*Nice work, Claire. Let's see you get out of this one.* "I think so. But to be honest *(HA!)* things are still a little fuzzy for me, you know what I mean?"

"Of course we do, dear," Sharon said. "But I must say, this is fascinating. Isn't it, Marly?"

"What?"

"I said, what Claire is experiencing—it's fascinating."

"Oh. Definitely."

But you didn't need to be psychic to know that Marly wasn't even remotely interested in what was happening to me. She was too busy watching Drew watch me.

"Hey," Adam said, "ask if you have to work up there, or if you get to goof off the whole time."

"Oh, I'm sure it's just like it is here, son," my father snapped. "You'll goof off all day, while some poor *schmuck* will have to break his back trying to support you."

"Actually"—I coughed—"he's telling me that it is amazing over there. Very peaceful."

"Oh jeez, Claire." My father groaned. "Enough with the crazy talk. You sound like a moron."

"No, you do." Shari Fabrikant sniffed. "I happen to believe that spirit attachments are very common in sudden-death situations. It wouldn't surprise me at all if Abe was still hanging around her."

And that was all the convincing people needed. If Shari said it was possible to communicate with the dead, who were they to argue? Milt, the betting man, was especially intrigued. He asked about the prospects for the Dolphins, and if it wasn't a bother, maybe he could get a heads-up on the Marlins, too.

Sharon wondered, if she gave Abe her mother's name, could he locate her and tell her that she loved her? And by the way, where had he left that antique diamond Jewish star that he'd wanted Marly to wear on her wedding day?

Marly was going for a prediction about how many children she and Drew would have, and by any chance could he tell her the sexes. Her little sister Marissa hoped to hear that, like Marly, a marriage proposal was in her future, but please not from Eric, her ex-body-building boyfriend who was practically stalking her at the gym.

Ben's wife Shari, the turquoise queen, asked something stupid and existential about the existence of God, while their freak-of-nature daughter Delia wanted to know if Joplin, Zappa, and Morrison were still making music. Adam thought that was an awesome question, and made a beeline over to check out the fellow rebel without a clue.

But my favorite inquiry came from Grams. One would think that she would be mostly curious about her health, or at least if she should move. Instead, she wanted Abe to solve a mystery. "Ask 'im what always happens to that other sock in the dryer."

Admittedly, we had a good laugh. But then I felt this dark, ominous cast come over me, and a name kept repeating in my head like a mantra. Was this how it worked for John Edward?

"I'm hearing the name John, or Jonathan," I blurted. "Does that mean anything to anyone?"

I don't know if Drew caught it, but Marly's milky complexion turned green.

"It probably means nothing," I continued. "But I keep hearing it. No one here has a connection to a John . . . Johnny . . . Jonah . . . Jonathan?"

"Wait," Drew snapped. "Marly. Didn't you used to date a guy by that name?"

"Yeah, like a hundred years ago." She glanced at her mother.

"I have a cousin Jonathan from Chicago," Sharon offered. "From my father's side."

"Oh, I know," Marissa, the good sister, chimed in. "My gynecologist's partner is a Dr. Jonathan. I've never seen him, though, because he specializes in infertility."

"No," I said, "I'm picking up that there's a personal involvement here. Friends who maybe lost touch, and now they're friends again."

"This is so wild." Sharon clapped. "You sound just like John Edward. But he's been doing this for a very long time, of course. And you're so new at it. Maybe you're getting your signals crossed."

"Maybe," I replied, "but I don't think so." I looked right at Marly.

"Why are you staring at me? Jonathan is a very common name."

"You still talk to him, don't you?" Drew's shoulders tensed.

"Can we please discuss this later?" she whispered.

"No. Let's talk about it right now. What's the story with this guy?"

"Oh my God. I can't believe you'd ask me something like that."

"I'm not accusing you. I just think it's pretty amazing that Claire picked up his name."

"Well, of course you do. Because if CLAIRE says anything at all, it's got to be important."

*Really?*

"And yet this morning, you said yourself that she was crazy."

*Oh.*

"What?" Drew shook his head.

"Yes. You said to ignore Claire if she acts crazy because she's not playing with a full deck."

"That's not what I said."

"You're right, Drew." Sharon smiled. "I think your exact words were, 'Right now, you could give Claire a penny for her thoughts, and still get change back.'"

"What are you busting his chops for?" Milt yelled at his wife. "Stay outa this."

"I'm just saying that Marly remembered correctly, dear."

"Drew. You and me." He signaled. "We're gonna have to form our own tag team to keep up with these two. You know what I mean?"

"Definitely," Drew gritted out.

"Oh God," I said. "This is so weird, because now I'm picking up a second name. A last name, I think. Jaffe? Or is it Yafi? No, wait. It sounds more like coffee. No, that can't be right."

"That's it!" Drew yelled. "That was his name. Jonathan Coffey. Right, Marly? The guy from Coral Springs who opened all those bagel shops, then skipped town? I remember because his name was in the paper for months, and when I showed you the story, you said it didn't surprise you because he was a real wheeler-dealer, and he probably did screw all those investors out of money."

"Yeah, like me." Milt groaned.

"Big deal," Marly cried. "So she got a lousy name right. It has nothing to do with me!"

"Drew, dear"—Sharon's voice rose—"you're upsetting her. Let it go. They saw each other a few times. It was nothing from nothing. Old friends catching up."

"Shut up, MOTHER!" Marly screamed. "Oh my God. What are you doing?"

"This is so bizarre," I interrupted. "I think he's trying to tell me the name of the restaurant . . . "Boccachino's . . ."

"Boca Chiante!" Drew yelled like a contestant. "Down Glades Road."

"I hate you so much!" Marly stormed off in tears before telling us to whom she was directing her wrath.

I assumed Drew would chase after her and beg forgiveness. But he didn't budge, even after Ben eyed him, bobbed his head toward the door, and said, "Go!"

"No." Drew shoved his hands in his jeans pockets. "I don't want to."

"Drew, c'mon. Go talk to her," Milt prodded. "Be a *mensch*. You didn't handle that very well."

"I'm sorry. How does this work? Marly lies to me, and I should go apologize?"

"I told you." Sharon headed for the door. "Nothing happened with them. You're being an ass."

"See, and I'm thinking, if my grandfather came all the way back from his grave to warn me, then maybe it's because there really is something I should know."

Sharon stopped. "Might I remind you that NONE of this would ever have happened if you hadn't been *shtupping* that idiot waitress from Kentucky. And for your information, it was Jonathan's partner who screwed up the books, not him!"

"And for your information, the real reason we broke up was because Marly cheated on me."

"What the hell are you talking about?" Milt exploded. "How dare you accuse—"

"Fine. I know she's your little angel who can do no wrong. But go on. Ask her about the time some guy from New York left a message on her answering machine that said his plans had changed, and he couldn't fly in for the weekend."

"That is bullshit, and you know it!" Sharon spit. "We have family in New York. It was probably her cousin David. They're very close."

"Really? So then why did she cancel her reservation at Mandarin Oriental? And why did it happen to be for the same weekend she told me she was taking Marissa to Canyon Ranch?"

The Beckers looked so stunned, it was as if they had just walked into their own party.

"Surprise!" I said under my breath.

Maybe this hadn't been such a bad birthday after all.

# Chapter 18

I WAS STARTING TO WONDER. HAD MY ACCIDENT CAUSED MY BRAIN TO scramble like a heavyweight match on HBO? Or through the miracle of telepathy, had I magically channeled information from the great beyond? I wanted to believe the latter, because not only had it been so much fun, it had empowered me like a sitcom character with supernatural powers who spent every episode creating havoc.

Whichever it was, head injury or psychic phenomenon, it was hard not to gloat. With my brain having doubled as a radio receiver, I could tune in to WABE, a fifty-thousand-watt, clear-channel station broadcasting from the top of God knows where. And although the signal had been weak, I was still able to pick up enough details to achieve a defense attorney's dream—reasonable doubt.

On the jury were Drew's parents, Ben and Shari, a couple in the center of their own relationship storm. Would they honestly want their son entering into a marriage that was starting out with a lousy forecast?

And now Milt and Sharon might also be having second thoughts about Marly marrying Drew, especially since they would be paying for the gala wedding reception that their daughter would insist have every bell, whistle, and shot girl this side of the Atlantic.

I hugged my pillow. I hadn't intended to sow seeds of doubt on the impending Becker/Fabrikant nuptials, but since the barn door was swinging, maybe the couple's special day would be postponed indefinitely like a J. Lo wedding.

Unfortunately, my giddiness was short-lived, for God was apparently an equal opportunity shocker. No sooner did the Beckers storm out and everyone else beg off than it was my family's turn to discover something so startling that, if chin-dropping was an Olympic sport, we would have taken home the gold.

Ben and Drew had stayed behind, I assumed because they were still in a daze about the newly discovered Marly mess, not to mention my shocking conversation with Abe. If there were going to be any further communiqués from him, of course they'd want to hear them firsthand.

But that wasn't what kept them from leaving. What they wanted was for me to open the wrapped box I'd mistaken for chocolates. Though Ben still thought the timing was bad, he agreed that the contents might help me better understand my connection to Abe.

Naturally, at the mention of Abe's name, my parents were berserk. I had already been through so much today, why keep bringing him up? And what about the doctors' repeated warnings that I could experience a serious setback if I became overstimulated?

Thing about it was, I knew that their carrying on was a big act. When it came to *The Lenny and Roberta Show*, nothing was more important than looking good in front of the live studio audience. But as soon as they were off camera? It was right back to being self-absorbed cretins. Honestly, I could have arrested them for impersonating caring parents.

That's why I said that it was still my birthday, and if I wanted to open the damn box, it was my prerogative. But when I ripped off the wrapping, and saw an old cigar box, I was crestfallen. So much for hoping to finding a priceless heirloom that would fetch thousands on eBay.

And good thing I was an actress who could feign delight when feeling disappointment. Otherwise I wouldn't have been able to convince Ben and Drew that I was excited about finding something in a smelly cigar box that had probably been lying dormant in an attic for fifty years.

"C'mon. Open it, Claire." Drew sounded anxious.

"Why do I have a bad feeling about this?" My father mumbled.

"Let me guess." I yawned. "It's cigars?"

Close, but no cigars. When I lifted the lid, there were dozens of photos. Black and whites. Polaroids. Class pictures. Grainy color shots. And oddly, it didn't hit me right away that I knew the girl who was posing because she was so out of context. In fact, when I finally recognized the clothes, the settings, and the seasons, I cried out like a wounded bird. "Oh my God! They're me!"

"What are you talking about?" My father grabbed a handful of photos. "Let me see those."

"They're all me!" I dumped the contents on my bed. "I don't understand. Where did they come from?"

"That's the thing," Ben said. "We have no idea. Last night we went over to my dad's place to clean up a little, and we found this box in the hall closet."

"Yeah." Drew nodded. "First we thought they were just unopened Cohibas—Cuban cigars were his favorites. Except that Pops always kept them in a humidor . . . until he started to get a little senile."

"Anyway," Ben sighed, "when we saw the pictures, at first we had no idea who it was . . . but then there was this one. I guess it was you maybe at the prom, or some big dance. You're wearing this long white gown."

"I took one look at the face and," Drew said, "Dad, that's Claire. And we were like, no way. How could that be?"

"Show me the picture." My heart pounded. "It might have been from my bat mitzvah. I wore this long white Jessica McClintock halter dress."

Ben searched the pile. "This is it. This is the one."

"Let me see." My mother leaned in to get a glimpse. "*Oy*. Lenny, it *is* from the bat mitzvah."

My father grabbed the photo. "Christ Almighty! I even remember when this was taken. We had just pulled up to the place, and the idiot photographer was already snapping away. See, that's me in the back . . . and I was yelling at him, not yet, let me at least put a comb through my hair, for God's sake . . . but would you look at that nice suit? A Hickey Freeman. Went for big bucks on that one."

"And what a party!" My mother blew into a tissue. "At the Crest Hollow Country Club in Woodbury. Maybe you've heard of it."

"Sounds familiar." Drew nodded. "But what I can't get over is that that was you at thirteen, Claire. You looked like you were in college or something."

"And what I can't get over is how I never knew there was an Abe Fabrikant, yet he somehow managed to have my entire life in pictures!"

"It's insane!" My father stood with hands on hips. "I feel so invaded!"

"You feel invaded? Oh my God. Are you serious? How should I feel? I'm the one whose face is in every shot. There's me at my first birthday. Me at the beach. Me riding my tricycle. Me on the first day of kindergarten. Me. All me. I'm the one who's been betrayed here, Dad. Not you. . . . I swear, I don't know how much more of this I can take."

"Believe me," Drew said, "we were expecting cigars. See, after his first heart attack, my grandmother made him quit smoking, which, of course, he couldn't do, so he'd hide his smokes all over the house. Then this one time she found a box of Magnum 46's. We're talking very rare, top of the line, almost impossible to get smuggled in . . . and she goes and throws the whole box into the trash."

I knew I should be listening to Drew's story, but I didn't hear a word.

"It was the first time I ever saw him cry." Drew looked up to see if there might be a sign that his Pops was listening. "Right, Pops? You even went to the city dump to go find the truck. . . ."

As Ben and Drew reminisced, I noticed that my father was hunched and bewildered, looking desperate for his favorite comfort food, a scotch and soda. Meanwhile, my mother looked as if she were in Temple *davening*. "This is so awful . . . this is so terrible . . . awful . . . terrible—"

"Wait a minute." My father sifted through the pile. "That shot from the bat mitzvah wasn't one of the actual photos. It was just a proof. See? Says right here. Glenmar Photography. May 1987 . . . So the only people who could have gotten hold of these was family. . . . Son-of-a-bitch. I bet Iris stole them and sent them. Anything for a quick buck. God, she's unbelievable!"

"Now you're talking crazy!" My mother gasped. "My sister would never do anything like that."

"Oh really? So all those times she went behind our backs and stole our cleaning ladies, and our babysitters . . . and that time she didn't give you the message to go over to your Aunt Ruth's to pick out the china she was getting rid of. You think that was being a good sister?"

"All I'm saying is she would never go out and find the family and not tell me. She couldn't keep a secret for five minutes. You think she could keep news like that for thirty years?"

"So fine, then." He sniffed. "Explain to me how the hell a man we couldn't find ended up with dozens of pictures of Claire. You think maybe the guy at Fotomat was in on this?"

"How should I know how he got them? Maybe he hired a private eye or something."

"No way." Ben puffed out his chest. "My father would never have stooped to anything so underhanded."

"Yeah. You didn't know my Pops," Drew added. "He never did a dishonest thing in his life."

"Shows ya what you know." Grams snorted.

"What?" My father's back stiffened.

"He didn't pay off no spy." Grams stared at the floor.

"Ma! What do you mean? Do you know something?"

Suddenly all eyes were on the elderly woman who was swaying in her chair.

"Mrs. Moss, please," Ben said. "Can you explain any of this?"

"I may know a thing or two."

"Grams! Oh my God . . . Stop playing these stupid-ass games. Do you or don't you know anything?"

My dad groaned. "The mouth, Claire. Watch the mouth."

"Who knew the son-of-a-bitch was going to die?" Grams blurted.

"What is she talking about?" My mother yelled at my father.

"How the hell should I know? She's your mother. Gert, What the hell are you talking about? Who wasn't supposed to die?"

"Abe Fabrikant! That's who!"

"Wait, wait, wait," I cried. "You swore up and down you never met him."

"That's right. I didn't."

"But you talked to him?"

"Once." Her lower lip puckered. "After Penelope disappeared on us."

"You what?" My father paced like a prosecutor. "You knew where he was?"

"Yeah, I found him."

"AND YOU DIDN'T TELL US?" he yelled.

"I did what I had to do," she whispered.

"Oh, for Christ's sake, Gert. Stop your nonsense. You couldn't possibly have found him. We didn't even know his name, where he lived. Today you go on the Internet, and boom, there's your guy. But that was the dark ages back then."

"From 1974 to 1978, he lived with his wife Esther at 4134 Collins Avenue, Miami Beach, Florida. Then they bought a home at 2385 Cocoa Plum Circle, Coconut Grove. Then after she died in 1992, Abe moved into a condo at 101 Bal Harbor Tower in Bal Harbor—"

"Whoa. Hold on here." My father held up his hand. "What are you all of a sudden? Directory Assistance? Is she right about any of this, Ben?"

Ben and Drew's eyes were locked in the stunned position.

"What is happening here?" I banged my fist on the bed. "I don't understand."

"That makes two of us." My father glared at Gert. "Of all the rotten things you've done over the years, this is unbelievable. You knew how hard we tried to find Penelope's family. You knew we called the police, we hired a private investigator, we even went to the FBI and filed a missing person's report. And what about all the time I took off time from work and *schlepped* into the city looking for people who might know her from school?"

"Oh my God!" I choked. "It all makes perfect sense now. You wanted to get rid of me."

"What the hell are you talking about?" Foam sprayed from his mouth like a perfect espresso. "We were crazy about you. We'd never seen a more perfect baby. But you gotta understand the circumstances, Claire. We were scared to death. And here you were, this tiny, helpless little infant. Your father was dead, and God knows where your wacko mother was, taking off in the middle of a night like a bandit."

"Yeah." My mother's head bobbed. "She leaves this *ferkakteh* note in the stroller saying she wasn't ready to be a mother, and could we please remember to buy formula because she was down to her last can."

"It's blowing me away that Aunt Penny did something so low," Drew said.

"Low?" my father yelled. "Are you kidding? It was downright criminal. I mean, you hear about ghetto kids abandoning their babies in Dumpsters. But she was supposedly this rich kid with brains."

"She always seemed a little selfish to me," my mother sniffed. "And very disagreeable."

"Yeah, and we were married, what, Roberta? Maybe six, seven months? We were kids ourselves. Who was thinking of starting a family? But it wasn't even that. We were scared to death that we would fall in love with you, Claire, and then one day out of the blue Penelope would just show up and say, 'Hey, everyone, thanks for your trouble, but I'm taking my daughter back now.'"

"We didn't know what the hell to do. So we thought, all right. Before this goes any further, let's try to find her family."

"And Gert, how the hell did you even find the Fabrikants? I spent thousands on that idiot PI, and all he came up with was some family in Michigan who claimed they had a daughter Penelope at NYU . . . but she turned to out to be black."

"I got lucky. That's how." Grams sighed. "'Cause Miss Smarty Pants was in such a rush to leave, see. She forgot to clean out one of the drawers in Gary's room. I found a bunch of receipts, some phone numbers . . . called 'em all."

"Ma, I can't believe you never told us. With everything that was going on, how could you not have said a word? That was selfish and irresponsible and—"

"Shows ya what you know!" She waved her bony finger. "I did what I had to do, see? You were all so busy trying to get everything back to normal, when there was no baby, no funerals, no *shiva* . . . but what good was that gonna do me? You think my life was ever gonna be normal again?"

"I don't believe this." My father slumped into a chair.

"I lost my one son. Over my dead body was I gonna lose my one grandchild. No sir. Nobody was takin' away my little Claireleh. I knew God gave her to me to make up for having to take Gary. Whadya think? I should go help you find the family so you could give the baby back to the idiot mother who didn't want her in the first place? What kind of life would she have had? The girl had no money, no husband. . . . I used to find them marijuana cigarettes in her jacket pocket. At least with us Claire could be from a nice Jewish family, she'd get a good education, a good upbringing."

"I can't believe what I'm hearing," my mother gasped.

"It's blowing my mind, Gert." My father's eyes misted. "Our whole lives would have been different if you'd just told us you found the father."

"No, you mean it would have been better," I cried. "You mean you wouldn't have had to raise me, or had all this aggravation."

"That's not what I mean, and you know it. I'm just in a little bit of shock here, okay? I'm not saying our lives would have been better, I'm saying that if we knew about Penelope's father, the whole damn story would have played out differently, and that's a hell of a thing to consider. You make a right turn instead of a left, and the rest of your life is changed forever."

"But the important thing," Ben jumped in, "is that it all worked out okay. Gert made a great decision. Claire was raised by a wonderful family."

"Thank you." My father closed his eyes and patted his heart. "We did our best."

"You sure did." Drew slapped him on the back. "Claire is a great girl."

*Great enough to dump your shallow, self-absorbed fiancée and fall in love with me?*

"There is something I'm curious about." Ben looked at Gert. "And I hope you don't mind my asking. But what exactly did you say to my parents?"

"What do you mean, what did I say?" Grams shrugged. "I told them the God's honest truth. After I got your father on the line, I says, 'Mr. Fabrikant? My name is Gertrude Moss of 2453 Lawson Lane in Valley Stream, New York, and I'm calling to tell you that your daughter Penelope has had a baby girl with my son Gary. But now he's dead from a car crash, and she ran away, and I was wondering if maybe you heard from her. . . . I'm sorry. I hope I didn't interrupt your supper.'"

"That's what you said?" Ben laughed. "'I hope I didn't interrupt your supper'?"

"'Cause I know how people get when their food is getting cold. They don't act nice."

"Did you speak to my mother, too? I can't believe she knew that their darling daughter had an unwanted pregnancy."

"Ben. Please." My father pointed to me. "Claire has feelings, you know."

I just looked at him. Suddenly he was Mr. Sensitive?

"Sorry, Claire," Ben said. "I'm just in shock. . . . You have to understand that my whole life all I ever heard was, Penelope is so beautiful, and Penelope is so talented . . . she could do no wrong, and I was the rotten bum."

"I never spoke to the girl's mother," Grams interrupted. "But believe you me, if I had, I would have told her a thing or two about raising good daughters."

"So wait, Ma," said my father. "What did Abe tell you?"

"Oh. Well. First I thought he was playin' tricks on me, asking what Penelope ate for breakfast, if she had any birthmarks. But he was just makin' sure I wasn't one of those people who make up stories to get money. . . . And that was it. I only talked to him that one time."

"Yes, but what did he say about the baby?" my father cried.

"What did he say? He said he couldn't take her, if that's why I was calling. And I couldn't call him no more on account of his wife's high blood pressure, but I could write him letters to tell him how Hannah was doing."

"And you did that?" I gulped. "You wrote to him?"

"Every month. Never missed a one. Not even when Harry died."

From the collective gasping, it sounded like we were all on respirators.

"But why, Grams?" I asked. "Why would you bother keeping in touch with a man who obviously didn't give a shit whether he had a granddaughter or not? Did he ever ask to meet me? Did he ever try to get his daughter to come back for me?"

"Why don't you ask him that?" my father sniffed. "You seem to have a direct connection."

"Would you listen to yourself, Lenny?" my mother yelled. "Enough with the wiseguy remarks."

"I'm sorry." I shivered. "I'm finding all of this very hard to believe. From everything I've heard about Abe, he was this wonderful, generous human being who couldn't turn his back on total strangers. Yet he didn't want to bother with his own flesh and blood? It makes no sense."

"Because he didn't want Penelope to have the baby, see?" Gert said. "He said she didn't deserve you on account of the fact that she was a selfish birdbrain who lived with her head in the clouds, and would make a terrible mother because she couldn't even take care of herself, let alone a small baby."

"My father actually said that?" Ben smiled.

"Yes, sir."

"So Grams, if he said he didn't want his daughter to have me, and he didn't want me, why did you keep writing to him? Why didn't you just hang up the phone after that first call and say to hell with this guy?"

"Because I made a deal with him, that's why. A deal with the devil, it turns out."

"You're calling my Pops a devil?" Drew frowned.

" 'Cause he promised if I would help raise the baby, and I wrote to him and sent him pictures, and told him how she was growing up, he would send me money for her."

"Oh, for Christ's sake!" my father exploded. "He was paying you all these years, and you never gave us a dime? You knew how I struggled with the business and three kids—"

"What money, Leonard? The son-of-a-bitch never sent me a lousy red cent! All these years I'm writing letters and sending pictures, the invitations to Claire's birthday parties."

"Did he used to write you back?" Drew asked.

"Only to give me his new address."

"So wait, Ma. Why did you keep sending him stuff if he never answered you?"

"Because I told you. We made a deal. He promised to give me money for Claire if I kept writing to him. So if I stopped writing, he'd think he didn't have to make good on his end of the bargain. That's why I figured, what does it cost me to send him letters? Some paper and a lousy stamp."

"This is such a shock." Ben shook his head. "Claire is right, though. That doesn't even sound like him. He was a very wealthy man, Mrs. Moss. And he never went back on his word. Are you sure you got the story straight? Are you sure he offered to send money?"

"Of course I'm sure," she hollered. "Do I look like I don't know what I'm talking about?"

"No, no. Of course not. It's just that it was a very emotional time in your life. You lost your son. There was a baby to deal with. Maybe you misunderstood his intentions. Maybe you heard wrong."

"I heard every blessed word of that conversation." Grams shook a finger in Ben's face. "Every blessed word . . . and Gertrude Moss never forgets a promise, you understand? He said, 'Don't call me on the telephone again, no matter what. This has to be our little secret. But I get mail from people all over the world, and anything addressed to me, my wife doesn't open. So send me letters, and I will help take care of Claire.' "

"Okay, but he didn't actually say he'd send money?" Ben asked.

"Well, what'd ya think he meant, sonny boy? He sure as heck wasn't planning to come help us change diapers. Of course it meant he would send me money. So she wouldn't be a burden on the family."

"Well, did you ever ask him in one of your letters?" My father sniffed. "What's the deal here, Abe? I'm sending you pictures every month, where's the dough?"

"No."

"Why not?"

" 'Cause I'm not pushy like you. I have my own ways of doin' things."

"Oh. Well, great job, Gert. I got stuck footing the bill all these years when a little financial support would have been very helpful. You have any idea what it cost to keep three kids in camp, and braces, then there were the bar and bat mitzvahs, sweet sixteens, college . . ."

"That's why he's a son-of-a-bitch!"

"Well, if he's such a son-of-a-bitch," my father asked, "why the hell did you say he wasn't supposed to die?"

Gert's lip puckered.

"Ma. What's the matter? What aren't you telling us?"

"I don't want to talk about this no more."

"What do you mean, you don't want to talk about this?" my father yelled. "You can't just open this huge can of worms and then decide you don't feel like telling us the whole story!"

"You're gonna be very angry, that's why."

"I'm ALREADY angry . . . what the hell difference does it make?"

"Lenny, sha! Stop scaring her. You want her to start burping?"

"Grams, c'mon," I whispered. "Spill it before I turn you upside down and shake it out of you."

"Please, Mrs. Moss," Ben said sweetly. "No one is going to be angry with you."

"Shows you what you know," she sighed. But a deep breath later, she finished her story.

"A few weeks ago, Abe finally gets around to sending me a stinking letter. Can you imagine? Took him thirty years to get off his fat heiny and write me back. And I'm thinking, see, I was right. I did what I promised, now he's finally going to do what he promised. But guess what? No check. Just a note saying he's coming to New York for a family party, and he's getting on in years, and he'd like to meet Claire."

"Oh my God." I felt my heart palpitate.

"So I write him back and I say, no, that's not possible, you can't just waltz into the kid's life after all these years and say hello, how do you do, I'm your grandfather. She don't even know she's adopted . . . which, believe me, wasn't my idea to keep secret. That I can tell you!

"Anyways, I got to thinking. . . . Roberta mentioned Claire was coming to visit me, so I wrote Abe another letter and said, I'll find out what flight she's on, then you can make your flight home the same one. At least you'll get to see what she looks like in person."

"Oh my God!" I screamed. "You set me up? You did this?"

"Jesus Christ, Gert!" My father smacked his forehead. "What the hell were you thinking?"

"So he writes me back, and he says, yes, that's what he's going to do. He's going to take the same flight as Claire, but would it be okay if he called the airline to request that they sit together?"

"No!" I burst into tears. "NOOOOO!"

"So I send him another letter that says, no, you can't sit next to her 'cause you might let it slip who you are . . . but I guess he didn't get that one in time 'cause now we all know where he sat."

"For God's sakes, Gert! What do you live in? A cave? Why didn't you just pick up the goddamn phone and say, 'Hey look. You lost the right to have any contact with Claire thirty years ago'?"

" 'Cause he told me never to call him at home." Grams shrugged.

"When his wife was alive, fine, that I can understand. But what the hell difference would it have made if you called him now? It wasn't even long distance!"

"Maybe I didn't want to, okay? 'Cause maybe I was thinkin' it might be nice if the two of them got to talking. Then it would be in God's hands. But ya think I would have done this if I knew he was going to drop dead on her lap?"

"You're out of your goddamned mind!" My father raised a fist at her.

"This is an unbelievable story." Ben's chin dropped.

Drew nodded. "Almost like a movie."

"Yeah, but you've only heard half the script," I wailed. "Grams, you gotta go home and get your gun." *How can I live with myself now? I blew my one and only chance to speak to my grandfather.*

# Chapter 19

IT IS TESTIMONY TO THE HUMAN SPIRIT THAT EVEN IN OUR DARKEST hours the light of hope can be ignited to warm our hearts and to renew our faith.

Not that I knew this from personal experience. If I had to guess, I'd say it had more to do with the fact that there were high doses of antidepressants downhill-racing in my bloodstream. It was also helpful that despite Gram's shocking admissions, she was there to cradle me in her arms, just as she had when I was a frightened child trying to forget a scary dream.

Yes, I was aware that she had single-handedly changed the course of my life by making a decision independent of my knowledge or consent. And yes, like a premeditated crime, she had sent me into a flying lion's den for a chance encounter with a grandfather I never knew.

But she was still my beloved Grams. Still the historian of my past, able to chronicle even the most insignificant days of my life, as she had been there to share them with me. So in spite of all that had just transpired, all that she had confessed, I could neither hate her nor hold her liable. At great risk, she had carried a burden for thirty years, in order that I be kept out of harm's way.

Yet as willing as I was to forgive her for her transgression, I felt no such compassion for my parents. Looking back, they loved me to the extent possible, but Grams loved me unconditionally. They were my legal guardians, but she raised me. They met my physical needs, she saw to it that I was emotionally strong.

Perhaps I owed my parents a big thanks, but I owed Grams my life.

It used to make me crazy whenever my agent called and said, "So what do you want first? The good news or the bad?" Frankly, it's a stupid question. Who wants to hear bad news under any circumstances? Half the time the good news isn't all that terrific, or at least not enough to offset the bad news.

So imagine how I felt the very next morning. Still numb from discovery, I was finally about to be released from the hospital, but not before being on the receiving end of all these good news/bad news scenarios.

"The good news, Claire," my neurosurgeon said, "is your recovery has been nothing short of miraculous. Normally in brain trauma cases like yours, I'd be recommending a few weeks in a neuro rehab center, but it doesn't seem warranted here. However, given everything that's happened to you, the shocking news about your family and the strange visitations from a deceased person, I am recommending that you seek intensive psychiatric treatment at a residential center in Boca that's doing wonders with cases like yours."

*Nope. Sorry. About the only thing I want from you is a prescription for enough anti-anxiety pills so I don't even feel a sneeze coming on.*

"Great news!" my father said as he helped me pack up. "Elyce has been calling to see how you're feeling, and then, this is so sweet, this morning she offered to let you use Ira's parents' vacation house in Hilton Head because they're off in Spain somewhere. She said it's right on the beach. A great place to recuperate. Then, Ira will try to get some time off so they can join you . . . give you two a chance to meet before the wedding.

"Only trouble is, the house is in the middle of a major renovation, and they're down to one bedroom, so you'd have to all squeeze in together. But I think you should do it anyway."

*Really? I was thinking I should fly to San Francisco, buy a really ugly bridesmaid's dress, climb to the top of the Golden Gate Bridge, and be the first jumper of the day.*

"Good news, Claire." Ben held my hand. "Penny says she's dying to meet you, of course, but she thinks it's probably best if you wait until you're feeling stronger before you plan any sort of reunion. Oh, and about that role in her new movie? She said to tell you that they really need to cast it this week, and apparently she already had someone else in mind. She thought since you knew the business so well, you'd understand."

*Oh, I understand, all right. I understand that Penny is a low-life bitch who should be shot out of a cannon and dumped into the pool during the* Vanity Fair *Oscar party.*

But then, in an unexplainable shift, either the planets magically realigned or the god of darkness left for vacation. Either way, I was finally on the receiving end of some legitimately nice news. And for the first time since that fateful morning I flew to Miami, I didn't see the world through eyes of despair.

It started with a get-well call from Pablo. Naturally he and Raphael were praying for my full recovery. But he also informed me that the office manager's job was still available, and I should just let him know when I was ready to start work.

"You didn't hold the job open for me," I laughed. "You couldn't get anyone else to take it."

"Actually, we did," Pablo whispered. "She lasted four days, which may have been a record."

Even Grams had wonderful news to cheer me up. She had gone back to look at Abe's apartment and loved it so much, she was moving in immediately. She'd also spoken to management and given the extenuating circumstances; they'd said if I wanted to live there temporarily, they would waive the bylaws that prohibited residents under the age of sixty-five.

"You just gotta promise a few things," Grams said. "No pets, no wild parties, and no fooling around with the men."

"Oh yuck. Why would they mention that?"

"Because you know the kinda mess animals make. Who needs dog poop all over the grass?"

But then came the granddaddy of the good-news calls, ironically because of my granddaddy. Right as we were walking out the door, the phone rang, and my father grumbled that I should let it ring because in exactly six minutes he would have to pay for another hour for the parking garage.

"Just let me see who it is," I said. "I'll make it fast." *Please be Drew calling to say he thought about it, and I was the girl of his dreams.*

"Oh, for crying out loud, Claire. Let the operator take a message. You gave them your cell number."

"Just go. I'll meet you downstairs. . . . Hello. . . . Yes, this is she. . . . Actually, no, it's not a good time. I've just been released from the hospital, and—"

"Who is it?" My father waited by the door.

"I'm sorry. Who is this again? . . . Uh-huh. . . . Oh my God. Really? . . . No, of course not. How would I have known that?"

"Claire, who are you talking to?"

"Shhh." I covered the mouthpiece. "Some attorney for Abe. . . . Yes, I guess I could meet you next week."

"Oh jeez. What did I tell you?" He smacked the wall with his palm. "Didn't I say if you got involved and the family sued the airline, you'd be looking at years of litigation and testifying?"

"Daddy, be quiet. . . . Excuse me. My father was talking to me at the same time. . . . Yes, I just turned thirty a few days ago. How did you know that? . . . I'm sorry?"

"Tell them you're not saying a word until you get your own representation," my father barked in my ear. "*Oy gevault.* That's what I need right now. More legal expenses."

"Oh my God . . . Are you sure? I can't believe it. . . . Okay. Yes. Of course. . . . Next Monday at eleven." I scribbled on the back of a prescription. "1500 Glades Road . . . third floor. Yes. I know Boca. Thank you. Thank you very much." I hung up and collapsed on the bed.

"What the hell did you say yes for?" my father yelled. "You can't meet with anyone next week. You're going home with us tomorrow, and I'm sure as hell not paying for another airfare to get you back down here. If they want to talk to you, they can take your statement by phone—"

"He left me money." I cried softly into a pillow.

"What?"

"There you are." My mother rushed in. "I've been looking everywhere for you two. Up the elevator, down the elevator . . . you told me to meet you at the car a half an hour ago—"

"Sha, Roberta!" My father waved. "Something just happened, and I want to hear. Claire, start from the beginning. Who was that on the phone, and what exactly did he tell you?"

"Grams was wrong about Abe," I whispered.

"What's she talking about?" my mother asked.

"That's what I'm trying to find out." My father sat beside me.

"He's not a son-of-a-bitch like Grams said. He did what he said . . . he put money away for me."

"Oh my God," my mother gasped. "How much money?"

"Oh jeez, Roberta. What kind of insensitive question is that to ask? Can't you see Claire is struggling right now? But now that you brought it up . . . Claire, honey. Did the lawyer happen to mention an amount?"

"Oh, 'scuse me." An orderly rolled in a linen cart. "I thought you left already."

"Well, we didn't." My father looked at his watch. "And this room is paid in full until twelve-oh-one P.M. . . . which gives us twenty-two more minutes. So if you wouldn't mind, please leave."

"Is anything wrong?" A supervisor entered.

"Yeah, this guy thinks he's at a Marriott or somethin'. He won't leave till checkout."

"Hey, look. We're in the middle of something important here. Just give us a few minutes, and we'll be out of your hair. For God's sake, my poor daughter has been here for over a week, and—"

"Lenny, stop. . . . Please excuse him. We just need another minute."

"Whatever." The supervisor signaled the orderly to return later.

"Now, are you sure this guy was legit? Did he say specifically that he was an estate attorney? 'Cause this is Florida, and the state is crawling with slimeball lawyers who read the obits like they're the comics, then try and get a piece of the action."

"I have no idea what he is. You were so busy screaming in my ear I couldn't hear. All I know is he said his name was Marvin Greenberg . . . and then he said something about a trust fund in my name."

"A trust fund?" My father's eyes lit up like a *menorah* on the eighth night.

"Yeah, and the thing that's so strange is, he said he was already in the process of trying to locate me, because legally he was required to notify me that on my thirtieth birthday, or upon the death of Abe, the money in the trust was mine. Which means I would have found out about him being my grandfather no matter what."

"Oh my God. This is so . . . I don't know." My mother sighed. "*Bashert?* Meant to be?"

"I'll tell you what it is. It's incredible." My father pounded his chest and looked up to thank God, like a ballplayer who just hit one over the fence. "Course I don't have to tell you the income tax on the interest could be . . . phew, don't even ask."

"I'll get the details on Monday, but he called it substantive."

"Substantive?" My father repeated the word like a dreamy-eyed Pinocchio.

"What's substantive mean, Lenny?"

"Are you kidding? It means our worries are over." My father laughed. "Let's say for argument's sake he put away, I don't know, ten grand a year for Claire. . . . If it earned an average of eight percent a year over thirty years?" He did a mental calculation. "Between reinvesting the dividends and compounding, that account could be worth well over a million by now."

"A million dollars?" my mother cried.

"That's right. And I don't have to tell you with how volatile the market's been, our investments have been in the toilet. . . . This could be a big, big help."

"What are you getting at?" I gulped. "I haven't heard anything official yet, and you're already talking like it's your money. . . . It's not your money, it's my money. The trust is in *my* name."

"Whoa. Hold on, there, Claire. Nobody's trying to take anything away from you, honey. I'm just saying, we need to be fair and reasonable here. We made a huge investment in you at our expense. Nobody gave us a dime. Did it strictly out of the goodness of our hearts."

"Oh my God. What are you saying?" I screamed. "To repay you for your kindness, I should hand over my entire inheritance to you?"

"No, of course not. I'm just saying that what we did for you was at a tremendous sacrifice. You have no idea how tough it was for us at the beginning—we had no money, no house, no savings and then we're strapped with a baby we didn't expect—"

"This isn't happening. Tell me this isn't happening."

"Lenny, she's right. This is too much for her to handle right now. . . . When did you say you were meeting the lawyer?"

"Monday morning."

"So fine. I'll fly home with Lindsey and Adam, and Lenny, you stay down here so you can go with her to the meeting."

"No! Sorry. I'm going alone."

"That's ridiculous, Claire." My father sneered. "What do you know about estate settlements, trust funds, probate . . . ?"

"I'll tell you what I know. I know that I can't trust you to make any decisions on my behalf because you're going to be too busy figuring out what your cut should be . . . and as far as I'm concerned, that is NOT your decision to make."

"You're unbelievable!" my father hollered. "Where's the gratitude? The respect?"

"Respect?" I closed my eyes. "You have the nerve to talk to me about respect? Oh my God. Look at the two of you, standing there like the parents of the year. What respect did you show me? You lied to me, you betrayed my trust, you never once bothered to consider how I'd feel if I found out the truth, all these years you've treated me like a burden and a nuisance—"

"We treated you all the same!" My mother shook her finger in my face.

"Bullshit! Everything I ever wanted, you made me feel like I had no right to ask for. But whatever Adam and Lindsey wanted? No problem. I had to pay for every dime of my first car . . . and what happened when Adam turned seventeen? Bingo. Daddy takes him over to the Nissan dealer, and says, 'Go on, son. Pick out something nice.' And for years I begged you to let me go to that great performing arts camp in Wisconsin, and you said, 'Nothing doing. Too much money.' But when Lindsey wanted to go to that stupid gymnastics camp . . . oh my God, the girl didn't know a cartwheel from a Ferris wheel, but suddenly money was no object."

"We were in a better financial position then," my father argued.

"And she was getting so fat. We thought a little exercise over the summer would help."

"Yeah, and you're also wrong about the car." My father sniffed. "Adam paid me back every month once he started working. Gave me a little bit out of his paycheck. Nobody got a free ride."

"He paid you back?" I laughed. "That's a joke. He still owes me the two hundred he borrowed from me when he wanted new rims. You're lying about this like you lied about everything else."

"How dare you open your mouth like that to me!" He raised his hand.

"No, how dare you treat me like an obligation, then suddenly at the mention of a payout we're like best friends."

"I can't believe you would say anything so awful. Can you believe her, Roberta?"

"Claire, you're talking nonsense. We treated you like our own from day one."

"Maybe from your perspective, but I've had a lot of time to think this past week, and I don't remember it that way. I don't remember you coming down on Adam and Lindsey like you came down on me. It's like with me, there was always this grudge or something."

"Oh, pull out the violin for poor little Claire." My father groaned.

"You make it sound like you were little Cinderella sitting by the ashes."

"Well, I'm sorry, but that's how I felt. I tried so hard to make you proud of me. I got great grades, I was captain of the volleyball team, I won all these civic duty awards, I never got into any trouble, and believe me I could have done that big-time."

"Of course we were proud of you," my mother said.

"Then why didn't you ever say it? Why didn't you ever say, 'Claire, we love you and we're proud of you'?"

"Oooh. Let's all go to Claire's pity party," my father snapped. "Sorry, dear. But this is all in your imagination."

"Oh, really? So you remember it differently? You remember putting your arm around me, lavishing me with praise, and telling me you were so proud to be my father?"

"I didn't say I was Ward Cleaver, for Christ's sake."

"And what about you, Mom? You really think you were there for me?"

"Of course I was. I took care of all your needs."

"Exactly. I never missed a dentist appointment. I was up to date on my shots. I got new shoes for school. You weren't my mother, you were my manager. You did everything for me, but nothing with me."

"How dare you attack your mother like this? She tried very hard with you."

"Oh really? Then how come she never took me out to lunch? Or to the city to see a show? Or just out shopping like everyone else's mother?"

"Well, pardon me, but I had two other children to take care of!"

"Yeah. YOUR children."

"You're completely out of line here," my father yelled. "And we don't have to take this."

"You were both so cold to me. All I ever heard was what I did wrong."

"I never missed one of your volleyball games," my mother pointed out.

"Yes, but did you ever cheer for me? Every time I'd look up, the other parents would be going crazy screaming, and there's my mother, blabbing with Elyce's mom. You never once got off your ass to say, 'Go, Claire!'"

"And where were you, Dad? You never even came to my games."

"I was working! That's where I was. Out busting my ass so I could support my family."

"Everybody's father's had jobs, but they found a way to come. And what about my senior year when I had the lead in *Grease*?"

"Oh jeez. Here we go again. How many goddamn times are we going to have to apologize for that?"

"My friends couldn't believe it. You missed all three performances, and then you didn't even send me flowers."

"Well, now, that was your mother's fault. I told her to do something nice . . . and didn't we watch the video like a dozen times?"

"Watch the video?" I yelled. "Oh my God! You think that's the same thing as being there for your child? The same thing as getting to hear the applause, and having everyone tell you how good you were? You think I wasn't mortified when everyone else's parents were waiting outside to say congratulations, and mine were hanging out at some stupid golf outing in Myrtle Beach?"

"It wasn't a stupid golf outing. It was the tenth annual—Oh, what the hell is the difference? You want to stay angry? Be my guest. But this is such crap. We did everything we could to give you a good home, a good education, and this is the thanks we get! A list of bullshit accusations."

"Mr. Greene, please." A nurse walked in. "I'm going to have to ask you to lower your voice. You're disturbing the other patients."

"Fine!" He waved. "We were just leaving. I don't need to stand around listening to my daughter, the ingrate—"

"Lenny, wait. Where are you going?" my mother called after him.

"Go on. Get out of here." I shooed her. "I'm not coming with you."

"What do you mean? We're going back to the hotel now. You have to come."

"Actually, I don't. I'll make other arrangements."

"What other arrangements? You have no place else to go."

"Sure I do. I can call Uncle Ben and Aunt Shari." I sniffed. "I'm sure they'd be happy to let me stay with them for a while."

"Uncle Ben and Aunt Shari?"

My father barreled back in. "Are you coming or not?"

"Claire says she's not coming with us. She's going to call that Ben Fabrikant."

"Good idea. Then we won't have to look at her anymore. Can we please get the hell out of here already?" He tapped his watch. "The meter . . ."

# Chapter 20

THIRTY SECONDS AFTER TELLING MY PARENTS TO LEAVE WITHOUT ME, I panicked. Not because I feared a life without their supervision. Hell, I'd been making my own decisions since junior high. Not because I was about to become a working girl. (Damn! I forgot to ask Pablo if pantyhose was a requirement, because that would definitely be a deal-breaker.) Not even because I was afraid of starting my life over in, of all places, Miami Beach, aka God's waiting room. No. What sent me into an emotional tailspin was that I couldn't remember where I'd left my new clothes.

Given my fragile neurological state, it hurt my head to think about things that had happened hours earlier, let alone an entire week ago. I had to close my eyes and force myself to focus. When was the last time I saw those three beautiful bags from Versace? Finally I remembered. Viktor had taken me to Drew's so I could use the shower, which meant I must have brought the bags upstairs. That was the good news. The bad news was that I had no way to retrieve them. Or worse, that a spiteful Marly could have already returned them. How depressing that I might never get to zip those black silken trousers, or step into those luxuriously rich mules with the tiny silver buckles.

Of course, if my father was right and Abe had left me a big, fat inheritance, money would be no object. But given how my luck was running, I'd probably get handed a check for a few grand, then watch the IRS chew it up and spit it out. All told, I'd end up with a few hundred in the bank. Hardly a life-altering amount.

Who knew, when Viktor was busy yapping about tax breaks, that I'd ever have a reason to stand on a soapbox like him? But speaking of Viktor, maybe I could call and ask if he would be willing to get my things at Drew's, bring them to the hospital, then take me to Ben and Shari's.

I felt bad about leaning on him so heavily, as he was neither my friend nor my employee. But what choice did I have? I was three thousand miles from anything resembling a support network, and now I was broke and homeless, which I would not have been if my parents hadn't stormed out.

Oh, fine. So maybe I'd been a bit hasty in insisting that they leave. But since when did they ever listen to me? Frankly, if they were as devoted as they claimed, they would have told me to stop talking nonsense and to go get my things so they could take me back to the hotel to rest.

But now that wasn't in the option column. Nor was using my room phone, as the line had already been disconnected. And with all the interference, my cell phone was out, too. My only choice was to trudge downstairs in my weakened condition, stand outside in Cancer Alley where the chain smokers congregated, call Viktor, and hope he'd be willing to be my knight in shining limo.

"Not so fast, Miss Greene." A nurse stopped me at the elevator. "You can't be officially discharged unless you're taken down in a wheelchair. Hospital rules."

"So, fine. I'll go down in a wheelchair. By any chance, could I be wheeled to South Beach?"

"There's no one to take you home? Weren't your folks just here a few minutes ago?"

"Yes, but I had to fire them. On account of gross incompetence, negligence—"

"You fired your parents?" She laughed. "Is that one of those California trends?"

"I assure you it was a necessary step. The only ride they wanted to take me on was the one to the bank so they could steal my trust fund."

"Uh-huh. Okay. I have no idea what any of that means, but obviously you need to call someone. I can't just leave you downstairs, dear. What about the rest of your family? The Fabrikants?"

"Oh yeah. I was going to call . . . Uncle Ben." *I will never get used to saying that.*

"Well, given your condition, memory lapses are normal."

"Yes, but how do you explain my parents' memory lapse?" I sighed. "For thirty years they forgot to mention a minor detail to me. . . . Could I please use your phone?"

"Of course. Do you remember his number?"

"Actually, I don't even know his number." I hesitated. "Or his address. In fact, I have no idea where the family lives, if they have room for me to stay . . ."

"Do you want to tell me what's going on here?" She eyed me. "I could call in Social Services, or have you speak to one of our patient advocates. They can do the impossible in situations—"

"No! It won't help! Believe me, they've never dealt with a situation like mine. . . ."

"Oh my. That is quite a story," she said after I told her my sad tale. "Wasn't there was a novel like that? Oh gosh. What was the name of that one?"

"Trust me, the only way it was my story was if it was science fiction."

"You're probably right." She laughed. "So what will you do?"

"I have no idea. For some stupid reason I accepted a job down here. But I have no place to live. . . . I was thinking of rooming with my grandmother in an assisted living center . . . that's a good idea, right? She'll follow me around Miami with plates of food. 'Here, darling. Eat something. It's been twenty minutes.' And how could I live in a city where I have no friends? I mean, I've met a few people. This guy, Viktor, who is very nice, and Drew Fabrikant, of course. It just blows me away that my perfectly unfulfilled life could go even deeper into the toilet."

"Maybe it would help if you called your parents to apologize."

The nurse checked her watch. "I'm sure they would be happy to come back for you."

"Apologize?" I started to cry. "Are you serious? Apologize for what? I'm not the one who did anything wrong. They're the ones who created this whole mess."

"Shhhh." She ushered me back into my room. "Let's not get ourselves worked up. Do you want to have a relapse?"

"I'm sorry." I sniffed. "This is so not like me. I never cry. Now I never stop."

"Well, look, dear. Maybe it's good that everything is out in the open now. You'll get counseling, make a fresh start. It's not the end of the world, you know. . . . Your mother seems like a lovely person. Your father's a bit high-strung, but you weren't abused or neglected. Believe me, I could tell you stories about foster children that would shock you."

"I know it could have been worse. But I don't even recognize my life anymore. I look at my parents, and the first thing that pops into my head is that they're frauds."

"You just need to give it more time."

"Everyone keeps saying that, but it's not going to matter whether it's next week or next year. I'm always going to hate them for what they did."

"Why don't you let me arrange for you to talk with one of the therapists?"

"What for? They're the ones who are crazy . . . I'm just trying to defend myself against a bunch of hypocrites. Do you know that I once got grounded for a month because I lied about where I spent the night? Meanwhile, they were lying to me about something far more horrible! They were the ones who should have been grounded!"

"I'm sure they thought they were doing right by you."

"Nope. Not part of their MO. They did what was right for them. It was a lot less messy than having to tell me the truth and take the chance I'd treat them differently."

"Would you have?"

"I don't know. Maybe. Probably."

"Then don't be so hard on them. They were just acting on instinct. Believe me, as a mother, I can tell you that my husband and I constantly questioned our decisions. Were we too easy on the kids, too hard, should we have pushed them more in school, made them pay for their mistakes? There's no manual for this. Parents have no idea how they'll handle a situation until the damn thing is staring them in the face. . . . Not that I agree with what your folks did. I would have done things differently, but gosh, maybe I wouldn't have. It's so hard to say."

"Yes, but how do you rationalize letting your child believe in something that's a total fabrication?" I cried. "It's like hoping they never learn the truth about Santa Claus, even though you know the day will come when they're gonna find out and have to deal with the disappointment."

"That's my point, dear. You found out the truth later than you would have liked, but at least now you're an adult. You'll be better able to cope with this."

"No, I won't. It's too late. All I understand is that my freakin' life has been turned into an asterisk, like a Sammy Sosa stat. He may have hit sixty-six home runs one year, but underneath in small print it's going to say, *In 2003, his bat was found to be corked.* So is he still a Hall of Fame slugger, or a major league cheater who should be kicked out of the game? My so-called parents raised me as their own, but underneath in small print it's going to say, *Thirty years later, Claire Greene was found not to be their biological child.* Don't you see? The truth changes everything."

"Not everything, dear. It's obvious they love you, no matter how you came into their lives."

"I'm not saying they don't have feelings for me. But right now I feel like I'm operating in this alternate universe. I look at my parents, and I think, don't go with strangers. I'm the same person I was last week, but my whole identity has been changed, like I was put into the Witness Protection Program. I have more family than ever, but I've never felt more alone. I mean, maybe at some point I'll be able to make sense of all this, but right now I am so sad, scared, angry, anxious, hurt . . . and do you know what else? I can't find my clothes!"

"I think you'll be fine." She patted me. "You're a smart girl. You'll get help. Now let's go see about your clothes. Were they in your room?"

"No, actually. I lost track of them before I got here."

"Miss Claire, there you are. What hez heppened to you?"

"Oh my God." I turned around. "Viktor?"

"I just saw yur parents drive off, but yur face—it was not in thi car."

"I have never been so happy to see anyone in my entire life." I hugged him.

"Looks like your ride is here." The nurse cupped my chin. "You take good care of yourself, dear. You'll be in my thoughts."

"Thank you so much for listening."

"It costs nothing. . . . Take care of her," she instructed Viktor. "She's marked *fragile*."

"I am so glad you're here." I wiped my eyes. "Why are you here?"

"This I ken't tell you because it was the oddest thing. I'm driving beck home after taking Drew and Marly to the airport . . . so much traffic you wouldn't believe—"

"Whoa. What do you mean, you took them to the airport? Where did they go?"

"No one told you? They fly to Bermuda to talk about their problems."

"Are you serious? They left the country? I can't believe they're actually going to try to get back together."

"I tell you thi whole family is crezy, em I right? Enyway, on the way beck from thi airport, I get idea in my head that sez, go to thi hospital."

"You mean you weren't planning to come here?"

"End now you are so heppy to see me, em I right?"

"Yes, yes. You're right. . . . What do you think it was? A feeling? A voice in your head?"

Viktor pursed his lips. "More like eh voice in my head."

"Oh my God. I bet it was Abe. I bet he was communicating with you."

"No. Sorry." Viktor howled. "I trick you, Miss Claire. There was no voice."

"What?"

"Ben called me in the car and said go get Claire."

"Really? But how did he know I—"

"Thet I ken't tell you. Maybe Abe called him instead of me."

"Very funny." I smacked his shoulder. "So where are you taking me?"

"Anywhere you like. To your grendmother'z place? To thi hotel for your parents?"

"No. No. I can't go there. . . . Viktor, I've made a mess of things. I don't have anywhere to go. Do you think . . . I was wondering . . . would I be welcome at Ben's house?"

"They have plenty room, off course. But maybe you would like my mother's house. It's no kestle, but there's spare bed in the base-ment from when my Uncle Vladimir was alive."

*Perfect. I'd love to sleep with a ghost and some mice.* "I appreciate the offer, Viktor. But you know what? Maybe I should just go back to California. I miss it so much, all my friends are there, my favorite beaches, the sushi, the Tae-Bo classes on every corner. I can't believe I ever left. . . . I would be so grateful if you took me to the airport."

"But in yur condition, ken you be flying?"

"Of course. It's not like I'll be needed in the copilot's seat. Please, Viktor. I really want to go home. I've been through so much. I just want to feel connected again. . . . I miss the girls with purple hair named Breeze. I miss knowing which restaurants serve the freshest arugula. I miss that when you walk into a Starbucks, the cute guy in the Dodgers cap who looks like John Cusack IS John Cusack."

"Fine. Viktor ken take you . . . it's just that we would all be very sed to see Miss Claire go."

"Thank you." I kissed his cheek. "I'll miss you, too. But I promise I'll come back to visit. See how my grandmother is doing in Abe's place."

"End maybe you come back for Drew and Marly's wedding, em I right?"

"Absolutely." *Over my dead body.* "Oh wait, wait, wait. There is one thing before we go. You know those clothes from Versace that Marly picked out for me? I left them at Drew's. Do you think we could stop there first, and then go to the airport?"

"Oh. Uh-huh. No. Because there's something I must tell you, princess. Thi bags? They are in my trunk. I was supposed to return them, but I forget."

"Return them?" I gasped. "No way. Why?" *Let me guess.*

"If you esk me, it is not right. But Marly said to take it all beck since you didn't need thi clothes for the funeral. But I'm thinking to myself, a gift is a gift."

"Exactly. A gift is a gift. Oh God. Please don't return them, Viktor. They are the most exquisite clothes I've ever come close to owning."

"So maybe I should hev talk with Ben? She did not pay, why should she say?"

"Yes, exactly!" I clapped. "C'mon. Let's go downstairs and call Uncle Ben."

But before I could figure out that a call to him would set off a chain reaction of questions about my plans that I did not want to answer, Viktor was speed dialing. And although I couldn't make out the conversation on the other end, I could see from his expression that it wasn't going well.

Yeesh. I was probably coming off as this selfish little brat who thought that I was entitled to lavish gifts for no reason at all. Which I did. But still, I didn't want this to be Ben's last impression of me before I flew home. Especially since he had already been so generous.

"He hez to speak to you." Viktor handed me his cell. "He is not heppy."

*Shit!* "Hi, Ben . . . Uncle Ben. Look, I'm very sorry. You're right, of course. The clothes should go right back. They were bought with a specific purpose in mind, and—"

"Thet's not it," Viktor whispered.

"What?" I said to Ben.

"Oh right. The meeting on Monday with the lawyer. I swear, the way my mind is working, or not working, I'd already forgotten about it. But wait. How do *you* know about that meeting?"

"Oh. . . . Uh-huh. . . . No. To be honest, I have no idea what an executor of the estate does. . . . Really? So wait. You'll be there, too? . . . Um, no. My parents aren't coming . . . long story . . . basically I'm not speaking to them. . . . Actually, no. I don't have a place to stay. . . . Are you sure? . . . Thank you. That is such a generous offer. . . . Yes, they just discharged me. . . . Okay, I'll ask Viktor to bring me over. Oh, and about those clothes? . . . Are you sure? . . . Thank you, thank you, thank you. . . . He says I can keep them because I'm staying for a few more days," I whispered to Viktor. "Oh . . . uh-huh. No, I'm sorry. I didn't know that. . . . Okay, well, not to worry. I know how to handle it. It's very California. . . . See you in a few."

"He told you?" Viktor asked.

"Yes. And I feel terrible. Is that why you didn't want me to stay there?"

"It's not too good, thi marriage. He goes beck and forth between condo and house. But now, less beck than forth."

"So wait. Is he living there at all?"

"Not so much, no. He wouldn't get divorce while Abe was alive, but now, I'm sure yes."

"Oh yuck. Maybe this wasn't such a good idea after all. Shari might not want me around."

"No, it's okay. She likes you. And her loverz? Not so terrible. . . ."

"Lovers?"

"Boy toys, flings, what you call them?"

"Oh gross. I get the point. I'm just not sure I could deal with any of that kind of stuff right now."

"You get used to it. Except for thi one from Areezona. Him I don't ker for. I tell Ben, wotch out. This one wants yur money."

"Are you serious? Ben knows about her lovers?"

"Of course. They hev understanding. She hez hers, he hez his . . . do-si-do and 'round they go. . . . Beck last summer, they fix up couple . . . lovers of therz they thought would be better together."

"Oh God. That's insane. It sounds like they both tested positive for stupid."

"Ectually, Shari is very smart girl. Except she is crezy with the woo-woo people."

"The who?"

"You know. Thi psychics, thi astrologers, thi gypsies with thi crazy cards. And then thi different loverz . . . you wouldn't beleeve what goes on in thet house."

"Oh God. Poor Delia. No wonder she walks around like a rebel without a clue."

"So now maybe you ken take her under yur wing. Be thi big sister, em I right?"

*Actually, I'd rather be the big sister-in-law. Any chance of helping me make that happen?*

This will probably sound stupid, but ever since I was a kid, responsible for garbage patrol at home, I've played the same silly game. Whenever I go to someone else's place, I secretly count the number of wastebaskets, and try to figure out who had the harder job—them or me. But multimillion-dollar mansions in Malibu would be considered quaint compared to the huge, scary, hundred-and-twenty-seven-wastebasket estate that Ben, Shari, and Delia called home.

It wasn't that they didn't have enough room for me—they had too much room. A choice of guest suites in the main house, or if I preferred my privacy, as Ben assumed I would, I could stay in one of the two guest houses on the property. And not to worry about getting back to the main house for meals, he told me. A quick call to the head groundskeeper, and a shuttle would be sent to fetch me.

Trouble was, I was already feeling so disoriented and alone. How could I spend the next few days padding around an eerily quiet, almost Temple of Doomish house that had a sitting room, which was not to be confused with the library, which was not to be confused with the living room, which was not to be confused with the great room? And that was just the first floor.

But what was even more disconcerting than trying to grasp the enormity of the place was realizing that it was virtually uninhabited. Unlike normal peoples' houses, there was no mountain of shoes by the door. No blasting stereos or TVs. No one screaming, "Where the hell is my North Face?"

The other thing I didn't quite get was how people with bottomless bank accounts could still end up with decor by the design firm of Taste Up Your Ass, Inc. Good Lord. Didn't the words *gaudy, ostentatious,* and *Hearst Castle* mean anything to Ben and Shari?

As they showed me around, calling attention to this work of art or that one-of-a-kind piece, I felt as if I were taking a tour with two vision-impaired guides. I kept thinking, don't you see what I see? You paid a fortune for this stuff, only to end up with a hodgepodge of Native American French country Hadassah, with a dab of southwestern art deco Tibetan monastery thrown in for good luck.

If I were smart, I would run back outside, hop into Viktor's limo, and make him take me to Miami International, where I would board a plane for Dayton or Dubuque, or some other place where common folk shopped at Levitz, and were elated if they got zero percent financing and the free end table with the purchase of a couch and two love seats.

"If you see anything you'd like to have, just let me know." Shari rubbed my arm.

"I'm sorry?" I nearly collided with the copper Buddahs with water spraying out their navels.

"We're putting the place up for sale soon," she sighed. "So before everything goes up at auction, if there's a piece you love, be my guest."

"Oh. Wow. That is so generous of you to offer." *Are you joking? You should be stocking up on charcoal and lighter fluid.*

"Yeah, absolutely." Ben nodded. "Just point and it's yours."

"You guys are being so sweet." I hugged them. "But at the moment, I don't have a place to hang my clothes, let alone something as beautiful as . . . as . . . that statue." *Is that Heather Locklear sucking on a gas pipe?*

"Of course." Shari took my hand. "What I was thinking? The last thing on your mind is decorating."

"Exactly." Ben coughed. "Why don't I take you down to the guest villa now?"

"No, Ben. I don't think Claire would be comfortable there."

"Why not? She'll have total privacy, plenty of peace and quiet."

"Actually"—I looked down—"I am feeling sort of spooked at the moment. I think I would prefer to have . . . you know . . . people around. Just in case of anything."

"Oh. Well, sure. I can understand that. And we've got plenty of room right here."

*Duh. The Beverly Hills Hotel is not this big.* "Anywhere you put me is fine. Really."

"What about Drew's room?" Ben asked.

*Oh my God . . . I love you.* "Oh no . . . I wouldn't want to disturb his things."

"I agree," Shari said. "And there are so many other choices."

"No. It's perfect, Claire," Ben picked up my suitcase. "There's a TV room, a nice big bathroom, a computer area . . ."

"A computer area?" I clapped. "That would be incredible. I haven't checked my e-mail in like a hundred years."

"Well, don't get too excited," Ben said. "It's still got the old dial-up service."

"No, it doesn't," Shari snapped. "Don't you remember? Last year I had Chuck wire the upstairs for high-speed Internet. . . . Oh, that's right. You've hardly been here."

"Apparently I missed the memo. Come on, Claire. Let's get you settled."

"Well, wait. Maybe she's hungry or thirsty. Claire, can we get you some lunch first?"

"A cup of coffee would be great . . . unless it's a hassle."

"Are you kidding?" Ben picked up my bags. "Nothing's ever a hassle for Shari. She's got one butler for regular, and another for decaf."

"Fuck. You."

"No, fuck you."

"Really. It's okay." I sighed. "I just want to lie down." *And wake up in California.*

# Chapter 21

I HAD A TERRIBLE MEMORY TO START WITH, SO JUST IMAGINE MY memory capacity after my big fall. I couldn't remember the name of a play from ten months ago. And I was in it! Mind you, a drive-by shooting lasted longer than the run of that show. But still, I wanted to remember its name because the character I played, Rebecca something, reminded me very much of Drew's mother. They were both so rich and bored, they had time not only to awaken their consciousness but to become active members of the Affair of the Month Club.

Not that I was passing judgement on Shari. In spite of her alleged extracurricular pursuits, I'd found her to be sweet and nurturing. And at least, unlike her wealthy, disenchanted sisters on the West Coast, she hadn't joined the local Buddhist Monk Society.

Thank God, because I couldn't have listened to one more Dalai Lama convert preach the need to rise at four A.M. for medication and prayer. (Did I say medication? I meant meditation.) Nor could I deal with another pampered princess who insisted that the key to inner peace and tranquillity was shedding all worldly possessions, only to pull up a week later in a Mercedes convertible.

On the other hand, what did it matter that Shari spent her days sipping wheat grass while trying to find her inner bliss? At least she knew who she was. Unlike me, who was suddenly minus an identity, thanks to the tsunami of all sea changes.

I might have sulked for hours in Drew's room, if not for a sudden rush of energy. An unexplainable force that nearly catapulted me off the bed and propelled me in the direction of his desk. At first I tried to resist the pull, but the thrust was too great. I was a puppet on a string who would dance at the whim of his master.

"Abe?" I whispered. "I mean, Grandpa Abe?"

No answer. Had I officially gone mad? How would I know? Would I receive a notice in the mail? Would a bunch of characters from a Woody Allen film show up with straitjackets? Trouble was, I didn't believe for a second that I was crazy. To the contrary, I knew with every fiber of my being that a force more powerful than free will had prodded me off the bed. A force that was tangible proof of my grandfather's nearness.

For as I stood amid a boy's bedroom with its scattered memorabilia and remnants of a treasured past, I knew what he wanted me to see. This wasn't just any boy's room. It was Drew's room. It was Drew's guitar and giant stuffed panda resting in the corner. His tennis racket perched against the dresser. His golden lacrosse trophies lining the bookshelves. His photos of friends and family gracing his desk.

And then it struck me. The chronicles of Drew Fabrikant's youth made me feel safe, as if by inhaling his scent and absorbing his saga I were bonding with the boy who had comforted me like no other. Who had befriended me and believed in me, purely on instinct, like a trusting young child. If only we could live in the warm shadow of innocence forever.

I don't know why this little fantasy made me crave a cigarette. I'd quit years ago, after my dermatologist showed me pictures of forty-year-old smokers who looked sixty after a lifetime of spewing nicotine on their snakeskinned faces. "This lady had more lines than a Barrymore," I believe was the sentence that convinced me to break the bad habit.

Then Sir Guilt rode in on his white horse. I needed a nicotine fix like I needed another hole in the back of my head. And I should not be traipsing through Drew's personal effects without his expressed, written consent. I would go berserk if I ever found out that someone had violated my privacy without regard for my feelings.

I shut the drawer and decided if there was to be any snooping, it should be on my own life. Of course. I should be checking my voice mail, something I'd been unable to do at the hospital because I couldn't get service. And what about my e-mail? (Lord knows how many hundreds of spams were awaiting me.) Good. Now I had a goal. Project Get Claire Back into Her Own Life.

I fetched my cell, plopped down on Drew's big, comfy bed, concentrated really hard so that I could remember how to retrieve messages, and waited to hear my mechanical man say, "You have [long pause] seventy-four messages." Good God. I didn't even know he could count that high.

Do I need to tell you how many of those messages were from Elyce? And seven calls were from Sydney: "Call me the instant you get this . . . I'm on the next plane. Just tell me where to meet you. . . . I miss you so much. . . . Baking brownies. . . . Please come home." Ten calls were from other friends in L.A., and one was from Pablo inquiring about my health, and if there was any chance I still intended to take the job. The rest were from my parents, who vacillated between sounding contrite and sounding indignant. "Call us, honey. We're very concerned." Then, "What nerve you have accusing us of being bad parents."

I'd heard enough. Time to switch to my other communication vice. And thank God Shari had been savvy enough to recognize the importance of quick connects. Within moments I was back on AOL. It was so good to hear my friend, the "You've got Mail" man. But was I reading right? I had 614 e-mails?

As I scanned the list, I had to laugh. There were a few dozen get-well messages, and the rest were spam. But good news. With all the money I could save by refinancing my mortgage, I could afford to buy a lifetime supply of Viagra to enhance the pleasure of my newly enlarged penis.

While in a delete, delete, delete mode, I did stumble on a money-making opportunity in an e-mail from a modeling agency that specialized in sending look-alikes to car shows. If I got in touch fast, I might still be able to reprise my former role as Darryl Hannah at the Buick booth in Chicago. Had I really once done that? Yes.

Nothing like stepping back into your old life after a short hiatus, and getting smacked in the face with the realization that your days had been filled with absurd, trivial pursuits. In fact, it seemed as if my entire existence bordered on banal and insignificant. Unlike my grandfather's life, which had had great meaning and purpose.

If I was truly as anxious to repent for my sins, I would make it my life's work to learn more about Abraham Fabrikant's good deeds. But not only learn about them, emulate them. As a loving tribute to the grandfather I never knew, I would carry on where he left off.

Maybe what I would do was try to get acquainted with my subject. Look through Drew's desk for things that would shed insight into this remarkable man's life, like pictures or birthday cards. And, of course, if I also learned a thing or two about darling Drew, something that clued me in on where his head and heart were at, I wouldn't complain.

"What the hell are you doing?" A loud voice startled me.

"Oh my God, Delia. I'm sorry." *How long have I been sitting here?*

"Man, he would be so pissed off if he saw you reading his stuff!"

"I am so sorry. I don't know what I was thinking. Please don't say anything to him. I promise I'll put everything back the way it was."

"Wait." She eyed my bags. "Are you staying here? 'Cause guests usually stay in the villas."

"I know. But I was afraid to be down there by myself. Your dad suggested it."

"Are you crying?"

"No. Uh-uh." I dabbed my eye. "I was just reading some of Drew's poetry. It's beautiful."

"It's not poetry, you idiot. They're words to songs."

"Oh. Of course. Lyrics. . . . Well, I think they're amazing."

"They all sound the same to me."

*Did someone forget to take her happy pills?* "I didn't even hear you walk in." I cleared my throat. "I guess I'm still so out of it."

"Whatever. . . . You better put that all back before my mother sees you. She doesn't even like it when I come in here. God forbid Drew's precious little things get touched."

"I think you're lucky to have a mom who's sentimental. When I left for college, mine didn't even wait till I was finished packing the car before she started hauling things to the curb. It's a good thing they didn't have eBay back then"—I smiled—"or I might have had to bid on my own stuff."

"Yeah, I feel real sorry for you. Just don't let her catch you going through his desk, or you'll be on her shit list forever."

"Yep. Got it. Thanks for the heads up." I quickly gathered the loose-leaf papers on which Drew had so poignantly captured his romantic voice, then carefully placed them back in the drawer.

"What are you doing here anyway? I thought you were going back to New York."

"I was. Then I changed my mind."

"Why? So you could spend more time with my brother?"

"What? No, of course not. My doctors wanted me to wait a few days before I flew. Besides, I thought I could use the time to make some decisions about what I want to do next." *Bitch*.

"Or see who else you could sponge off of." Delia checked her hair in the mirror.

"Okay, look. I know I'm not exactly of sound mind and body yet, but are you mad at me?"

"I don't even know you."

"Exactly. So what's with the attitude?"

"I just don't think you had any right going through my brother's drawers."

"And I agree with you. I fucked up. I'm sorry."

"Whatever."

"But those songs he wrote . . . I thought they were amazing."

"No one knows about them, okay? So like don't go running to tell my mother because she'll have no idea what the hell you're talking about."

"Are you serious? She doesn't know her son is a poet?"

"He's not a poet, okay? He's a podiatrist. Not that he ever had to actually touch anyone's smelly, disgusting feet. . . . Daddy to the rescue."

*Now, here's a case where a little Ecstasy might be helpful.* "And what about you? What do you do? Do you go to school?"

"Duh. No. I'm over that."

"Oh. So do you work for your dad?" *'Cause I hear there's a lot of that going around.*

"When I feel like it."

"So . . . like what is your thing?"

Delia shrugged. "I was thinkin' I'd tell Aunt Penny I should be in one of her movies."

"Seriously? You'd like to be an actress?" *That's awesome, because there is such a shortage of real talent out there.*

"I didn't say act. I just want to be in a movie."

"Oh, you mean as an extra."

"No." She sniffed. "I'd want to talk and stuff. I just don't have to be the star like Aunt Penny. I could play one of those girls who dresses like a slut and talks like a lawyer. Like Julia Roberts did. How hard could that be?"

*Oh, I know. Nothing is easier than learning a hundred twenty pages of dialogue.* "I don't know if you know this, Delia, but I'm an actress. Maybe I could give you a few pointers."

"Yeah, but Drew said you weren't in anything he ever heard of."

"Well, no. But I was supposed to do a film with Adam Sandler. Then he had this whole big fight with the studio, and the deal fell apart. Which unfortunately happens a lot."

"It's never happened to Aunt Penny."

*Don't mess with me. I know where to get a gun.*

"So what are you girls gabbing about?" Shari walked in.

*About the penalty for murder in Florida.*

"Um, we were just deciding who we hate more." I smiled. "Brittney Spears or Christina Aguilera."

"*Hate* is such an extreme word, don't you think?" Shari smoothed her daughter's hair.

*You wouldn't say that if you knew my agent.* "You sound like my mother."

"That's 'cause they all take this class called, How to Annoy the Shit out of Your Kids."

"Delia, spare me the antics. . . . Claire, I really came up to see if you were ready for some lunch."

"Thanks, but I'm not hungry right now."

"Actually, my concern is all those prescriptions they gave you. It's not good to take medication on an empty stomach."

"Oh my God, Mother. You are so damn annoying. Does Claire look like she's two?"

"It's fine." I smiled. "I should be taking my pills with food. How did you know?"

"Your mother called to remind you. And I wasn't going to say anything, but your father called before, too."

"Are you serious? Why?"

"To ask if we could pick you up at the hospital. I guess you wouldn't leave with them?"

*So much for Viktor's divine inspiration.* "Uh-huh."

"This is none of my business, of course. But they're very worried about you. Don't you think it would better for everyone if you tried working out your issues?"

"And don't you think it would be better for everyone if you minded your own business, Mother? If Claire wants to be pissed at her family, what's it to you? Besides, the way you and Daddy have screwed everything up around here, you're hardly the one to lecture about keeping a family together."

"I can't hear you." Shari turned on her heels. "Claire, I'd be very grateful if you came down for a bite to eat."

"I will. I promise."

"You don't have to be so nice to her." Delia played with a paperweight on Drew's desk.

"Why not?" I sat on the bed. "She's been very sweet to me."

"Only 'cause she hasn't figured out you're full of shit yet."

"Excuse me?"

"None of them have. Except me."

"I'm sorry?"

"Yeah. You're like this pathological liar."

"Oh my God, Delia. What a horrible thing to say. I can't believe after all I've been through that you would try to hurt my feelings like that." *Uh-oh!*

"If that's the best you can act, no wonder you're not famous. You know before, when you told my mom we were talking about Brittney Spears? Why did you lie?"

"I don't know. You told me not to say anything about Drew's poetry, so I said the first thing that popped into my head."

"Like you did when you met my dad and Drew? You just made stuff up?"

"Okay." My heart pounded. "You know what? I don't know what your drug of choice is—"

"It must be the same as yours, 'cause you may think you fooled everyone, but I heard your bullshit little story, and I don't know who you talked to on that flight, but it sure as hell wasn't my Pops."

*Shit.* "I don't know what you're talking about, Delia. Were you there? Because I don't remember seeing you."

"I didn't have to be there. I knew my Pops, and there was no freakin' way he would have sat there doing stupid crossword puzzles with you."

*Houston, we have a problem.* "Really?" I swallowed. "Why not?"

" 'Cause they made him feel dumb, that's why."

"Dumb."

"Yeah, dumb. After he escaped Germany and came to America, he used to get the crap beat out of him every time the kids at school heard his accent."

"I'm sorry. I'm not following you."

"He never liked speaking English 'cause he was always afraid of being teased, or people thinking he wasn't smart because he didn't know the right words to say. . . . That's why he hated doing speeches and stuff, even though he was asked like all the time. Believe me,

I knew my Pops. The last thing he would have done was sit there figuring out a seven-letter word for *appetizer*."

"He was just trying to be polite."

"Not his style." Delia glared. "That's how I know you're as fake as your Louie."

Why I bothered staring at my own pocketbook I had no idea. It *was* a fake. Although compared to the ones sold by the street vendors with the cheap zippers and glued-on logos, it was a good fake.

"I never said we spent hours at it. All I said was—"

"It makes me want to puke that you're trying to take advantage of my family."

"I swear, Delia, I'm not trying to do any such thing. I told them the truth."

"Really? Even that whole business about Pops having friends where he lived?"

"I didn't say they had sleepovers." I gulped. "I just said he found some men to play cards with."

"No. Sorry. Thanks for playing." She honked. "This is a guy who spent his whole life raising money, meeting with world leaders . . . he never would have sat on his ass all day playing cards."

"He said he liked having the company."

"He could give a shit about company, okay? I know for a fact because I visited him before he left for New York, and he told me he doubted anyone would even notice he was gone, because he hadn't made a single friend. Everyone there was too busy complaining about their aches and pains and their ungrateful children. Nobody liked to talk about books or movies. It was killing him to be so idle. In fact he said that as soon as he got back, he was telling my dad to start looking for another place for him."

"I . . . um . . . don't remember him saying anything like that."

"Course not. It's hard to remember shit that never happened."

"Delia, this is insane. You're making it sound like I made this whole thing up."

"Yeah, 'cause you did. . . . I even called the airline and talked to one of the flight attendants, and she told me everything."

*Oh God. She knows how to play "Liar Liar."* "What's 'everything'?"

"Like that after he had the heart attack, you had to check his wallet for ID because you had no idea what his name was?"

I blinked hard, hopeful that it would hold back my tears. Never did I think that the dawn of my undoing would be at the hands of a little brat whose only skill was nailing counterfeit pocketbooks.

"Which means that this whole big thing with your parents is a bunch of crap," Delia yelled. "How can you be all bent out of shape that they lied to you, if you're exactly like them?"

*Is she right?* "Is . . . does . . . do your father and Drew know anything?"

"Hell if I know. It's not exactly like we sit around the kitchen table talking over Cheerios."

"I don't know what to say, Delia." I blew into a tissue. "I feel so . . ."

"I could give a shit how you feel. I just don't want you staying at my house, okay? I don't like you, I don't trust you."

"You know what? Right now I don't like me or trust me, either. But I still need you to believe me. . . . He looked like a typical old guy. I had no idea who he was, that he was rich. The only reason I got off the plane in Jacksonville was because I was trying to stop feeling so damn guilty for ignoring him the whole flight." *Oh crap!*

"What?" Delia choked. "Are you saying you never even talked to him?"

I looked down.

"Oh my God. You're an even bigger asshole than I thought."

"I'm not an asshole, okay? You have to believe me. I'm really a nice person. I was just depressed. I needed to be alone. The way I was feeling that morning, I wouldn't have talked to anyone."

"I can't fucking believe you! You ignored him the whole time, then got off the plane and made up that whole bullshit story? You're a psycho!"

"I was just trying to help, okay? I thought if I told your dad and Drew that Abe didn't die alone, that he'd made a friend, they'd be comforted by that, and they were. But then they were so happy to hear what I was saying, I guess I got a little carried away."

"You guess? Oh my God. You fucking told them that my Pops was proud of both of them."

"Well, I'm sure he was."

"You are so pathetic. You put words into a dead man's mouth. No wonder all this bad shit's happening. It's 'cause you deserve to get your ass kicked. You're a horrible person."

"No, I'm not. I swear. I'm a good person who made a mistake, okay?"

And that was that. Without any sort of drumroll, I folded like a house of cards, collapsing on the floor like a battered rag doll. I didn't have the strength to argue, or the mental prowess to smash a return over the net like Venus Williams. Delia won. She beat me. She said I was a horrible person, and she was right. I deserved all of this pain and misfortune.

"It doesn't matter whether you believe me. But this is the absolute truth. When I was in the hospital, I was praying to die. I kept thinking, how am I going to live the rest of my life knowing that I did something so shitty? Especially to such a good, kind man. It's like finding out you snubbed Santa Claus the day after he delivered millions of toys to needy children. And then on top of that to find out that he was my grandfather. And that my own grandmother set it up so that we'd meet on the plane. And that I blew my one and only chance to ever talk to him. . . . Delia, I swear, if you want me to be punished for what I did, you are getting your wish. There is nothing you could say that could make me feel any worse than I do right now.

"My life is completely fucked up. It's like I've been disconnected from everything I know, like when they pulled all those tubes out of me in the hospital. . . . No way am I ever going to be able to think of my parents as my real parents. They're just going to be the people who took me in out of pity. . . . And maybe I'm supposed to feel grateful to them, but I don't. I'm so angry that they hid the truth from me. I will never be able to see that as anything other than arrogant and cruel.

"And then to find out that my real mother is this big, famous Hollywood star who I've always idolized, and she was right under my nose all these years while I was out there killing myself to get these nothing parts, and that my father died when he was even younger than me? It's fucking crazy.

"But that's not even the worst of it. You're right about something else. I do have feelings for Drew. I think he's wonderful. He's smart and funny and sensitive . . . and after reading the lyrics he wrote, I'm even more crazy about him. But what difference does it make? He's in love with another woman, not to mention he's my first cousin. So there is no chance I'll ever be with the one man I know I could love forever.

"I really want to die, Delia. I do. . . . I don't think I'll ever get past all of this. It's too much. It's just too much."

"What's going on in here?" Shari rushed in. "I was just in a deep meditative state when I realized I heard crying."

I couldn't look up at her. Couldn't face another Fabrikant who was about to make a horrible discovery about me.

"Um. Nothing," Delia said quietly. "She's just sad right now. I guess everything hit her at once."

*Hello?* I peeked, and saw that Delia was both pale and shaken. Did that mean she had a heart after all?

"Oh, you poor thing." Shari knelt down to hug me. "You poor, poor thing. . . . But don't worry, Claire. You've come to the right place. We'll take good care of you. Whatever it takes. We'll help you heal. Won't we, Delia?"

"Yeah." Delia smoothed my hair. "Definitely."

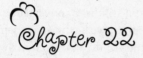

# Chapter 22

I<small>F A FILM DIRECTOR WAS SHOOTING THE FOLLOWING SCENE, HERE IS</small> what audiences would see up on the big screen:

Angle on: A compassionate mother and daughter, S<small>HARI</small> and D<small>ELIA</small>, caring for a grief-stricken young woman (C<small>LAIRE</small>) too incapacitated to care for herself. Their gestures seem instinctive, as if they are following ancient customs and traditions.

Angle on: Claire being tucked into Drew's sumptuous bed and brought a tray of food. She is void of emotion and oblivious to her caregivers' efforts.

Angle on: Shari and Delia speak to Claire in hushed tones so as not to agitate her.

Cut.

The thing is, that scene actually took place. Only I wasn't there. Well, I was, but I wasn't. I have no idea how, but somewhere between Delia deciding she felt sorry for me and Shari deciding she was going to make it her mission to help me heal, I left the physical plane of existence and witnessed this entire scene from an aerial view.

I'm not joking. I actually watched Shari grab a pair of sweats and a University of Miami T-shirt from Drew's dresser, help me change, tuck me into bed, then instruct Delia to bring me a tray of food.

I was sure I was dreaming, except that the images seemed so real. Normally my dreams look like outtakes from *Candid Camera*: mortifying situations at the hands of a prankster. Which made me wonder:

If I wasn't dreaming, was I dead? Had God decided he'd heard enough of my *kvetching* and said, "Fine, Claire. You don't want to live anymore? You're outahere."

But how could I be dead? I could still hear conversations. Could still smell the jasmine tea, and the toast with strawberry jam. Could still feel the sadness in my heart, and the dread of tomorrow.

So if I wasn't dreaming and I wasn't dead, then what was I?

Sydney and a bunch of her Looney Tune friends were into this thing called astral travel, where they'd all sit around and try to leave their physical bodies for dimensions unknown. Frankly, I thought all of that paranormal stuff was a bunch of hooey, which is why I would tell her that no, I wasn't interested in visiting a parallel universe. I was having a hard enough time getting along in this one. And that if she and her friends were so interested in group travel, they should check out Caribbean cruises.

But what if I was wrong? What if it was possible to check out for a while? To leave your body, while your soul traveled? It might explain how it was me, Claire, curled in bed, crying in Drew's pillow, and at the same time, me, Claire, fluttering overhead like the Flying Nun. Might explain how the longer I hovered, the more vivid the colors in the room turned, as if a brilliant, sacred beam of light was shining through.

Then I saw it. The vibrating, silver cord connecting my physical body to my soul like a fibrous web. And it hit me. Ready or not, I was having an out-of-body experience. And no sooner did I give credence to this possibility than my astral travel agent appeared.

"Oh jeez, Grandpa Abe. You scared me to death."

"That's not a very popular expression over here," he laughed.

"Really? Because no one wants to be dead?"

"Because there is no such thing as dead. We retain the same energy force here that we do on earth, only without physical form. . . . Now tell me. How does it feel to be light and free?"

"I don't know. Like yogurt? I guess it feels nice. Are you sure I'm not dead?"

"No, Claire. You are very much alive."

"And very confused . . . I have a hell of a lot of questions for you."

"There is no hell, as there is no heaven."

"Gee. Doesn't that pretty much put the Catholic church out of business?"

"It puts every religion out of business. Once you cross over, you have returned home to the peaceful universe from which you arrived, and it is safe, and free of judgment."

"Okay, now I get it. This *is* a dream, and we're in a remake of *Oh, God.* You're George Burns, and I landed the Teri Garr part."

"No."

"So then what *is* happening? Please don't tell me this is an out-of-body experience."

"I prefer to call it soul travel."

"Is that anything like *Soul Train*? Because I loved that show growing up."

"Sorry, no. But you'll be happy to know that you are about to embark on a distant journey, where you will reunite with the spirits you have known and loved through many lifetimes."

"How distant? Enough to rack up frequent flyer miles? Because if I am traveling to another dimension, that should be worth a lot, right?"

"It is worth more than you can imagine, Claire. I am going to help you return to the light, and remember why you chose this life path."

"Wait, wait, wait. You're saying I purposely picked a life that involved pain and misery? Because that I'm not buying. Who would be stupid enough to volunteer for a life as pathetic as mine? See how miserable I am down there? I'm sad, I'm scared, I'm—"

"Going to be fine."

"How can you be sure?"

"Because you are surrounded by guardian angels who are guiding and protecting you."

"Well, I hope they're not expecting a raise anytime soon, because it seems to me that they've been asleep at the wheel. My life is a disaster. Can't you see that?"

"I can see that you are struggling to make sense of your karmic lessons."

"Wait. . . . How do I know you're not just any old spirit? If you were my grandfather, you'd know exactly what I was going through. . . . Where's your German accent? Do you have identification?"

"I have no pants. Where would I keep it?"

"Good point. But can you prove you're him? Can you tell me about my life down there?"

"Yes. That is my other granddaughter Delia, a twenty-two-year-old lost soul, and her mother, Shari Deveraux Fabrikant, a fifty-two year old lost soul. You are Hannah Claire Fabrikant Greene, a thirty-year old actress from Long Island who recently made some startling discoveries about your past after the man seated next to you on a flight—that would be me—passed over on your lap."

"So I guess it is you. But then why are you being so nice to me? I treated you like—"

"I know."

"I am very sorry," I said. "You have no idea how bad I feel. I was already so miserable. . . ."

"And I am sorry, too. It is why I could not leave you."

"Why should you be sorry? You at least tried to talk to me. I'm the one who blew you off."

"No, dear. I did it first—when you were born. I'm the one who made the terrible mistake of abandoning you when you needed my help. I could have done so much more."

"Hey, yeah. That's right. You could have done so much more. You could have made Penelope take responsibility for me. You could have sent Grams the money you promised. You could have—"

"Done the courageous thing instead of choosing to do nothing at all. . . . It was a difficult time for me. . . . Helping strangers, but not my own family. . . . I couldn't bear the truth that I had raised a selfish, irresponsible daughter who shared none of my values. But I knew that with a nice family to raise you, you'd be better off than most. And that was that. Until one morning I woke up and said to myself that before I die, I must meet you."

"So wait. You knew you were going to have a heart attack on the plane?"

"No." He laughed. "That came as a surprise."

"Oh wow." I shivered. "I don't know what to say."

"Think how I felt. But it's not words that matter now, dear. It's understanding and forgiveness."

"Are you saying that you forgive me? Because that would really help me so much."

"Yes, I forgive you, Claire. And I understand why you didn't speak to me. . . . Do you feel better?"

"Yes. Definitely."

"Then don't you think that if you could forgive and understand the people you are angry with, they would feel better, too?"

"I don't care how they feel. They did something far worse than me."

"No, they did something far better. They didn't look the other way. They opened their hearts. Raised you as their own. Shared whatever they had."

"Yes, but they taught me never to lie, and then they deceived me big-time. They're hypocrites."

"It takes one to know one, dear. Didn't you refuse to acknowledge me, and then lie to my family? Your parents didn't lie to you, Claire. They just chose to shield you from the painful truth. It's not the same thing."

I could not answer.

"Let me save you from a lifetime of hurt. Forgive yourself. Forgive your family. Forgive my daughter—"

"NO!"

"Why not?"

"Because . . . I don't know . . . This may sound stupid, but . . . I think I like anger. It's safe."

"Anger makes you feel safe?"

"Well, maybe not safe. It's just that I understand it better because I got so much practice as a kid. I mean, think about it. When you're little, and you're mad at someone, or things aren't going your way, you get to scream, slam doors, have a tantrum, be mean, and everyone puts up with you.

"Then you grow up, and all of a sudden it's not okay to react that way anymore, except that it's the only response that feels normal. Oh, and anger gives you the perfect excuse to act crazy, get stoned, not pay your bills, eat Doritos in bed. . . ."

"But it can also be an excuse to hide from the truth and feel self-pity."

"True."

"Claire, anger is a luxury you can't afford, because the price tag is paid in the currency of pain."

"Were you this smart on earth, Grandpa?"

"I wish I had been."

"But you have to admit, I do have a lot of good reasons to be angry."

"I think you have a lot of good reasons to be grateful."

"Can't I be both?"

"Not if you want to move on."

"Hey, look." I pointed to myself. "I'm smiling. . . . How come they don't know I'm gone?"

"You're not gone. You are there. And here."

"I gotta tell you. As neat as this little talk is, it's still a little creepy."

"It shouldn't be. You often return to the other side."

"I don't believe you."

"Have you ever noticed that when burdened by a problem, somehow things look different in the morning? Maybe you wake up with an idea or an answer?"

"I guess. Yeah, that's happened."

"Where did the ideas come from? Was it coincidence that you suddenly knew what to do?"

"I don't know. Are you telling me that thoughts are put into our heads?"

"Exactly. And have you ever dreamt you were flying, but there was no plane? Or felt you were falling, but didn't get hurt? Have you ever been awoken by a sudden jolt?"

"I think so."

"That was your soul reentering your body. Sometimes it goes smoothly. Other times there is an urgency to the return, and the vibrations are so strong, the landing can be quite abrupt."

"Really? . . . and what exactly do we do over here? Look for long-lost relatives?"

"Sometimes you reunite with those you have loved and lost. Other times you come in search of reassurance, courage, patience, answers. Every journey is different."

"So what's going to happen when I go back? Will all my problems be over?"

"That is quite up to you."

"Okay. Well, can you tell me this: Is there any chance I'll hook up with Drew? I really want to know, because I'm in love with him."

"Yes, I see that."

"But you have to tell me before my heart breaks. Is he going to marry Marly or not?"

"Don't you think it's best to return, and find out for yourself what is meant to be?"

"No, I think it's best that, if you already know how this ends, you should give me a heads up."

"Are you always this pushy?" He laughed.

"Usually I'm worse. . . . Just tell me. Heartbreak or husband?"

"I do see love in your future."

"But with Drew? Not some other guy?"

"I see that you are happy, and if this is what it takes, then perhaps it is God's will."

"So then let's go back. I don't need to do any exploring. I'm ready to start the rest of my life."

"I will miss you, Hannah Claire."

"Miss me? No, wait. I want you to come with me."

"It is time for me to return home as well."

"But we just met. And I really don't think I can do this alone."

"You will never be alone. I will be in your heart."

"Well, can't you at least stay until I get my life back together? I have so many questions. Did you really leave me money? Should I live with Grams in your apartment? Should I work for those crazy guys over at Casa deMiro? Will I ever get a decent role in a film?"

"You haven't asked about your family, dear. Don't you want to know about them?"

"It doesn't matter. I'm never going to feel close to them again."

"It matters a great deal, because they love you. And even though they made mistakes, just as you did, they need forgiveness, just as you did."

"But they're not my real family."

"Of course they are. Family is not about the people to whom you are born. It is a covenant with the people with whom you have been bound by God to share your life and your love. Family is not about blood, it's about heart. Never give up on family, Claire. They are the heartbeat of your journey. The keepers of your soul."

"But—"

"There are no buts. It is a universal truth."

"I guess I understand. But I still want you to watch over me."

"I will."

"Then can we work out a sign so I know that you're watching?"

"Yes. Why don't you tell me your favorite flower?"

"Oh. Um. I'm not really a flower person. . . . They're all nice."

"Then a favorite song."

"Much better. I love music."

"I love music myself. How about 'My Sky'?"

"Never heard of it."

"It's one of my favorites. If it's okay with you, I'd like that to be our song."

"And I'm thinking, shouldn't it be one we both like?"

"Soon it will be."

"Well, wait. What was the name of it again?"

" 'My Sky.' "

"Who sings it?"

"I do."

The summer between my junior and senior years in college, I back-packed through Europe with two of my sorority sisters. After the first month, we would often wake up in the morning, clueless as to where we'd slept. Venice? No, that was Monday. Barcelona? Possibly.

That's how it felt when I awoke from a deep slumber in Drew's room and checked out my surroundings. I needed time to remember why I was in his bed. All I knew was that what woke me was a sudden thud, which oddly felt like a gymnast's dismount from the balance beam. Fortunately, there were no judges commenting on my nice extension or holding flash cards stating my score.

It was an even greater relief that I wasn't being judged for a beauty contest, for my hair was greasy, my clothes were rumpled, and my b.o. smelled like eau de gross. And yet I felt a lightness of being, as if my feet could touch the ground but keep me afloat at the same time. The image in the mirror shouted, "Do something with yourself," yet my skin had an angelic glow, and my eyes shone.

What really struck me as odd was the time. How could it be only three P.M.? I felt so well rested, surely I'd been out for more than a half an hour. Either this was one great bed, or Delia had used the same "tea" as that I had for Grams.

Except that something was nagging at me. Something I wanted to recall, but what? Maybe it would come to me when I jumped in the shower. For whatever reason, everything usually came to me in the shower— Oh right. How could I forget? The last thing that came to me in the shower nearly killed me.

Better not take chances, I thought. I'd clean myself up and hopefully find bread crumbs leading to the kitchen. I was positively famished and just wanted to sneak downstairs to throw some lunch together without running into a dagger-throwing Delia.

As I tip-toed through the empty hallways, praying that I didn't inadvertently end up in the lion's den, I suddenly forgot what ailed me. I was too preoccupied checking out the unusual floor plan.

Honestly, who lived like this? Whose house had a circular staircase leading to an indoor garden, which led to a meditation room with a large balcony overlooking an atrium, which was situated next to a media center and a glass enclosed gym? It didn't even seem like a house. More like one of those full service, business hotels that offered an array of facilities that sounded perfect in the brochure.

Hopefully I would run into the concierge, who could direct me to the kitchen.

Fortunately, my own global positioning ability was working, for as I turned down the next hallway, eureka!, I found the kitchen. At least I think it was the kitchen. I had never seen one that was two stories high, sporting a balcony and an ocean view. And was that a café on the second floor? It looked like a mini-Starbucks, with comfy couches, magazine racks, tables and chairs, and a magnificent oak coffee bar.

I could just imagine waking up every morning, shuffling down the hall in my pj's, and being greeted by a perky young boy who was standing by with my latte and a newspaper. Maybe Ben wasn't kidding when he made that remark about Shari having one butler for regular, and another for decaf.

As I explored the sea of cabinets, and a refrigerator the size of my entire kitchen back in L.A., it dawned on me that it had been weeks since I'd eaten a real meal. I just hoped that Shari wouldn't think badly of me if I stole the leftover sushi.

I was in the middle of devouring eel when a housekeeper walked by with a laundry basket. By virtue of the fact that she did not ask what I was doing there, I assumed she knew I was the sick guest in Drew's room.

What I did get out of her was that the Mrs. was outside. Sure enough, when I peered through the glass wall facing the back of the house, there was Shari, perfectly posed, practicing what looked like pranayama yogic breathing with her trainer. Talk about being breathless. He was stunning.

Had I not been enjoying my lunch, I might have asked to join them, but then the phone rang. Having no idea if anyone was home, or if there was a secretary on staff who took messages, I didn't answer. But by the third ring, I figured it was the least an appreciative guest could do.

Bad move. Very bad move. If only I hadn't picked up.

# Chapter 23

"Oh my God." I hung up the phone and stood soldier-still.

"Claire." Shari clapped. "Welcome back to civilization. How are you feeling?"

I turned to see her and Handsome Yoga Man prance through the sliding doors, rolled mats and towels in hand. "I didn't know you came down." She hugged me.

"I can't believe it." I sank into a kitchen chair. "She hung up on me."

"Who did? If it was Delia, don't give it a second thought." She wiped her sweaty brow. "She is so rude with that call waiting. Honestly, she doesn't even bother saying good-bye."

"It wasn't Delia. It was Penny. And she hung up on me."

"Oh, I'm sure you're mistaken, because lately we've been getting so many wrong numbers."

"No, it was her. It's right here on the caller ID . . . P. Nichol. And it's a 323 area code, which is L.A. I'm telling you, it was her, and she hung up on me."

"Now, why would she do that? Did you have . . . words?"

"What words? All I said was hello, and then she said, 'Delia?' Puff of smoke. 'It's Aunt Pen. Mom home?' So I said, 'No. Hi. It's not Delia, it's Claire.' And then she hung up on me."

"Oh."

"Why doesn't she want to talk to me?" I burst into tears. "What have I ever done to this woman other than be born? I'm the one who should be hanging up on her, not the other way around. I mean, it's one thing to decide you don't want a baby at nineteen, but grow up already—the cat's out of the bag. I'm her flesh and blood. How do you hang up on your only child?"

"I guess this isn't a good time." Yoga man rubbed Shari's shoulder. "And I really have to run."

"No, wait." She reached for his hand. "I wanted you to meet my niece, Claire. Claire, this is my yogi, Ron."

*Why do I always look like crap when I meet the hottest men?* "Hi. Nice to meet you, Ron." I extended my tear-soaked hand.

"Nice to meet you, too, Claire. Hey, look. I'm sure you'll be okay with Shari helping you figure things out. She's great." He kissed her smack on the lips far longer than any teacher ever kissed me.

So Viktor was right again. Shari kept a stable of lovers, and this one must have been the flavor of the month. Maybe instead of her leftover sushi, I should go for her leftover men.

"Have a good weekend." Ron patted my head. "See you Monday morning?" He winked at Shari.

"A good weekend?" I repeated. "It's only Tuesday."

"Actually, it's Friday." Shari wiped her sweaty brow.

"No way. I just took a quick nap. I slept, what? An hour tops."

"No." She laughed. "You've been asleep for three days."

"Three days? How is that possible? I can't even hold a job for that long."

"Well, you did wake up every once in a while, and we'd tried to get some food into you, but you always fell right back, and Dr. Zhivago said to just let you do what your body was telling you."

"Who?"

"Dr. Zhivago. From your neurology team at the hospital."

"I'm sorry. I have a doctor named after a movie? Who's his partner? Dr. No?"

"To be honest," she whispered, "I doubt that's his real name, but who really knows?"

"Whatever." I slumped into the chair. "What am I going to do?"

"There is nothing you can do. Just try to relax, compose yourself, take long, deep breaths."

"Shari, my life is getting sadder by the day. I don't think proper breathing techniques are going to solve much."

"I suppose you're right." She grabbed a water bottle from the refrigerator. "I just thought if you could find a calm center, you could think more clearly. How about we start by getting you back on schedule with your medications? I'd like to have you in the best possible shape for your doctor's appointment Monday, and then, of course, Ben is taking you over to meet the attorney handling Abe's estate."

"I just don't get it. Why couldn't she at least say, 'Hello, Claire? How are you feeling? What are your plans?' How do you just say nothing and hang up?"

"I'm not one to defend her, believe me. Over the years we've had our differences. I just think this all happened so fast—"

"Fast? She's had thirty years to think about it."

"She's overwhelmed right now."

"What should I say?"

"I've known her for many years. She's not the easiest person to deal with."

"SHE'S MY MOTHER!"

"Just give her some time. I'm sure she'll come to her senses, although she can be beyond stubborn. One time we asked her to fly in for an awards dinner honoring Abe, and I don't know, it was something with a trunk show in Milan, there was a conflict, and she told Ben to change the date of the dinner, but he said no, this was planned a year in advance, and they'd already sold sixty tables. Do you know that she still wouldn't change her plans? It was a mess . . . Abe was so disappointed. So you see, it's not you. She's just difficult— Oh. There's the garage door. Delia's back."

"Great." I gulped. "Did she happen to mention anything about me?"

"Well, yes, of course. She's been very concerned."

"No, I mean did she say anything to you about a conversation we had?"

"Hey." Delia walked in, armed with shopping bags and dry cleaning. "Look who's up. How's it going?"

"Much better, thanks." *I wonder what it's like to have nothing to do all day but spend Daddy's money and pick up clean clothes.* "How about you?"

"Same shit, different day." She threw everything down on the counter and opened the fridge. "Hey! Where's the sushi from last night? I'm like dying for it."

"It's there," Shari said. "Check the second shelf."

"Um, no, it's not. I'm really sorry, Delia. I was starving, and it looked so good . . ."

"Okay. Whatever. I'll just call and order more. No biggie."

*No biggie? Did I miss something here? First you wanted to kill me, now you're being nice?*

"So do you like want to do something?" Delia downed some black olives.

"Who? You mean me?"

"Oh, no. Delia. That's really not a good idea. Claire is very weak now. She needs—"

"I'd love to." I jumped up. "I don't care what, as long as it feels normal. Dinner. A movie. . . ."

"Too boring. I thought we'd go hang out in SoBe."

"Sounds great. What is it?"

"Duh. Like where have you been? It's South Beach. Like you know, SoHo? I thought I'd show you my dad's new place. It's very cool. It's called By the C, right next to the Ritz-Carlton? Then we could go hit the bars . . . woo-hoo . . ."

"But, Delia. It's four in the afternoon," Shari whined.

"Exactly. By the time we get done looking around, it'll be Happy Hour."

"Happy Hour?" I clapped. "I love Happy Hour. It sounds great. Thank you, Delia." I hugged her. "Thank you so much."

"Well, wait, Claire. Do you really think this is such a good idea? Mixing alcohol with prescription medications?".

"I'll be fine, I swear. I haven't taken anything yet. And tomorrow I promise I'll be the world's most perfect patient. . . . Just give me ten minutes to jump in the shower."

"Take twenty." Delia guzzled a Diet Coke. "We've got nothing else to do."

"Nothing crazy, Delia," Shari warned. "I don't need you bringing Claire back here completely hung over. She's in a very vulnerable state right now."

"That's exactly why she should drink, Mother."

*You got that right, sister,* I thought as I ran out. "Can somebody please tell me how to get back to my room?"

Up until the day I slipped in my grandmother's shower, then fell into a coma in Drew's bed, I'd had no encounters with near-death experiences. But after riding shotgun with Delia Fabrikant in her little Mercedes coupe, I was now three for three.

Apparently the girl thought that red lights were only suggestions and that speed limits were strictly for tourists. She maneuvered through the streets of Miami as if her steering wheel were hooked up to a PlayStation, and her goal was to beat her high score at "Need for Speed."

As I grabbed the armrest, it hit me that the only reason she'd been so keen on taking me out was so that she could literally take me out. Death by driving. The perfect crime. What jury would convict a girl with no priors?

Of course, *I* would know her motive. Revenge for ignoring her grandfather and lying to her family. But I would be dead, so who would I tell? Honestly, how could I have been so stupid to fall for such a cheap, manipulative trick? Had I learned nothing from watching *Law and Order*?

But then, miraculously, Delia pulled into a VIP parking spot at By the C, put the top up, and announced that the celebrating had officially begun. "Party time, here we come!" She wiggled her ass.

"What exactly are we celebrating? Arriving in one piece?"

"No, silly. We're celebrating that you came back from the dead."

"So then why did you just try to kill me? You drive like shit!"

"Oh chill. I'm on these roads my whole life. I could drive them if I was blind."

"You mean you're not?"

"Would you stop? I'm trying to show you a good time and you're ruining it."

"Sorry. You're right. We made it here without a single head injury."

"I can't believe you're not even going to ask me something," Delia interrupted.

"Ask you what?"

"About why I'm being so nice to you. Don't you think it's weird? Or did you forget that I was ready to kill you before you like blacked out?"

"No, I didn't forget. And yes, I am curious. Why are you being so nice to me?"

"Because I realized the other night when you had your little meltdown that you're right. Your life is so screwed up. I mean, I still hate what you did, but it's like you're so pathetic. What's the point of making you feel even shittier?"

"Thanks?"

"And then I was thinking about my Pops. He loved family. We were the only thing that mattered to him. You had to see how crazy he'd get if like me and Drew were fighting, or I was yelling at my dad. He used to say, 'Delia, never give up on family. They're the heartbeat of your journey. The keepers of your soul.' So like now that you're family, I was thinking how pissed he'd be if I wasn't nice to you."

"Wait. What did you just say?"

"I don't know. A bunch of things."

"No. I mean about what Abe used to say to you about family. About the journey."

"He had a lot of sappy sayings." She shrugged. "After a while they all sounded alike."

"No, the thing about the keepers of your soul. . . . It's so strange. I think I've heard that somewhere before. I just can't think of where."

"Whatever. . . . Anyway, I decided he'd be proud of me if I didn't tell your dirty little secrets. So I'm letting you off the hook. But no more bullshit lies, okay?"

"Absolutely."

"Oh. And then before we go in, there's one other thing I have to tell you. It's one of those good news/bad news deals."

"Great. Love those." I winced.

Delia leaned in and signaled that I should do the same. "I'm pretty sure it's over with Marly."

"What?"

"Yeah. Drew's coming back from Bermuda tonight. But not with her."

"Oh my God. Why?"

"I don't know. My dad talked to him this morning, and he said he was packing it in, and that he and Marly were taking different flights back."

"Delia, that's not just good news, that's great news! But wait. I'm sorry. Aren't you and Marly friends?"

"Are you kidding? I hate the stupid bitch."

"You do?"

"It's a long story. I knew her before Drew did. We used to hang out in high school."

"Oh. So wait. What happened? How come you're happy about them splitting?"

" 'Cause she's a freakin' mess. She used to go down on everybody's boyfriends, she lied about everything. One time I got this Gucci wallet from my dad, which she ripped off from my pocketbook, and then told everyone her uncle brought it back from Italy."

"Seriously? Did Drew know?"

"Yeah, but he said those were in her wannabe days. That she's not like that anymore."

"So what do you think happened now? Did they have a fight?"

"Who the hell cares? All I know is, now I won't have to be in their stupid bridal party and wear some shitty pink dress that she thought was so amazing."

"You are so lucky. I wish I could get out of my bridal party obligation. . . . I've tried everything, but this friend, Elyce, she just won't take no for an answer. . . . Anyway. What's the bad news?"

"Oh yeah. Well, um . . . Drew's coming home tonight, but he mentioned something to my dad about this chick Nicole. She's one of our bartenders. They hooked up a few years ago, and then Marly came along. He asked if she's on tomorrow."

"Oh. Uh-huh. Well, I'm sure he's hurting right now. Old friends are good for times like that."

"I hate her fucking guts. She is so two-faced. I hope to God she doesn't hear about Drew and Marly, 'cause she'll rip off her clothes and hump him right on the bar. . . . He is like so pathetic. He could have anybody, but he keeps picking these loser bitches."

"Why are you telling me this, Delia?"

" 'Cause if you love him, you gotta tell him. I want you to tell him."

"Why? I'm obviously not his type, and let's not forget a basic fact here. We're first cousins."

"Yeah, but my father isn't his real father. I mean, he adopted him and everything. But it's not like your kids would have three heads."

"I don't know. It seems kind of gross. . . . People would talk."

"So? Who gives a shit? You told me before you really loved him. Did you change your mind?"

"No."

"Then you have to tell him, because I think if he knew, he might . . . give it a chance."

"I don't understand why you're rooting for me. You just told me I'm pathetic."

"I know. But it's not your fault. It's just because of all this shit that's happened you. Other than that, I guess you're okay. I mean, anyone who would go bare-ass naked in front of Marly is a rip."

"Oh God. Drew told you?"

"No, she did. She was like in shock. It was so great. I wish I could have seen her little face all scrunched up."

"It was pretty funny, actually. But what difference does it make? I don't want to be anyone's rebound girl. I've been there too many times before, and it never works out."

"Just leave it to me, okay? If you want my brother, I'll make sure he doesn't screw this up."

I know a lot of crazy, let-loose, give-the-dog-a-beer kind of people. But after partying in Hollywood for six years, mingling with celebrities, eventual celebrities, used-to-be celebrities, and my-shit-doesn't-stink-because-I work-for-celebrities, I thought I had seen just about every form of aberrant behavior there was.

So when I tell you that Delia Fabrikant turned out to be a sweet kid, but a total wack job, I think I speak with some authority. I mean, Sydney had an unpredictable, lunatic side to her, too. Enough that I used to worry about one day getting a call from the police saying that she was standing on a thirty-six-story ledge, just to find out who her friends were. But compared to Delia's let-loose antics, Sydney looked like an honor roll student at Encino Valley Middle School.

From the minute we set foot into By the C, Delia morphed into a younger, hipper Norm on *Cheers*. She was greeted by every customer, waiter, bartender, and manager, and before I could even adjust my eyes to the darkened room, she was off table-hopping, tongue-kissing, drinking, snorting, and dancing. At five-thirty in the afternoon. With her father working upstairs in his office.

After watching Delia's signature greeting to men—sticking her hand down the front of their Pavlovian pants—I realized how lucky I was to have been raised by Mr. Don't You Dare, a shrewd accountant who made me accountable for every decision I ever made.

Which made me think. If my dad had ever gotten wind of the fact that I was the neighborhood Bianca Jagger, he would have made me write a letter of apology to anyone I might have offended, and then grounded me for life.

He never would have tolerated such infantile antics. He never would have allowed me to discredit my good name. He never would have let me do anything that would disparage my reputation or make me feel unworthy.

And for that I had to raise my glass to Lenny Greene.

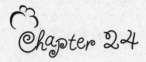

# Chapter 24

You know what they say about getting what you wish for. I was thrilled when Delia invited me out for a night of fun. I finally got to wear one of those amazing Versace outfits. Met some cute guys. Pretended that it was just another night in SoBe to enjoy the heat and the beat.

So imagine my disappointment when the evening turned into a raucous booze cruise on land, and I realized that my sole function was to serve as Delia's personal hair holder when she vomited. If only I could be back at the Fabrikants', curled in Drew's bed.

It made me wonder how long I could exist in this surreal holding pattern. Unlike my formerly frenetic life, when I ran from shit job to even bigger shit job, from sea salt manicures to human hair extensions, from cocktails in Santa Monica to beach parties in Malibu, now I had no reason to get up, no place to go, no immediate plans for the future. The only thing on my "To Do" list was checking in with Grams to see how she was managing in her new place. Or so I thought.

When I headed down to the kitchen the next morning (a much easier feat the second time), instead of finding Shari, I saw Drew standing over the sink with a bagel in one hand and the newspaper in the other. How adorable he looked in his white pressed T-shirt and khaki shorts. How well behaved, too, making sure his crumbs didn't touch the floor.

It was hard to believe that he and Delia were raised by the same people. Oh no. I also realized that this would be my first face-to-face with Drew since Delia heard my confession. She had promised not to tell, but what if she'd let it slip? And what about his breakup with Marly? Did I know about that, or was I supposed to play dumb? It was too much for my still-fragile brain to handle. Better to tiptoe back to my/his room, call Delia's cell, and find out what I could and could not say.

"Claire!" He turned around. "Hi, there. I was hoping you'd come down so we could talk. I almost gave up on you."

*Don't ever give up on me.* "Drew? Oh wow. What a surprise to see you here. I mean, not that this isn't still your house, it's just that no one was expecting you until tomorrow." *Shut up, shut up, shut up.* "How are you?"

"Good." He kissed my cheek. "But you look great. Amazing, actually."

"That's not saying much. If you recall, last time you saw me, I was headed to Psycho U on full scholarship."

"No, you weren't." He laughed. "You were just overwhelmed and—"

"Can I ask you something? 'Cause I really need to know. Are you mad at me?"

"Why do you always ask me that?" He hoisted himself up on to the counter. "Do you have this kind of complex with everyone? No, I'm not mad at you. In fact, I'm very happy to see you."

"Just checking. So . . . um . . . how was Bermuda? I hear it's nice this time of year."

"You can lay off the fancy footwork. Delia told me she told you about me and Marly."

"Oh . . . well, then, I just wanted to say that I'm really sorry."

"No, you're not. You're as happy as everyone else."

"Fine. I cannot tell a lie." *Ha!* "I am a little happy. Now I can throw out my Marly voodoo doll."

"You hate her that much?"

"It's not important. Um, by any chance did Delia happen to say anything else about me?"

"Yeah. She said you're staying in my room."

*Is that all?* "I know, and I am really sorry. I had this big fight with my parents before they went back to New York, and I had nowhere else to go, so your parents invited me to stay here, which was really nice, but then I was afraid to stay down in the villas alone, so your dad said it was okay to stay in your room, but I'll go get my things and move out now. I don't want to invade your—"

"No, no. You don't have to do that. Stay as long as you like. . . . Are those my clothes?"

I looked down at my boxers and Miami Marlins T-shirt. "Uh-oh."

"No, it's fine. I just feel like Papa Bear. Someone's been sleeping in my bed and wearing my boxers and looking better in them than me." He spoke in a baritone. "And I hope she's hot."

"Oh, she's hot, all right. Especially when she's running a fever." I laughed. "But oh my God, Drew. Your bed is so comfortable, I slept for three straight days. In fact, the whole room is great. I feel safe in there."

"That's funny, because I always felt safe in there myself. Probably because it was the only normal room in the entire house."

"Are you serious? You didn't like growing up here?"

"What's not to love? I was the only kid on the block with a Little Tykes Rolls-Royce."

"That must have impressed the little girls."

"Nah. They were so rich, their piggybanks had vice presidents."

It was so wonderful to laugh again, and to feel relaxed. And excited. I hadn't just been imagining that Drew was wonderful. He was wonderful. Now the question was not how long could I stay in his room, but how long could I stay in his room before I begged him to join me? Just inhaling his soap scent and looking at his lean, muscular body made me weak.

But even better than getting to look at him over coffee was getting to talk to him. Most men presume that they should be the focus of conversation, but Drew was more concerned with my frame of mind and my relationship with my parents. He talked about how angry he was with Delia for wasting her life. Anything, apparently, to avoid discussing his feelings about Marly, because I did try to go there, and the door to that subject was closed.

On the other hand, you should have seen his eyes sparkle when I asked about Abe. It didn't even faze him when I used the collective, "our grandfather." He just smiled and shared stories about the great man's passions. And all the while I was thinking that any guy who could write song lyrics and who could share the pain of his loss was someone I could spend the rest of my life with.

It was in the midst of listening to the tales that I heard Drew say something about a poem that Pops loved so well, he'd made a copy and tucked it into his wallet. He often forgot to walk around with money, but he never left home without his tattered copy of "My Sky."

"Wait. I think of I've heard of it," I said. "But it's a song, not a poem. Right?"

"No. It's a poem. From the Holocaust. It was written in a concentration camp."

"No, I'm pretty sure it's a song. . . . I just don't know why I know that."

"I guess the title sounds like a song, but trust me, it's a poem. It's in this book he gave me when I was like eight or nine. He was the only grandfather I knew who didn't read fairy tales to his grandchildren. Instead he read us stories from the Holocaust, which wasn't exactly the kind of thing you should do before putting a little kid to sleep. But that was my Pops. He drilled it into our heads that life was precious, and we couldn't ever forget the six million who died."

"Do you remember the name of the book?"

"Yeah. Absolutely. It was called *Reason to Believe*."

"Oh. Now, that's weird. I had that book, too. I think someone gave it to me for Chanukah one year, and it was like, oh wow. Thanks so much. It's just what I wanted."

"Yeah, well for a while he was reading it to me every night. Then my mother made him stop because she was sure it would turn me into some kind of psycho revenge killer or something. Did you ever read it?"

"I doubt it. And yet for some reason, the name 'My Sky' rings a bell. It's like ever since Abe died, things keep coming to me that I have no way of knowing, and I have no idea why."

"Me either. But maybe your dad was right. We need to call in the local exorcist."

"Very funny."

"No, really. It's like Pops didn't die. He's still here, and he's getting through to you. Like in the hospital when you got all those messages. And before that, you said that you felt his presence a lot."

"Yes, but I have no recollection of him telling me about this poem . . . but I would swear on my life that it's a song."

"No. Believe me, if there was a recording of it, we would have had it, especially since he was so into music. When he was a kid, he was this supposed piano prodigy. His big dream was to be a composer, but then the war happened; he lost everyone and everything, somehow made it out of the concentration camps, got brought to this country with the help of an uncle, and by the time he got to America, he'd lost all desire to play—"

"Oh wait, wait, wait," I interrupted. "I'm starting to remember something."

Drew jumped off the counter and slung his leg around a kitchen chair. "Hit me."

"The day we met at the airport, I was holding his wallet, remember? And you were so glad that I had it because you thought it was stolen?"

"Yeah."

"Then you said something about a poem he kept in his wallet. You said it was like his American Express card. He never left home without it."

"Okay."

"And you mentioned the name. You said it was 'My Sky'. That's where I heard it." I clapped.

"To tell you the truth, I don't remember that. The whole day is still a blur. But did I say it was a song?"

"No."

"And you think it's a song because . . ."

"I wish I could tell you. I don't know. Maybe I dreamt it."

We sat quietly, contemplating the insanity of this conversation. Nothing was making sense, yet neither of us thought the other was crazy. It was just giving us a reason to bond. And it was nice. I liked watching Drew, deep in thought, slicking back his hair. I liked watching him stare off into space, then look at me with that dazzling, dentist-chair smile. So I don't know what possessed me to break the mood by saying something stupid.

"This is by far the strangest house I've ever been in," I blurted.

"I agree." He laughed. "But why do you think so?"

"I don't know. Maybe because it's so quiet? I feel like I'm the only guest in this huge hotel."

"You are the only guest."

"I know, but people do live here."

"Only two. My mom and Delia. My dad pretty much moved out."

"I heard."

"But what the hell? The place is up for sale. Soon it will be someone else's hotel."

"Will you miss it?"

"Maybe, maybe not. I love the walk down to the ocean. And I guess I'll miss my room."

"Oh, I know. Look at me. I've only been here a few days, and I'll miss it, too."

Drew jumped up.

"What is it?"

"My room. I just thought of something."

"Tell me."

"He did once write some music for a poem."

"Are you serious? You mean for 'My Sky'?"

"I'm not sure."

"But what does that have to do with your room?"

"I remember now I had gotten this little dinky tape recorder for my birthday one year, and he asked if he could borrow it because he wrote this song, and he wanted to be able to remember it."

"Okay."

"So he sat down at the piano, he made the tape, and then he handed it to me and said, 'Here. I want you to have this.'"

"That was sweet. So what was on it?"

"Who knows? I never even listened to it. But I bet it's in my desk somewhere. Which, if I know my mom, it's part of the Drew Fabrikant permanent exhibit . . . velvet ropes and a sign that says don't touch."

"Your desk?" *Noooooo. Don't look in your desk. You might notice things got moved around.*

"You know what?" Drew said. "Why don't we go up there and look for it?"

"Um . . . maybe later? It's sort of a mess."

"Are you kidding? You think it was any different with me? Until I moved out, I had no idea what color the carpet was. C'mon. Let's go check it out. I know a shortcut."

"A shortcut? Are you serious? You have a shortcut to your room?" I giggled. "At my house, it takes me exactly six seconds to go from the front door to my room. Ten if I stop for my mail."

"Then I'm insanely jealous." He grabbed my hand and ran. "If we leave now, we can get to mine before sunset."

Drew wasn't joking. There really was a shortcut to his bedroom. Could you imagine living in a place so big that you had choices on how to get around? Not that I had time to think about this, for as soon as we reached his room, he closed the door.

"Are you mad at me for something?" He looked me in the eye. "I really have to know."

"No, of course not. Why would you even say that?"

"To show you how annoying it is every time you ask me the same thing." He stroked my hair.

"I'm sorry. I don't mean to be annoying. I just really like you, and your opinion of me means everything to me."

"And I feel the same . . . which is why I have an important question for you."

"Okay."

"Would it be all right if I kissed you?"

*Duh. Hello? Can't you hear my heart pounding?* "I think so."

"But you're not sure?"

"Just tell me this. Am I the first girl you ever made out with up here?"

"No. Sorry." He laughed. "There have been hundreds, maybe thousands of girls up here. I was importing them from Taiwan. But none that I cared about as much as you."

"That's what you said to all of them."

"No. Only one."

"Marly?"

"Actually, no. Now that I think of it, she was never up here."

"Are you serious? How come?"

"I don't know. I guess she never expressed much interest in my past."

"I love your past, and I want to know everything. . . . So who was the one girl who mattered?"

"Oh. Um . . . that would be Lyssa Schneider. We were fourteen. She was amazing. Beautiful. Smart. She could make me laugh, no matter what was going on with my life. Just like you do."

"And this was your make-out headquarters?"

"Nope. Never touched her. I wanted to, but I was afraid if I made a move, she'd hate me and leave. That's why I'm asking permission now. I don't want to do anything that would make you leave."

I grabbed Drew, placed his arms around my waist, and gently kissed him, rocking to a rhythm of desire that I had never felt before.

Normally a first real kiss is awkward, something you rush, so that you can establish mutual lust, and then explore more interesting territory. But I never wanted this moment to end. I wanted to remember how soft his lips felt. How perfectly they aligned with mine, like a matched set. How safe I felt in his strapping arms, as if our bodies were meant to be joined.

But mostly what I loved was that he did not presume that kissing me also gave him the keys to the kingdom. It did not give him permission to unfasten my bra or run his hand down the front of my panties. Nor did he presume that I would want to unzip his shorts.

"Thank you." He brushed my hair from my cheek. "That was . . . I don't know. The greatest kiss of my life."

I smiled.

"I swear, if I didn't get to do that, I would have always wondered what it would be like, and it would have killed me."

"Me, too."

"There is something about you, Claire. I feel this unexplainable connection, and I have since the minute I saw you in the airport."

"Me, too."

"But I don't know . . . it just wouldn't make any sense, you and me. We're related now. I've been through this a thousand times in my head. You're like the forbidden fruit."

"No. No, I'm not. . . . I've thought about this, too. There are no bloodlines here. We're cousins by coincidence."

"Cousins by coincidence." He laughed. "Sounds like a support group."

"This isn't funny . . . and it's not fair. You can't kiss me like you just did, get me so crazy I want to rip my clothes off, then tell me, you're great Claire, but I can't be with you."

"You want to rip your clothes off?"

"Well, no. Not if it's just so you could satisfy your curiosity of what it would be like to make love to me so you could get it out of your system, and then go back to screwing Nicole—" *Oops.*

"How do you know about Nicole? Never mind. I know. It was Delia. I swear that girl has the biggest mouth."

"Shhh. Stop. It's not about Nicole. It's not about anyone but you and me."

"We don't even know each other."

"But I know what's in my heart, and you do, too. That's why you kissed me. Because something is happening here, and even though the circumstances that brought us together are bizarre, this is real. Every time I see you, my heart races. My knees get weak. My head practically explodes with this deep desire. . . . And I know I sound like a Hallmark card I wouldn't be caught dead sending, but I really believe that we were meant to be together, no matter how odd it appears to everyone else."

"I don't know what to say. . . . It's been such a crazy few weeks. . . . I thought that Marly and I had gotten past all our old problems, but they won't go away. . . . The whole time I was with her in Bermuda, I was wondering how you were managing. And then I'd think, how the hell am I going to build a life with her if I can't stop thinking about you?"

"Now, that's more like it."

I kissed him again, and he held me as if he would never let go. But this time I heard music. A strange melody that sounded eerily familiar, yet I couldn't place.

"Do you hear that?" I whispered.

"The music?"

I nodded.

"Are we both losing our minds? It's a like a waltz or something. Where is it coming from?"

I pointed to the sky. "And how weird would that be if we found out it was called 'My Sky'?"

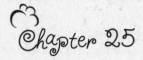

# Chapter 25

You had to see the look on Drew's face when he discovered an old black cassette tape in the top drawer of his desk. Oddly, it had been there all these years, right under a pack of unopened baseball cards and the invitation to Jeremy Finkelstein's bar mitzvah at the Fountainbleau Hotel.

The cassette wasn't labeled, but when he held it under the light, we were able to make out the scribbled message: *To Drew. Love Pops. March 1, 1987.*

"This is it." His hand was shaking.

"Are you sure?"

"Yeah. I remember it now. It's definitely the tape he made me."

"We have to listen to it. Do you have a cassette player?"

"Not anymore. That's like trying to find an eight-track player. . . . I guess we could run out to Target and buy one."

"You love Target?" I clapped.

"I don't know if I love it, but I'm always running in there for something."

"Oh, me too. See how much we have in common? Don't they have the cutest things?"

"No, you're the cutest thing." He stroked my cheek. "Marly would never have been caught dead in a store that discounted."

"Perfect. Then there's no chance I'll ever run into her. . . . Hey, wait. What about your car? Maybe you have a cassette deck in there. I do in mine."

"No, but you know what? You're brilliant. I'm almost positive Pops' Caddy has one."

"Great. Give me a few minutes to shower and change, we'll go get his car, and then, if you don't mind, I'd really like to go visit Grams. I'm worried about how she's doing."

"Actually, she's doing great. I saw her this morning."

"Are you serious? You went to visit my grandmother?"

"Sort of. I mean, yes, I wanted to see how she was doing, but I went over there to pick up some more boxes. She kind of moved in before we had a chance to clean everything out."

"Oh. So how is she?"

"Happy as a clam. She's made so many friends already, you'd think she was there for years."

"My grandmother made friends? Are you sure you had the right apartment?"

"Yeah." He laughed. "It was the right place. If you want, we can run over there later."

"I can't believe how wonderful you are. You just got back from a trip, and the first thing you did was something so sweet."

"It wasn't exactly the first thing I did," he sighed. "The first thing I did was change my locks."

"Uh-huh. . . . Does that mean things with Marly are going to get ugly?"

"If I had to guess? Yes."

"Do you want to talk about it?"

"That's a definite no . . . but here's another thought. I might actually have the cassette player Pops used to make this. If I did, it would be in my room somewhere. I swear my mother threw nothing out, like it was a shrine. . . . Feel like going through my stuff to look for it?"

"Oh no. I couldn't do that. I wouldn't want to invade your privacy."

"Nice try." He tousled my hair. "I already know that you went through my drawers."

"What are you talking about?" *My acting ability should get me out of this one.*

"Delia told me she found you going through my desk."

*Or maybe not.* "Why, that little . . ."

"I told you she had a big mouth. And you, Claire, are very naughty." He winked.

"Are you going to send me to my room?" I whispered.

"You mean my room. But that's right—since you were caught trespassing, you should be punished. Unless I decide to give you time off for good behavior."

"I'd rather have time off for bad behavior." My hand went right to his crotch, and he laughed.

"Better be careful there. Messing with the judge could get you in trouble."

"Exactly." I let my fingers do the talking.

"Whoa. Down, girl." He moaned. "How about we start with first base?"

"I like first base." I kissed him. "But I'm also a great home run hitter."

"I'm sure you are. . . . But maybe this is a little soon. We should wait."

"No." I tugged at his T-shirt.

"No?"

"I've waited my whole life to meet someone like you." My hand traveled south on a heat-seeking mission. "I think that's long enough."

"But don't you want the first time to be romantic? Some wine, some good music . . ."

"This is romantic. We're sneaking a quickie in your old room."

"I don't want a quickie. I want a longie."

"We can have both." I wrestled with his shirt and shorts until they made a heap on the floor.

"Uh-oh. You're making a mess." He laughed. "My mom's going to get mad."

"Good. Maybe she'll sentence me to more time in your room." I lowered his briefs until the very essence of his being was in my hands.

"You . . . I . . . This . . ."

"Shhhh."

"Oh my God." He groaned as I fell to my knees. "You don't know what you're doing to me."

"I think I do."

"Claire, no, really." He closed his eyes. "Oh my God. You are amazing. . . . But c'mon. This is too important not to do it right. We should wait . . . we need condoms . . ."

"Third drawer on the left." I giggled.

"You mean the ones from ninth grade?" He tried not to laugh. "I think they've expired by now."

I stopped. "You're serious about this. You don't want to make love to me?"

"I'm dying to make love to you. But not here. Not now."

"Then can we stop at Target and stock up on condoms?" I stood.

"As many as you can fit in the basket." He kissed me.

"Okay. You're right. We're not kids anymore—we can actually do this anytime we want."

"Thank you."

"But will you at least take a shower with me? To make sure I don't fall again?"

"Sure." He smiled. "I wouldn't want you to get hurt."

"And, of course, there are still some spots I can't reach. . . ."

"You mean behind your ears?" He swatted my butt.

"Not even close." I ran my hands down his bare chest.

You have no idea how much I love shopping at Target. Or *Tar-czay*, as it's called in L.A. They have the coolest pocketbooks and accessories, and no one can tell that you bought them in a place that also sells light-bulbs and motor oil.

But nothing is better than making a Target run for toiletries and condoms with a man you are so hot for, you're counting the seconds until you can rip off his clothes and rub him down with the whipped cream you bought in aisle eleven.

Drew, on the other hand, had a great deal more integrity than me.

He was not only a man who stuck to his shopping list, but to his guns. Even in the shower he was a man of his word. He kissed and caressed every inch of my body, then dried me off as if I were a tender infant. But he wouldn't commit to the final act, and you know as well as me, a naked man can't hide his rock-hard desire.

How could I not love a guy who showed that much restraint? Or even better, who was such a good little shopper, that he knew that Target's 100 percent Egyptian cotton towels were of a much better quality than the ones sold at leading department stores? I swear, by the time we reached the checkout, I was weak with anticipation.

But no more so than when we went back to his place, picked up the keys to Pops' car, and drove down A1A to the ocean. I couldn't imagine him wanting to go to a crowded beach right now, and sure enough, he took a circuitous route, ending up at a spot not only breathtaking, but secluded.

"You wanted to be a first." He turned off the engine. "I've never brought anyone here."

"It's so peaceful. . . . How did you find it?"

"I didn't. Pops did. He used to bring me here so we could fish. We never caught much. I don't think the fish could find the place. But we'd talk a lot, and he'd tell me great stories."

"Drew, you were so lucky to have had him in your life."

"Yeah. He was an extraordinary man. I'm still in shock that he's gone. I can't tell you how many times I've reached for the phone to call him . . . how weird it was going over there this morning, and having your grandmother answer the door. . . . I mean, don't get me wrong, I'm really glad it worked out for her . . . but the reality hit me hard. My Pops is gone," he sighed.

"It's my Popsy, and I'll cry if I want to . . ." I sang quietly.

That made him laugh. "Claire, I swear, you are amazing. You are the most beautiful woman I've ever seen naked, you're sweet, you're smart, you turn sad moments into good ones . . ."

"That's why I think you should marry me."

"Are you ever going to let me take charge of anything?" He smiled. "I mean, will you at least let me lead when we dance?"

"I'm sorry. You're right. I'm being way too forward."

"Yes, you are . . . but other than that, you're perfect."

"Oh, then please marry me?"

"Do you mean tonight?"

"Sure."

"Can't."

"Why not?"

"Because I have a date."

"A date!" I smacked his shoulder. "Are you kidding me? You just broke up with your fiancée not two days ago, and you already asked someone out? Is that why you wouldn't make love to me? Because you were saving your strength for Nicole?"

"No, Claire." He leaned over to kiss me. "It's you. You're my date. . . . But good to know you've got a jealous streak."

"Oh my God. I'm so sorry, Drew. I don't know why I keep acting like this."

"Don't get me wrong. I feel strangely connected to you, for someone I didn't know two weeks ago. And even though I've never really thought much about destiny, I'm starting to think that we were supposed to meet exactly when we did.

"You had done the whole Hollywood thing, and were ready for something different. I was trying to figure out if I was doing what made me happy, or if I was just doing what everyone expected me to do. Get married. Run the family business. Live well. . . .

"Then you came along on what would have been a really sad day, and somehow you turned my entire life upside down and my heart inside out."

I sighed. Had I ever known a man who could be this honest with his feelings, or so unafraid of showing emotion? Doubt it. But as much as I wanted to jump into his arms and never let go, he was right. Nothing would be gained by my pushing so hard for the relationship shuttle to launch. If it was meant to be, the takeoff would happen without my bringing in a rocket booster.

Which is exactly what I told him, to his great relief.

"Good. Now let's listen to the tape." Drew popped it into the cassette player, turned up the volume, and took my hand. Given the great anticipation, we expected to hear something. Anything. But we waited. And waited. And nothing.

"Damn." He leaned back. "Maybe these things have a shelf life or something."

"Or maybe it was always a blank tape, and the one you were thinking of is somewhere else."

"No. He wrote on it. Remember?"

Just as he reached to turn off the sound, we heard a crackling, then a clicking, then a whistling sound, as if someone were blowing into a microphone. "Hullo? Hullo? Testing. Vun, two, three. Testing. Vun, two, three. . . . I think it's vorking now."

"Oh my God. That's him." Drew cranked up the volume. "It's him."

"Thank God."

Naturally, I was relieved for Drew. Photographs were wonderful keepsakes, but what could be better than having a grandparent's voice on a tape to replay whenever you needed comfort?

And yet the sound of Abe's voice gave me a chill, as it was the first time I was hearing it. Delia had told me that his accent was thick German. But what she hadn't conveyed was the warm inflection in his tone. His upbeat tempo. His loving words. He sounded just like a grandfather.

"Dis is some music I write for a poyim I love called 'My Sky.' "

"Oh my God. It is a song! I knew it."

"This was our favorite poyim. You remember it, Dreweleh? About vaking up every morning and looking up at thi ski? This is a good message for you. Always be heppy to be alife . . . and lift your head high. You get eh much better view. [chuckle] I love you. Pop Pops."

"Oh my God," I whispered, "I love him."

Tears were already streaming down Drew's cheek when Abe began to play a sweet, delicate melody on the piano. For some reason I happened to notice the waves. It felt as if the ocean could hear the music, too, for it flowed to the same gentle rhythm. Even the clouds glided by in a fluid motion. The perfect synchronization of music and nature. And then Abe sang, his rich voice filling the air of his beloved Cadillac, the car in which he spent the good years driving to this very spot.

*Sunrise pulls back the curtain on a sky full of hope*
*And the promise of brightness over yesterday's ash*
*When faith, nestled in its vast white sails*
*Is the dawn of your dreams, the breath of air divine*

*They can snatch your bread, but not your patch of sky*
*They cannot take away what they did not create*
*They can break your heart but not your soul*
*Signs of life will never die*

*God made the sky to give us reason to look up*
*To lift our head and feel hope*
*To find brightness day and night*
*There is always reason to believe*

Drew played the tape over and over, and each time it resonated differently for me. Finally, instead of focusing on the words, I listened to the melody, and something struck me. Was it the music I'd heard in my head when I was making out with Drew in his room?

"That was . . . I don't know." He wiped his eyes. "Amazing."

"I know," I replied. "So beautiful. . . . And you're sure you've never heard it before?"

"I'm positive . . . although, this is weird—it actually sounds familiar."

"I know. Me, too. And this is going to sound crazy, but I'm wondering if it's the song I heard when we were in your room."

Drew's sun-kissed skin turned ashen.

"I can't explain it." I shrugged. "But I know I've heard it before."

"Now that you mention it, it did sort of sound like that . . . kind of slow and sad, like a waltz. But a nice waltz. . . . I can't believe I'm even having this conversation. What do you think it means?"

"Either that it's true that too much pot kills off your brain cells, or that our grandfather is trying to tell us to enjoy life and be happy."

"How can I be happy? I'm so pissed at myself. He wrote that music for me, and I never even bothered listening to it. I just threw it in my desk with the rest of my crap."

"You were a kid. Don't be so hard on yourself. He knew how much you loved him."

"I suppose." Drew sighed. "Have you . . . ever done anything you deeply regretted?"

*If you only knew.* "Sure."

"It's such a god-awful feeling, isn't it? It's like you'd do anything to take it back."

"Oh, I know."

"Although it's hard to believe that you'd ever do anything you regretted. You seem like such an honest person."

*Believe me. I'm no honest Abe.* "Thanks."

"No, I mean it. You're so up-front about everything. What you're thinking. How you feel. None of the girls I've been with are like that. They're all so cagey and manipulative. You never really know if they mean what they say."

*Oh shit. This is going somewhere.* "Uh-huh."

Maybe I was being paranoid. Most people with guilty consciences were. Besides, Delia had obviously told Drew that I had gone through his desk. Why wouldn't I think that she also told him about the flight?

"So anyway," Drew said, "you thought you had that book of poems, too?"

*Or maybe I was wrong. He was changing the subject, bless his heart.*

"I sort of remember getting it one Chanukah . . . I'm not sure from whom. But I know I never even opened it. I probably assumed it was boring and didn't give it a second thought. Now think how bad I feel. That poem was amazing. If I ever go home, I'll look and see if it's still in my room somewhere."

"You are going home." Drew took my hand. "And you are going to talk to your parents."

"Excuse me?" I just looked at him.

"I have to be honest. If you can't resolve your issues with them, it's a deal-breaker for me."

"Wait, wait, wait. This isn't your decision. What I do with my family is my business."

"You're right. But I can't help it. It makes me crazy when families fight and this one's not talking to that one. Life is short, and in the end, they're all you have. And even though I agree that your parents made mistakes, they're not bad people. Pops had this expression—"

"'Family are the heartbeat of your journey, and the keepers of your soul.'"

"Yeah. How did you know?"

"I'm not sure."

"And then this whole thing with 'My Sky' and music . . . where the hell did that come from?"

"I wish I could tell you. . . . It's almost as if I had a special conversation with Abe."

"You mean on the plane?"

"No. We didn't talk on the plane." *Oh my God.*

"What?" Drew let go of my hand.

*OH MY GOD!* "I mean we didn't talk on the plane about that stuff. We talked about other stuff."

Drew couldn't look at me, and suddenly, without warning, the tide changed. Gone was the affection and humor. Gone was the sexual current in the air. I couldn't even read his expression. But when an interminable few moments went by and he said not one word, it didn't take a psychic to figure out what was happening. He was angry with me. Which could only mean one thing.

I took a deep breath. "You know about the flight, don't you?"

"Damn you, Claire! I was really hoping it wasn't true."

## Chapter 26

Truth or dare. To thine own self be true. To tell the truth. Truth or consequences. True or false? Too good to be true. Do you solemnly swear to tell the truth, the whole truth, and nothing but the truth?

Those may be the most familiar expressions of all time. But obviously they meant nothing to me, because I'd just been caught in the championship edition of "Liar Liar." And much as I dreaded it, it was time to find out if the loser was going home with a consolation prize. Her self-worth.

"Did Delia tell you?" I finally found the nerve to ask.

He shook his head.

"Then who?"

"No one. I just knew."

"I'm sorry?"

"The truth is, I suspected it at the airport."

"No way. How?"

"Because I knew my Pops, and nothing you said made any sense. He never did crossword puzzles, he had no friends where he lived, and he never would have chewed your ear off talking about his family because he wasn't big on talking to strangers. He always thought his accent made him sound uneducated. Most flights he'd either read a book or take a nap."

"I don't get it. Then why were you so nice to me? Why did you ask me all those questions about him? Why did you lend me Viktor? Why in God's name did you ask me to speak at the funeral?"

"I don't know. At first I thought you were this parasite bitch who was trying to sponge off us, and I was going to tell you to take a hike. But then it hit me. There you were making things up as you went along, and not asking for anything in return. You just wanted us to feel better."

"Yes."

"And then, because you were trying so hard, I realized I was starting to root for you. I really wanted to believe you . . . not to mention you were the most beautiful girl I'd ever seen. I was afraid if I didn't keep the conversation going, I might never see you again."

"Oh my God."

"There was just something about you that blew me away. It was more than chemistry. It was . . . I don't know . . . like this force that drew me to you. I swear, I couldn't take my eyes off you."

"But you were engaged!"

"Tell me about it."

"And you begged me to speak at the funeral!"

"It's crazy. I know."

"I can't believe you. All this time I've been sick to my stomach feeling guilty for what I did to such a wonderful man, and not only did you know, you had your own agenda."

"I'm not proud."

"So how does that make you any different than the girls you can't stand because they're so cagey and manipulative?"

"I don't know. How does that make what you did to me any different than what your parents did to you? You all perpetuated a big lie until the day you got caught."

"Oh jeez. Delia said the same thing to me. . . . It's true. We're both such big hypocrites."

"Not exactly the thing you want to have in common, is it?" He shook his head.

"No, it's not. . . . But you really should be ashamed of yourself." I smacked his shoulder.

"Me? What about you? You're not exactly on the short list for sainthood."

"Touché" I laughed.

Drew put on a CD and reached for my hand. The warm gesture immediately calmed my nerves. Was this a signal that we had endured a grade-one relationship hurricane? That the wind gusts were dying down?

"I am curious about one thing, though," I said. "What would you have done if I'd just wished you well when we got to Miami? Just said good-bye and taken off?"

"I don't know. I probably would have told myself it was for the best and gone on with my life."

"So then, in a way, you're glad I lied?"

"Yes."

"And you don't hate me?"

"At the moment, I'm too busy hating myself for being such a lousy grandson."

"You were a wonderful grandson, Drew. . . . But before, when you were asking me if I'd ever done anything I'd seriously regretted? Was that a setup so I'd confess?"

"Busted." He shrugged. "After everything that's happened with Marly, I just couldn't deal with more lies . . . more secrets. I never want to be in a relationship again that isn't based on trust."

"You're very wise." I kissed him. "And even though I'm still in shock that you knew about the flight, I do like the idea that we've gotten everything out in the open. . . . Now there are no more secrets."

"Um . . . see, that's not entirely true." Drew sighed. "There's something else I haven't told you."

"Well, it couldn't be any worse than this."

"It's right up there."

"Are you serious? You're not sick, are you? About to be indicted?"

"No, nothing like that. . . . It's . . . Marly . . . You're going to go nuts when I tell you."

"Is she sick? About to be indicted?"

He shook his head.

"Oh God. I know that look. . . . Don't tell me she's . . ."

"Yeah."

"No!"

"That's why we flew to Bermuda."

"For what? An abortion?"

"No, of course not. To try to work things out. If we're having a baby, we need to—"

"I think I'm going to be sick, Drew. . . . And you had no idea?"

"Actually, I did. I was just hoping the test was negative."

"How far along is she?"

"She was only a week late. But she took two different tests, and they both came out positive."

"Were you there when she took them? Do you know for sure?"

"She didn't lie, if that's what you're getting at."

"She wouldn't be the first girl to go that route."

"I saw the test results while she was puking her guts out."

"Oh . . . so then how could you just leave her in Bermuda? That was a pretty shitty thing to do."

"It wasn't my idea. She kicked me out. She called her mom and had her fly out there last night."

"That's a little bizarre. You'd think she'd want you to be with her."

"It's complicated, Claire. . . . We were fighting pretty bad. . . . I'm not sure I'm the father."

"Oh my God. Marly cheated on you? She's crazy. . . . What are you going to do?"

"The only thing I can do. I'm going to help her in any way I can. And after the baby's born, I don't know, I guess we'll do the blood tests to prove that I'm the father."

"And if you are?" I held my breath. "Are you going to marry her?"

"I don't know."

"Do you still love her?"

"That's not the issue, Claire."

"Sure it is. Why should you have to alter the course of your entire life just because of a baby?"

Drew's jaw dropped.

"Oh my God. What am I saying? What is wrong with me?"

"No kidding. I mean, you of all people . . . I thought after everything you've just been through, you'd be the one insisting that babies deserve to grow up with their biological parents."

"You're right. I can't believe those words even came out of my mouth. I had no idea I was such a hypocrite. Of course if this is your baby you must be there."

"That's better."

"But . . ."

"I know . . . unfortunately, it changes everything."

For two people who had talked nonstop all day, the conversation finally ran dry. Well, that wasn't altogether true. There was plenty we could have said, but given that it was only two in the afternoon and we'd already reached our quota of huge, scary surprises for the day, it seemed easier to opt for silence.

About the only thing we were willing to discuss was deciding how the rest of the day would play out. I said that I wanted to spend the afternoon with Grams. Drew loved that idea because he really needed to get to the office for few hours to catch up on some paperwork.

But then I was sorry that we were doing the whole lay-low thing because I was suddenly dying to ask what exactly he did for a living. I knew, of course, that he worked for his father, but I was curious: Was it a real job with responsibilities, or was it a toy job like Delia's? Show up whenever the tide rolled in to check messages and pick up a paycheck?

Something else occurred to me as Drew drove me over to Grams' place. Not only did I have no idea what Drew did, I didn't know his age, rank, or serial number. Had not the slightest clue when his birthday was, and, more importantly, his astrological sign. Didn't know if he was a morning person or a night owl, an athlete or a fan, a dreamer or a doer. Who were his friends? What were his hobbies?

Nor did he really know anything about me. But given my recent track record of repelling the opposite sex, maybe that was just as well. In fact, before I said or did anything that turned him off and sent him running back to Marly, it was probably good to be taking a quick breather. Think about the day's events. Then, when we saw each other again, we'd have clear heads.

So I broke the silence barrier by telling him that I'd thought about it, and I was going to spend the night with Grams. That would give us both time to collect ourselves. And not to worry about bringing me a change of clothes. I'd bought enough toiletries, shorts and T's at Target to stay for a week.

To my surprise (and disappointment), Drew didn't protest. There was no whining, no oh-come-on's, I thought we were going to open that first box of condoms tonight. He simply said he thought it was the right thing for me to do.

Me and my big mouth.

I wasn't sure what the world was coming to when a guy who had just broken his second engagement to the same girl didn't seize the opportunity to have hot sex with a girl he'd shown "big" interest in only a few hours earlier.

Or when I rang Gram's bell, and she asked what I was doing there. What grandmother wouldn't welcome the opportunity to spend some quality time with her beloved granddaughter, the very one who nearly died in her shower?

Apparently my timing wasn't great. She and some of her new lady friends were being taken to the movies, and when they got back were going to play cards and have coffee and cake with the fellas. "You can come see the picture if you want," she offered.

No, thanks. I wasn't in the mood to spend a few hours in a dark theater with a bunch of old ladies who farted without shame, and who had zero hearing, so every five minutes they'd lean over to complain to their friend that they were tired of the actors who whispered. "Why can't they speak up?"

"What time do you think you'll be back?" I asked.

"In time for supper. You want to come back?"

"Come back? I can't leave, Grams. I don't have a car. I got dropped off here."

"Oh. So do you want to make dinner?"

"Who, me? You know I'll end up setting off the smoke alarms."

"So what are you going to do? You can't stay here."

"Why not?"

"Because it's restricted. You gotta be sixty-five or older."

"To live here, Grams. Not to visit."

"Oh. Uh-huh. Maybe watch some television, then."

"I can't believe you're leaving me here. You know these women four days. Now total strangers are more important than your own granddaughter?" *Surprise. Two can play the guilt game.*

"Did you call your folks yet?"

"No."

"Then I don't need to spend no time with you."

"Are you serious? You're mad at me? Why aren't you mad at them? They're the ones who made all the mistakes."

"Oh, stop singin' the same song already. I heard enough of your broken record. So they made a little mistake. What's the big hoo-ha? Did they beat you? Did they lock you in a closet? No. They took very good care of you, and believe you me, they did me a big favor, because I couldn't have handled a baby in the house. Your grandfather, may he rest in peace, he said, nothing doing . . . like you was a little puppy I wanted to keep. I don't know what I woulda done if Leonard and Roberta said no. So don't go mouthin' off about how they hurt your feelings or they lied to you . . . they saved your life. If I was you, missy, I'd pick up that phone right now and talk to them. They've been worried sick about you. . . . What are them bags for?"

"I'm sorry." I scratched my head. "What?"

"Whadaya got in those bags?"

"Oh. Just some things I picked up at Target. I thought I would stay with you tonight. There's so much I have to tell you, and—"

She checked her watch. "*Oy.* Now I'm late. Gotta meet the ladies downstairs, or I'll miss the van. We're going to see that picture with what's-his-name. The one who was married to that actress I like. You know who I mean. The one who was in that other picture I liked. Call your parents, Claire. Then we'll talk."

And that was that. My grandmother, who'd never known from

close female companionship because she had no use for other people's *mishegas*, was abandoning me in favor of a bunch of white-haired ladies she just met.

Did you ever?

But an hour later, I was actually happy that she'd left me to my own devices. I walked around the apartment, and remembered how excited I had felt the night that Drew first brought me over here. Little did I know then the extent to which thirty years of living could be suddenly hit by a Hummer and flattened by the force.

How I was still standing was a mystery, I thought, as I scoured the kitchen for the makings of an edible lunch. Something that wasn't no fat, no sodium, no thanks. Thank God for tuna. And the nice garden view off the little balcony.

As I sat outside, feet propped on a plastic Parsons table, I realized that it was the first time in almost ten days that I was alone at the same time that I was of sound mind and body. The first time that there was enough clarity of thought to try and make sense of the enormous changes in my life that were about to unfold. Even though it was in the low eighties, I got such a chill.

I thought about both Grams' and Drew's insistence that I call my parents to basically make amends and move on. Easy for them to say. I thought about Drew's dilemma with Marly and the baby and shuddered at the thought that I had actually suggested it was okay for him to look the other way. But mostly I thought about me.

Life as I knew it was over. So now what? Should I stay in Miami and take a shot at a relationship with a man who could decide to marry the mother of his child? Or should I try to forget Drew, stay down here anyway, and start my life over? Maybe work for Pablo at Case de Miro for a little while, just to have a place to go in the morning?

Perhaps it would be best if I packed up and returned to New York, home of the world's finest therapists (or rather, the most therapists). After serving time on the couch, I would consider adopting a foster child, so that I would have someone with whom I could commiserate when talking about how much life sucked for kids with substitute parents.

Or maybe I should just return to my old life in L.A., spend my days reading the trades, hunting down producers, then begging them for a chance to be cast in their new whatever. . . . Scrap that. I couldn't just show up in Santa Monica and pretend that I'd taken a short hiatus to visit the folks.

Mostly I couldn't fathom being in the same town as my mother the big star, knowing that she could put my career into play with one lousy phone call, but since she couldn't even be bothered to speak to me, it was doubtful she would do something helpful on my behalf.

Clearly none of the above options were appealing. But they did remind me how much I missed Sydney. Unlike my grandmother, she would be happy to hear from me, and she always knew the right thing to say when I was confused.

I grabbed my cell and went back out on the balcony. Turns out I was half right. Sydney was thrilled to hear from me and to learn that I was feeling better. But rather than being the shoulder I needed, she monopolized the conversation.

I'd forgotten how complicated her life could get, between her crazy boyfriends, her crazy parents and their assorted spouses, and her crazy jobs that always seemed to require tasks that bordered on insane, if not illegal.

I listened patiently, as I always did, but it bothered me that she was failing to appreciate the enormity of what was going on in my life. And that, for once, what was happening to me was more important than what was happening to her.

When I realized that the part of the conversation where I would unburden myself was never going to happen, and maybe with Sydney it never had, I begged off, citing the need to get ready for my daily brain scan/spinal tap/blood transfusion. It's possible that got her attention, but I wouldn't know. I had already hung up.

Who else could I call that would be willing to listen to me? Viktor, certainly. But the poor man had already been saddled with enough of my problems. He deserved a rest. Elyce? She could be a good listener, but after dodging so many of her calls, I knew I would be subjected to endless wedding chatter.

Yesterday she'd left a message that her other (more dutiful) bridesmaids had decided to splurge on a four-day cruise to the Bahamas in lieu of a bachelorette party, and I should let her know right away if I wanted a single or a double cabin.

I thought of a few other people who might be decent candidates for a heart-to-heart conversation, but no one who really understood me. Until a name popped into my head.

"Good afternoon. Greene and Levinson."

"Hey, Linds. It's me. What's up?"

"This isn't Linds. It's Diana. Who is this?"

"Oh. Hi. I'm sorry. I thought you were my sister. This is Claire Greene. Where is Lindsey?"

"Who?"

"Lindsey Greene. Leonard's other daughter?"

"What department is she in?"

"Department? Last I looked, it was just my dad and his partner, Marvin."

"Can you please hold? The phones are going crazy. Don't people know it's Saturday?"

"Never mind."

I hit "end," and then punched in the speed dial number for a cell phone number that I should have called first. "Hi, Daddy."

"Claire, is that you?"

"Yes."

"Well, what do you know? Nice to finally hear from you. To what do I owe the honor?"

I thought about bantering with him, but it was a little like needing to pee really bad. There just wasn't time.

"Everything is a mess," I blurted. "And I don't know what to do."

Then, just as with the hundreds of calls to my father that preceded this one, those were my last coherent words before the dam burst, and I cried like only a Daddy's girl could.

# Chapter 27

When I first moved to L.A., I immediately went into therapy, under the pretense that I had to be crazy to live there. In one session, I was asked to describe my father, and I remember passing go, not stopping to collect my two hundred dollars. "He's pigheaded, close-minded, arrogant, rude, impatient, and a major pain in the ass," I said.

"And what are his attributes?"

For that I had to stop and think. "He always knows what to do," I replied.

And it was true. No matter what kind of problem I presented him—a school problem, a personal problem, a work problem—he relied on his accountant, life-is-black-or-white mindset. There was no place for emotion in the equation. Every problem could be reduced to a simple, logical solution.

And so, just as I had done all my life, I unburdened myself on my father once again.

I told him about my growing affection for Drew, and the sad possibility that he would end up staying with Marly and the baby. I told him about the phone call from Penny that ended in a hang-up. About my confusion about where to live and what to do with my life. But mostly about how conflicted I was about him and my mother. That I couldn't understand why everyone was insisting that I should be the one to try to work things out, as if this whole situation were my fault.

To his credit, he never interrupted. Never made a snide comment.

He just listened. Churned the issues in his computerlike brain, then spit out his answers with militarylike precision.

"Okay." He cleared his throat. "First thing is Drew. . . . I like the boy, I do. He's a sweet kid. Seems like he's on the ball. But this isn't the best time for either of you to get involved, and timing is everything. The right person at the wrong time still doesn't add up. I'm not saying don't ever be with him, although it's going to look strange to a lot of people, the whole cousin thing, but the lawyers will cut to the chase on that one. . . . I'm saying for right now you've got enough on your head without adding more complications. If there's really something there, it'll still be there six months from now, too."

"Six months? Are you serious? I can't wait that long. I really, really like him, Daddy. He's not like anyone I've ever met before. He's smart, and cute, and—"

"Rich." My father snorted. "God, does that family have money. You don't even know. . . ."

"Yeah, but it's not like he flaunts it. He took me shopping at Target this morning, and he bought just as much stuff as I did."

"Really? Who paid?"

"Daddy! . . . He did."

"You know, I thought you'd go for him. I even said to your mother, you watch, Claire. She's going to go for this one."

"Really? Why?"

"Are you kidding? He's tall, dark, and handsome, he's going to inherit an estate one day, that's, phew . . . what a life you'd have. . . ."

"It's not the money I like. I like him. Who he is as a person."

"So, fine. If he's that terrific, be friends. Just don't go jumping into the sack with him. Especially if he's trying to figure out what to do with the other one . . . and what a nutcase she is."

"I know. She is so full of herself."

"Well, whatever. You don't want him thinking about her while he's *shtupping* you."

"Daddy!"

"What! You know what I'm saying. . . . If this is meant to be, it'll be."

"I guess."

"Now, as for your mother and me—"

"I know what you're going to say. I owe you both an apology."

"You bet your sweet ass! Your mother is devastated. She can't eat, she can't sleep—"

"I'm sorry, but she—"

"No. Uh-uh. There are no buts. You said some pretty shitty things, kiddo, and it broke her heart. . . . We know your issues. So, fine, we should have told you. But we can't take it back. We made the decisions we thought were right at the time, and now they're coming back to haunt us. But don't question our love for you. Don't question our pride or our devotion. There wasn't a day that went by that we weren't in your corner trying to be good parents.

"God! It just killed me when you said we were too cheap to send you to that acting camp. But you weren't aware that I found out from a buddy of mine that the owner was operating under bankruptcy protection. So what should I have done? Sent in the four grand, and waited for the letter that says, *Sorry. We're not opening this season. For refunds, the line forms to the left, and maybe you'll get twenty cents on the dollar?*"

"I didn't know that."

"No, of course not. There are lots of things you didn't know. That's what parents do. They shelter their kids from the things they shouldn't have to know." He sighed. "Look, I can understand where you're coming from. You see what Mom and I did as some kind of Watergate cover-up. But that's not how it was, kiddo. . . . You were a newborn when this happened . . . too young to ever have any recollections. . . . I don't know. At the time it seemed like the smart thing to do. To just love you and raise you as our own and say to hell with the past. I think we honestly expected we'd tell you one day. Everyone we talked to, the Rabbi, family, friends, this child psychiatrist we went to . . . they all said the same thing: When the time is right, you'll tell her. But the years went by, and that time never came. . . . And don't get me wrong. You were a bright kid. Maybe too smart for your own good. I knew if we told you even a little bit, you'd ask a million questions, and we'd end up telling you more than you could have handled.

"And then there was a point, I don't know, you were maybe sixteen, when we realized we'd lost our big chance. By then you were in your angry, rebellious stage, and hitting you with something like this would have been the push you needed to do something stupid like get into drugs or go run off with that idiot biker you liked, what was his name . . ."

"Kevin Albright."

"Yeah, That guy. I swear, when I found out you were sneaking around with him, I almost locked you up and threw away the key. What was he, like nineteen, twenty? My precious Claire, riding around town on the back seat of a Harley with some unemployed grease monkey who couldn't keep his hands off you. You have no idea how many sleepless nights I had over that one.

"Anyway, dear. What I'm trying to say is I love you, I have always loved you, and from the day I held you, I gave you my word to honor and protect you, and to try to give you the best life that I could."

"You did, Daddy," I cried. "You gave me a great life. It was perfect, actually. I had everything I ever needed. A great family, lots of friends, a nice house, I got to go to camp every year, you bought me anything I asked for, we took all those great trips. . . ."

"Now, don't cry, sweetheart. Please. You know what that does to me."

"And I'm so sorry. I know I said some awful things. I was just in shock. Everything came from out of nowhere, and you know how bad I am when I get blindsided. I completely freak out."

"We know. But it would sure be a big help if you called your mother for Mother's Day. Tell her you love her and you're sorry."

"Oh God. Is that tomorrow?"

"All day."

"Should I send flowers?"

"No. She just wants to know you're okay and that you don't hate her."

"I don't hate her. Not that I don't have my issues with her. But I guess I did sort of go a little overboard."

"A little overboard? Jesus, Claire. The only thing you didn't accuse her of was trying to steal your boyfriends."

"Hmmm. I always thought she had her eye on the biker guy," I laughed. "Anyway, I promise I'll call and apologize."

"I'm sure she'd love to hear it. . . . And as for the other mother, if you could even call her that—"

"Oh my God, I still can't get over the fact that she hung up on me. Who hangs up on her only child?"

"I think you should go out there and talk to her," he said.

"What?"

"Yeah. Tell her how you feel. Lord knows you've got a big enough mouth. You shouldn't have a hard time figuring out what you want to say."

"You can't be serious."

"Why not? You're never going to get better until you do, and it's not as if you need her for anything. You already have a mother."

"I don't know, it would just be too weird."

"Well, don't not do it because you think we'd be upset. We're not threatened by the old coward. I just think if you don't go duke things out with her now, it'll eat you up inside forever."

"I guess. . . . I mean, it's not like I haven't thought about what I'd say to her."

"Exactly."

"But it's so obvious she doesn't want to talk to me. What am I supposed to do, camp out at her front door and hope she lets me in?"

"I bet Ben could set something up for you. He seems like a pretty decent guy."

"He is. But what are you saying? I should ask him to make an appointment for me so I could speak to my own mother?"

"Not an appointment. I don't know, tell her you want to meet for a drink. Keep it casual."

"I can't believe you're telling me to do this, especially after you walloped her in the face."

"Oh . . . didn't know if you knew about that little episode."

"Yeah. I heard. Anyway, I couldn't go out there right now. I don't have enough money for cab fare, let alone airfare."

"I figured as much. . . . But what the hell? Consider it a peace offering. It's the least I could do . . . and JetBlue flies to Long Beach now."

"You really love that airline, don't you?"

"If they don't go, I don't go . . . but no, really. Look into making a reservation. . . . And as for your meeting with the lawyers on Monday—"

"Okay, now, that I am definitely sorry about. I promise you, whatever I get, I'm sharing with you and Mommy."

"That's lovely, dear, thank you. But here's something you don't hear the old man say every day. You were right. It's not our money, it's yours. If you want my advice on investing or whatever, fine—"

"Thanks . . . but do you think . . . would you . . . is there any chance you could come in?"

"For what? The meeting on Monday?"

"Yes."

"No. Can't. I've got a full day already. But it's at a lawyer's office. Just have them put me on speaker phone before you get started. It'll be like I'm right there."

"I guess that works. . . . And I meant what I said before. I have no idea how much I'm getting, but consider it family money."

"Well, that's very sweet of you, dear, but let's find out how much you'll owe Uncle Sam before you start handing out checks."

"Thanks, Daddy . . . for everything. I do love you and Mommy."

"We know."

"And I appreciate all of your advice."

"It's my job."

"Except there is one thing I can't do."

"What?"

"I'm not going to be able to stay away from Drew. In fact, right now all I can think about is *shtupping* his little brains out."

"Good God, Claire. I'm your father . . . show some respect."

"Sorry."

"And at least promise to use protection. Nothing's worse than being second in line for child support."

I was glad to hear Gram's key in the door. I couldn't wait to tell her about the nice conversation with my Dad, and that things looked like they might be okay after all. But when she walked in, she was so pleased with her afternoon adventure, it was as if she'd forgotten I was there.

Mind you, I was thrilled that she was finally enjoying herself. I was just surprised how little she cared about hanging with me. Gabbing like old times. Feeding me until I wanted to puke. Instead, she announced a change of plans. She was meeting friends for supper, then they were going over to the clubhouse to hear a comedian.

"He used to play up at Grossingers," she informed me. "Want to come?"

"No. It's fine. I'll just . . ." But I couldn't think fast enough to finish my sentence.

"Whatsa matter?"

"Nothing. I think I'll call Drew, and see what he's up to."

"So now you're friends with Abe's grandson?"

"Yes. He's been very nice to me."

"Well, if you ask me, I think he's sweet on you."

"You do?"

"Sure. I seen the way he looks at you . . . not like he looks at that *meshugina* he's marrying."

"Maybe not. They're sort of an on again, off again couple."

"Smart kid. . . . 'Cause if you ask me, she could use a good *zetz* across that little heiny of hers."

"I know . . . but, um . . . what would you think about Drew and me?"

Grams stopped fussing with her hair in the mirror.

"I mean, nothing has happened yet, of course." *Except for one hot shower. And I do mean hot!*

"They got laws against that sort of thing, you know."

*Taking a shower together?* "Oh, you mean the cousin connection.

But it's not like that, Grams. We're not blood relatives. Drew is actually Ben's adopted son, so it's okay."

"You really like this fella." Her hips swayed.

I nodded.

"So whadaya think is going to happen?"

"I wish I knew. Things are pretty complicated."

"Too bad we're not in the old neighborhood no more. There was a fella we would go to . . . he had special powers, see."

"Are you serious, Grams? You went to a psychic?"

"Course not. The sons-of-bitches take your money and give you nothin' but cock-and-bull stories. And how come, if they're so smart, you don't hear about them winnin' the lottery? But this fella, he wasn't like that. He owned a coffee shop. And in between customers, he'd tell us things."

"Oh my God . . . not the one on 188th?"

"Yeah. You know the place?"

"I'm not sure. Is it a Greek restaurant with flies . . . what was the name of it?"

"House of Athens," Grams said.

"Yeah. That was it. Oh my God. I can't believe it, I just happened to walk in there the afternoon I got out of the hospital the first time. I ordered lunch, and the owner comes up to me and says something about the food being only so-so, but the predictions, they're the best."

"That's him! *Oy.* I hope this don't mean he's getting famous, 'cause he always said as soon as he got famous, he'd have to start to charging."

"This is unbelievable. I remember now. He asked me if I believed in love at first sight, because he said he could tell that I was in love but didn't want to admit it."

"Well, whadaya know!"

"Amazing. . . . I was falling in love with Drew. I just couldn't admit it. . . . Poor man, I basically told him to go back to making his moussaka because he didn't know what the hell he was talking about."

"Uch. Too bad you can't go back there now. See what else he sees.

God forbid, maybe a baby already. 'Cause I don't have to tell you you're not getting any younger."

"Oh yeah. There's definitely a baby in the future . . . it's just not mine."

A half hour later, Grams took off again to meet up with friends. This from someone who used to complain that her back went out more than she did. Now her social calendar was busier than mine.

I looked at the clock again. Six-fifteen, and no word from Drew. I stopped my world for him. The least he could do is call. Yes, I'd told him I wanted to stay here for the night. But still. For a guy who'd just had his hands all over my naked body, and then shared some mighty huge secrets, you'd think he could at least pick up the phone to say hi.

This was why I hated the start of relationships. I never knew where I stood. What was expected. If initiating something was thoughtful or pushing it. And if he didn't call me, what did it mean? Was he legitimately busy or legitimately avoiding me?

And it's not as if I didn't understand the line of work that Drew and his family were in. They owned nightclubs, for God's sake. And not just any clubs. The hottest clubs in all of south Florida. Maybe the entire goddamn Western Hemisphere.

So it wasn't like when Drew said he had work to do in the office, I expected him to be hanging out at the water cooler taking bets on who'd be the next survivor to be voted off the island. Of course his job description included schmoozing, drinking, and flirting. Anything to keep the party going and the shot girls flush with twenties in their hot pants.

And it's not like, when he finally answered his cell, I expected to hear the sound of clicking keyboards coming from the secretarial pool. Good thing, because I wasn't the least bit thrown when it sounded like a large, raucous party. "Hi. How are you?"

"Great," he yelled over the din. "You?"

I'm sorry. Was this the same man who only hours earlier was mourning the loss of his grandfather? Who professed his prurient desire to be with me, rather than his ex-fiancée who might very well be the mother of his first child?

"I'm fine," I replied. "I just wanted to see how you were holding up."

"What?"

"I was thinking about you." I spoke in my crowded-bar voice.

"I can't hear you, Carly, honey. Call me back tonight."

CARLY? Who was Carly?

"Nicole," he hollered. "Check it out. Dooley's hot for you. Look at him. He's licking your leg."

"I gotta go." I ended the call.

As if that snippet of conversation weren't enough of a mood crapper, I realized that it was six-thirty on a Saturday night and I was sitting by myself in an assisted living center. But not to worry. This could still be my lucky night. Maybe I'd find a hot game of bingo going on, and beat the pants of the old folks who could neither see nor hear. How hard could it be to win enough money to cover the cost of a cab to Miami International?

An alluring thought, if not for one small matter. I didn't want to leave town yet. Certainly not before my meeting with Abe's attorney on Monday, which offered the potential for better winnings than a decent night of bingo. But mostly not before getting to tell Drew thanks, but no thanks. I thought he was great, but I didn't have the stomach to get involved with a guy who got in trouble if he *didn't* drink on the job. To say nothing of a guy who was about to become a father to a baby with whom he might not have a biological link. I'd already seen that movie. "Taxi!"

But rather than chickening out, I toughed it out. If you could call getting a pedicure on a Saturday night toughing it out.

After I had hung up on or with Drew, depending on how you saw it, I invited my one and only friend in town, Viktor, to have dinner. In an act of cunning, I suggested the Greek coffee shop where he'd once come to get me. But you know as well as I, it had nothing to do with the grape leaves. More like the tea leaves. I was desperate to find out from the owner if there was any hope for my future.

Unfortunately for me, Viktor was enjoying his rare night off with friends. And not that I begrudged the man a life. I was just a teensy bit hurt that he intimated that his dealings with me were strictly job-related. Apparently I'd confused the friendly bond we'd forged with his being nice in exchange for a paycheck.

He did, however, remember to tell me that Delia and her mother were worried about me, and that I should call to let them know I was fine. Which is how I ended up soaking my feet in hot bubbles on a Saturday night. Seems that they, too, were alone with nothing to do.

"I know this great Korean nail salon that stays open late every night," Delia said. "Want to go get pedicures?"

"A pedicure?" I cheered like a three-year-old who just got invited to the circus.

"You don't have to have an orgasm over it. It's not that exciting."

"It is to me," I said. "I haven't done something that normal in ages. I just can't believe you and your mom want to do this. It's Saturday night."

"Down here every night is Saturday night. Well, actually, Monday and Tuesday night are more like Thursday night. Wednesday night is the new Friday night. Thursday and Friday are what Saturday night used to be, and Sunday night is still Sunday night. Chinese food and HBO."

"Thanks for the lonely-girls update," I laughed.

"Yeah, but you're not gonna be lonely for long."

"Not true. At the rate I'm going, my Saturday night steady is going to be a Korean guy who knows how to exfoliate."

"I don't get it. I told Drew you were into him. I thought, you know, he'd—"

"Don't get me wrong, Delia. He's really sweet, but we've both got a lot of stuff to deal with right now, and he's a busy guy."

"No he's not. I'll talk to him again."

"No, don't." I spit out.

"Okay. But, um . . . there's something I need to tell you. You just got this huge flower delivery."

"I did? From who?"

"I don't know."

"Oh bullshit, Delia. You know everything. Are they from Drew?" Delia didn't answer.

"C'mon, don't play games. Just tell me who they're from. I'll bet they're from my dad, 'cause we had this really nice conversation before, and—"

"Okay, look. They're not from your Dad. Or Drew, either. They're . . . um . . . from Aunt Penny. Well, she's my Aunt Penny. I don't know what she is to you."

I got a chill. "She's nothing to me . . . absolutely nothing. . . . Is there a card?"

"You know what? I'll just bring it when I pick you up."

"No. Read it to me now."

"You sure?"

"Delia, read me the fucking card."

"Okay. Well, it's not very long or anything. It says, *Claire, call me tomorrow. Penny Nichol.*"

"Oh wow. That is so touching. Short, but with that nice Hallmark sentiment. Don't you think?"

"Whatever. She's—"

" 'Call me tomorrow,' " I repeated. "Oh my God. Tomorrow is Mother's Day! How presumptuous can you get? Like hell I'd ever call her, let alone on—"

"They're really nice flowers, Claire. It's one huge mother of a bouquet," she laughed.

"I wouldn't care if she sent me a float from the Rose Bowl parade. I'm not calling her."

"I wouldn't do that. Aunt Penny gets pretty pissy when you don't do what she wants."

"Well, that's nothing compared to how pissy I get when someone abandons me!"

"She's trying to be nice. Maybe just call her to say hi."

"Nope. Sorry. She hung up on me already. Only one insult per customer."

# Chapter 28

Seriously, who does that? Who has a baby, ditches the kid, then thirty years later sends flowers and a card that says call me? What did the fabulous Penny Nichol think? That she was in some sappy film by Nora Ephron that had your predictable let's-kiss-and-make-up scene, followed by a happy ending? Roll credits?

As I waited for Delia and Shari to pick me up, and wrote Grams a note telling her where I was going, I had a chilling thought. Abe had become a great humanitarian, in spite of witnessing untold atrocities and the insidious underbelly of evil. Yet his biggest disappointment may have been that he had spawned a daughter who had beauty and talent, but a defective heart. Who came from a loving home that cherished family, but who in a slap-of-the-face act chose a life that shunned motherhood and commitment.

In fact, who could have guessed that of all the heroic acts that Abraham Fabrikant performed in his eighty-four years, his greatest act of compassion would be deciding to let me grow up in a normal environment? How wise and fortuitous he was to understand that if he forced his daughter to raise her daughter, I would be subjected to emotional abuses that could scar me for life.

Oh yeah. I would definitely be calling my mother to wish her a happy Mother's Day.

No, not that one.

\* \* \*

When I awoke the next morning in Cousin Drew's bed (yes, he was back to being Cousin Drew), I tried to remember what I did last Mother's Day. *Oy.* How could I have forgotten? I'd spent it with Sydney and her mother. And Sydney's stepmother. And her ex-stepmother, too. In fact, it was practically raining mothers at Pedal's, the trendy Santa Monica bistro, where we'd been invited to brunch with Sydney's father.

How very chic, I'd thought at the time. And so very California to have a civil assemblage of women all connected to one man, feasting on cold, poached salmon and green apple martinis. The fact that two of the women had recently had their antidepressants upped, and the third had just been released from the hospital after a little bout with attempted suicide, did in no way diminish the cordial chatter about the one issue on which we were all united: the urgent need for cow cloning so as to guarantee an endless supply of the all important botulinum toxin that made frown lines disappear.

But this Mother's Day would surely go down as the mother of them all. Too bad Hallmark didn't sell one card for the woman who forgot you existed, and another for the woman who woke up one day, got word that she was being called up for active duty, and had to report to Camp Motherhood at once.

Or maybe they could set up a special hotline offering advice on solving sticky mother problems. Like the one the folks at Butterball ran on Thanksgiving for those last-minute questions on preparing the holiday turkey.

I would e-mail my suggestions later. Meanwhile, I would try to fall back asleep, as I'd spent most of the night tossing and turning over what to do about my own sticky Mother's Day problem.

"Knock, knock." I heard Shari's voice on the other side of the door.

"Hi." I sat up. "C'mon in."

"Did I wake you?" She stuck her head in.

"No, I've been up. . . . Happy Mother's Day."

"Thank you, Claire. I came up to . . . I'm not sure how to tell you this . . ."

"What?"

"Penny is on the phone for you."

"What the . . . Why?"

"I don't know. She called earlier, and I said I wouldn't disturb you. But she just called again, and I said, 'All right, let me go up and see if she's awake.'"

"I can't believe her. She disappears for thirty years, and now it's like she's stalking me."

"She's not stalking you." Shari laughed. "She just seems anxious to, you know . . . talk."

"I'm sorry. I don't mean to put you in the middle of all this, but there is nothing to talk about."

"I know you're hurt and upset, but please don't be like this. It's Mother's Day."

"Exactly. All the more reason to tell her to leave me the hell alone."

"Maybe you could just pick up for a minute and listen to what she has to say."

"No way! And if this offends you, then I'll be more than happy to pack my things and go."

"No. No. Of course not. You're a grown woman. I respect your decision to handle this however you think best. It's just that . . . I've never heard Penny like this. She actually seems nervous."

"Good. She should be."

"It's so rare for her to show her vulnerable side. That's why I thought you might—"

"Wait, wait, wait. You just said you respected whatever decision I made."

"I do. Absolutely. It's just that it's . . . you know . . ."

"Mother's Day. Which is why I plan to call my mother, and my grandmother, and my friend Sydney's mother. I'll call your mother. I'll call everyone I've ever met who is a mother. I'm just not speaking to the woman who had the nerve to call at . . . what time is it?"

"Nine-thirty."

"Nine-thirty on a Sunday morning so she can try to smooth over a little misunderstanding we had when I was born. 'I'm sorry. Was I suppose to raise you? Silly me. I completely forgot.'"

"Actually, she happened to mention something about a possible film role."

*Damn!* "I don't care. If she wants to bribe someone, let her call a congressman."

"Oh c'mon, Claire. I thought you were a bigger person than this. You do realize it's only six-thirty her time. And, my God, she must have been up at the crack of dawn when she called the first time."

"You don't understand. The very idea of hearing her voice makes me want to—"

"I swear, you are just like her!"

"I'm sorry?"

"I'm saying, you are most definitely her daughter. You're as obstinate and pigheaded as she is . . . you can't tell her a goddamn thing."

So, fine. Maybe I had inherited Penny's stubborn streak. All the more reason she should have understood that when I said I didn't want to speak to her, I meant it. And nothing would change my mind. Not her *ferkakte* flowers, not the other calls she made that day, not the e-mails she sent (thanks for giving her my screen name, Delia), not the insistence of the entire Fabrikant family.

In fact, the greater the pressure they applied, the angrier I got. No one had any right to ask, let alone push me into doing something that felt so inextricably, undeniably, I'd-rather-eat-bugs-on-*Fear-Factor* wrong.

I was not trying to punish Penny, as Shari remarked (well, maybe a little), I was not trying to humiliate her (Ben's two cents), not trying to hurt her feelings (Drew), not even trying to guilt her into being nice so she ended up buying me a house, a car, and taking me to Paris for a shopping spree (do you even need to ask who said that?).

And with apologies to Dr. Phil, I saw no need to work on my "ka-muni-cation" skills. I was simply exercising my rights as a wronged person. Whatever lay ahead for me wouldn't involve her, so why open the door?

My father was right, I told him when I called home. I had a mother. I did not need another who was clueless, insincere, and beyond fashionably late to the party. Although, to my surprise, even

*The Lenny and Roberta Show* urged me to at least 'listen to what the woman has to say.'

As did Sydney: "Get over it. You were fucked. Let the bitch make it up to you." Viktor: "She is not so bed, really. Maybe you tell her she hez to find job for you in the movies, end then yule talk. Em I right?" Even Grams: "Whadaya got to lose? And tell her to make it up to you, she has to come over here and sign autographs at our big dinner dance next week. That son-of-a-bitch Vic Damone dropped out. I never cared much for him anyway."

Still, I turned my back on Penny, just as she had turned hers on me. Didn't care that it would deprive Grams of being a hero for delivering a big celebrity to the dance. Didn't care that I was offending my gracious hosts. Didn't care that I was spurning a woman who could call any of the biggest Hollywood producers and demand that they send me scripts. I chose, instead, to be "Penniless."

For here is what no one but me seemed to get. No matter how grown up I appeared, I had officially reverted back to the emotional equivalent of a five-year-old who spent the whole day stomping and screaming, "It's not fair. It's NOT fair!"

It's not fair that there was no justice in life. That Penny hadn't suffered for her crime of abandonment. Instead, she was at the top of her game, earning millions every year, being glorified by the media, and living lavishly in a dream mansion. Surely anyone who left her tiny baby in a crib with a diaper bag and a note was not deserving of such riches.

And it wasn't even that she'd been young and stupid when she made her dreadful mistake. It's that she had grown up and laughed in the face of destiny without apparent remorse or regret. Otherwise she would have made herself known to my family. Not disguised herself in name and appearance, then built a fairy-tale existence to pretend that she was born without a past.

It just wasn't fair.

Midway through a lovely Mother's Day dinner at By the C, I leaned over to Cousin Drew and asked a huge favor. Could I please borrow his car, as there was someplace important I wanted to go after we dropped off Grams? He said yes, but followed with an immediate offer to have either he or Viktor take me wherever I wanted to go. How to tell him that that wouldn't help me?

For one thing, I didn't want Drew to know I was headed to a Greek coffee shop in order to consult with the psychic owner. For another thing, I would be too ashamed to ask Viktor to take me to the very place I'd offered to take him to dinner. Then he'd know my invitation was premeditated.

"Have you ever driven a Porsche before?" Drew asked.

"Many times." *Once.*

"All right, then. But under one condition. Tell me why you've been acting so cool to me."

"I am not acting cool," I whispered. "I just think we should both try to get our lives in order before we jump into a new relationship."

"You mean because of Marly," he said.

"I mean because of Marly, and what's going on with Penny and I, and because I'd like to fully recover from my injuries, and decide where I want to live, and—"

"I've rethought things, too. And I don't care what happens with Marly, or Aunt Penny, or your injuries, or your career. I want us to be together."

"Well, that sounds really swell. But it seems to me as if your life is all set here. You've got a big business to run, an endless supply of girls who dig you—"

"Whoa. Slow down. What girls? For the past two years, I was mostly with Marly."

"Look, Drew. I think you're amazing. And whenever I'm with you, I feel safe, I feel happy. It's just when I'm not with you, the doubt creeps in. I wonder what you're doing, who you're with . . . who the hell Carly Honey is—"

"Carly Honey. . . . Do you mean Carly Deveraux?"

"I don't know. Who's that?"

"My cousin on the other side. My mom's brother's daughter. They just moved to Atlanta, and she calls me almost every day to bitch about how much she hates it."

"Oh. Guess I blew that one. . . . I called you last night and you thought I was her. I just figured—"

"That was you? I'm sorry. I should have looked at the caller ID. I just assumed you were with your grandmother and you needed some time alone. . . . And that is one hell of a jealous streak you've got . . . a little scary, actually. This is a crazy business, Claire. But for me, it's only business. I'm not into the whole bar scene anymore. In fact, I hate it. It's one of the reasons I want to get out and do my own thing. The girls are all like Delia. Out-of-their-minds crazy, and after a while it's so degrading. All they want from you is drugs and sex."

"Actually, it's no different in L.A. Did you know it stands for lotsa ass?"

"Hey, that's what Miami needs. A catchy slogan like that."

"No, wait. You haven't heard my favorite. It was one of those local public service announcements about sexual harassment in the work-place. The tag line was the best. 'Ladies, don't forget. Harass is not two words.' "

Drew laughed, then kissed me for all the world to see. Or at least his family and employees. But how embarrassing when they all cheered, and Ben scribbled something on a napkin. It said, *9.5.*

"You can do better than that, son. Your dismount was a little shaky."

Was it just my imagination, or was everyone genuinely happy for us? The answer came in the form of a tune. I could swear I heard Delia hum, "Ding dong, the witch is dead."

"I'm sorry I jumped to conclusions," I whispered. "I've never thought of myself as the jealous type. But when you want some-thing so badly, you panic just thinking that something will mess it all up."

"So that whole business before about needing time to get your life together—that was a crock?"

I nodded.

"Good, because if I can't have you, then I'm down to only one other first cousin, and she's definitely not my type."

"Oh. Not blond?"

"Not straight."

When it was time to leave, Drew offered to come along on my errand, but I begged to go alone. I knew how to get there, promised it wouldn't take long, and that I would tell him about it when I got back. Except that, as with everything else in my life, my little excursion didn't go according to plan.

After driving around for ten minutes, the only parking spot I could find was three long blocks from the House of Athens. The streets were dark and deserted, and by the time I finally arrived, an out-of-breath mess, the CLOSED sign was hanging over the door. And yet there was a light on in the back.

I took a shot and rang the bell, but nothing. I banged on the window. Still nothing. I grabbed my cell and called the phone number on the door. No answer. Then, just as I was about to head back to the car and pray that I could remember where I'd parked, an older, heavyset woman spotted me.

"Closed." She pointed to the sign.

"I know. It's okay. I don't want to eat, I just wanted . . ."

What? What did I want? To ask the owner if he remembered me? The girl with the good aura?

I must have looked pretty pathetic, because the woman opened the door. "We're closed, ma'am. We open again tomorrow at eleven."

"I know. I'm sorry. I didn't actually want to order anything, I wanted to talk to the man who was here last time."

"Who? Costa? My son?"

"Yes. Yes. That's his name. Costa. Is he here?"

"Not now, miss. His wife had a baby two days ago. A beautiful little girl." She smiled.

"That's so nice. Congratulations."

"Daphne Athena Christina Eugenia Amandes."

"Oh, that's lovely." *She'll be ten befor*

"So what did you want to ask him? Yo

"Not just big problems. Huge problems
fused in my whole—"

"Come in, come in. I'm just mopping up. You

"Sure. Absolutely. I'm a great little mopper." *I
the smell of ammonia, but that's another story.*

"You got the job, honey," she said after an hour
spraying, dusting, and sweeping.

"You do this every night?" I collapsed into one of the boo

"For twenty-six years. Tonight I have no help because I send
all home to be with their families. The days are long, but it's a g
life. Next month we're all going to Greece to visit my mother
family."

"That's wonderful. . . . I'm sorry. I don't even know your name."

"I'm Althea. And you are . . . ?"

"Claire Greene. From New York." We shook hands. "Nice to
meet you."

"So you come a very long way for us. Why didn't you say so?"

"Well, actually I've been here for a few weeks . . . very unexpectedly."

"Uh-huh. You have good auras around you."

"Oh my God. That's exactly what your son said. But what does it
mean? Because if it's supposed to be bringing me good luck, someone didn't get the memo."

"Oh my dear, you've had nothing but good luck. You've got great
beauty and intelligence, passion and abilities, love and friendship,
good health. . . . You're a very wealthy woman."

"Really? I always thought rich girls had more than four hundred
and seventy-seven dollars to their name."

"Wealth is not only measured in dollars and cents, my dear."

"That's what I've been trying to tell Mastercard."

Althea smiled. "You have wonderful colors around you, which
tells me not only have you been blessed, but that you are guided and
protected. I think by a male spirit . . . maybe a grandfather?"

my lap, only I didn't

a laughed. "One day
My family is waiting

ll that cleaning . . .

n within. The radiant
n great psychic aware-

any of this coming, 'cause
stayed away from shower stalls."
do you need? Should you marry him? Yes. Should
talk to your mother? Most definitely. Should you put your inheritance away for a rainy day? It never hurts. Anything else?"

"Yes. . . . Wait. How did you know all that? Where do you get
your information?"

"The same place as you, dear. I just listen to the voices from the
other side."

"But it's not just voices. I hear music. I feel energy around me. I
see the image of my grandfather in front of me. I know things I have
no way of knowing."

"It's just like your name, which is so perfect for you. You are
Claire. For clairvoyant."

"Clairvoyant? Me? Are you sure?"

"I am most certain. When you walked through the door, I felt the
great power of your spirit guides enter with you. It's the sign that you
often return to the other side for answers."

"Return to the other side? You mean actually come and go? Like
astral travel?"

"Don't let the name scare you, dear. It is all quite natural. But I do
sense that you have visited very recently. Perhaps, if you try, you will
be able to remember the journey."

*Claire Voyant*

*e she learns how to spell it.*
*u have problems?"*
*I've never been so con-*
*'ll give me a hand?"*
*used to vomit from*
*of scrubbing,*
*ths.*
*them*
*od*

*Chapter 29*

WHEN I WAS A KID, I USED TO CRINGE EVERY TIME MY FATHER THREW up his hands and asked, "How can I make plans if God just laughs?" Or when my mother would iron his shirts to the tune of "Que sera, sera, whatever will be will be." As an already anxious nine-year-old, it was disconcerting to think my parents, my God-assigned protectors, were walking through life with an undertow of dread that at any moment the Almighty One could capsize their comfortable four-bedroom, split-level boat.

By the time I reached high school, I was so sick of their we-control-nothing attitude, I purposely dated a geek named Stephen Wishnick who believed in free will. It was so liberating to subscribe to his more enlightened ideology that we were here to program our own destinies, much like getting to decide which TV shows we wanted to tape on this new thing called a VCR.

Naturally I shared this with my father in the hopes of setting him straight. Why let the poor guy spend his golden years in an ignorant, misguided state?

"Free will, my ass." He twirled a Salem in an ashtray. "There's no such thing. It's all decided before we get here. Like Rabbi Rubin says every Yom Kippur. Who shall live and who shall die. Who by trial and who by fire."

After leaving Althea's House of Predictions, it hit me that he'd probably been right. Free will was a crock. A concept we embraced to convince ourselves that we were independent operators, entitled to make decisions and choose actions as we saw fit.

So after all these years, why had I suddenly changed my mind? Because a total stranger had just zoned in on my most pressing issues: men, marriage, money, and mothers. Of course, a cynic—me, for instance—could say that those were the most universal of dilemmas, and the woman just got lucky.

But something about the way Althea hit all those bull's-eyes led me to believe that she wasn't just a good guesser. She knew what was causing me to lose sleep because she was the universe's answer to a diligent studio executive. She had read the script, screened the dailies, and knew how the story ended. Which really pissed me off. I hated the idea that the paths I chose, and the outcome of those choices, were all in the script. The script written, executive-produced, and directed by God, with maybe a bunch of cutthroat associate-producer angels trying to exert their limited powers in order to satisfy their own agendas.

As an actress, one would think I would love the notion of our lives being preordained. Our destinies a wrap. But I knew better than anyone that a great life was about as rare as a great script. And all too often, we didn't even realize when we were holding one in our hands.

In general, it's not a good idea to be behind the wheel of a borrowed Porsche when you are DWU: Driving while unhinged. Particularly if you don't know the area and, therefore, the best exit to your destination. If only I'd remembered that while trying to find my way back to the Fabrikant estate.

You know the scene. You take your eyes off the road to read the signs for one split second, and boom. You're exchanging phone numbers with a guy who is not likely to take you to dinner after the tow truck pulls away.

I was shaking when I dialed Drew to tell him, fully expecting to hear this otherwise genteel man flip out.

"Are you sure you're okay?" Drew asked for like the tenth time.

"I'm fine. I'm just so so sorry. I should have listened to you and let you drive. I don't know what I was thinking."

"As long as you're okay," he insisted. "It's only metal and money."

*Yeah. A* lot *of metal and money.* "I'll pay you back, I swear. Whatever your out-of-pocket-costs are. This was entirely my fault."

"Claire, relax. It's okay. We're like a twelve-car family. I have other things to drive."

"Yes, but it's a Porsche. It's seven years' bad luck to wreck one."

"Not for the body shop."

"Are you always this understanding after your car's been towed?"

"Are you kidding? You know how many times I cracked up my car and had to call my dad to come get me? He was never happy, but as long as I made the call, it meant I was okay, and he just taught me to deal with it."

"A great attitude." I coughed. "Now let's see how you handle the really bad news."

"What?"

"You know the guy I hit?" I closed my eyes. "Seems it's a very small world."

"Oh no. How small?"

"Pretty small, apparently. I'm not a hundred percent, but he may be Marly's Uncle Alvin?"

"Oh shit. Not Alvin Becker. Claire, you idiot! The guy is a lunatic!"

As I listened to Drew carry on that I was an irresponsible, stubborn jerk, it didn't faze me one bit. I guess I hated the idea of dating a man who only had one speed (Mr. Nice Guy). Imagine the pressure on me to follow suit. I'd have to spend at least one week a month biting my PMS tongue. At least now I had proof that he could go ballistic like the rest of us mere mortals.

"Thank you," I sighed. "I feel so much better already."

Can I tell you what saved my ass when I finally got back to the house? My ass is what saved my ass. Seems Drew had been planning an official welcome-to-my-room party, complete with scented candles and mood music. But after the stressful events of the night, he begged off.

Unfortunately, between the phone calls from Penny, the dinner kiss, the hour of scrubbing, the strange reading, and the accident, I was so wired myself, I really wanted Drew to stay. So when I saw that he was torn, I went with my instincts and locked the bedroom door. The music he had chosen turned out to be just right for a lap dance.

Funny how the scent of vanilla, and a little striptease can get a man to forget what ails him. By the time I was down to my tiny black Cosabella thong, Drew was no longer thinking about smashed fenders and broken headlights. But he wasn't the only one feeling pleasure.

To my delight, he had been a good little boy and paid close attention to instruction-happy Samantha on *Sex and the City*. (God bless HBO: Hot Breathing and Orgasms). And even though I knew I should stay focused on the moment, I found myself thinking about the call I would make to Sydney. We may not have had a special coffee shop like Carrie, Miranda, Charlotte, and Samantha, but we knew how to dish.

I couldn't wait to tell her that dating Drew was like having four of the best boyfriends on the show: He had a big, hard body like Smith, a big, wonderful heart like Steve, and big, deep pockets like Harry. But best of all, he was my Mr. Big. I just looked at him and I got weak. No doubt in my mind—I was not walking away from this guy after six seasons.

"I swear, you get more amazing by the day." He stroked my hair.

"So you're not mad at me anymore?"

"I'm furious, but at least I found a way for you to repent."

"If I had known being a sinner was this much fun . . ."

"Down, girl." He kissed my hand. "As it is, I'm not going to be able to walk in the morning."

"Oh, I'm sorry. I thought you'd be good for another three rounds."

"Not tonight, coach . . . I'm out of practice."

"Okay, that makes no sense. Didn't you and Marly— I'm sorry. It's none of my business."

"Claire, we had sex . . . but not like this."

"And you were going to marry her anyway?"

"Things were different with us. Basically, she was bisexual."

"WHAT?"

"Yeah, as long as I'd buy things for her, she was sexual."

"Oh. . . . You scared me," I laughed. "But seriously, I don't get the relationship. I mean, I know what was in it for her. The big house, the fancy cars . . ."

"It's not what you think. Marly and I were great together . . . just not in bed."

"And that was okay with you?"

"She took care of me in a lot of other ways. She didn't make any demands. She was a good listener . . . and we had an understanding."

"An understanding."

"Yeah. If we needed to shop elsewhere on occasion, it was okay."

"You're joking, right? You actually gave each other permission to screw around?"

"Basically."

"Oh my God. That's insane. Does the term *sexually transmitted disease* mean anything to you?"

"We were careful. But to be honest, it's how I grew up. I know it sounds strange, but my parents had the same arrangement."

"With the operative word being *had*. Now they're getting a divorce."

"For a lot of reasons."

"Well, you would know better than me, and I'm no expert. But it seems to me that infidelity isn't exactly the cornerstone of a good, healthy relationship."

"I'm not saying it works for everyone."

"Okay, well, just so you're clear? It wouldn't work for me. And if we're going to be together, we would have to have an understanding, too. It's just us. I couldn't share you."

"And I couldn't imagine ever needing anyone else but you."

"Thank you, but this conversation just took a very scary turn. We grew up so differently. My parents fight like crazy. You've seen them. But I can't imagine either of them ever playing around . . . not that anyone else would want them. And yet, no matter how loud they hollered and carried on, they still believed in the institution of marriage, in the holiness of the vows. And I do, too. But what if you can't accept those same values?"

"Claire, I was faithful to Marly."

"But you just said that you had an understanding that you could shop elsewhere."

"Yes, but I didn't. I accepted what we had, even though it wasn't perfect."

"Why?"

"Because I needed to believe in love. I needed to know that if you cared that deeply for someone, you could get past just about anything."

"Well, obviously she didn't feel that way. She's pregnant, and it might not be your chid."

He didn't answer.

"How is that even possible? You make it sound like she wasn't even interested in sex, yet she cheated on you? Why?"

"She had her reasons. Can we talk about this later?"

"I'm sorry I'm prying. . . . It just seems so strange that she—"

"Had certain needs I couldn't give her. Okay? Can we please just leave it at that?"

"That's what a guy says when he's impotent. But you certainly aren't that . . . at least for me."

"I'm begging you, Claire. I really don't want to talk about this right now."

"But wait. I know she loves you. She practically covered your whole place with those pillows she made. *Marly and Drew together forever . . . And they lived happily ever after . . .*"

"Claire, stop it already. I can't do this. I can't be in a microwave relationship—press a button and zap, all your questions are answered in the time it takes to heat a cup of coffee. My life is complicated. There's a lot you don't know. And I'm not going to spill my guts just because you've turned into Curious George. Jeez! I can't tell you how much I hate it when girls I go out with think they're entitled to know every goddamn thing I ever said or did. Then they have to sit there and analyze it, and discuss it, and worry about it, and call their girlfriends, and have them sit there and analyze and discuss it. I'm a guy, not a bug under your microscope."

"Okay. I get the point. I'm sorry. I'll never ask you another personal question again."

"Like hell!" He got up to put on his shirt.

"Wait? Where are you going? Don't leave. We were just having a little argument."

"Yeah, well, it's not as little as you think."

Have you ever been at a party where you were the only one not enjoying yourself? When you were counting the seconds until it was socially acceptable to bolt? That's how it was at the neurology consult. After being subjected to a litany of follow-up tests, the brain boys were positively ecstatic with the reports. One for the books, they called me. Miracle Girl. Lucky, lucky, lucky.

Seems that in spite of their earlier fears about my recovery, they simply couldn't believe the speed at which I had resumed my normal brain functions. There were no residual effects from the fall. No language deficits. No more memory loss. No physical impairments. No visual problems.

*Little do you know*, I thought as they babbled on. I was both blind and stupid because I didn't see that Drew had begged me not to pursue my line of questioning. I didn't understand that he had a right to his privacy. I just drove right over his emotional divide, then crashed, as I did with his car.

"You must be so relieved." Shari hugged me. "It's even better news than we thought."

"I know. It's amazing."

"And it was so funny how baffled they were. Like patients can't ever recover unless it's a result of something they did. Doctors can be such arrogant putzs, can't they?"

*So can nosy girlfriends.* "Definitely."

"Why don't we call your folks now? I'm sure they're anxious to hear the great news."

"Good idea. . . . Do you think you could you do it? I'd like to call Drew first."

"You want me to call your parents, while you call my son? Isn't that a bit backwards?"

"Yes, but my parents don't hate me, and he does." I started to cry. "Last night I did something so stupid. . . ."

"Oh, I'm sure it will be all right, Claire. C'mon, don't fall apart now. It's been such a great day. You've got your health back. You're going to be fine."

"I'm not going to be fine unless Drew forgives me."

"What did you do?"

"I blew it, that's what I did. I opened my big mouth and tried to get him to talk about his relationship with Marly, and he got very angry. . . . I mean, I nearly totaled his car, and he was, eh, no big deal, I have others; but I wouldn't stop prying, and he went off on me. And now I'm afraid that it's over, and it never really even began."

"Oh. Not good."

"It's not?" I gulped.

"Drew is an extremely private person, Claire. He's not good with digging deep into the psyche for answers. And don't get me wrong, he's honest and open . . . but with limitations. His father was just like that, so I know what you're going through. You couldn't pry a button off his shirt with a crowbar."

"So what am I supposed to do? I can't handle his being angry with me."

"I know my son. Just give him time to cool off. He'll forgive you."

"No, he won't. I saw the look in his eyes when he left. I pushed too far, and now he's checked out for good."

"Well, you certainly don't have to worry about his going back to Marly, if that's what you're so upset about."

"Yes, he will . . . she's pregnant."

"What?"

"Oh my God. Oh shit. What did I just do?"

"She's pregnant? Are you sure?"

"Oh my God. I can't believe I just did that. On top of everything else, I betrayed his trust."

"Claire, get a grip. He actually told you that Marly was pregnant?" I nodded.

"Oh for God's sake . . . I can't believe that little . . . All this time he's been doting on her and supporting her. And then she goes back to Jonathan anyway and gets pregnant?"

"Wait. How can you assume Drew's not the father? I'm so confused."

"Claire, stop rambling. It's almost impossible for Drew to be the father."

"It is?"

"He's got something called varicocele. Lousy sperm production. He's damn near infertile."

"Infertile?" I stood there with my mouth open. That's what this was about? But how could he be infertile? We bought condoms. He said that after the baby was born, he was going to order a blood test to confirm the identity of the father.

Naturally, I had a million questions. But I was so afraid of repeating my utterly inconsiderate performance from last night, I asked nothing. The last thing I wanted to do was alienate the one person who could explain everything when the time was right.

You know how broke I was. Let me refresh your memory. I had a total of $477 in my bank account. Oh, and a few savings bonds from my college graduation hidden somewhere. Maybe add another three, four hundred to the pot. And then my former fiancé, Aaron Darren, had invested a small amount for me in this upstart pharmaceutical company in New Jersey that was going to go public after they got the patent approved for their noninjectable version of Botox.

That was basically it. I was thirty years old, and for all intents and purposes, I had squat. No stock portfolio, no real estate, no life insurance. Not even an IRA. But I did have debts. Yes, sir. Plenty of those. A car loan, credit card bills up the wazoo, back rent, and a small—well, not so small, a $10,000—loan I borrowed from Sydney's father when I thought I was going to need a down payment on a condo.

But did I return the money when the deal fell through? Of course not. Did I at least use the money to pay off my Visa bills? Are you serious? I blew it on a much-needed vacation to Italy, some new clothes including this red Badgley Mischka gown that would be perfect for the Oscars if, God forbid, I was ever actually there, and finally this exquisite dyed Persian lamb coat from Maximilian that was marked down to an amazing you'll-never-see-a-deal-like-this-again four grand.

Not smart choices for anyone, let alone an accountant's daughter. Someone who grew up with a better-than-average understanding of tax brackets, deductions, maximum contributions, cap gains, and the whole alphabet soup of personal finance. A lot of good it did me.

Until the day I ended up in an attorney's office, listening to a conversation between two estate lawyers, Uncle Ben, and my dad via speaker phone. It was the first time I was sorry that I hadn't paid closer attention to my father's business dealings.

But no matter that I didn't understand the exact details of what they were hashing out, one thing was crystal clear: I was going to walk out of this office a wealthy woman. Not Oprah rich, but I heard figures being bandied about that riveted me to my seat.

Bottom line? A man I had never met, let alone knew existed, had invested money in my name every year of my life. Set up a trust fund, with an honest-to-God trustee, whose job it was to invest and reinvest my assets, so that one day, as compensation for being abandoned, I would have enough money to live comfortably. Very, very comfortably.

You heard me. I, Claire Awful Person Greene, had just inherited a portfolio worth almost two million dollars. Do you have any idea how much money that is? Me, either. But my dad did. And as I listened to his booming voice crackle through the loudspeaker, talking about lump sums, and tax liabilities, and costs basis, and seeing tax returns of the trust, I had never been happier to have him in my corner. He knew exactly what to say, unlike me, who would have sounded like a blithering idiot.

"Thank you, Daddy," I said to the silver metal box on the desk after the meeting ended.

"My pleasure, dear."

Was he crying? *Oh God, don't cry*, I thought. *I'll never be able to keep it together.*

"This is a wonderful day for you, Claire." He blew into his hanky. "A wonderful day. I'm so happy for you. You've got your whole life ahead of you and not a care in the world. Now you'll be able to afford whatever you want, travel wherever you want. . . . You deserve all the happiness in the world."

"Thank you," I said. "I love you. . . . I'll call you back in a little while."

"No, call your mother."

"Which one?" I teased.

"You only have one, dear." He laughed. "And she's great, isn't she?"

"The best."

# Chapter 30

Of course I wanted to celebrate the single, most extraordinary day of my life. Lunch was on me, but I had no takers. Uncle Ben couldn't have been happier for me, but he was already late for a meeting, so the best he could offer was to drop me at the house and promise a celebration later.

Mondays were Shari's standing (or should I say lying) appointment with Yogi Ron. And from the way it looked the week before, she wasn't going to pass up hot action on her yoga mat just to have shrimp salad with me.

Delia rarely woke up before one. And why give her an excuse to celebrate and get crazy? Not that she needed an excuse. Seventy-five and sunny was good enough for her.

Grams turned me down, too. Seems the jackpot was huge on Bingo Monday, and after that, she didn't want to miss the napkin-folding class.

Viktor was on his way to the airport for a pick-up. Pablo was busy training the new office manager ("Couldn't wait for you forever, darling."). And I tried Drew's cell three times, but he never answered. Which made me so nauseous, I couldn't even leave a message.

And those were all the people I knew in Miami. So I had been rich for all of an hour, but had already learned that money couldn't buy you love. Or someone to have lunch with. Most of all, it couldn't mend a broken heart. It could only pay for the therapy.

Maybe I was supposed to take this dearth of companionship as a sign that my work was done here. I had come to Miami to help Grams, and that mission was accomplished big time. I had never seen her this happy. As for me, I could use a beach chair and a nice Robert Mondavi Merlot. In a keg.

I wondered if with my newfound wealth I could pay a therapist to join me on the beach, rather than *schlep* to some sterile office, with its requisite three P's: plants, paintings, and pillows. I was very aware that I needed to speak to someone professionally. But in which city? Miami, New York, or L.A.?

It didn't take long to answer my own question. I no longer had a reason to stay here, and the sooner I left, the easier it would be on everyone. Ben and Shari, Delia . . . Drew. So I headed upstairs to pack my bag and book a flight home.

I thought about crying, as it certainly felt like a good moment to let it all out. No one else was around, and given the emotional importance of the day, a rush of tears would be cleansing. Or at least better timed than my breaking down at the airport.

As I packed the clothes I'd arrived with (Had I really worn those awful gym shorts the day I met Drew? Yes!), I compared them to the designer duds Marly had picked out for me for Abe's funeral (Could I buy Versace whenever I wanted? Yes!), and the casual things Drew and I got at Target (Would *we* ever get to wear our matching T-shirts? No!).

I was just about to zip my suitcase, when I heard the doorbell. I assumed one of the maids would get the door. But when the chime rang again and again, it occurred to me that I was the only one home.

From Drew's window, I had a slight view of the circular driveway, and spotted the familiar white limousine. Of course. Viktor had come over to congratulate me on my hitting the inheritance jackpot. And, knowing him, to give me his expert tax advice so I didn't have to share my winnings with the government.

"Perfect timing, old boy," I said as I flew down the stairs. "You're my ride to the airport." I opened the door, only to be blinded by the midday sun. Best I could make out was that unless Viktor was a closet drag queen, the visitor was a tall woman holding a small designer dog. "Can I help you?" I petted her pooch.

The woman took a long drag of her cigarette, put the dog down, and signaled for Viktor to leave. Oddly, the dog seemed right at home, and waddled in. Which drew my attention to the expensive Persian rug on which he or she peed, and the high-heeled feet of the dog's owner. Huge, gangly feet. Size ten, I was guessing. Just like mine.

"Oh my God." A tremor ran through me.

"Hello, Claire." She removed her sunglasses and took another drag. "How are you?"

I gawked so long, the dog growled. But I was completely stymied. Torn between wanting to slap the Hollywood legend and wanting to ask if she'd pose for a picture with me. She had such striking features up close. Such defined beauty.

"What . . . are you doing here?" I could barely speak.

"Mohammad wouldn't come to the mountain." Puff puff. "So I've come to Mohammad. . . . I don't like it when my phone calls aren't returned."

"And I don't like to be hung up on. But did that stop you?"

"I see we've got some anger stored in us."

"Not me. You?"

"Endless," she laughed. "Now, are we going to stand here all day or find a place to sit down?"

"You can sit wherever you want. I'm upstairs packing."

I made it to the fourth or fifth stair when I heard that familiar, husky, movie-star bellow. "Get down here, Claire. I want to speak to you."

"Oh wow." I stopped. "You sure got that 'Mom's mad' part down. Been rehearsing?"

"I'm surprised to hear you speak to me like that. I'd heard you were a lovely girl."

"I am. Just not to people who lose interest in me as a baby, then show up thirty years later for a speed date. You know, check out the chick for five minutes to see if she's worth buying a drink.

"Furthermore, I hate cigarettes, so don't walk in here and blow smoke in my face, and expect me to heel like your dog."

"Oooh. A feisty one." She fluffed the dog's fur. "But we like 'em feisty, don't we?"

"I would appreciate it if you would leave."

"Then what do you propose I do for the rest of the day? Sip mint juleps by the pool?"

"I don't care. You can't just waltz in here, exchange air kisses, and pick a place for us to lunch."

"I can't!"

"You are unbelievable! Why would you think that I would want to spend time with you? Did I return your phone calls or e-mails? No. Did I thank you for the flowers?"

"No, and I found that rather rude. Who raised you? Barnyard animals?"

"Barnyard animals?" I nearly jumped over the banister to choke her, but unexpectedly I laughed. She was making a joke, and sick as it was, it was funny.

"Oh, so you can smile. I was afraid all that Botox had rendered you unable. It's a very serious problem these days. The studios are going crazy."

"What do you want from me?" I wiped the grin off my face.

"Nothing, really. Just a chance to share some trade secrets. Talk about old times."

"Old times." I gasped. "That's funny to you?"

"Take it however you want. . . . Come with Mama, Bubby. Let's go clean up your mess and find us some lunch."

I shook my head as Penny and the pup strode single file to the kitchen.

"Now, that is funny," I said. "You didn't want a kid to call you Mama, but a dog was fine."

"At least this one's not a bitch." She sniffed.

I hurtled up the staircase and locked Drew's door. The nerve of that woman, walking in unannounced, expecting me to welcome her with open arms. But still, I was in shock. That woman also happened to be my idol and, God help me, my mother.

Damn her. I was supposed to be relishing the most fantastic day of my life. A clean bill of health, money in the bank, and a grandmother with nothing to complain about. But this little stunt of Penny's was overshadowing the joy.

So typical of the Hollywood elite. There was no limit to the crap they got away with because the reporters and paparazzi were feeding the frenzy. But Penny Nichol didn't know me. I was not going all ga-ga over her because she was this big celebrity.

And yet it was impossible not to look at her and think of all her magazine covers, her *Letterman* appearances, her starring roles in films and how rare were her box office bombs. . . . I may have come off as a big mouth, but she should only know how my heart pounded in fear.

There was only one way out of this mess. I would beg Viktor to come get me. And then, voilà, the red light on my cell flashed. Wouldn't it be funny if it was him? Or, even better, Drew?

"Don't be such a baby," Penny puffed. "Come down and talk to me. I'm not going to bite you."

"Shit!"

"I'm making fresh coffee, and fortunately for you, I always travel with my own beans . . . Manolo Gold. Don't you just love their French roast?"

*Oh my God, yes. And I would so love a taste of home.* "It's okay. Very overpriced."

"How do you take it?"

"Black, one sugar."

"Oh, me, too. Coincidence? I think not. Just don't blame me if it's not how you remember. There is nothing I can do about the dreadful-tasting water down here. I don't even know how people brush their teeth."

When I walked into the kitchen, I said not one word. I just stared at this stranger, who was yet so familiar-looking. Not because I'd seen her on the big screen. It was the angled chin. The wide forehead and half-moon cheeks. The long, sinewy fingers. The mile-long legs. The fair-haired girl. If not for the thirty years between us, it was like looking at me.

It reminded me of that moment in Drew's bathroom when I first met Marly and her mother, and felt so depressed by how similar their appearance is. I had always been envious of mothers and daughters who shared physical traits. The genetic before and after. But now that I'd discovered my biological partner with whom I could join the club, I no longer wanted to be a member.

"I'm sorry I left you." Penny poured me a steaming hot cup. "It was wrong of me."

"Uh-huh." I stopped stirring. "Of course, you do realize that what you did was not only morally wrong, it was illegal? In fact, in all fifty states abandonment is illegal."

"Oh that. I wasn't talking about back then. I was talking about last week. I should have stayed a little longer. At least introduced myself."

"Wait, wait, wait. You're apologizing for not keeping me company in the hospital, but you have nothing to say about running out on me as a baby in the middle of the night?"

"Correct. I have no regrets." She lit another cigarette. "I did the right thing."

"Oh God. Put that thing out. It's bad enough having to sit here with you. Don't make it worse by blowing smoke in my face."

"You must be a fantastic delight in Paris, darling. . . . Fine, I'll exhale over here. Is that better?"

"No. Shari hates smoking as much as I do, and it's her house."

"Oh, like she actually spends time in this ostentatious museum. . . . It's Monday, right? Who is it today? The yoga guru? Or is he Tuesdays? Hard for me to keep track."

"You call me a bitch?"

"Oh please, Claire. Get off your high horse. I'm not a bitch. I'm honest. Don't you like honesty?"

"Yeah, honesty is great. My favorite virtue, right up there with integrity and courage." I looked at her. "And if you think I'm all impressed that you flew back just to talk to me—"

"It was nothing. John Travolta and his lovely wife, something or other. I think it's with a K . . ."

"Kelly Preston."

"Right. Sweet kid. Does some respectable work. They offered me a ride on their private jet."

"Unfortunately, it was a wasted trip. I'm on my way out the door, and the last thing I wanted today was to engage in obnoxious banter with—"

"To the contrary, you're the one who's behaving like a little snot. If you have something to say to me, just say it, for God's sake. Speak up. . . . Come 'ere, Bubby Baby." She whistled. "Come to Mama. Sit like a good little girl. We're about to be crucified."

"You'd like that, wouldn't you? To have me spill my guts, so you could go back and tell everyone what a great lady you are because you let me get everything off my chest. Well, sorry to disappoint. But you're not worthy of that much of my time."

"I see. . . . Good to know you're not easily intimidated."

"By what? Your fucking stardom? Believe me, I'd kill for the success you've had. But not at the expense of being shallow and heartless."

"Is that what you think? Well, then, you don't know anything about me."

"And how would I? From your annual holiday card?"

Bubby Baby must have sensed her master's need for a little show of support, and jumped into my lap. "Hey, there." I let her lick me. "You're a good girl . . . aren't you?"

"You're a dog person?" Penny said.

"Love 'em. She actually reminds me a little of my Millie. I miss her so much."

"Oh. A shih tzu like her?"

"A Bijon."

"Dumb as a brick, aren't they? I had one once. Had to train him not to pee on himself."

"I had the same problem with a guy I dated."

Penny laughed and took another puff. "You look like me."

"I know."

"Several friends told me about a young actress from New York who was practically my twin . . . but in a million years it never dawned on me that it was you."

"Well, now you know. . . . Do you mind if I ask a few questions?"

"Go right ahead."

"Did anyone know you were coming today?"

"My brother did. Yes."

"So when he dropped me off, he knew we'd be here at the same time."

"Seems that way."

"And Shari, Delia, and Drew? They knew, too?"

"It's possible Ben told them."

"So basically this whole thing was a setup to get us to talk?"

"Very perceptive. You'd be perfect on *CSI*. . . . I could make a call."

"Some other time, thanks. . . . Why did you leave me?"

"You do the lawyer thing very well, too. I know the show runners on *Law and Order*."

"Please stop trying to bribe me. I'm not six. You can't con me with a lollipop."

"A thousand apologies. I'm a bit nervous."

"You're full of shit. Nothing makes you nervous."

"Why not? This whole situation is dreadfully awkward. Neither of us wants to be here. I vote for let's get it all out in the open and get the hell out."

"Fine. Then just tell me this. Why did you do it? Why did you just take off in the middle of night and never come back?"

"Because it was what was best for everyone. I was nineteen. I was flat broke. I wanted fame and fortune. What would I have done with a kid?"

"You could have taken me home to your parents. They would have helped you."

"You watch too much television. They would never have accepted the idea that their precious daughter dirtied the good family name. And like hell I wanted to live in Florida again. I waited my whole life to get out of there. New York was where I belonged."

"So basically I would have been an intrusion."

"Big time."

"Did you feel nothing for me?"

"I felt everything for you. Which is why I did what I did. After Gary was killed, what was I supposed to do? Move in with his parents, go to school, try to raise you on my own? It would have been a disaster. And frankly it wasn't how I wanted to spend my days. I knew I had talent and beauty . . . I had great hopes for a career."

"So then if a baby was never an option, why did you chicken out of the abortion?"

"Easy. I hate needles. And I was terrified of bleeding to death on the table. . . . I didn't suddenly find God, if that's the answer you were looking for."

"So you're nineteen, pregnant, and the guy's family seem like nice people."

"A little whiny and high-strung, but basically, yes. I figured they'd get whatever help they needed from your grandparents, and it would all work out fine."

"And you never looked back."

"Pretty much."

"Did you ever think about me? Wonder how I was doing?"

"At the beginning. Then after a while I had my own, new reality. A little bout with a drug dependency . . . an abortion after I got raped down in the Village . . . not my proudest decade, for sure."

"Did you know that my grandmother found your father and stayed in touch all these years? That she was sending him pictures and graduation announcements?"

"No."

"Did you know that he was putting money away for me in a trust fund?"

"I hadn't a clue."

"Does it bother you?"

"Not at all. The family is loaded. Why shouldn't you be in on it? . . . . Is it my turn to play twenty questions yet?"

"Sure," I sighed. "This isn't especially satisfying."

"When did you know you wanted to become an actress?"

"Oh. Um. I guess when I was maybe seven or eight. Every year I got picked to be Queen Esther in the Purim play. I took tap and ballet. I wrote little skits that Adam, Lindsey, and I used to put on for the kids on the block."

"When did you know you were good?"

"When I was maybe seven or eight."

"And when did you decide to move to L.A. to pursue a film career?"

"When I was maybe seven or eight."

Penny laughed. "So you might say it was in the genes?"

"I guess it's possible."

"Well, knowing what I know, I'm not the least bit surprised that you had the calling . . . given your true bloodline." Penny stood to look out the window.

"My true bloodline? Just because you were an actress didn't mean I would be. I might have been a . . . I don't know . . . whatever my father was going to be if he hadn't died."

Penny took an extra long inhalation. "Your father was a brilliant, gifted actor."

"My father was a Vietnam vet who worked at his parents' shoe store on the weekends."

"Have you ever heard the name Helmut Ehrlich?"

"Absolutely. I studied him in school. I think I still have his book. *The Passion to Act*." ·

"He would have found that rather amusing."

"You knew him?"

"Oh very well. He was a professor of mine at NYU. We got quite friendly. I was his prize pupil for a while. He let me hang out with him and Lee Strasberg, Uta Hagen, Herbert Berghof. Those were the days . . . the HB Studio, the Actors Studio, Washington Square. Uta was an amazing cook."

"Oh my God. Those were all the legends. I can't believe you knew them."

"We had an affair, Helmut and I. Well, Helmut and everyone, actually. L' Affair du jour."

"What was he like?"

"What was he like? A passionate Hungarian. A married Hungarian . . . who got me pregnant."

"That seemed to be a real theme with you. . . . So, wait. You had two children out of wedlock?"

"No . . . only one."

"Only one? I don't understand. . . . If he got you pregnant and you had that baby . . . then that would mean. . . . Oh my God." I clutched my heart. "OH MY GOD!"

"Exactly."

"What are you saying?" I screamed. "That Helmut Ehrlich is my father?"

Penny took another puff.

"How can that be? Gary Moss was my father. You and Gary had a baby . . . that's what happened."

"I couldn't tell Helmut. He was the goddamn chairman of the department. He would have had me kicked out of the program. I had just met Gary at a bar, he seemed like a sweet guy, we had a few laughs, I slept with him a couple of times. . . ."

I could barely catch my breath. "You were already pregnant?"

"Basically."

"So, what? You lied to him? You told him you were pregnant and it was his?"

"Basically."

"Oh my God. Do you realize what this means? Do you even have a clue what you've done?"

"I'm aware. . . . But as I said, no regrets. It all worked out fine. You were raised by decent people. You had siblings. A nice place to grow up. They did a good job."

I tried to locate the exact location of her jaw where my father had taken his swing so I could smack her again, but she ducked and I connected with her shoulder instead.

"Oh! Oh! Oh! Jesus Christ!" She bent over in pain. "What is it with you people? You can't have a lousy conversation without getting into the ring?"

"You stupid . . . fucking . . . bitch!" I massaged my sore hand. "How dare you come here and drop that ugly bombshell on me? You deceived my family. You let them think I was their responsibility because you were too spineless to do the honorable thing. You made these innocent people carry a heavy burden all these years. And for what? So you could run off and sleep your way to stardom?"

"I just thought you'd like to know the truth . . . about where your ability comes from."

"My ability . . . is that all you think I care about? No wonder your father was so ashamed of you. He knew you were a despicable human being. Worse than the—"

"Oh, please. I'm none of those things. I did the absolute best thing for you, and he knew it. That's why he looked the other way. He knew what kind of life you'd have had with me. Dragging you from place to place to live. . . . You'd have been at the mercy of whatever stoned friend I could find to watch you. You'd have been in drug rehab at twelve, right alongside Drew Barrymore.

"And I knew I wouldn't get any support from Helmut. A week after he dumped me, he was screwing a TA from Pittsburgh . . . My parents would have insisted I give you up for adoption, and God knows where you would have ended up then. . . . So don't sit here in judgment of me. I was fucking nineteen. I made a damn good decision. I knew it would give Gert something else to focus on other than the death of Gary. I knew Lenny would be an amazing father . . . you had to see him when I'd ask him to feed you. Singing to you, talking to you, he hated to let go. He wouldn't even let Roberta hold you. He'd say, 'She's fine with me. Go run your errands. I'm okay.' It was such an amazing connection. And I thought, who am I kidding? I can't give you what these people can give you . . . and I left. That's why you ought to thank me, Claire. I never interfered. Never created a single problem for your parents after I left. And I never looked back because it only would have hurt you more."

# Chapter 31

No, I DIDN'T WANT A BEER. I DIDN'T WANT TO RUN OVER TO SPA Villmè for a Java Lulur body wrap. I didn't even want Mary, the massage therapist, to rush over to give me a hot stone rub. What I wanted was for everyone to leave me the hell alone so that, like a rabid animal, I could find a nice hole to crawl into, and die.

Was that so hard to understand? Apparently yes. For as I looked around the now-crowded kitchen, every Fabrikant there was fully aware of what these past three weeks had been like for me. So you'd think they'd get it when I said very nicely, "Please. I just want to take a walk."

But no. Everyone thought that they knew better. Ben was insistent that I call my parents right away to share this latest development in the continuing saga of *The Greene Family Goes Downhill*.

Shari wanted to take me over to meet her favorite therapist. And, if she was in session, then to her meditation center for a deep cleansing, which would purify me by getting rid of the toxins in my system (loosely translated: a seaweed enema . . . doesn't that sound divine?).

Delia thought she knew the perfect cure for my blues: new shoes. ("The spring line of Christian Louboutin sandals are so, so hot!")

Only Drew, very quiet Drew, understood my need for solitude. He offered to take me to Abe's spot at the ocean, and to let me sit in the Caddy as long as I wanted. It was the single sweetest gesture any human being ever offered me.

"Stop babying her already." Penny lit another smoke. "I really don't understand what the big fuss is about. So she got some shocking news. It's not like it's cancer or anything."

"Shut up, Penny," Ben said. "She's been through enough, for Christ's sake. Why the hell did you have to open up this can of worms anyway?"

"I have my reasons."

"Oh Good Lord." Shari sat with tea bags on her eyelids. "What did you do now?"

Suddenly the room grew still. At any moment, I felt like Ricky Ricardo was going to enter stage right and yell, "Lucy, you have some 'splaining to do."

"Relax. It's nothing terrible," Penny said. "In fact, it's great news. I want to talk to Claire about a possible film deal. Well, at this point we're only talking about optioning the story, but I think this is right up Sherry Lansing's alley."

"Oh awesome. A new movie." Delia's eyes lit up. "Can I be in this one? You promised."

"Nothing is firmed. It's just the talking stages. First we'd have to hire the screenwriter to draft the screenplay. My agent was just telling me about this kid he signed from New York who—"

"I'm sorry," I interrupted. "Have I missed something here? What does any of this have to do with me?"

"Well, that's just the thing, Claire. I think your story is truly amazing. It's got everything: Comedy, drama, suspense . . ."

"What story?"

"Your story. The whole left-at-birth thing. . . . Growing up with people you assumed were your parents . . . sitting next to a man who dies in flight, and it's the grandfather you never knew . . ."

"Oh my God." I tried to take another swing.

"Claire. Stop." Drew held me down. "She wouldn't do anything that stupid."

"What's stupid about it? Naturally, I've been keeping it very low-key. But so far there's quite a bit of interest. In fact, Tom and Rita both thought it was a fabulous premise."

"Who're Tom and Rita?" Shari asked from under her tea bags.

"I know." Delia raised her hand. "Tom Hanks and Rita Wilson. Right, Aunt Penny?"

"My life is not a premise," I gritted. "And I'm telling you right now, the story is not for sale."

"Well, technically, dear, it's not only your story. It's my story too."

"I'm going to kill her." I forced Drew to let go. "Listen to me. And listen good, before I take every dollar I inherited today and use it to hire the world's best lawyers to sue your arrogant, inconsiderate ass.

"You will not option my story, or any part of it. You will not mention this to any member of my family. And you will never, ever discuss the details of my life with any producer, director, screenwriter, cameraman, grip, or gofer. It is off-limits! Do you hear me? Off-limits!"

"I have to be honest, Claire. This was not quite the reaction I expected." Penny lit another smoke. "I thought you'd be thrilled at the prospect of starring in a film. . . . And I'm sure I could get Rob Reiner to direct. Maybe he'll turn it into *When Claire Met Penny*. Can you imagine how great it will be? Your first time out of the box, and you're a big star? Isn't that what you've always dreamed of?"

"I think what Claire is trying to say is that it's all happening a little too soon," Drew said. "You need to give her some time."

"Fine. But we can't sit on this for too long. Concepts get ripped off like that." She snapped her fingers.

"I don't think any of you understand." I closed my eyes. "There is nothing to jump on because there will be no deal. No screenplay. No meetings with the studios. No discussions with Rob Reiner. . . . Can't you see that I'm struggling here? That I'm in pain?"

"Which is why I'm trying to help you work through it. And frankly, what better way than to see your story come to life on the big screen? Look what it did for Erin Brockovich."

"Oh my God. This is unreal. Somebody please stop her from saying another word. . . ."

I ran to Drew's room, called a cab, then threw myself on his bed.

How had a day that started out a dream come true so quickly turn into such a nightmare?

I was so sure after I'd left the lawyer's office that the worst was over. That I would finally be able to catch my breath. Weigh my options. Take baby steps into my new, financially secure life. Honestly, after all that I had been through, was I not entitled to a little reprieve before I got bombarded? And by own mother, no less.

What was wrong with this woman anyway? Did she think I'd jump at the chance to share my humiliating tale with millions of movie-goers? So that, what—they could sit there eating their nachos, laughing at what a moron I was because I never figured out I was adopted?

And what about my parents? Did they deserve to be blindsided again by Penny, the scheming ingrate? What did she think, that I'd casually tell them over dinner, oh by the way, I found out Gary wasn't my real father? You were duped. You didn't have to raise me. You just got caught holding the bag. . . . And here's the real kicker. For more details, drive to your nearest multiplex.

Well! Penny Nichol may have thought she had an exclusive on my story, but over my dead body was she going to pursue this. Not at the expense of having my family learn the awful truth about the baby they raised in order to honor the legacy of their son and brother.

Perhaps the only positive from this disaster was that for the first time it made me realize the precarious position they'd been in when I was left in their laps. As decent human beings, they did the only thing they could. They took me in, accepted me, raised me, and protected me.

And in a show of love, they chose to keep the truth at bay. Why hamper my childhood with thoughts of what could have been if the circumstances were different? What purpose would it have served if I knew that my mother was out there leading a great life unencumbered by me?

I finally understood. *The Lenny and Roberta Show* did right by me. And as a token of my love and respect, I would do the same for them.

They would be spared the shock until the day they died. I owed them nothing less.

"Hey." Drew stuck his head in. "Mind if I come in?"

"It's your room," I sighed. "I'm about to leave anyway. It's all yours."

"You're leaving?" He came in. "Why? Because of what Penny just said?"

"It's everything. . . . Let's just say it's time for me to go home."

"No, I understand. Definitely. But not today. We never got a chance to talk."

"Well, don't blame that on me. I'm not the one who took off."

"You're right, and I'm sorry. It was stupid and I want to make it up to you. And what about your grandmother . . . and my parents . . . Delia? You can't leave without saying good-bye."

"I called the cab already. They'll be here any minute."

"You called a cab? I would have taken you."

"Aren't you still pissed at me?"

"Furious. You stole my room, you wrecked my car, and now you're breaking my heart."

"I'm breaking your heart? How?"

"Because there's so much I want to say to you, and you're not giving me the chance."

"I'm really confused. After last night, I wasn't sure we'd ever talk again."

"I'm a guy. Just assume that nine times out of ten I'm going to make things worse. But you, you're amazing. You see a situation, and you get it right away. You don't have to think about it. You just know where you stand."

"That's not true. . . . Especially these past few weeks. I've been nothing but dazed and confused."

"Well, you didn't act that way downstairs with that whole movie deal. I couldn't believe it. You didn't even bat an eye. You turned her down flat, and it's everything you ever wanted."

"Because there was nothing to think about. It was the most despicable, insensitive idea I've ever heard. You abandon your baby, leave her with people who think she's family because you lie about who the father is, and then come back thirty years later and say, hey, wouldn't this make a great film?"

"I know. It's awful. But I love the way you just figure these things out so fast and know what's right. What's important. You're my hero, Claire, I swear. You're so brave and smart."

"Does that mean you want to marry me?"

"No. . . . I mean yes. . . . Maybe one day, sure." He laughed. "But generally I like to know my fiancées for more than a few weeks."

"You are going to marry me. I had a dream about it, remember?"

"I do. When you were in the hospital."

"You said, I do." I clapped. "You said, I do."

"You are the pushiest girl I ever met."

"Yes, but you just told me that you like that I always know what I want."

"I know. I'm just going to have to learn to deal with it. But only if you'll stay one more night. Then I promise I'll get up at the crack of dawn to take you to the airport. In fact, I'll pay for your ticket. . . . No wait. I'll even buy two tickets, and I'll go home with you."

"You'd go with me to Plainview?"

"Are you kidding? I hear Plainview is beautiful this time of year. The cars. The houses. All those 7-Elevens on every corner."

What could I tell you? The boy made me laugh.

"I'm begging you. Don't leave yet."

"But I don't belong here anymore. I don't have a place."

"Right here." Drew pointed to his heart. "This is your place. This is where you belong."

I sighed. "What about the cab?"

"Hey, you're a rich woman now. You can spring for a twenty to send him away."

What could I say? I was relieved that Drew wasn't holding a grudge. But what made me think that this relationship would ever be anything other than crazy and chaotic? I might lose my mind and never find it again. And yet . . .

"Tell you what," I said. "Let me go home, spend some time with my family. You were the one who said it was a deal-breaker if I couldn't work things out with them. And then maybe in a few weeks we'll make plans to meet somewhere in the middle, and—"

"No."

"No?"

Drew grabbed me as if he were rescuing me from a burning building, then kissed me with the fervor of a hero until I collapsed in his arms. I had never felt this much hunger, passion, and fear all rolled into a single moment of intimacy. A kiss that might not have ended if not for the sound of a cabby honking his horn.

"Don't go anywhere." His hands rested on my shoulders. "I'll lend you the twenty . . . Be right back."

And with the speed of Hermes, I heard him fly down the stairs and out the front door.

I had to laugh. Whatever anger he'd felt last night had magically dissipated. And good thing. Because I may have called a cab, but I'd only planned to take it over to Grams'. Damn right I wasn't flying home before I had a chance to say good-bye.

Oh, so fine. There wasn't much arm-twisting to get me to stay. After a kiss like that, and the anticipation of the lovemaking to come if I could just refrain from any more stupid remarks, I was glad that I did. It gave me time to thank Ben, Shari, and Delia properly for all their hospitality and TLC.

And it gave me a chance to run over to Grams' place to wish her good luck, although she could only spare me a few minutes. Seems that she didn't want to be late for Bridge Night, and a certain fellow named Norman Singer from down the hall who had his eye on her.

Uch. Trust me, you don't want details of this budding courtship. After listening to her mention something about a trick or two she learned from Lillian the Lover, I got queasy and said. "TMI, Grams. I don't even want to think about it."

Staying the night also gave me a chance to have a special evening out with Drew. We'd go for a nice quiet dinner, and then he'd promised his friend Peter Loftin that we'd stop by a party he was having at his mansion, Casa Casuarina.

"Why does that sound familiar?" I asked.

"Because a few years back it was in all the papers. It was Gianni Versace's house. I thought you knew it was a few doors down from By the C."

I didn't know that, but as I had found out these past few weeks, there was a lot I didn't know. At least we would be getting a chance to talk first, because Drew was smart enough to find a beautiful, quiet restaurant on the Intercoastal where no one knew him.

Over cocktails, it dawned on me that as much time as we had spent together, we had never actually gone out on a date.

Drew chuckled. "Yeah, but don't forget. I was engaged for most of those three weeks."

"I guess that does sort of get in the way of dating."

"Plus I had a funeral to attend, three nights of *shiva*, and the rest of the time you were in the hospital or in a coma in my room."

"That certainly explains where the time went."

"And then there's the whole matter of the first cousin thing, but I think we're past that."

"Are you kidding?" I laughed. "It turns out I'm not even related to myself."

"I always knew Aunt Penny was crazy, but I still can't believe she actually lied about who the father was, and then made the wrong family responsible. . . . She's awful."

"Yeah." I sipped my wine. "But let's just hope Marly doesn't try to pull the same stunt." *Uh-oh*.

Drew looked away, and I knew I'd done it again. Opened my big mouth. Damn me!

"Um . . . yeah. Look, about that whole thing . . . I've been putting it off because I didn't want to ruin our first date. But we do need to talk."

"I'm sorry I said that." I reached for his hand. "It was mean."

"Forget it. At least I know I can count on you to be brutally honest. I wish I had your guts."

"Drew, you don't have to explain anything. I know."

"Know about what?"

"About your varicose veins."

"My what?"

"This morning when I was with your mom at the doctor's, she happened to mention something about . . . your problem . . . the infertility."

"Why were you talking about that? I hope to God you didn't tell her about Marly and the baby."

"I, um . . . well . . . I am so sorry."

"Damn you!" He slammed his fist down.

"It just slipped. I was telling her how bad I felt because you were mad at me, and I thought I'd blown the chance to be in a relationship with you, and one thing led to the next. . . ."

"I didn't need this right now. I really didn't, Claire. Everything is such a mess. We wanted to handle this on our own without getting the families involved. . . . That's one of the reasons we broke up. So much goddamn interference."

"I'm sorry . . . I really am."

"Have you noticed that all you ever do is apologize? I'm sorry for this, and I'm sorry for that?"

"I know, and I'm really sorry."

"Ahhhhhh." He laughed, and pretended to squeeze my neck. "I could strangle you sometimes. But then I'd miss you so damn much. . . . I can't believe you told my mother."

"She did seem a little shocked . . . because of your problem and everything."

"My problem, Claire, is that everyone knows my goddamn business. I can't even take a piss in this town without someone hearing about it. And I don't know what it is with all you girls. You're like a bunch of yentas . . . yak, yak, yak."

"I'm not a yenta."

"Fine. You just happened to be talking about me, and my medical problems, and my sex life, and God knows what else. . . . Oh, and incidentally? I don't have varicose veins. I have something called varicocele. . . . It's a problem in the scrotum that messes with your sperm production, and it makes your balls two different sizes. . . . I hope I'm not ruining your dinner. But hey. Here's a hot news story that just came off the wire: I went and had my plumbing fixed."

"You did?"

"Yeah. It was a real first. I didn't even tell Marly. But six months ago I flew to New York and had the surgery."

"Why New York?"

"Because no one knew me or would call me twenty times a day to ask if I pissed yet. And mostly because a good friend of mine from podiatry school, David Goldstone—his brother is this big-deal urologist in New York who specializes in male infertility. I figured, what the hell? My dick is worth the trip!"

"What did Marly say after you told her?"

"I haven't."

"Are you serious? Why not?"

"Because I needed to know if she was marrying me because she loved me or because she was being pushed into this by her parents."

"I don't understand."

"She knew I was going to have a big problem getting her pregnant. Basically, I was told that without the surgery there was like a one percent chance. But if she really loved me, she would have taken her chances that the surgery would fix the problem, or just accepted that we'd have to adopt. And if this marriage wasn't about love, but about money and security and a hundred other lousy reasons to get married, then she'd end up sneaking around and going back to this guy Jonathan."

"The bagel guy."

"Yeah. The bagel guy."

"And that's what she did?"

"Seems that way."

"But it could be yours . . . because you had the surgery."

"I'm not a hundred percent yet, but it is possible it's mine. She just doesn't know that."

"And that's why you want the blood test after the baby is born."

"Yeah."

"Oh my God. It's like my story all over again. Will the real father please stand up? What are you going to do? Are you going to tell her?"

"Eventually."

"Do you mean to tell me she never noticed that . . . the boys were fixed?"

"She didn't exactly spend a lot of time down there."

*Ah, so Viktor had been right.*

"This whole thing is insane."

"I know. And I'm sorry. So, so sorry," he mimicked me.

We just looked at each other and tried to keep a straight face. But when you're falling in love, even the stupid stuff is funny.

# Chapter 32

CAN YOU BLAME ME? ON MY FLIGHT TO NEW YORK THE NEXT DAY, I specifically requested not to sit next to any one over the age of sixty-five. "I'm not prejudiced," I told the agent at the ticket counter. "But after my last flight, I just don't want to take any chances."

"That bad?" he said.

"Your clothes would go out of style before I finished telling you what happened."

"Couldn't be any worse than what happened to this lady a few weeks ago," he laughed. "Some old man dropped dead on her tray table."

"Oh my God. Are you serious? That's awful."

"Yeah. It was ugly. . . . I hope she's okay. That's a hell of a thing to have happen."

"I have a feeling she'll be fine," I said.

As for why I was traveling alone, I decided not to take Drew up on his kind offer to go home with me. I really felt like I should spend some time alone with my family. And I had so much to contemplate, it would be easier if I wasn't under pressure to keep him entertained.

Besides, I had one last hurdle, and that was how to handle the Penny bombshell. Frankly, I was still in shock myself. In the past few weeks, I'd thought that my father was three different men. The man who raised me, my Uncle Gary, and finally, the real sperm donator, a

Hungarian philanderer who took more than a passing interest in his students.

Anyone wanting to do a remake of *Three Men and a Baby*, could come to me for ideas.

But seriously, it was upsetting to discover that I was the offspring of a lying, scheming witch who slept her way to the top of her class, and a lying, scheming professor who pursued extracurricular activities when the wife wasn't looking. For all I knew, there were lots of little Ehrlichs in the world.

Anyway, you know at first I was adamant about keeping the true identity of my father a secret, just as my parents had kept the story of my birth under wraps all these years. And now that I understood the painful should-we-or-shouldn't-we hand-wringing they went through, I not only respected their judgment, I wanted to follow their lead.

Trouble was, Penny was adamant about making this stupid film based on her life no matter who got trampled in the process. "With or without you, I'm pursuing this," she told me last night. "Maybe Streep and Keaton are getting sent scripts, but the rest of us old ladies are fighting for scraps. The only way to get work is to produce the damn film yourself."

So I would have "the talk," but it would have to wait. For somehow, even though my plans to return home were literally last-minute, my parents pulled off a surprise welcome-home backyard barbecue in my honor, complete with friends, neighbors, and, in a shocking move for my dad, relatives.

How quaint the backyard looked, with its small cedar deck and the hunter-green patio set from Fortunoff's, which came with the free matching umbrella. And how happy the guests looked in their casual attire, downing wings and potato salad as if they hadn't eaten since lunch.

This would have been a very different affair at Drew's house. Gourmet catering with mouthwatering epicurean delights in the garden. A jazz quartet. Guests in silk Armani and designer shoes that cost more than three times the food being served.

I began to wonder if it was even possible for our backgrounds to mesh. Only last night, I'd dined on wild striped bass with shiitake port sauce at Casa Casuarina, while mingling with socialites, bankers, fashion designers, fellow models, and a countess from Italy.

Ha! The only thing from Italy at this little soirée was the sausage, and my Aunt Shirley's pocketbook. No, wait. What was I saying? There's no way she spent twelve hundred dollars for a Gucci bag. It had to be a fake.

I could only imagine the wedding, then. A smorgasbord of Prada and Pay-Less. Of Marc Jacobs and Macy's. Of ultra-wealthy business entrepreneurs and my father's cousins, the garment district guys who played poker on the train and who lived from season to season. Could this marriage be saved?

Meanwhile, I had a very important matter to attend to before I could ever envision a future with Drew. So after the last of the paper goods were tossed and the leftover cold cuts wrapped, I made the very grown-up decision to tell my parents the truth after all.

They did not deserve to open *Newsday* one day and read an article about Penny Nichol's latest film. A biopic of her college days, and the unfortunate tryst with her theater professor that produced a child who ended up being raised by some boy's unsuspecting family on Long Island.

I shuddered at the thought, and recalled that moment in Grams' bathroom when I realized what she had been trying to tell me. That I was not Claire Greene, the girl I knew. I was Hannah Claire Fabrikant, the girl who never was. It would certainly go down as the most terrifying moment of my life, second only to learning the true identity of my father.

And although it was getting late, I knew I would have to come clean with this revelation sooner rather than later. I was not the type of person to hold something in. In fact, I don't know what ever made me think I could keep this quiet for the rest of my life. I would die trying not to mention anything, and then blow it with my big mouth.

No. I had to do this right. Sit them down, carefully choose my words, and hope that it didn't cause my father chest pains that required a visit to the emergency room. But that's the funny thing about coming clean. It never goes as you expect.

"I knew it. I knew it, I knew it." My father swatted a mosquito on his arm as he paced the deck.

"Are you serious?" I said. "How could you have known?"

"Roberta, didn't I say to you first thing? How do we even know it's his kid? We don't know this girl from Adam, where she's from, who her family is. It's like she showed up from out of nowhere, and suddenly she's telling us she's pregnant with Gary's child."

"I thought your father was crazy," my mother said. "Who lies about something like this?"

"Oh, and then it was the way she seemed to pop," he said. "We had a bunch of friends having their first kids at the time, and with those girls, it took a while to show. But Penelope had this big belly right away. I don't know, the timing seemed off. Like maybe she was more pregnant than she said."

"It's coming back to me," my mother added. "Your father kept telling me, she's an actress, she knows how to make you believe her. . . . But still, I thought, how could it not be Gary's baby? He was walking around so happy. I mean, sure, of course he was scared, but he was crazy for her. And why not? A beautiful girl like that giving him the time of day, and now they were going to start a family together. . . . And then Grams was so tickled about the whole thing. You had to see her. Knitting up a storm with the booties and the blankets."

"So, let me ask you something, Claire." My father looked up at the stars. "Did Penny happen to tell you the truth? Who the real father was?"

"She told me everything. . . . And it's so weird. It turns out he was this big, important theater professor at NYU . . . a married professor . . . Helmut Ehrlich."

"Never heard of him."

"Oh, I did. He was one of the great acting coaches of our time. Right up there with Lee Strasberg. In fact, I think I kept the book he wrote. . . . Can you imagine? There I am, a student in the IU Theater

Department, cramming for an exam, studying from a book written by the man who fathered me twenty years earlier."

"Oh my," my mother said. "Don't they always say truth is stranger than fiction?"

"Well, at least thank God, it sounds like a Jewish name." My father shrugged.

"She said he was Hungarian. I don't know about the Jewish part. Not that I care."

"It would just be nice to know if you were a purebred. That's all." He chucked my chin. "So what's the story with this guy? Is he still alive?"

"You know, I didn't even ask, because it wouldn't matter to me. I already have a father."

"Thanks, honey. I guess I'm just curious. And it's been a whole week since I smacked anyone in the jaw. I just thought—"

"Don't you dare," I said. "This wasn't his doing. According to Penny, she never told him she was pregnant. It's not like she asked for his help and he turned his back on her."

"I suppose. I don't know . . . the whole thing is so crazy. The way one person's decision can turn so many lives upside down, and you don't even know about it. And yet I don't even care that we were taken advantage of. I'm grateful you were ours to raise. We got the better end of the deal."

"You brought us a lot of joy and pleasure." My mother wiped her eyes. "Really. You were a wonderful baby. Not even the least bit fussy. And you were such a happy child. Always laughing and playing. You got along with everybody. You were so smart in school.

"I know you think I wasn't proud of you because I wasn't like those big-mouth mothers who had to shout it from the rooftops when their kid scored a basket . . . I didn't need to broadcast it. I was proud of you in my own way.

"When I would see you standing so proud and tall with your friends at school, you were always so kind to everyone. If they needed cheering up, you'd try to make them laugh with your jokes. You were a very special girl, Claire. Always worrying about the next one. Asking if there was something you could do to help. Those were the moments I *kvelled*."

"Thank you both," I said. "You were great."

As we soaked up the clear night sky, and the sounds of cars passing on the Northern State, we tried to let register all that had taken place. I couldn't get over how well they'd taken the news, and I hoped that they would remain calm for part two.

"A movie?" My father whistled. "*Oy*. I'll tell you this. The woman has balls."

"It is a good story, though," my mother said.

"You can't be serious," I replied. "Do you realize what you're saying? She wants to make a film that shows what idiots you were for taking in a baby you had no connection to."

"Would we . . . get to be in it?" she asked.

"Oh my God." I laughed. "That's what this is about? She treated you like shit, but it's okay as long as you get your fifteen minutes of fame?"

"Why not?"

"The reason why not, Mother, is because once again, she's trying to take advantage of you. She's trying to capitalize on your good heart, and tell your very personal story."

"I don't know, Claire. Maybe your mother is right. It could be very good for you. I can't think of anything that you've ever wanted more than to be a film actress. And if you're around while they're writing the story, you'll be our eyes and ears. You'll make sure we come off as the good guys, not the *schmucks* from Valley Stream."

"I can't believe you two. You're crazy. And you don't know who you're dealing with here. Penny is a wack job."

"No, dear," he said. "You're forgetting that we do know her. We spent six long months with her while she was living at Grams' house before you were born. And she is a handful. But what do you care? You'd be getting your breakout role. . . . So who do you think would play me?"

"I don't know." I laughed. "How do you feel about Alan Arkin? Or maybe Jerry Stiller?"

"What are you talking about? Jerry Stiller, my ass. I'm much better-looking than him. Don't I remind you more of Pierce Brosnan?"

"Only if I'm played by that Sally Jessica Parker." My mother waved her hand. "She's adorable."

"Sarah, Mom," I sighed. "Sarah Jessica Parker. And I'm sure she'd be honored to play the very challenging role of Roberta Greene."

"I'm gonna be a big star in the movies." My father danced with me to the old Beatles tune.

"Oh my God." I laid my head on his chest. "Shoot me now."

What's a visit to Plainview without a stop at the old Plainview Diner? I had invited good old Elyce to breakfast as a way to make it up to her for not returning her seven hundred phone calls. Although, after expressing my apologies, I did plan to tell her that, much as I was happy for her and Ira, my circumstances were so crazy now, I simply couldn't be in the wedding party.

But that plan went down the drain when she walked in with her cousin Julia Farber. The same Julia Farber whom I'd run into with her mother at the Jacksonville airport on the day that Abe died. Just my luck. Now I could be double-teamed by the bride and her attendant, and not be able to bow gracefully out of the obligation.

But the Lord works in mysterious ways, as I'd learned all too well. Seems Elyce and Ira were suddenly on shaky ground. Or at least Ira was. Elyce cried over her egg-white omelette that he was starting to get cold feet. That he'd gone fishing with his father for a few day to think about things, and although he hadn't asked her for the ring back yet, she was afraid that was coming.

"I'm so sorry, Elyce." I'd patted her hand. "Because I was really starting to get excited about your wedding. And that cruise to the Bahamas we were going on? Sounded like a blast."

"Well, it's not over yet," she sniffed. "We're trying to work things out. . . . But I don't know. I'm so scared that he's going to keep changing his mind, and then we'll get closer and closer to the date, and have to call it off at the last minute. . . . At least, thank God, we didn't order the invitations yet."

"I think he still wants to marry you, honey." Julia sipped her coffee. "He's crazy about you. He's just a typical guy. They never know how good they have it . . . I'm sure he'll come to his senses."

"But what if he doesn't? What if he wants out? I love him so much. I'll just die."

"Maybe Joel can talk to him when he gets back from his urology conference. . . . We've been engaged for a year, so he'll know exactly what Ira is going through," she explained to me. "And he's very well known for his work in male infertility, so he's great at talking to men about their personal problems."

Wait a minute. Urology. Male infertility. "What's his last name again?" I held my breath.

"Who? Joel? It's Goldstone."

"Where have I heard that before? It was just recently, too. . . . Oh my God. He doesn't happen to have a brother . . .?"

"Who? You mean David?"

"Yes. That's it. David Goldstone. . . . Is he a podiatrist?"

"Yes, which, thank God, Joel didn't go into like he was supposed to. His father's a podiatrist, too. But I'm so glad he became a real doctor."

*Oh, shut up. I'll give him two years before he's cheating on you.*

"Anyway, Claire. How do you know David?"

"Long story." I leaned back into my seat. "And I also think I know someone who used Joel."

"Really? Isn't it such a small world?"

"And getting smaller every day."

Drew waited five days before calling to tell me that he missed me terribly, and wouldn't wait any longer to visit. Could I please pick him up at La Guardia at six-thirty, and not to worry about putting him up, he'd made a reservation at a hotel in the city. "This is working out great because I was supposed to do a follow-up visit with my doctor two months ago, but I never made time."

"Yeah, that really does work out great . . . but can you do me a favor?"

"Anything."

"If the doctor happens to ask what you do for a living, do you mind telling him you're a brain surgeon?"

"Oh, this oughta be good."

"Yeah. See, because do you remember when we were in Jacksonville, and you were boarding the plane with your dad, and I was talking to this girl?"

"Not really."

"Well, I had just run into a sorority sister of mine from Indiana, Julia Farber. Anyway, she was bragging about her brilliant fiancé who was this big-deal urologist in New York, and—"

"Whoa. Don't tell me it's the same guy?"

"Joel Goldstone?" I held my breath.

"Yeah. That's him. So, wait. You know him?"

"Never met the man. But he's marrying Julia, and to shut her up, I told her that—"

"I was a brain surgeon." He laughed.

"And so is your dad. In fact, you're in practice together, and you speak at all these conferences."

"At least you didn't make me a proctologist. . . . Anything else I should know?"

"Um, yes. When I had breakfast with her this morning, I remembered we were engaged."

"When did you tell her that?"

"That day in the airport."

"Hold on. You're saying I knew you for all of an hour, and you told her we were getting married?"

"I had a premonition."

"But I was already engaged."

"Okay, fine. I made a wish."

# Chapter 33

In preparation for Drew's arrival, I tore through the house trying to clean up the place. And with each passing minute, felt pure dread that he would see it for what it was. A worn, shabby split-level with a dated kitchen, tiny bathrooms, and the plainest landscaping in all of Plainview.

Maybe the trick would be to pick him up, help him check into the hotel, and try to skip the Long Island part of the excursion. That's what I would do. Buy theater tickets. Make dinner reservations. Go to a Mets game. Anything to avoid giving him a tour of my home, which would take him a total of three minutes.

I felt guilty for feeling shame. I had never really given much thought to how we lived before I'd moved to California. But after partying in some of the grandest oceanfront homes there, and then spending a week at the Fabrikant estate, it would be hard to play show and tell.

Drew, however, wouldn't hear of it. We could head back to the city later, but first he wanted to see my family again, have dinner together, and then, spend some time in my bedroom, as I had done his.

You know what I was thinking. That he wanted to even the score by making love in my old room. But it would never work. Unlike at his house, where you had to drive to the nearest bedroom, Lindsey, Adam, and my parents would be right on top of us, divided only by paper-thin walls.

But being the sweetheart that he was, it turned out his motives for being in my room had nothing to do with getting into my pants. "I can do that anytime," he teased. "You're easy." Instead, he was hoping that we could search the house to see if I still had my copy of *Reason to Believe*.

Having a mission helped. I forgot about being self-conscious, and Drew seemed so happy to be with me, clearly he hadn't come to evaluate the decor. And too, digging through boxes of old albums, photos, and memorabilia from school gave me a chance to introduce the me he never knew.

Not once did he complain about the cramped space in my bedroom, or the cold floor in the basement, or the musty smell in the attic. His eyes were on me, and I honestly couldn't think of a time when I had ever felt such warmth and compassion coming from another human being.

It was in this spirit of kinship that we discovered a box of books in the garage marked CLAIRE SCHOOL. I couldn't believe I hadn't thought to look there sooner, as I had walked past that box every time I came in and out of the house.

"You think it's in there?" he asked.

"I'm keeping my fingers crossed, because I'm starting to lose hope."

"Maybe we could ask your parents if they have any idea."

"Are you kidding? You saw the house. There's crap everywhere. You think they're going to remember where I put a book I got twenty years ago that I never even looked at?"

"I guess. I'm just so curious to see if . . ."

"If what? I mean, I agree it would be great to find it. But why does this matter so much to you?"

"Because I would take it as a sign that we were meant to be together."

"A sign? You mean the fact that the only reason we met was because a man died on my lap, and I decided to get off the plane to express my condolences to the family . . . that doesn't tell you anything?"

"It tells me a lot. But the thing is, Claire, there are no more copies of this book anywhere. I've tried to buy one online, and it's just not available. So I would love if it turned up here. Then maybe if we end up living together, we can each keep a copy by our side of the bed. And every day, it will be a reminder not only of our grandfather, but everything that was important to him."

Never did I imagine that the most touching words I would ever hear would be spoken to me in a dirty garage while a twenty-year-old refrigerator hummed in the background.

I kissed him, and in answer to my prayers, I remembered correctly that I'd once been given the book, only to stuff it in a box without ever having read it. For had it been opened, I would have seen the almost illegible inscription: *To Claire. Love, Grandpa. Chanukah, 1986.*

"That's definitely his handwriting." Drew studied the black scrawl with the eye of a scholar. "Is this the most unbelievable thing? He gave you the same book, the same year as me. And look where the bookmark is." He lifted the red satin ribbon.

I opened it to the page, but of course I already knew.

"My Sky," we said in unison.

"You think he's watching us right now?" I asked.

"Without a doubt."

"And do you think this is a sign that he wants you to marry me?"

"I don't know." Drew kissed me. "You talk to him more than me. Maybe you should ask."

There is nothing like falling in love, and in the process discovering something magical about yourself. That you are worthy of unconditional devotion and affection. That you deserve to be respected. That through the eyes of another soul, you are the answer to the question, is there a God?

I learned this, not on the day that Drew and I sat on the cold garage floor at my parents' house, but over the months that followed as we spent time together at each other's homes and allowed our fondness for one another to deepen.

I also learned that what often disguises itself as love is nothing more than a desire to share your burdens, and not your heart. Marly wanted to lay on Drew's financial security blanket and to have someone to take on her troubles as his own. Drew had hoped that in Marly he had a partner with whom he could build a quiet life, away from the daily grind of entertaining the tourists.

But after confessing that he'd had the procedure to reverse his varicocele, and she owned up to being more in love with another man, their second attempt to reach the altar was aborted like a rocket launch at Cape Kennedy.

It was not all that was aborted. In an act of both defiance and cowardice, Marly ended her pregnancy, as she did not want to take the chance that the man she hoped to marry one day was not the father of their child.

Her loss. Her pitiful, grievous, incalculable loss.

For several months, Drew and I commuted in order to be with one another. But there was a point at which the *schlep* seemed both interminable and unnecessary. And aside from the frequent number of bad hair days, Florida was the more desirable location to live. Better weather, endless action, and as Pablo had so aptly pointed out, no state income taxes. And believe me, after my windfall, I was paying much closer attention to what happened to my assets.

Only trouble with moving down there was that I could not bring myself to stay at Drew's place. Just knowing that he'd shared his bed with Marly made me want to sleep on the floor.

I tried to bring myself to get past the grossness of sleeping there, because, let's face it, the upside was getting to use that awesome shower every day. And yet, each time I came to town, I preferred to use his former bedroom as home base, until one day the house was sold to a Latin American businessman and I was evicted.

Now what? Follow Shari and Delia to their new condo in Boca? Buy my own place? I could actually afford to do that now. Which was the thought I had in mind when Drew and I took a ride in Pops' Caddy out to his cherished oceanfront oasis, Sunday paper and coffee in hand.

"I've been thinking about something, and we need to talk." Drew took the real estate section from me and turned off the CD.

"Sure." I sipped the last of my coffee. "You're not mad at me, are you?"

"No, I'm not mad at you." He rolled his eyes. "Even when you infuriate me, I can't be mad at you. I don't know what it is. . . . I think it's because you're so cute."

"Works for me."

"Anyway, I've been thinking. Since Pops was your grandfather, too, maybe you would want to talk to a lawyer about legally changing your name."

"Changing it to what? Annabelle?"

"No," he laughed. "Your last name. Changing it to Fabrikant. As a way to honor his memory."

"Oh. I hadn't thought about that. But it's probably not a good idea. My parents would be hurt."

"I guess you're right."

"Besides, it's not like I'd have to take his name in order to honor his memory. I've been trying to do that in other ways. I've been answering all his mail, and volunteering with Delia."

"I know. And I'm really proud of you two. . . . I guess it was a stupid idea. I shouldn't have said anything. Unless maybe . . ."

"What?"

"I don't know. Unless we could think of a way to legally change your name to Fabrikant that would make your parents happy."

"Don't even go there. They'd never understand."

"Well, there is one way."

"No, there isn't, Drew. Stop."

"Sure there is. . . . You could become my wife."

"What?"

"Yeah. I was thinking, if Claire married me, then she'd legally be a Fabrikant."

I just stared at him for a minute. "Really? You want me to be your wife?"

He couldn't stop grinning.

"WOO-HOO!!!!" I bounced up, grateful the Caddy's top was down. "DREW WANTS TO MARRY ME!"

"This shouldn't be coming as a huge surprise," he laughed. "You've only been asking me since we met."

"I know." I clapped. "But this is the first time you're asking me, and it's totally different. . . . I'm so happy. And you're sure? You've thought about it, and you really want to marry me?"

"I know that I would be the luckiest man alive if you said yes."

"Should we . . . I don't know . . . maybe ask Pops if he's okay with the idea?"

"Claire, the man died just so that we would meet. I think that's a pretty good sign. . . . And think about it. We're in his favorite car, at his favorite lookout point . . . and you know how crazy he was about keeping family together," he teased. "You don't think he'd give us his blessing?"

"I love you, Dr. Andrew whatever-your-middle-name-is Fabrikant. . . . What is your middle name?"

"Steven."

"Thanks. I always say a girl should know her fiancé's full name. . . . Oh, wait. There's just one thing."

"Now what? I thought I had the job."

"You do." I laughed. "You're definitely hired. It's more a favor than a question. Will you keep writing those beautiful poems, or lyrics, or whatever they were?"

"Probably not. I wrote all that stuff in high school. I doubt that it's any good."

"Well, I'm telling you you're a great writer, and you should definitely pursue it."

"Thank you . . . It's probably because Pops read so much to me when I was a kid. . . . I did once think about writing a book. But right now I'm trying to close a very big deal, Claire whatever-your-middle-name-is Greene. . . . What is your middle name?"

"Susannah."

"That's pretty. Claire Susannah Greene, will you marry me?"

I started to cry.

"So that's a yes?" He kissed me.

"A definite yes." I wiped my tears with my shirt.

"Okay, then open up the glove compartment."

"Oh my God. Really? This is it? The moment I've been waiting for?"

"I don't know what you're talking about," he teased.

I tried opening the latch, then jiggling it. But it wouldn't budge. "It won't open." I pounded the door in case it only responded to the impatient Type A touch.

"It has to open." Drew just stared. "It did before. Oh God . . . why me?"

"Well, wait. Try using your car key. I remember that's how my grandfather opened his—"

"No, it's only for the ignition. There's a separate key for the trunk, and . . . wait. Hold on. That just gave me an idea."

"I promise not to accept another man's proposal until you come back," I said as I watched this wonderful guy open the trunk, grab his jacket, sift through his pockets, and produce a small blue box.

"What's this?"

"Open it."

"Are you serious? You drive around with a spare engagement ring?"

"Lots of pretty girls in Miami," he laughed.

I shoved him.

"Okay, I confess." He watched me fumble with the box. "There was nothing behind door number one. I did that to keep you guessing. . . . It's almost impossible to outsmart you."

"Ooooh. You are so mean to pull a trick on me when I'm about to become engaged." I closed my eyes and made a wish.

"What do you think?" he asked as I gazed at the diamond.

"Oh my God. It's absolutely exquisite. And so huge. It looks like it could seat six."

"My dad went nuts picking this out with me. Nothing was good enough. He loves you."

"Oh, that's so sweet," I sighed.

"Just tell me that you'll wear it for the rest of your life."

"I will. . . . But I'm more excited about wearing your name for the rest of my life. I can't believe it. I'm really going to be a Fabrikant."

"Claire, I love you. And I mean this from the bottom of my heart. Nobody, and I mean nobody, is more deserving than you to carry on the family name. . . . You were born to have that name."

I had been in L.A. for maybe three weeks when I made my first real friend, another new girl in town. A stunning young woman from Kauai, Hawaii, named Christine Osaka. We had both shown up at an open cast call for *General Hospital* and were scared to death.

Although I had some previous TV experience, and she had just finished her year as the first runner-up to Miss Hawaii for the Miss America Pageant, we were both in a panic that we would be swallowed whole by the vagaries of the Hollywood machine, and latched on to one another for dear life.

To our delight, were both chosen for walk-on parts for several episodes, and spent a glorious few weeks on the set, exploring our new hometown and figuring out ways to get attractive men to pay for dinner without having to later invite them into our pants.

It was a heady experience, and I was so grateful to be sharing this period of discovery with a girl who didn't hate me for my good looks, because she was hardly chopped liver, but also because she had brains and a spirited heart that taught me so much about courage and resilience.

I will never forget how she described the fall of 1992, when Hurricane Iniki bore down on her hometown with 150-mile-an-hour winds, causing the fifty thousand residents to be without food, shelter, or running water for weeks. To say nothing of the years it took to repair, rebuild, and begin life anew.

She often talked about what it felt like to be clocked by a wind gust that could pick you up and throw you against an immovable object, and something called the aloha spirit, which brought people together in times of need to help you rebound.

I thought of Christine a lot in the months that followed my personal hurricane. The powerful storm that blew in from out of nowhere literally lifted me out of my existence and dumped me into an unsettling place that caused me great fear, pain, and consternation.

I remembered her saying that it took her parents a lifetime to create a comfortable home, and less than a minute to have it be destroyed. But that you were only given two choices when the storm passed. Either rebuild or die.

I knew, of course, that I had weathered my storm, and prayed that it was my last direct hit. Not that I expected to go through life unscathed. I just hoped that, having survived the maelstrom, I would never be knocked off my feet like that again.

But in the event I ever was, I would handle it, because I had learned much about fortitude. Just as my friend Christine had, watching the roof of her house pull away, and her neighbors' possessions fly through the night sky. For life isn't about what picks you up and throws you around. It's about what you do after you land.

And it's not about who made you, but who shaped you. Not about who brought you into this world, but who took you by the hand and showed you the right path. Not about where you came from, but where you chose to go from there.

Those were not just my lessons, but my grandfather Abe's as well. A man who survived far more horrible atrocities than I, yet somehow managed to carry on without benefit of family, education, or money. Who looked right into the eye of the storm and created a life full of hope and meaning.

I don't know if he was familiar with the aloha spirit, the coming together of a community to help others survive tragedy. But God bless his beautiful soul. It was inherent in him to have the wisdom to prevail, the desire to live, and the ability to do good deeds, so that when his time came to pass, he would leave the world a far better place.

I never got to speak to my grandfather, and for that I am eternally sorry. But I could not be more proud of his legacy and of carrying on his name and his dreams. For that is the true meaning of life. To do for your children, and your children's children, so that one day they will do for you.

## *New York Times* Weddings/Celebrations

### Claire Susannah Greene
### Dr. Andrew Steven Fabrikant

Claire Greene, a daughter of Leonard and Roberta Greene of Plainview, New York, is to be married today to Dr. Andrew Fabrikant, the son of Benjamin Fabrikant of Miami Beach and Shari Deveraux Fabrikant of Boca Raton, Florida. Rabbi Marc Gellman of Melville, New York, a friend of the bride's father, is to officiate at the ceremony, to be held at Casa Casuarina in Miami Beach.

The bride, 31, is a film actress who will be starring in the upcoming motion picture, "Claire Voyant." It is the story of her life, and is to be executive produced and directed by Ms. Penny Nichol, the Hollywood film star and the bride's biological parent. Mrs. Fabrikant graduated with a degree in Theater and Drama from Indiana University, Bloomington. Her father, a certified public accountant on Long Island, is a founding partner of Greene and Levinson. Her mother is a homemaker and film extra who will be appearing in "Claire Voyant." In the film, her character, Roberta, will be portrayed by the actress Marsha Mason. The role of Leonard will be played by actor Jerry Stiller.

The bridegroom, 29, known as Drew, is a podiatrist in private practice in South Beach, and is the author of the forthcoming book, "Feet First: How to Get A Jump-start on Healthy Living" (HarperCollins). He graduated from the

University of Florida, Gainesville, and earned his Doctor of Podiatric Medicine and Surgery from Barry University in Miami Shores. His mother is a personal trainer and yoga instructor. His father is the owner and chief executive officer of FabFood, a concern that owns and operates seven nightclubs and restaurants in south Florida. He is also the director of the Abraham Fabrikant Institute, a not-for-profit organization that provides financial assistance to foreign citizens who are under threat of persecution for their religious beliefs.

Members of the bridal party are to include the bride's sister, Lindsey Greene, who will serve as maid of honor, the bridegroom's sister, Delia Fabrikant, Sydney Sloan of Los Angeles, and Elyce Berg, a childhood friend. Also in the bridal party are the best man, Dr. David Goldstone, the bride's brother, Adam Greene, the bridegroom's cousin, Jake Deveraux, and Viktor Petrovsky, a longtime family friend.

The bride's grandmother, Gertrude Moss, of Coral Gables, and her companion, Norman Singer, also of Coral Gables, will serve as fleur de matron and ring bearer, respectively.

The bride and bridegroom will walk down the aisle to "My Sky," a poem written anonymously during the Holocaust that was put to music by their beloved grandfather, Abraham Fabrikant, known as Pops.

And yes, you read right. Claire and Drew had the same grandfather. . . . Don't ask. It's a long story. A very long story.

# Let's Talk
## Hot Topics for Book Discussions

YOU'RE ON A FLIGHT, WHEN SUDDENLY THE ELDERLY PASSENGER SEATED next to you, a complete stranger, collapses on your tray table and dies. Would you:

a. Scream, cry hysterically, then pass out.
b. Keep a cool head, and try to administer medical help.
c. Wonder what you did to deserve this fate, and vow never to take this airline again.
d. Forget it. Don't even want to think about this. The idea is just too awful.

I don't know about you, but I chose "d." Sure, I may have been able to dream up the unthinkable, but I wouldn't want to live it. Unfortunately, as we all know, the unthinkable happens every day. But only in fiction is the outcome carefully scripted. In reality, we never know what will come of life's most turbulent flights. All we can do is try to hang on through the bumpiness, and pray for a swift, smooth landing.

To that end, perhaps you would like to discuss the issues explored in *Claire Voyant* as a way to share your thoughts and experiences on dealing with some of life's challenges.

## *Adoption and Family Secrets*

- Claire's parents and grandmother were prepared to take a lifetime of secrets to their grave. Was that their right, or should they have come clean years ago? In other words, what's more important—the truth, or protecting someone from the truth?
- Lenny Greene admitted that he and Roberta had had every intention of telling Claire the truth about her adoption, but just never found the right time. Is there a "right time" in which to reveal the truth?
- During the thirty-year period that Claire was left in the dark about her true past, who was hurt more by the secrecy? Her family who knew, or Claire, who hadn't a clue?
- Did Penny Nichol, who gave up her baby at nineteen and left her with a family she knew had no biological link, do the right thing? Or should she have toughed it out, regardless of how it might have altered the course of her life?
- If you have ever been the keeper of a family secret and the truth was finally revealed, what were the effects on those who had no knowledge, versus those who were withholding it?

## *Marriage and Family*

- Lenny and Roberta fight constantly, but have remained married for thirty years. Is theirs a good relationship in spite of the bickering, or should they just have admitted they were miserable and split?
- Claire's parents agree on nothing. Her best friend Sydney's parents have each married and divorced several times. Drew's parents, Ben and Shari, are big fans of infidelity, and ultimately split. Drew and Marly have been twice engaged, but the road to the altar is a bumpy one. Her friend Elyce doesn't care that her fiancé, Ira, has cold feet. She'll marry him anyway. You'd think that Claire would have seen enough to be turned off to marriage,

yet she can't resist the idea that the perfect husband is out there. Knowing the difficulties, what is it about marriage, and remarriage, that keeps people knocking at the door and begging to be let in?

- Penny Nichol had her share of affairs but never married. Given her tendency to look out for number one, was it smart that she stayed single, or might she have been one of those for whom marriage made her a more compassionate, less self-absorbed person?

- Will Claire and Drew beat the odds and have a long, happy marriage?

## Karma, Destiny, and the Afterlife

- Immediately after Abe Fabrikant dies, Claire sees his image, hears his voice, and feels his presence. Is that even possible? Do spirits return to the physical plane and try to communicate with us?

- What about out-of-body experiences? Makes for good reading, but is it even remotely possible? Or is astral travel as common as flights between New York and Florida?

- After everything that happened to Claire, she concluded that she was wrong about free will, and that her father was right about the script having been written beforehand. What do you think? Are the circumstances that happen in our life simply random events, or was the journey already mapped out?

- Some say that karma, like pepperoni, tends to repeat on you. In other words, if you don't learn from your experiences and your mistakes, those same issues will continue to plague you. Although we face many challenges, have you ever noticed that there seems to be a theme? A particular issue that we grapple with over and over again? Relationships? Health? Money? Career? Is this just an unlucky streak, or is there a message here?

## Love

- In the course of the story, Claire's relationship with Drew is very complicated. There is the matter of their being related, although not biologically, the matter of their very different backgrounds, the matter of Marly, the pregnant fiancée, etc. If two people are in love, is there such a thing as problems being too insurmountable for marriage? Or can love conquer all?

- Love and guilt are explored on a lot of levels. Both Claire's adoptive parents and her grandmother Gert learned to live with their guilt for keeping secrets by rationalizing that they raised Claire as their own and prevented her from a lifetime of misery. Drew worshipped his Grandfather Abe but could not deal with the fact that he never thanked him for his kindness and generosity. Claire and Drew fall in love, but the relationship begins with several instances of hiding the truth. Was Erich Segal right? Does love mean never having to say you're sorry?

- Penny Nichol claims that her abandoning her baby was done as an act of unselfish love. That it was best for the child because Penny was too young and immature to handle the responsibility. But was it love or cowardice?

## Finally . . .

- True or False: Saralee Rosenberg, the author of *Claire Voyant*, is a wonderful new writer who makes you laugh and cry and lock yourself in the bathroom until you finish the next chapter. Seriously, please let me know what you thought of this book, and also *A Little Help from Above*. E-mail me at my website: *www.Saraleerosenberg.com*. I try to respond quickly to anyone who writes, unless they're asking for money.

# AVON TRADE... because every great bag deserves a great book!

**HELP WANTED, Desperately**

ARIEL HORN

Paperback $12.95
($17.95 Can.)
ISBN 0-06-058958-2

*Claire Voyant*

Saralee Rosenberg
Author of *A Little Help from Above*

Paperback $12.95
($17.95 Can.)
ISBN 0-06-058441-6

**kissing in technicolor**

jane mendle

Paperback $12.95
($17.95 Can.)
ISBN 0-06-059568-X

**THE LAST OF THE HONKY-TONK ANGELS**

A NOVEL

MARSHA MOYER
author of *The Second Coming of Lucy Hatch*

Paperback $13.95
($21.95 Can.)
ISBN 0-06-008164-3

**MICHELLE CUNNAH**

**CALL WAITING**

Paperback $10.95
($16.95 Can.)
ISBN 0-06-056036-3

MELISSA NATHAN

*Persuading Annie*

Paperback $12.95
ISBN 0-06-059580-9

---

**Don't miss the next book by your favorite author.**
**Sign up for AuthorTracker by visiting *www.AuthorTracker.com*.**

**Available wherever books are sold, or call 1-800-331-3761 to order.**

ATP 1104